**Praise for Gill Thompson's gripping and heartrending**

'A warm-hearted tale of love, ... human spi... **Kathryn Hughes**

'Heartrending. Riveting. Definitely on my list of *Ten Best Books of the Year*'
**Sharon Maas**

'The characters and their moving stories will haunt you long after you finish the last page'
**Shirley Dickson**

'A mother's loss and a son's courage . . . A heartrending story that spans the world'
**Diney Costeloe**

'A heartrending story'
**Jane Corry**

'[Thompson] secures her position as a leading light in wartime drama . . . A story to haunt you'
***Peterborough Telegraph***

'Beautifully written . . . an extraordinary novel that has stayed with me long after I turned the final page'
**Carol McGrath**

'Beautiful and evocative . . . an intelligent, thrilling novel which will stay with me for a long time'
**Louise Morrish**

**Gill Thompson** lives with her family in West Sussex. She is a Royal Literary Fund Fellow at the University of Chichester.

*Also By Gill Thompson*

The Oceans Between Us
The Child on Platform One
The Lighthouse Sisters
The Orphans on the Train

# The Orphans on the Train

## GILL THOMPSON

REVIEW

First published in Great Britain in 2023 by Headline Review
An imprint of HEADLINE PUBLISHING GROUP

First published in Great Britain in paperback in 2023 by Headline Review
An imprint of HEADLINE PUBLISHING GROUP

1

Cataloguing in Publication Data is available from the British Library

ISBN 978 1 4722 7998 9

Typeset in Garamond MT Pro by Jouve (UK), Milton Keynes

Printed and bound in Great Britain by Clays Ltd, Elcograf S.p.A.

HEADLINE PUBLISHING GROUP
An Hachette UK Company
Carmelite House
50 Victoria Embankment
London EC4Y 0DZ

www.headline.co.uk
www.hachette.co.uk

*To my dear friends and fellow writers*
*Stephanie and Jane,*
*with grateful thanks*

# Prologue

When she has in mind to do something, nothing will hold her back. And she's been marking this day in the same way for twenty years now, despite the bitter weather.

The best thing is to start swimming as quickly as possible. So she wades into the freezing river until her hips are submerged, then launches herself forwards. It's like being encased in ice and she makes a series of rapid strokes until she starts to feel her limbs again. Yet, despite the cold, the feeling of weightlessness is joyous.

The Clyde is the colour of pewter, with a drift of dark twigs and decomposed leaves at the edges. A breeze puckers its surface, causing little swirls and ripples. Underwater, cold currents push and pummel her thighs, and feathery mare's tail brushes her toes, but she keeps swimming, knowing the burning pain will ease as she gets acclimatised. She dips her face in and tastes pure chill, her lips freezing in an instant. She won't be able to swim under water for long today, it's too risky at this time of year. She loves the river but she respects it too.

She takes a large gulp of air, ducks down, pushing aside a slippery tangle of weed with her fingers, and swims for a few strokes. The browny-grey water turns her skin to ochre and her shoulders smart with the cold. In the slow gloom, a grayling flicks its tail and glides away. Sometimes there are brown trout and barbel too. Once, on an early-morning visit, she encountered an otter. This part of the river is fresh water; further down it becomes brackish, then saltier still when it nears the Firth of Clyde. Her chest starts to tighten and she pushes up to the surface in a rush of bubbles.

The river is different from when she was younger. It's cleaner now, for a start. When she came here as a bairn it was heavily polluted from the pits and the ship-building industries. She shudders to think how she swam in all that filth. There are a couple of shipyards still operating, although there are rules now about effluence. But the pits are long gone, and with them the miners and the old way of life. For a moment, the sadness almost overwhelms her but she casts it from her mind and into the water.

This anniversary takes her to another river – far away in time and space – and she needs to honour the events that took place there. She can still see the two terrified girls trembling on the bank, and hear the gunshots that catapulted them into the waiting waters. Today she is swimming for pleasure and as an act of homage; back then she was swimming for her life.

# Part One

# 1

July 1939

As Kirsty pushed open the door to the swimming baths, the familiar sharpness of chlorine laced with something earthy made her spirits soar, even though she smelled it every day.

'Evening, hen.' Maggie had her handbag on the counter already. She snapped it open and extracted the keys, then locked the office door behind her.

'Evening, Maggie. Were many in today?'

'Aye. Loads of 'em. It'll be the warm weather.' The summer heat still lingered in the atmosphere, that and the chemicals making the air gauzy. Kirsty felt as though she was looking at Maggie's flushed plump face through a veil.

'Bound to be lots of men in later then.'

'Aye. Make sure you clean up after them well, lass.' Maggie grimaced. 'Bye for now.' She pushed open the outer door and went into the street.

The miners usually came for their baths on a Friday night, washing the grime of the pits from their bodies before heading home by way of the pub. It was Kirsty's job to sluice the black tidemarks off the tiles after they left. It was mucky work, but there were rewards. Da would be there. He'd come in with his cronies, full of bluster and banter, but making sure to wink at her as he walked past. Kirsty would keep well away from the baths while the men were washing. She'd busy herself mopping down the side of the pool, or swilling out the toilets; anything rather than be thought to be gawping at their nakedness, or eavesdropping on their smutty talk. At fourteen, she was so easily embarrassed.

But as soon as the men had left, blackened skin now miraculously returned to its underground pallor, it would be their time, hers and Da's. They'd have the pool to themselves. And she'd be allowed to swim.

She looked at her watch then frowned as she opened the cleaning cupboard and pulled out the metal bucket, which scraped across the floor with a clatter. It was after five. The miners were usually here by now. But that was probably nothing to worry about. Doubtless the foreman had kept them late or maybe they were working deeper in the mine and taking a while to get back up to the surface.

She took her bucket over to the sink and filled it with warm water. Then she delved into her pocket to retrieve the bag of soap shavings she'd shoved in earlier. She always grated the carbolic at home, so all she had to do was tip in the flakes, then swirl her fingers around until the water lathered. She went back for the mop, dipped it in, then squeezed out the excess of frothy liquid. By the time she'd done the toilets, the miners would be here. Then she could scuttle back to the pool side while they bathed.

But by half past five there was still no sign of them. She tried to shake off the pinpricks of anxiety creeping up her spine. She couldn't help being a worrier, although she wished she wasn't. Losing Ma at a young age made her terrified of losing Da too. Mining was such a precarious job – so far underground with all those explosives and the constant threat of a roof collapsing or a sudden rockfall. 'Don't be daft, Kirsty,' Da would say whenever she expressed her concerns. 'Hamilton pits are well maintained. There's never been an accident in my lifetime.' But that didn't help. It only took one miscalculation . . . one careless slip.

There was nothing more to do in the changing rooms so she wandered into the pool area. Normally she loved being on her own in the cavernous space, enjoying the silence, the deep expanse of blue-green water, the invitingly smooth surface. Da, who'd done a lot of swimming when he was younger, had once told her that every pool tasted different. Hamilton water was soft and sweet; the Motherwell baths, where he'd trained as a lad, were more acidic. Doubtless it was the different quantities of chemicals, but to Kirsty it was a source of wonder.

She leant over the side and trailed her fingers through the water, creating tiny ripples. When the pool was full, the water heaved and surged, a cauldron of thrashing limbs. It was hard to believe something so turbulent could now be so serene. Soon she'd be in the pool herself, revelling in its delicious coolness, the water wrapping itself round her like silk. She loved swimming: it cheered her up when she was sad; it calmed her when she was anxious; it soothed her when she was angry. She'd started to learn after Ma had died and Da had taken on a couple of lifeguard shifts at the baths at the weekend. At first she just stood in the shallow end, letting the water lap around her, too scared to join the other swimmers. Da sat on the side, watching her through glazed eyes – or with his head in his hands, ignoring her completely. But one day, he emerged from the changing room in his trunks, climbed down the steps and joined her. 'Not like that, lassie,' he said as she bobbed up and down in the pool, slapping at the surface with her palms. He picked her up and laid her across the water, a strong hand supporting her tummy. 'Now kick your legs.' She made a cycling motion. He laughed. The first time he'd done that in months. 'You're not on a bike. Like this.' He let her go, grasped the rail at the side of the pool, stretched his legs out, then beat them up and down in a steady rhythm. Kirsty held onto the side next to him and did the same. 'That's much better. Well done.'

Da's encouraging smile came back to her now from across the years. He'd always taken her swimming after that. Friday nights, after the miners had washed, was their time. Within a few months she was swimming properly – first widths, then lengths. Now she could do all the strokes, and even tumble turns and racing dives. He said she was a natural, like him.

But where was he? Where were all of them? The pool clock said a quarter to six now. They were never that late. The air in the pool thickened and her breath snagged in her throat.

As she made her way back to the changing rooms with a thrumming heart, she heard the outside door bang. Relief surged through her. At last. She imagined the miners pouring into the lobby, moaning about some last-minute crisis that had eaten into their leisure time, desperate to get their breeks off and wallow in the warm water. But when she opened the door, only one figure greeted her. And it wasn't Da. Or any of the other men.

'Oh it's you, Maggie. Have you forgotten . . .?' At the sight of Maggie's expression, the words died in her mouth.

'Kirsty.' Maggie reached out a hand and drew Kirsty

8

towards her. 'There's been an accident.' Her face was as white as the tiles.

'No-o-o-o-o-o!' If she shouted hard enough perhaps she could stop Maggie telling her anything; she could push her words into reverse until they ceased to exist. Then Maggie would just smile and admit she'd left her keys behind, or her jumper . . . or there'd be something she'd forgotten to tell her. But not this, please not this. The one thing she dreaded above all.

She put her hand to the wall as the floor tilted under her feet. Maggie pulled up a chair and pushed her gently down. There were two deep ridges between her eyebrows.

Kirsty swallowed down a rush of bile. 'What happened?' she whispered.

'I'm afraid I don't know much. I popped into the Black Bull on the way home to ask my Archie what he wanted for his tea. But I could hardly get in for folk rushing out of the pub. Rumour is there's a fire at the colliery.' Maggie's voice was heavy with shock. 'I thought you'd want to know, lass.'

Kirsty's knee was jiggling up and down uncontrollably. Maggie put out a hand to steady it. 'Shall we go over there together?'

Kirsty nodded mutely. She couldn't breathe. A huge weight was pressing on her chest.

'Come on.' Maggie helped her up, wrapped an arm round her and guided her out of the building.

As they stumbled up Saffronhall Lane, and along Montrose Crescent, Kirsty was dimly aware of other people joining them. Mrs McKay, who lived further down Beckford Street from them, shot her a frightened glance as she overtook her, walking rapidly down the road, her heels clip-clopping on the cobbles. Mr McKay worked with Da at the colliery. Kirsty glimpsed the Pattisons up ahead: she'd been at school with Jamie. His da was a miner as well. So many of them were. All the men she'd expected to see at the baths were now trapped underground by the fire, possibly dead. She breathed in the scent of her own sweat and fear. There were so many ways you could die when you worked in the bowels of the earth: suffocation, drowning, gas, being buried alive . . . The latter was probably the worst fate of all. Stabs of heat and intense cold pulsed down her spine with each new thought.

The closer they got to the mine, the thicker the crowd became. Mothers dragged bawling toddlers by the arm; a few pushed prams or carried babies in shawls. Young women with blotchy faces and linked arms marched silently along the road. The acrid smell of smoke filled the air and Kirsty's stomach contracted as she saw a thin black spiral in the distance. It seemed certain then that there had been a fire – and that it was possibly still raging. Despite the abundance of people, the roads were eerily quiet. Nobody dared speak, but it was obvious what they all feared. All Kirsty could hear was the pounding of footsteps, and the crashing of terrified thoughts in her head.

Gloomy groups of people stood around talking quietly, or stared anxiously at the pit entrance. A chain of men scooped water from puddles and passed buckets along the line.

'Wait here, hen.' Maggie squeezed Kirsty's shoulder then walked over to one of the women standing near the front.

They spoke intensely for a few minutes then Maggie returned. 'The rescuers from Coatbridge are on their way. And the fire extinguishers have been sent for.'

Kirsty's throat tightened. 'It's all taking so long.'

'Try not to fret yourself,' Maggie said. 'It may look worse than it is.'

But Kirsty could do nothing to allay her sense of foreboding. Why couldn't Da have worked in a shop or served drinks at the Black Bull? Why couldn't he have taught swimming or been a lifeguard full-time? Miners were constantly at risk. Even if they never met with an accident, few of the men had long lives. The work was too strenuous, the conditions too hard. Those elderly miners she did know suffered from 'black lung' disease, caused by years of inhaling all that coal dust. It scarred the lungs, making it difficult to breathe. Even if you did live to old age, you couldn't enjoy it.

But Hamilton was a mining town. And most of its men worked down the pits. It was a way of life.

After a while, the banksman appeared, a bag of tokens in his hand. He spread them on the ground and the crowd surged towards them. At the beginning of the day, each miner was given two small metal tokens, one round and one square. When he went into the cage to go underground, he would give one to the banksman, recording the fact he was in the mine, and at what time. It was a way of accounting for the numbers of men below. At the end of a shift, the miner would give his second token to the onsetter who would record the time he left the pit. Da's token number was one hundred and fifty-one.

Kirsty moved forward on legs that felt suddenly strawlike. Perhaps Da hadn't been underground after all. Maybe he'd been sent off on an errand and was even now making his way back from another colliery, having spent the day safely in some mining office. She fixed her eyes on the metal shapes glinting in the late sunlight as she took in the numbers. 96 . . . 34 . . . 23 . . . 17 . . . Each one confirmed a family's deepest fear. The air was punctured with moans and gasps whenever someone recognised a number. The crowd thinned as people turned away, racked with grief. Kirsty continued to scan the tokens. 74 . . . 120 . . . 236 . . . 149. Her stomach twisted and she swallowed down a surge of nausea. 151. Da was in the mine. Maggie drew her back and stood with her arms round her as they continued to wait.

The sun sank lower in the sky, flushing the pithead with mellow light. Waves of unease came off the crowd. Every so often some words floated back to her: *outbye, weighting, powerhouse, brushing squad* . . . They were all terms Kirsty was familiar with from years spent listening to Da talk to his mining friends. Not that she ever paid them much attention. Now it was confirmed Da was underground, she suspected he was in No.1 pit; she'd dimly registered him mentioning something about preparing the coalface for Monday's production when she'd handed him a bowl of porridge that morning, but she hadn't given it any further thought. She racked her brains to see if he'd told her anything else. It might be vital to know where he was, but she couldn't recall another detail. He'd been more intent on holding forth about politics. They'd been listening to the radio. The German Chancellor had just summoned the British ambassador to Germany to discuss the Polish situation and Da said he was a bloody eejit. Kirsty wasn't sure if he'd meant Adolf Hitler or Neville Henderson. Either way, Da was convinced that war was inevitable. For months Kirsty had been worried about him being called up and going off to fight like Granda had in the Great War, coming back injured like he'd been – or worse. But now the events in Europe seemed remote and irrelevant; the real danger lay much closer to home.

A thin breeze threaded through the crowd, ruffling people's hair, and causing some of the women to shiver and pull their cardigans more tightly around them. The crowd was much larger now, spilling over the main road and up to a railway embankment that overlooked the workings. The lights from the surface machinery and the glare of the coke ovens picked out the dread and worry on people's faces.

A hush descended.

'The rescue squad is here,' Maggie said, pointing out a group of men in full-length overalls and stout boots climbing down from a truck. They were wearing breathing apparatus and carrying lamps.

'About time too,' muttered Kirsty, a glimmer of hope flickering in her chest as she watched Mr Fleming, the colliery manager, lead the men over to the entrance to No.1 pit, before they disappeared down below.

Still the crowd waited.

But all too soon the men returned, shaking their heads.

'The smoke must be too thick,' said Maggie.

'What good's a rescue squad if they can't rescue anyone?'

A few people turned round at the sound of her raised voice.

'It's all right, lass. At least there's some fire extinguishers already down there.' Maggie pulled her closer. The Glasgow police and fire brigade had brought some across earlier.

Kirsty felt so helpless standing on the surface, not knowing what was going on deep underground. She tried to summon Da's face when he'd gone off that morning. There were lines around his eyes now, and his chin-stubble was flecked with grey, but he'd still looked eager to be joining his mates – or his freens as he called them. 'It's all about teamwork, ye see,' he'd say. 'You look out for yer freens and yer freens look out for you.'

A ripple through the crowd made Kirsty snap to attention. 'They're coming out.' Maggie was looking towards the entrance to No.1 pit where one miner was being carried out on a stretcher, followed by a straggle of weary men, shocked eyes staring out of grimy faces, clothes plastered with dust. Some of them were limping. On others, rivulets of blood created livid stripes across their powder-coated skin. Kirsty's stomach was a cold mass of fear.

The crowd, which had become lethargic from worry and exhaustion, now came alive. People shouted and pointed. A young woman Kirsty didn't recognise sprinted across the ground and hurled herself into one of the miners' arms. He buried his head in her shoulder, his body sagging. Kirsty swallowed and looked away.

Children were running to greet their fathers; whole families hugged each other; women and even some men were sobbing. But as miner after miner emerged, and Kirsty frantically scanned each figure, the ice in her gut expanded until her whole being was frozen with fear.

'Kirsty?' Maggie's voice was laden with concern.

Kirsty shook her head as her world crashed around her. 'I can't see Da anywhere,' she whispered.

# 2

'I'm here to discuss the arrangements,' the man from McGuire's told Kirsty. He looked sad, as though it was his Da who'd died, although that was probably part of his job. 'I called round to Beckford Street to speak to you, but your neighbour informed me I'd find you here.'

For a moment Kirsty failed to grasp what he was talking about. 'What arrangements?'

'They want to know where your Da's coffin is to go,' said Maggie gently. 'And what you want to do about his funeral.'

Kirsty tried to look at Maggie but her face was all blurry. She blinked hard. 'What do you think I should do?'

'Well it's up to you of course, hen. He'd be welcome here. But it might be easier to have him resting at your own place. Where he belongs. I can come over there with you.'

'Aye. Thank you.' Recent events had been so harrowing that Kirsty had barely thought about her home in Beckford Street but now she saw the squat little house nestling between two others, reaching right to the pavement with a wide cobbled street in front. A home where she'd grown up. Where Ma and Da had lived after they were first married and where, later, they'd taken her back from the hospital as a wee bairn. Perhaps Ma had nursed her at the old kitchen table, while Da pottered around trying to make the tea, his strong miner's fingers fumbling in the drawer for the teaspoons and the strainer. She wasn't even sure when the rent was due. Normally Da managed all that stuff. There was so much she had to deal with and she didn't feel much more than a bairn herself. Perhaps Maggie would help her.

The funeral director bowed his head and wrote something in his notebook. 'And the funeral?'

Again Kirsty looked at Maggie.

'Shall we talk about that later and let you know?'

'Very good.'

Kirsty had a feeling that the man would agree to whatever they suggested, with a bow and a half-smile. Perhaps undertakers practised doing that secretly in front of the mirror.

Maggie saw the man out. Later on she accompanied her over to Beckford Street. A few people stopped them on their way to express their sympathy. Kirsty wasn't sure what to say. When Ma had died, she'd been too young for people to offer her condolences; Da had handled all that, although she could remember her head being patted a lot. But as ever, Maggie shielded her. 'Thank you for your kind words,' she said to each person who told her how sorry they were. 'Kirsty is very grateful.' And Kirsty just nodded mutely. It seemed that everyone had a favourite memory of Da or wanted to express their gratitude for when he'd helped them to mend a fence, or carried a bag of coal, or taught their child to swim. Apparently, anyone and everyone had a claim on her father. She knew they meant well, but he was her da and she wanted him to herself. Even if he only existed in memories now.

Da had died from carbon monoxide poisoning. Apparently the direct current breaker had tripped and a fire broke out in his pit. Fire extinguishers were sent down and the men tried throwing in bags of cement and stone dust but the fire was like a furnace by then; nothing seemed to be able to stop it. The roof girders were red-hot. That's why the rescue squad was driven back. Some of the men in the closer passages were rescued, but Da was further back and didn't make it. Every time Kirsty closed her eyes, red and orange flames leapt behind her lids, and she heard again and again Da's desperate gasps for air as the deadly gas overwhelmed him. Would she ever be able to sleep again?

Even after just a few hours, the house smelled musty. At the sight of Da's chipped blue cup from yesterday morning, still on the draining board, and the neatly folded copy of the *Daily Record* on the kitchen table, waves of sadness surged through her. She slumped over the table, her head in her hands, and sobbed and sobbed. How was she going to cope without Da? There was no one left in the world who loved her. Maggie stroked her hair until she'd cried herself out, then gave her a warm hug. 'You poor lass.'

Kirsty wiped the snot and tears from her face and gave her a watery smile. 'I'm all right,' she said, trying to ignore the wobble in her voice. 'What do we need to do?'

Maggie spoke gently. 'Let's sort out the perishables.' She opened the larder door and scooped a few items into her basket. 'These won't last long, love. Best take them back with us.'

Kirsty nodded, her vision still clouded with tears. It was hard to take any interest in a block of cheese wrapped in grease-proof paper or a handful of carrots and potatoes, but Maggie was probably right. They needed to be practical. Even if what she really wanted to do was to howl and howl until exhaustion drove out the pain.

The McGuire's van arrived soon afterwards. Kirsty stood in front of the limp net curtains in the window, watching the men unload Da's coffin and bring it to the door in a sombre procession. She answered their knock, Maggie hovering behind her.

'Can you bring him into this room please?' She pointed to the parlour. It seemed so strange to refer to Da as though he was alive, when he was lying in a wooden box. The coffin looked strangely small – hard to believe her da could fit in there. He wasn't a tall man but he was strong and muscular which made him seem big. As a little girl she used to wrap her arms around his legs, tip her head back, and look up at his broad, smiling face. 'My da,' she'd say.

The undertakers did as she requested and set the coffin on a little stand at the back of the room. She took a deep breath as they prised open the lid. Then there was Da, like a waxwork, his face creamy pale, no trace of dust or soot, purple-lidded eyes closed, his mouth curved as if he'd just told her a joke. A strangled sob escaped her mouth. She'd been holding out a shred of hope that they'd made a mistake, that Da hadn't been killed after all, that it was another man's corpse they'd brought up. But it was definitely him – recognisable yet different. If it wasn't for the tiny scar just above his left eyebrow and the mole on his chin, Kirsty would have thought he was a mannequin. She reached out, conscious of a vaguely chemical smell, then touched his hair, smoothing it over his forehead. It sprang back as though all the life from his body had gone into it, giving it energy when the rest of him was cold and motionless. Da had never been one to sit still. Even if he was reading the paper he'd be scratching his nose or jigging his foot up and down, filled with a restlessness she found irritating at times.

Yet she'd give anything now for a twitch of his eyelid or a shrug of his shoulders, the gestures that made him so familiar. Not this impersonal, lifeless figure. She wiped away the tears that slid down her face and tried to swallow the raw, searing grief that hauled at her guts and sawed her nerves until all she wanted to do was curl into a ball alongside Da.

'We've put him in a shroud,' the undertaker said, indicating the white robe Da was dressed in, like an adult choirboy – so different to his usual dirty mining clothes. 'But if you want to choose anything different for him – a suit maybe – we can arrange that.'

'Maybe his mining gear?' she said to Maggie.

Maggie shrugged. 'It's your decision, dear.'

Kirsty wondered what they'd done with the overalls Da had been found in, the second, vital, token still in the pocket. Were they too grimy for him to be seen wearing? There were some spares in his wardrobe that she could get down. But it was the mine that had killed him. Would he want to be remembered in that way?

She ran upstairs to find the clean clothes, but as she rifled through the wardrobe, an image sidled into her mind of Da in his lifeguard's chair at the pool, wearing his woollen black bather with the 'crab back' top. At once she knew what to do. She retrieved the outfit from the drawer, then returned to the undertaker. 'Please put him in this.'

The man raised an eyebrow and glanced at Maggie, who shrugged again. 'Well, dear, it's a little irregular, but if that's what you want . . .'

'I do,' said Kirsty. 'And it's what my father would have wanted too.' She was sure of that now.

'All right.' The undertaker held up the costume, stretching it this way and that. 'If you'd care to leave the room for a few moments, I will see to it.'

'Thank you,' Kirsty said, and followed Maggie into the kitchen.

The rest of the day was filled with a succession of visitors paying their respects: Beckford Street neighbours in ill-fitting suits who patted Kirsty's shoulder and told her how much they'd miss Da; other miners who removed their caps at the door and shuffled past the coffin guiltily, murmuring their condolences, while their faces betrayed their relief that they'd been the ones to survive the accident; members of the pit management who looked in briskly then departed straight away as though terrified she'd ask them awkward questions. Most people looked a little uncomfortable when they peered into the coffin and saw how Da had been dressed. But Kirsty didn't regret her decision: she wanted to remember him as a swimmer and a lifeguard: that would be people's last memory of him.

When the final visitor had gone, Maggie took her back to Cadzow Street, insisting Kirsty shouldn't be on her own for the time being. Kirsty felt guilty leaving Da behind but told herself he wouldn't know. And she did feel anxious at the thought of staying in the house again. What if she forgot to lock the back door? Or woke in the night to the sound of creaking floorboards? Or the wind whistling down the chimney? She wasn't ready to deal with all the memories yet. When she was at Maggie's she was able to keep herself in check; she had an awful feeling that if she was on her own she wouldn't be able to stop crying. It felt as if there was a huge bucket of tears deep in her body that was pushing to get out. Of course, she *had* cried last night: sobbing into her pillow so that she wouldn't disturb Maggie and Archie, but she knew there was much more to come. She didn't want to think about the scary questions either: who was going to look after her? How would she manage on her own?

Archie hadn't come across to Beckford Street with them and was out when they got back. Perhaps he was at the Black Bull already.

'Sit down, hen, I'll make some tea.' Maggie filled the kettle and placed it on the stove before setting cups and milk on the table. They'd been drinking tea all day with the visitors, but one more wouldn't hurt.

'Now,' said Maggie once she'd put the filled teapot on the table and sat down facing Kirsty. 'We have to organise the funeral. You can't leave yer da in limbo.'

'I know.' Kirsty had dreaded this conversation. She hadn't gone to Ma's funeral; Da had asked Mrs Campbell next door to look after her. Da wasn't much of a one for the kirk after Ma had died, and he'd never mentioned any funeral arrangements. Best just to get everything over as soon as possible.

'Did your da have a favourite hymn?' asked Maggie. She stood up again, rummaged around in a drawer then returned with a stubby pencil and a small exercise book.

'I don't think so,' Kirsty said. 'He never mentioned one if he did.'

'What about Gresford?'

'What's that?'

Maggie ripped out a page from the exercise book. 'There was an explosion in a colliery in Wales back in thirty-four. Terrible business.' She picked up the pencil and doodled on the paper. 'The place was called Gresford. Nearly three hundred miners died. Chap called Saint was a putter there.' A putter was a young boy or girl who was harnessed to a box loaded with coal and made to pull its weight from the coalface to the haulage road. 'But he was also a good musician. After the disaster he wrote this piece and dedicated it to the miners who died.' Maggie sniffed. 'Right sad it is.'

Kirsty shrugged. 'Fine.'

'We'll meet up with Reverend Murray tomorrow. See if he has any more ideas.'

'Aye.' Kirsty felt exhausted. When people spoke about heartache, she hadn't really understood what the word meant. But now she knew. It was a physical pain, as if the air was slowly being wrung out of her chest. She wanted to lay her head down on the table and sleep until the whole nightmare was over. But it wasn't an option; she had to go on.

Suddenly she sat up straight. 'Aunt Ruth.'

Maggie looked at her enquiringly.

'Ma's sister.'

'Oh. Why didn't you mention her before?'

Kirsty wiped a hand across her eyes. 'We never saw her after Ma died.'

'Do you think we should get in touch?'

Kirsty shrugged. 'I suppose so.'

Maggie stirred her tea thoughtfully. 'What did your mother die of?' she asked after a long pause.

'Tuberculosis.' It was ironic that Da breathed in coal dust

22

every day from his work in the mine, yet it was Ma who'd had the cough. The doctors tried everything, even collapsing her lung once to see if it would heal, but nothing worked.

'You poor orphaned lass,' said Maggie.

Kirsty's breath caught in her chest. Yes, she was an orphan now. There was no one living who'd love her as much as her parents had. Aunt Ruth had made it very clear she wouldn't take responsibility for her when she was a bairn; she certainly wouldn't be interested now she was a teenager. And Maggie was kind but she couldn't stay with her and Archie for ever.

'How old were you when your ma died?' Maggie asked.

'Four.'

Maggie squeezed her shoulder. 'Just a wee yin.'

'It's hard to picture her now. Sometimes I get little flashbacks. I can remember her doing up my coat before taking me to the park. And making me swallow cod liver oil to ward off colds in the winter.' She shuddered and Maggie laughed. 'But Da and I have been on our own for a long time now.'

'And has your father ever had a lady friend?'

'Not as far as I know,' she said. Poor Da. He'd been so busy looking after her and trying to put food on the table that there'd been no time in his life for romance – even if anyone could have matched up to Ma, which she doubted. And now he'd died without a chance to find anyone else. Hot tears pricked her eyes at the thought.


As Kirsty had anticipated, Aunt Ruth didn't attend the funeral. She sent a stiff little note offering her 'sincere condolences' but nothing further. And Kirsty didn't expect to hear from her again. As far as she knew she had no other living relatives.

Reverend Murray made up for Aunt Ruth's absence by his kind manner. He'd never met Da but managed to make it sound from his sermon as though he had. He said Da was a good man who'd worked hard and had many friends – at the mine and at the baths – and that he'd been a wonderful father, all of which was true. Then he read a Bible verse from a book called Job which talked about walking *in the recesses of the deep*, which was what Da had done for all of his working life. And Maggie had been right about Gresford. Reverend Murray had conjured up a few brass players and they'd played the piece so beautifully that the tears had spilled down Kirsty's cheeks. 'It's the song to be played when words are not enough,' Maggie had told her. And she was right. There were no words to express the hollowed-out feeling in her chest, the unbearable ache for Da's arms around her, the knowledge she'd never again see him bounding into the swimming baths, his face lighting up at the sight of her, or ruffling her hair and dropping a kiss on her head as he set off for work. No words could express what people tried to say to her through their sorrowful looks and kind expressions, but the mournful sounds of the music did that for them. It was a fitting tribute to Da.

'Well done, lass,' the reverend said, laying a hand on her shoulder as she left the church. 'I'll come and see you in a few days.'

# 3

Kirsty was given a week off from her cleaning work at the baths but Maggie still had to go in to do her shifts at reception. Kirsty was unwilling to stay on her own with Archie, whom she found a bit scary with his loud voice and bushy black eyebrows, so she went back to Beckford Street and started sorting out Da's belongings. Maggie had told her to bag all the clothes up and she'd arrange for the Salvation Army to collect them.

She took a deep breath, then went up the stairs and into Da's room, trying not to look at the double bed with its paisley eiderdown that he must have smoothed straight on the morning he died. Instead, she went over to the old dark wood wardrobe that had once housed Ma's skirts and blouses. She took down the breeks, shirts and overalls Da wore down the mine, folded them into a ragged pile, and stuffed them into a holdall Maggie had given her. Then she packed up the smarter attire he put on to go to the pub with his pals and the clothes for special occasions. An image crept into her mind of Da standing in front of the hall mirror in his kilt and sporran, off to receive some life-saving award, as she brushed down his velvet jacket. 'You look like a right knab,' she'd told him, straightening the triangular tip of a handkerchief poking out of his breast pocket. And Da had laughed and puffed on a pretend cigar.

She pressed her face into a checked shirt. It still smelt of Da. Suddenly a sob caught in her throat and she clapped the shirt to her mouth to stifle the frightening howling sound that followed. The bucket of tears overflowed and she sat there, crying and sobbing and wailing until she felt weak with misery. Why was Da dead in a coffin and not warm and strong and alive and wearing his clothes? When the crying fit passed, she took another deep breath and wiped her eyes with the back of her hand. Packing away Da's things felt as though she was packing him away too. She knew his body was in the coffin, but somehow it was as if a little bit of him was still occupying his clothes. Once they'd gone, she'd have even less of him. She picked up the white handkerchief, which had been pressed and folded into a neat square, picturing it again in Da's top pocket. She slipped it into her own pocket. Then carried on folding and packing.

One evening, Maggie came home with a basket of shopping. Panting slightly, she thumped it down on the kitchen table, then went to take off her coat and hat.

'Have you ever done any baking, lass?' Maggie drew flour and a tin of treacle out of her bag.

'Not really. I think Ma did some with me when I was very little.' A dim memory stirred of Ma scooping out spoonfuls of treacle and wiping down her sticky fingers with a cloth. Then the smell of gingerbread wafting through the house.

Maggie went to the bread crock and drew out the remains of a loaf. 'Nothing can bring our loved ones back, but it helps to keep occupied. I'll teach you to bake and then I'll teach you to cook.'

Kirsty managed a wan smile. 'Thanks, Maggie.'

'We'll start with clootie dumplings,' Maggie announced,

slapping the heel of bread down on the table in front of Kirsty. She rummaged in the cupboard for a bit then produced a grater and a thick slab of wood. 'Now. You make the breadcrumbs while I find the other ingredients.'

Kirsty followed Maggie's instructions a step at a time. Maggie was right. There was something about keeping active, concentrating on what she was asked to do, that helped to take her mind away from the constant thoughts of Da. And presumably she was helping too.

Before long, they'd produced a neat mound of dough and wrapped it in muslin. 'There we are, your first dumpling,' Maggie said. She lit one of the rings on the stove and placed a large pan on it, then tipped in hot water from the kettle which she'd boiled while Kirsty made the breadcrumbs. Next she lowered the parcelled dumpling into the pan. 'That'll take a couple of hours. I'll leave it to cool overnight then we'll have a slice with our breakfast.'

For a second Kirsty thought how much Da would enjoy it too. Realisation that he'd never eat anything she'd made again washed over her as she went to wipe her hands and she also had to use the tea towel to blot her face. Then she took out Da's hanky and twisted it tightly round her fingers. As though she was binding a wound.

The next morning, Kirsty woke early. Her limbs were restless, her muscles quivering. She thrashed around in bed in an attempt to get comfortable, then threw off the bedclothes impatiently. It was useless trying to get back to sleep. Thoughts were crashing round her head: why did Da have to be a miner? Why did there have to be a fire at the colliery? Why was he the

one to die? White heat flared in her chest at every new injust-
ice. There were children now sitting cosily around the breakfast
table, smug in the knowledge that their father had survived the
disaster and could carry on working and providing for them.
Children with mothers who looked after them too. Yet she had
no one – only a distant aunt who wanted nothing to do with
her. What had she ever done to deserve this? She rammed her
fists into her eye sockets until green sparks flashed across the
darkness. Suddenly the prospect of another day in the kitchen
was too tame. She'd been grateful for the chance to keep her
mind busy, but now she needed to use up the energy pounding
inside her, and drive herself to exhaustion. Anything to get rid
of all these violent feelings.

She sat up in bed. There was only one activity that would
fulfil this deep need.

She'd told Maggie she couldn't face going back to the baths,
and it was true. She knew her stomach would heave at the smell
of chlorine; that she'd be stabbed with sadness at the sight of
the empty lifeguard's chair and all the memories of Da that the
baths evoked. But swimming outdoors was another matter. She
longed for the rush of adrenaline, the bite of cold on her body,
the buffeting of the wind, the friction of the wave-whipped
water on her skin. She needed to go to the Clyde.

She put on her warmest clothes, then tiptoed along to the
bathroom and eased a towel off the rail before rolling it up
under her arm. There was no sound from Maggie and Archie's
room as she carefully made her way downstairs and into the
kitchen. Breakfast could wait – she wasn't hungry and it would
only delay her. It was tempting to rush straight out of the house
but she decided Maggie would only worry if she found her

bedroom empty, so she scrawled a note to say she'd gone for a walk and would be back soon, then left it on the kitchen table. There was no need to mention the swimming; it might alarm Maggie, and she might even get back before anyone came down.

She set off through the early-morning streets. There was a sharpness in the air, the sky washed with pink dawn light. Suddenly impatient to get to the river, she started to run, the towel clamped under her arm, her chest burning, her breath ragged. Soon she left the cottages, houses, shops and pavements behind and was sprinting along a dirt track, past bushes and brambles, swiping at the low-hanging branches which threatened to lash her face.

She smelled the river before she saw it: a familiar earthy odour. Then she was slip-sliding down the muddy bank towards a sheet of grey-brown. There was no one around at this early hour to see her, so she tugged off her clothes until she was down to her underwear, then waded in. Even in late summer the river was freezing, icy currents stinging her skin and stabbing her legs. Jagged stones tilted and shifted under her bare feet and she plunged, gasping, into the biting water. At first it was like being trapped in a glacier, her limbs rigid, her nerves jangling, but she knew that the only way to keep warm was to swim as fast as possible, so she set off in a surge of spray, flailing across the surface so furiously she created small tidal waves. She spat out the foul water that slopped into her mouth.

She swam for as long as she dared, the early frantic strokes giving way to deeper, more measured movements as the initial numbness eased, but still with all the strength she could muster. There was something about punishing her body that unlocked her mind. The more she swam, the more her thoughts and pain welled up then cascaded into the river. By the time she staggered back up the riverbank, her skin puckered and wrinkled, her body glowing, she felt lighter, freer. She rubbed herself briskly with the towel she'd taken from Maggie's bathroom, put on her clothes, then set off back to Cadzow Street.

She found Maggie in the kitchen, her hands on her hips and a frown on her face. 'Kirsty. Whatever were you thinking of?'

'I'm sorry,' Kirsty said. 'I just had to get out of the house.'

Maggie glanced at her damp hair. 'Funny sort of walk that has you looking like you've been swimming.'

Kirsty's face flushed. 'I didn't want to worry you.'

'Hmmm.' Maggie filled the kettle and set it on the stove. 'While you're in our house, we're responsible for you, lass.'

'I know.' Kirsty drew out a chair and slumped at the table. 'I was just so angry at everything that's happened.' That was the emotion she'd felt that morning. She realised it now. Anger. Fury at the way life had treated her. That's why she'd needed to swim – it was the only way she could think of to get rid of the feelings boiling up inside.

'And do you feel better?'

'Yes, I do.' It was strange. The anger had gone as quickly as it had arrived. She just felt exhausted now, as if a huge hand had delved deep inside her, scooped up all the rage and thrown it away.

Maggie made the tea and passed Kirsty a cup before joining her at the table. Archie was nowhere to be seen. 'Then we'll say no more about it.'

'Thank you.'

'But don't ever do that again.'

'I won't.'

'Now,' Maggie took a long sip of tea, 'are you ready to do some more baking?'

Suddenly, the hot little kitchen didn't feel stifling any more, but cosy and welcoming. She no longer needed to escape. 'Aye,' she said.

Over the next few days, Maggie taught Kirsty how to bake oatcakes, bannock bread, drop scones and Dundee cake. She'd come home each evening with a bulging basket of shopping and together they'd set to work. Before long the kitchen would be full of delicious smells. Once the bakes were cool, they'd pop them into tins and Kirsty would take them round to the minister's house the next day – for the Mothers' Union, or the Sunday School, or the coffee morning. Wherever they could be used.

Soon Maggie announced that Kirsty was ready to move on to cooking and she added Cullen skink and cranachan to her repertoire, as well as Forfar bridies which they ate at home with Archie. He consumed them with relish, gravy dripping down his chin which he dashed at with the back of his hand.

One night, Kirsty woke up with a parched throat. She opened her bedroom door quietly and crept onto the landing, intending to go down for a glass of water. But she stopped at the sound of raised voices. A shaft of yellow light spilled out of the half-open kitchen door below, casting sinewy shadows on the hall wallpaper. Kirsty sat down, her face pressed against the bannister. Archie and Maggie were arguing,

Archie's loud indignant tones answered by Maggie's softer, pleading ones.

'And how much is all this extra food costing?' Archie thundered. 'Every time you come home from work you bring yet more items. And both of you in the kitchen every night until all hours.'

Maggie's voice was gentler, but no less audible. 'And aren't you enjoying the benefits, Archie Gordon?'

'I must admit, the standard of cooking has improved. That lass has a way with food. But she can't stay forever. You've done your bit. There must be someone else who can look after her. Where are all her relatives?'

'I've told you. There's only one. An aunt. And she's made it very clear she's not interested.'

'Well, the lass needs to learn to stand on her own two feet. There's a war coming. It'll be every man and woman for themselves then.'

'Archie, Kirsty's *fourteen*.'

'Aye, and I was down a mine at fourteen. If she's old enough to leave school and have a job, then she's old enough to look after herself.'

'Have a heart. She's just lost her da.'

'I know. And you've shown her plenty of sympathy. But you have to be cruel to be kind. Otherwise she'll start playing you for a fool.'

Maggie's voice was raised now. 'How can you be so heartless?'

'I won't be spoken to like that in my own house!'

Kirsty recoiled at the sound of a blow and a muffled cry. She retreated to her room and lay on the bed, her heart racing. Had she outstayed her welcome? Archie obviously thought so and he was lord of the manor. Poor Maggie. There was clearly a more brutal side to her husband.

She made a batch of petticoat tails on her own the next morning; Maggie was at work, having left the house with a muffler round her neck, and Archie had announced he was going round to a friend's. While the shortbread was cooling, she went upstairs and packed her things. She hadn't brought much with her: a couple of slacks and blouses, two skirts, her stout shoes, some slippers, her night things and, of course, Da's handkerchief that she still carried in her pocket, or up her sleeve, transferring it from garment to garment. She left her suitcase ready at the end of the bed then set off for the manse where the minister lived to deliver the petticoat tails.

Reverend Murray answered the door. When Kirsty had first met him, she'd wondered if that's what God looked like. He had shaggy grey hair and an equally shaggy grey beard. His eyes were piercing through round brown glasses. Sometimes Kirsty felt he could scrutinise her every thought with his sharp looks, even though he'd only ever been kind to her.

'Come in, my dear,' he said pulling the door wide and setting off down a dark passage. The manse was chilly, even though it was summer. Probably all those old windows and stone walls. Kirsty followed him down the hall and into a gloomy little parlour containing a dark oak table piled high with books and papers. The floorboards were dark too. There'd been some attempt to lighten them with a tapestry rug, but even that was drab in the dingy room. The reverend sagged into an old armchair and invited Kirsty to sit opposite him. 'Mrs Anderson has just made some coffee. Would you like some?' Mrs Anderson was the housekeeper. Kirsty didn't know if Reverend Murray had ever had a wife. She certainly hadn't met one.

'Yes please.' She took the cup the reverend poured for her from a tartan-patterned thermos he'd retrieved from the floor beside him.

The minister had been as good as his word and popped round to see her a few times since Da's funeral, but Kirsty was always conscious of Archie glowering at him from the kitchen or Maggie hovering anxiously. It was easier to walk over to the manse, and the petticoat tails gave her an excuse. She handed him the tin.

'These look wonderful,' he proclaimed, prising open the lid and peering inside. 'I think I should sample one before passing them on to my parishioners. What d'you think?' His eyes twinkled behind the glasses.

Kirsty smiled. 'Of course.' She wondered whether Mrs Anderson ever indulged him with sweet things.

'You really are becoming a very good cook,' he said with his mouth full and crumbs flying in all directions.

Kirsty took a sip of her coffee. 'Thank you. I enjoy it.'

The reverend brushed the debris from his beard. 'Does baking help keep your mind off your da?'

'A bit.'

'I've seen a lot of grief in my time here.' His face was thoughtful. 'It strikes me that the folk who cope best are those who keep busy. It doesn't do to sit and brood, however bad the pain.'

'That's what Maggie said when she taught me to cook.'

'She's a wise woman.'

'Aye, that she is.' For a second Kirsty wondered whether to tell Reverend Murray about Archie but she didn't think Maggie would be happy about that. It was probably best she left it up to her. Perhaps the minister already knew. There must be so many secrets going on behind closed doors, and ministers, whom people confided in, doubtless knew more than most.

'So, lass. What are your plans now?'

'I can't stay with Maggie and Archie for much longer.'

The reverend sat forward. 'And do you feel ready to be on your own?'

There was something about the minister's expression that made Kirsty feel she could tell him anything. 'Not really. And besides, I can't afford the rent.' She hadn't been able to face going back to the baths yet and they'd stopped paying her wages after the first week. Da had a bit put by, a wad of notes which he'd kept in the bread crock, but it would soon run out. And then where would she be?

'Mm.' The reverend sat back in his chair, his fingers pressed together. Kirsty wondered if he was praying but his eyes were wide open. Perhaps he was just thinking hard.

'I may know someone who can help you,' he said. 'I had a visitor from the Scottish Mission earlier. A lady. She's home on furlough from Hungary, although she came from Scotland originally. Dunscore, I believe.'

Kirsty didn't know where Dunscore was and she couldn't imagine how this woman could help her but she waited for the reverend to elaborate.

'She is matron of a girls' home in Budapest – that's the capital of Hungary.' Kirsty already knew that from geography lessons at school, but she just nodded. 'She mentioned she was looking for a live-in cook's assistant. Perhaps you'd be interested in the post?'

All sorts of thoughts went through Kirsty's mind. She'd never left Scotland in her life. Hungary was miles away. But then again it might be the best thing for her to go somewhere new. Somewhere with no memories. And she really did enjoy cooking. It would be good to learn to cook properly, although she had no idea what they ate in Hungary. But what would happen to her dream of being a swimming teacher?

Then another thought struck her. 'What about the war? Would it be dangerous to go to Hungary?' Kirsty rarely read a newspaper, and Da's death had blotted everything else out, but Maggie usually listened to the wireless in the kitchen and Kirsty had heard the reports that Hitler was becoming more and more carnaptious.

Again the thoughtful expression. 'I hope to God we're not headed for another war,' the reverend said. 'But Hungary has declared itself neutral. You'd probably be safer there than in Britain.'

Kirsty felt reassured. The reverend was clearly a clever man. He probably read newspapers and listened carefully to the wireless. If he said Hungary was safe then she trusted him. Talk of war made her feel a bit uneasy, but in some ways the worst had already happened to her. Da was dead. He couldn't be conscripted, or sent away to fight in Europe, or captured or mortally wounded . . . She'd already experienced the gnawing anxiety and terrible shock that others might have to face. There'd be no more funerals to arrange. She swallowed. 'How can I find out more?'

'The lady is called Jean Mathison. She's giving a talk at

Queen's Park in Glasgow tomorrow. I was going to go across and hear her anyway. If you like I can take you with me then we can speak to her afterwards.'

'Thank you. I'd like that.'

'Excellent. I'll pick you up from Cadzow Street just before seven.'

As Kirsty left the room, she glimpsed Reverend Murray prising open the tin again.

Maggie seemed surprised when Kirsty told her the news. 'Is that what you really want to do?'

Kirsty pushed a strand of hair off her forehead. It was humid in the kitchen. A pan was boiling furiously on the stove, filling the room with steam. 'I don't know. It's an option. I thought I'd go and find out more.'

Maggie leant over the sink to open a window. 'Good idea. You can meet this Miss Mathison and see what you think.'

'Aye.'

When Maggie turned round, Kirsty thought she looked a little relieved, but she couldn't be sure.

At five to seven the next day, the minister drew up in the black car that she'd often seem him driving around Hamilton, as he'd promised.

Maggie came to the doorstep to greet Reverend Murray and see them off.

'Don't worry, I'll look after her,' the reverend assured Maggie.

'Of course. Thank you. We'll see you later.'

In spite of her frequent need to take out Da's handkerchief,

Kirsty couldn't help but feel a little bubble of excitement at being in a car. Da had never owned one – none of the miners could afford that – and he and Kirsty had travelled everywhere by bus or on foot. It was nice to run her hands over the brown leather seat and see the world flashing by out of the window. Hamilton was a town of broad cobbled streets and stone houses, some of them dating back to the eighteenth century. Da had told her that Queen Victoria's mother had once visited the duke at Hamilton Palace. She wondered what Budapest might be like. Would it be hard to leave Hamilton? A few weeks ago she'd have thought it impossible. But so much had changed now. It might be good to go somewhere where every street didn't remind her of Da, where people didn't know anything about her, where grief might be easier to deal with and she could lose herself in the physical demands of cooking. So much depended on this evening.

# 4

The church was made of blackened stone with a high pointy steeple. A long queue of people snaked round the building, and by the time Reverend Murray and Kirsty entered, the dark wood pews on the ground floor were already packed. The air vibrated with the sounds of low voices, shuffling feet and rustling cough-sweet papers.

'We'll go up to the balcony,' said the reverend, leading Kirsty upstairs to another level of seating which ran along three of the walls of the church. The smell of furniture polish and flowers came up with them. Kirsty felt more invisible there. She could watch the service without feeling embarrassed that she didn't know the words of the hymns or when to stand up and sit down. It was interesting to look down on the people below too – like a little bird, high up in a tree, observing life on the ground. Most of the women wore hats, and Kirsty wondered if she should have borrowed one from Maggie. Suddenly her best cream blouse and tartan skirt looked a little shabby compared to the tweed suits and smart dresses – another reason she was glad she couldn't be seen. She hadn't been in a church since Da's funeral. She was relieved they hadn't sung the same hymns. That would have been too hard to bear.

After a while the minister announced the evening's speaker. 'We are delighted to have Miss Jean Mathison back on furlough,' he said. 'She's here to talk about her work for the Scottish Mission in Hungary.' He smiled as a woman approached the stage.

Kirsty peered over the balcony. The lady looked to be around Maggie's age – in her forties – and was quite sturdily built. She hesitated by the pulpit steps then climbed slowly up. But once there she squared her shoulders and raised her chin.

'I expect you're wondering what a lass from Dunscore is doing in Budapest,' she started in a quiet but firm voice. It was the kind of voice that might soothe a distressed child but could still quieten a roomful of girls. 'I'm the matron of a girls' home for Christian and Jewish children established by the Scottish Mission.' She paused to clear her throat. 'The mission came about by chance, really. Two missionaries were returning from Palestine. One was kicked by a camel in Egypt and by the time they got to Budapest, he was too ill to carry on. They were put up at a hotel, where the second man also became ill. The wife of the Austro-Hungarian governor, a devout German Protestant lady called Duchess Maria Dorothea, found out about the poor missionaries and promised them support if they agreed to establish a mission to the Jews in Hungary, a cause close to her heart.'

She looked out into the congregation, then took a deep breath. 'It's a cause close to my heart too. My pupils, many of them Jewish, are frightened. They're frightened because their parents are terrified.' Reverend Murray leaned forward, his sharp eyes focussed on Miss Mathison. Beneath them, the shuffling and fidgeting stopped. Silence fell.

'The Jews of Europe are in huge danger. Back in November last year, in Austria and Germany, Jewish shops and businesses were smashed up. Synagogues were torched, homes vandalised. Over thirty thousand Jewish males were rounded up and taken away, just because they were Jews, without any further cause for arrest.'

Her voice started to waver. She cleared her throat. 'I'm afraid I don't know how our Jewish population in Hungary will cope. Many will lose jobs in an already worsening economy. Many will no longer be able to afford fees for our mission school, which is actually the one stable thing in their children's lives. Already we've had fifteen of our boarders' families reduced to begging for food. And we're thankful to the Church of Scotland for its generous provision.' She smiled warmly at the congregation. 'I'm not sure how widely known this is in Scotland, but I am here to tell you that for these poor persecuted people, the situation is desperate.'

Kirsty didn't follow all of Miss Mathison's comments, and she didn't know much about the Jews, but one thing did stand out to her: people were suffering and the speaker was asking for help. This lady was clearly kind and Kirsty wanted to get to know her.

A large crowd surrounded Miss Mathison at the end of the service. While Kirsty and the reverend waited patiently, a man remonstrated with her, his loud voice carrying over the throngs of people.

'But surely you are dramatising a situation that is simply the result of the political unrest throughout Europe at present? It's happening to any who are vulnerable in society.' Kirsty glimpsed the man through the crowd. He had a shiny red face and was standing very close to Miss Mathison. 'I understand your need to publicise your work. I'm sure the Jews are suffering but so are the poor in every country in Europe,' he continued.

Miss Mathison flushed. 'I'm sure that is so,' she said quietly. 'But many of my pupils and their parents are Jewish. Therefore, I will help Jewish people.'

'Shouldn't you be helping other Christians?' another man said.

'There are Christian pupils at the school too. I treat them both the same.'

The man shrugged and left and the crowd thinned out. Eventually Miss Mathison and the minister were standing in front of her.

'Reverend Murray,' she exclaimed in a warm voice. 'How lovely to see you again.'

'Dear Jean,' the reverend replied. 'You spoke very powerfully tonight.'

Sadness tugged at the corners of Miss Mathison's mouth. 'Clearly not everyone agrees with me. But I am very concerned.'

'I can see that. Such challenging times.' He drew Kirsty forwards. 'This is Kirsty McClean. She lost her father recently in the mining accident at Hamilton and her mother died several years ago.'

Kirsty felt bright blue eyes upon her. Her body started to feel warmer and her mind less busy. The tight knot in her stomach loosened.

'Let's go somewhere more private,' Miss Mathison said. She drew them into a small room on one side of the church and gestured for them to sit down. 'That's terrible, my dear. My mother died when I was very young, and my father passed away just recently. It's so hard to be an orphan, isn't it?'

Tears pricked Kirsty's eyes; she wiped them with the pad of her thumb. She wanted to lay her head on Miss Mathison's shoulder and feel the soft wool of her jumper against her cheek.

'Kirsty was wondering about the position you have at the school for a cook's assistant.' Reverend Murray looked at Kirsty who nodded. She was still interested. In fact, even more so since she'd heard Miss Mathison speak. Even though it would mean putting aside her dream of being a swimming teacher, at least for the time being.

'Ah yes. Poor Mária is struggling to cope on her own. She'd really welcome some help.' The blue eyes sharpened. 'Can you cook, Kirsty?'

Kirsty explained about Maggie's tuition. 'I don't know anything about Hungarian food but I'm very happy to learn.'

Miss Mathison smiled, revealing even teeth. 'I knew very little when I first arrived in Budapest. I had to learn how to manage a boarding school of girls. I don't mind someone with no experience. But a willingness to learn is crucial.'

Suddenly all Kirsty wanted to do was to make Miss Mathison smile at her all the time. She imagined her popping a piece of Kirsty's home-made clootie dumpling into her mouth and pronouncing it delicious. 'I'd work very hard,' she said.

'You sound ideal, although I'll need references of course.'

Reverend Murray patted his stomach. 'I can certainly vouch for her baking,' he said.

Miss Mathison laughed in a musical kind of way.

'But I'll type up something more formal for you,' the reverend continued. 'And is there anyone at the baths who could supply you with a reference, Kirsty?'

Kirsty briefly wondered about Maggie, but she wasn't technically her employer, and she'd become more of a friend now. 'I'm not sure,' she said. 'Perhaps someone from the council?' The man from the council came in each week with Maggie's pay in a little brown envelope. He used to pay her too, she thought with a pang.

'That won't be necessary,' said Miss Mathison. 'Reverend Murray's word is good enough for me.' Again, Kirsty heard the mix of gentleness and authority in her voice. 'Now, I leave for Budapest at the beginning of September. Why don't you go home and have a think about it? You'll need to consult any relatives and guardians. Europe is quite unstable at the moment so everyone needs to be happy about you going. But if you're still interested in a few days, then inform the reverend and he'll get in touch with me. Then I'll sort out the paperwork.'

'Do you think there'll be a war?' asked Kirsty, feeling for Da's hanky inside her pocket. Perhaps Scotland would be safer after all.

'I don't know,' replied Miss Mathison thoughtfully. 'But if there is one, Hungary has proclaimed its neutrality. There are some people that side with Germany but I think we'll keep out of any conflict. I'm certainly not frightened and I wouldn't be offering to take you if I had any deep concerns.'

Kirsty nodded. She couldn't think of anyone who'd object to her going. Aunt Ruth would probably be all too happy to sign the permission form. Maggie, though kind, would be relieved she could just go back to pacifying Archie. It would do her good to get away from Hamilton for a while. Being in a different place might give her something to think about other than Da. She could always come back, and there'd be many more jobs she could apply for once she'd gained some cooking experience. And perhaps, after a while away, she'd be able to face going to the baths again and continue with her swimming. But she didn't feel up to it yet.

* * *

44

'You know you're always welcome here,' Maggie said as they sat at the kitchen table later, each with a cup of tea. She looked away as she spoke.

Kirsty squeezed Maggie's hand. 'I know. But I think you have enough to do looking after Archie. That and your job at the baths.'

'I'm sorry.' Maggie rubbed absent-mindedly at her neck. 'But all this talk of war is so alarming.'

'Neither Reverend Murray nor Miss Mathison thinks there'll be a war. And anyway, Hungary is neutral.'

'I suppose so.' Maggie looked unconvinced. 'You'll have to tell your Aunt Ruth. And give notice on Beckford Street. But I could help you with that.'

Lots of thoughts started to rush around Kirsty's head. 'Miss Mathison goes soon. What am I going to do with all the stuff in the house?' Thank goodness she'd packed away all Da's clothes – apart from the handkerchief she still kept with her. And Ma's belongings had long gone. But there were still all the household items, and things of her own that she wouldn't need in Budapest, but didn't want to give away.

'I'll ask the Salvation Army to take any bits and bobs you don't want. And you can store the rest here.'

'Are you sure Archie won't mind?'

Maggie's mouth twisted. 'I'll put them in our Susan's room. He never goes in there. There's space in the wardrobe.'

'Thanks, Maggie.' There was no doubt the next few days would be busy, but it would be good to have tasks to complete. They might stop her endlessly thinking about Da.

Perhaps going to Hungary really was the right decision.

# 5

September 1939

Kirsty had never left Scotland before. When she and Miss Mathison first boarded the train for the south of England, she'd looked out of the window, fascinated by the way the view changed hour after hour. The Scottish hills, purple and brown with heather and bracken, gave way to lakes and ploughed fields and towns, to factories with huge chimneys billowing smoke, until the landscape flattened as they neared London. They took a grimy tube train across the city before getting on another train to Dover. From there they boarded a boat across the Channel, where she shared a cabin with Miss Mathison, her stomach churning as the boat lurched across the sea.

By the time they reached France, her head was aching and her shoulders were stiff with tension. But there was worse to come. As they stood on the platform, waiting for the Paris train, Miss Mathison suddenly gasped and grabbed Kirsty's arm.

She followed Miss Mathison's gaze. A man next to them was reading a newspaper, his upper body hidden behind the spread of pages. The headline was huge on the cover: *L'Allemagne enva-hit la Pologne*. Kirsty had only studied basic French at school, but even she knew what it meant: Germany had invaded Poland. Ice inched up her spine. Had she made a terrible mistake? She could have stayed safely in Scotland instead of heading towards enemy territory. Even if Hungary remained neutral, they still had to get there. The trains could be bombed. They could be trapped in a war zone. Or injured . . . or killed. Her stomach swooped with each terrifying possibility. But when she turned back to Miss Mathison, her fearful expression had been replaced by one of calm confidence.

'We'll be travelling through France, Switzerland and what used to be Austria,' she said. 'We won't be crossing Poland or Germany. And we'll be quite safe once we get to Budapest. The Hungarian regent, Miklós Horthy, made an alliance with Germany. Adolf Hitler will leave us alone.'

Kirsty tried to stretch her mouth into a smile.

Even so, the journey was grim. She sat tightly pressed against Miss Mathison on train after train as they progressed slowly through Europe. There were no porters, few toilets and no hot food. Just endless packed carriages full of anxious people. They were constantly asked for their papers. Thank goodness Miss Mathison had added Kirsty to her passport as a minor and arranged all the documentation she needed.

At one of their stops, a family boarded with a dog and two chickens, who barked and clucked for much of the journey. It was stiflingly hot and airless with so many passengers. Kirsty had piled on extra clothes to save space in her suitcase and before long her forehead was slippery with perspiration. A couple of times they had to spend the night on the platform, waiting for delayed trains. They couldn't leave the station to stay in a hotel in case the train arrived and they didn't dare desert their luggage, so there was nothing for it but to sit on their bags, trying to snatch a few minutes' sleep, and hope the train would turn up soon.

It was a relief to hear Miss Mathison's calm Scottish brogue amongst the babble of foreign voices. There was a palpable sense of panic in the air. It seemed everyone was trying to move south, away from the threat of a German invasion.

But Miss Mathison still didn't seem perturbed. She folded her hands in her lap and turned her face towards Kirsty. 'I'll tell you a bit more about the school. Not all the girls are Jewish. There are Christian children there too.'

'I don't know much about Jews.' Kirsty was worried Miss Mathison would think her ignorant and childish – or even foolhardy for applying for the job without finding out more details.

'They're only people, the same as us. Just different beliefs and customs.' Miss Mathison's eyes had a faraway look. 'But there's a lot of anxiety for Jewish people just now. The Hungarian government has passed laws against them, making it difficult for them to work. It's hard for the girls when their parents are clearly so worried.'

Kirsty nodded. She knew what it was like to have huge upheaval in her life – and to find kind souls who tried to help her through it. Perhaps there was something she could do to help these girls too. Maybe she could teach them to cook, as Maggie had taught her, to help keep them busy and distract their minds from their troubles. She pictured herself in the kitchen demonstrating how to make shortbread, with a row of adoring girls in front of her, hanging on her every word.

Another thought struck her. 'Do you speak Hungarian?'

Miss Mathison laughed. 'Aye. And you will too in time.'

Kirsty couldn't imagine speaking another language fluently. 'I wouldn't know where to start.'

'I was lucky. I was good at German and French at school. I love languages but Hungarian is particularly difficult. After a while you pick it up just by listening to people talk. That's how I started. Then Miss Roda, the headmistress of the elementary school, taught me the basics and I kept studying it on my own. I'm pretty confident now.'

Kirsty swallowed. She'd only really mastered a bit of French. And Hungarian was probably nothing like it. There was so much she had to learn – a new language, cookery skills, how to find her way around a completely unfamiliar place. Her mind flickered with unease.

Miss Mathison patted her arm. 'I'll teach you, my dear. It will seem strange at first but you'll soon pick it up. Of course, you'll be on the staff, and you'll take your orders from Mária, but I expect you'll make friends with some of the girls. That'll help a lot.'

Kirsty nodded and looked out of the window. The train had ground to a halt yet again and more people were piling in: anxious-looking mothers carrying young babies, small children looking confused and unhappy, or bawling loudly, elderly women dressed in black. Luggage was crammed into overhead racks or piled up in the aisles until it was impossible to move. The train air thickened with odours: stale food, perspiration, cheap perfume and old clothes. She became aware of a sweaty smell coming from her armpits, and tried to avoid lifting her arms. There was a babble of sound, lots of people talking to each other in a language Kirsty didn't understand. They were in Switzerland now. The language must be German.

'What are they saying?' Kirsty asked.

Miss Mathison took a sharp intake of breath. 'It seems Britain and France have declared war on Germany,' she said, in a strangely high voice. 'I'm very sorry, my dear. I had hoped it wouldn't come to this. Mr Chamberlain was so determined he could keep the peace. I wouldn't have brought you if I'd known how precarious things would become.' She put a hand to her chest. 'There are rumours that the transport services are all cancelled as the trains are needed to carry German soldiers.'

Kirsty's heart raced. 'What are we going to do?'

Beside her, Miss Mathison's face was pale although her voice was steadier.

'I don't think we can go back,' she said. 'Britain is a target now. We'd be in more danger at home. We have to keep pressing on and pray we'll arrive safely in Hungary. Switzerland has always been neutral.'

Kirsty's throat tightened. What choice did she have? Miss Mathison was determined to return to her charges. It would be foolish to attempt the journey back to Scotland on her own. And she was right. It was probably better to risk the journey with her, knowing the destination was safe, than retrace her steps and make herself more vulnerable.

Miss Mathison patted her knee. 'We're two orphans on a train, you and I. We've already come through a lot in our lives. We'll get through this.' She pushed a damp tendril of hair out of her eyes. 'Let's focus on the school, dear. We have around four hundred pupils ranging in age from six to sixteen, and of these around a tenth either live in or are day-boarders, having all their meals with us but just going home to sleep.'

Kirsty's brain struggled to take in the numbers. She was

mesmerised by what was happening in the train but she knew she needed to come up with some sort of response.

'That's a lot of people to cook for!'

Miss Mathison laughed. 'And there are thirty members of staff as well of course. No wonder poor Mária is overwhelmed.'

Kirsty wondered what Mária would be like. Her brain conjured a huge woman with a red face and greasy hair, shouting at her in a language she didn't understand. She swallowed. Miss Mathison seemed to think she'd make friends with the girls but what if they looked down on her for working in the kitchen? She imagined sitting by herself in a chilly bedroom, listening to the pupils having fun outside. And there'd be no kind Maggie to keep an eye on her – although no Archie either. But Miss Mathison seemed gentle and caring. She was a fellow Scot too. Perhaps it would be all right. As long as they survived the journey.

The train wound on, through narrow valleys and past sparkling lakes with snow-capped mountains in the distance. There was something about Swiss scenery that reminded her of Scotland. Perhaps it was a good sign.

They had another night-long delay at a place called Leoben in Austria, huddling together on a derelict platform while an icy wind swept around them. Kirsty was relieved she'd packed her Arran sweater. She'd been tempted to leave it out – the weather was still mild in Glasgow – but Miss Mathison had told her the Budapest winters could be very cold. Certainly Austria was when the sun went down and it was still only early September. All the station staff had gone home for the night so once again there was no food or warm drinks to be had. The waiting room, which would have been warmer, was locked.

The only sign of life, apart from their equally dejected fellow passengers, was a few pigeons pecking in the dust.

Eventually, word got out that a train was about to arrive. They staggered to their feet, rubbing their stiff limbs, and picked up their luggage. 'Not far to Budapest now,' Miss Mathison murmured through lips that were blue with cold. Kirsty followed her into a carriage, hauled her case onto the luggage rack, and soon fell asleep.

She was woken by the sound of people standing up, grabbing their bags and their bairns and chatting unintelligibly.

Miss Mathison handed over her case. 'Here you are, dear. We're safe at Keleti station at last. I doubt anyone from the school will be here to meet us. We'll have to get a taxi. I have a few *pengö* in my bag.' She rooted around and produced some coins.

Kirsty followed her down onto the platform, swapping her suitcase from one hand to another to relieve her aching fingers. They joined the press of people who'd already got off the train. Most of them, like her, were carrying luggage: bulging carpet bags, their patterns muted with age; scuffed brown cases; backpacks and wicker baskets heaped with provisions. Even small children wore knapsacks, making them stagger along the platform like human beetles. Kirsty looked around her. The station was huge, with stone arches topped by semi-circular windows running down each side. She tipped her head back. More windows were cut into the vaulted roof, light pouring down through its intricate metal struts like a second sky, illuminating the weary faces of the passengers in their crumpled clothes. The air smelled of sweat and steam.

They trudged towards the exit, their fingers whitening on the handles of their heavy cases, unwilling to shout above the clattering of shoes and bags, the sharp sounds of whistles and the noisy babble of hundreds of people. It was reassuring to be in the warm taxi and heading towards the school.

'Nearly there,' said Miss Mathison. Her face sagged with tiredness, folds of skin drooping under her eyes and there was a pinched look to her mouth. Kirsty felt a surge of affection towards her. It wasn't her fault that war had broken out or that the journey was so uncomfortable. She might have been frightened herself, deep down, but she always made sure Kirsty was all right. A bit like a mother would. Da would have liked her.

Kirsty looked out of the window as the taxi ground through busy streets. It was the end of the day, people bustling home from work or popping into the shops that lined the roads. Above them loomed tall buildings in a light-coloured stone, with myriad windows in the same arched shape she'd seen at the station.

'Buda and Pest used to be two separate cities.' Miss Mathison leant her head against the car seat and half closed her eyes. 'The great river Danube runs between them. Buda is on the west and Pest is on the east. Now there is a bridge between them and the two cities are joined – Budapest!'

'And which side is the school?' asked Kirsty.

'It's in Pest. Most of the girls live nearby, quite a few in the Jewish quarter. The school is on Vörösmarty utca. Utca means street. And Vörösmarty is the name of a Hungarian poet.'

Kirsty nodded. She wondered if the Danube was anything like the Clyde. 'Do people swim in the river?' she asked.

'I believe they do. But in the summer, we go to Lake Balaton. It's about eighty miles from the school. The biggest lake in Central Europe. We stay for several weeks and all the girls swim there.'

Despite her tiredness, and the need to keep reaching for Da's hanky, Kirsty still felt a ripple of excitement. 'Would I be able to go with them?'

Miss Mathison smiled at her. 'I'm sure we can arrange it,' she said. Then she put a hand on Kirsty's arm. 'And one more thing. Everyone calls me Matron at the school. Perhaps you should do the same.'

'Of course,' Kirsty said. 'Miss Mathison' was a bit of a mouthful. 'Matron' would be easier. Funny how all her names began with the letter 'm'. Like the word 'Ma'.

The taxi drew up outside a grand building with many floors. It was huge. Kirsty had been imagining something like her old school in Hamilton which was about a tenth of the size. The lower levels were cream coloured; higher up the windows were surrounded by brown and dark green stone. There were triangular shapes on the roof, and tall, thin pillars with ornate tops.

Miss Mathison – Matron – laughed at Kirsty's surprised expression. 'Welcome to your new home,' she said.

The taxi driver handed them their luggage and Matron dropped some coins into his palm. She opened a heavy wooden door and ushered Kirsty inside, then frowned as several men hurried towards her, their faces full of concern.

'Matron!' exclaimed one in English. 'Now that Europe is at war, we were hoping you wouldn't return. And we certainly didn't expect you to bring a companion.' His eyes darted towards Kirsty. 'We must insist you go back to Scotland. These are dangerous times to be British women abroad. We can no longer guarantee your safety.'

# 6

'Are you all right, dear? You've turned very pale.' Matron put an arm round her.

Kirsty tried to smile but her legs felt as though they might buckle at any moment. She was dimly aware of background noises: high chattering voices, heels tapping on stone floors and distant stairs, cutlery and crockery tinkling.

'We're quite safe now we're in Budapest. The mission governors are just fussing. The Germans are much more interested in attacking Britain than us.'

Kirsty's heart started to race. 'What about my friends back home?' She'd been so caught up with her own safety on the train that she hadn't thought about the impact of war on Scotland. She had a sudden vision of Maggie quaking behind the reception desk at the baths as the bombs rained down, the streets of Hamilton pounded by the boots of German soldiers; the little house in Beckford Street blown to smithereens . . .

The grip on her shoulders tightened. 'We can only hope and pray.'

Kirsty looked into Matron's calm eyes and her heartbeat steadied. 'I feel a little better now.'

'Good girl.' She picked up her suitcase. 'Let me show you to your room, and then I'll introduce you to Mária.'

Kirsty followed Matron up a winding staircase to a small bedroom on the fourth floor.

'Here you are. The girls' dormitories are on this floor too but I thought it would be best for you to have a room of your own. You'll have to get up very early to help prepare breakfast, although there may be times in the day when you're able to rest. The bathroom's just down the corridor.'

'Thank you,' said Kirsty. She looked round the room. It had a narrow bed with a dark wooden headboard pushed up against the wall. The bed was covered with a yellow counterpane. There was a chest of drawers and a small cupboard. The window, framed by brown curtains, overlooked a pretty garden that was bordered by the building.

Matron heaved Kirsty's suitcase onto the bed. 'Do you feel well enough to unpack, dear?'

'I think so.' She still felt shaky after their arrival at the school but the initial waves of panic had receded.

'Here are some hangers.' Matron opened the door of the wardrobe. 'And there should be plenty of space in the drawers. You can put your suitcase under the bed when you've finished.' She walked towards the door. 'I'll pop back in half an hour or so.' Her footsteps receded down the corridor, leaving Kirsty alone.

She was tempted to sit on the bed and give way to the feelings of helplessness that were beginning to engulf her, but she'd caused enough upset already. It wouldn't do to appear with red eyes and a tear-streaked face. So she took a deep breath and started to unpack, sliding the warm jumpers and underwear into the drawers, and hanging her blouses and skirts in the wardrobe. In the middle of her clothes, to cushion the glass, lay a framed photo of her parents on their wedding day: an impossibly young Da in an over-large suit, smiling shyly, and Ma in a long white dress and veil, laughing into the camera. Kirsty swallowed and placed the picture on the chest of drawers. 'I'll try to make you proud,' she whispered.

By the time Matron returned, all Kirsty's clothes were packed away and she was standing by the window, watching a group of girls playing hopscotch in the garden. They looked to be about nine or ten. It was a game she'd played often at the same age. Funny how children nearly fifteen hundred miles apart could enjoy the same activities. She wondered if bairns all over the world played hopscotch.

'That's Katalin, Flóra, and Ema,' said Matron, following her gaze. 'They are sweet girls. All Jewish. I suspect we are going to have more now so many Jews are flooding into Budapest to seek sanctuary.' Her eyes were thoughtful behind her brown glasses. 'Such troubled times for them all. I shall do all I can to support the families.'

Kirsty remembered Matron's talk at Queen's Park in Glasgow. There was clearly a lot she didn't understand about politics and religion, but she did trust Matron, and if she could, she'd support her too.

Matron led Kirsty down the stairs to a cavernous kitchen that smelled of stewed plums, infusing the air with their sweet-sharp aroma. Shelves crammed with large tins, jars and equipment ran round the walls. Above the shelves were white tiles, grimy where the shafts of sunlight hit them. For a second Kirsty was transported back to the Hamilton baths and the memory of wiping down the tiles after the miners had bathed. Perhaps her cleaning skills would be required again. She willed herself to leave Glasgow behind and continue surveying the room. There were two enormous ranges and a large wooden table in the middle. A diminutive figure stood by one of the ranges, stirring something in a pot. She wore a white apron and a large chef's hat, which looked slightly incongruous on her small head.

'Meet Mária, my dear.'

The figure turned, revealing a flushed, olive-skinned face and dark eyes – not at all as Kirsty had imagined her. She jerked her head at Kirsty and muttered something in what must be Hungarian.

Matron laughed. 'She says she hopes you're a hard worker.'

'I am,' Kirsty replied and Matron translated.

To Kirsty's alarm, Mária marched up to her, grabbed her arm and wrapped her fingers round her bicep. She nodded briskly then stepped back, making another comment.

Matron laughed again. 'Mária approves of your muscles! She says you'll need them in this kitchen.'

Kirsty smiled at the cook to indicate she'd understood. All that swimming had clearly paid off. Many girls her age were still quite scrawny, but she knew she had the broad shoulders and strong limbs of a swimmer. Her muscles would indeed come in useful.

Mária was still gabbling away to Matron, so Kirsty wandered round the kitchen, looking at all the food and equipment. Everything was giant sized: the huge tins of peas and peaches (identified by garish pictures on the labels); the bulging sacks of flour; the massive jars of pickles. It was so different to

Maggie's small kitchen with its modest food stocks. Kirsty chewed at a fingernail. She just hoped her limited cooking skills were up to it.

She became aware that the conversation had stopped.

Matron approached her. 'Mária's asked me to teach you a few words.'

Mária locked eyes with her, rummaged in a crate and picked up a potato. '*Burr-gon-ya*,' she said.

Kirsty repeated the word.

'That's good,' Matron said, 'but draw out the first syllable a little more: *Bu-rr* . . .'

Kirsty did so and was rewarded with a nod from Mária.

The cook went round the room, picking up and labelling food: '*sill-var*'. Those were the plums she'd smelled earlier, now cooling in a large bowl on the table. '*Leest*' (pointing to the sack of flour), '*reesh*' (rice), '*voy*' (butter), '*soo-kor*' (sugar).

Each time, Kirsty repeated the word back to Mária and Matron corrected her pronunciation. 'I'll get a little book for you to write the words down in,' she said. 'Then you can go over them on your own in the evenings.' She must have noticed Kirsty's hesitant expression as she added, 'Don't worry – it's overwhelming at first, but you just have to keep at it. After a while you'll even dream in Hungarian!'

Kirsty doubted that. At the moment her dreams were still of Da: perched in his lifeguard's chair at the pool, watching the swimmers intently; going off to the pit that fateful morning with a grin and a wave; his face distorted with terror as he choked to death at the bottom of a tunnel . . . If she did start to dream in Hungarian, perhaps it would wipe out the nightmares.

Matron squeezed her arm. 'Are you all right, dear? You still look very wan.'

Kirsty nodded. 'It's all a bit daunting.'

'Of course. Especially after the journey we've had. I think Mária could do with a hand preparing supper. Then I'll take you into my office and we'll start your first Hungarian lesson.'

'Thank you.'

As soon as Matron left the room, Mária handed Kirsty an apron and a chef's hat and watched while Kirsty tried to tuck her hair underneath the brim until no auburn strands were visible. She gestured to Kirsty to sit down, then reached for a huge saucepan, filled it with water and deposited it on the table. Some of the water sloshed over the side.

Kirsty froze, uncertain what to do.

The cook heaved up the crate of potatoes she'd pointed to earlier and dropped it next to the pan. Finally, she rummaged in the drawer for a knife and handed it to Kirsty.

No language was needed to explain what would occupy the next hour or so.

By eight o' clock that evening, Kirsty's head was throbbing and her back ached. Mainly through miming, she'd helped Mária prepare a meal of potato and sausage stew followed by cold cooked plums. Around thirty pupils, ten members of staff and the school principal, Doctor Molnár, had filed past the hatch for Kirsty and Mária to serve them. Some of the girls had shot her curious glances; others had openly stared. At first Kirsty tried to smile as she scooped up ladlefuls of stew and endeavoured to tip them onto the plates without spilling any of the gravy. But it was hard to concentrate on her task while making eye contact so after a while she abandoned all attempts at engagement.

Matron was last into the dining hall. She rushed up to Kirsty, pushing back strands of her hair that had escaped their clips. 'This looks delicious. Bit different to Scottish mince and tatties, eh? How are you doing, dear?'

Kirsty scraped the remains of the meal from the dish and handed her a plateful. 'All right, I think. We've been miming a lot.'

Matron laughed. 'That's how I started. But you'll soon pick up the words. Don't forget we have a lesson later. I'll come and collect you when you've finished here.' She went over to a group of girls, who greeted her warmly, and sat down at their table. Soon they were all deep in conversation.

Once everyone had finished their dinner, Kirsty helped Mária clear the tables and stack the bowls and plates by the sink. Matron had explained that a couple of local girls would come in later to do the washing up. They appeared just as Kirsty had wiped down the last table, and Mária set them to work. She made a dismissing gesture to Kirsty and Kirsty responded gratefully. She'd spent long hours keeping house for Da and working her shifts at the baths, but this was far harder. And she was already exhausted from the journey. She untied her apron and hat and hung them on the back of the door, where the cook had retrieved it from earlier. Then she wandered down the corridor to look for Matron.

'In here, Kirsty.' Matron's face appeared at a door then ducked back in again.

Kirsty hesitated. She could hear a man's voice in the room, posh and blaring. Did Matron have company? She didn't want to intrude. But as she peered in, she realised that what she'd heard was the wireless. The disembodied voice floated out, announcing that the Germans had occupied somewhere called Krakow.

Matron snapped the wireless off. 'That's enough of that,' she said. 'Now, I've found you a notebook.' She pulled open a drawer and took out a small pad and a sharp pencil. 'Here you are.' *Kirsty McClean, Hungarian vocabulary*, it said on the front. It was like being back in school. 'We won't do much this evening. I know you're tired. But we need to get into good habits from the start.'

Kirsty stifled a yawn as Matron carefully wrote down the words Mária had taught her earlier, and began to test her.

She was up at six the next morning, thanks to the alarm clock Matron had lent her. Her bedroom had chilled overnight and she was glad to pull her Arran jumper on over her blouse before she tiptoed along to the bathroom to wash her face and clean her teeth. But the jumper soon came off in the heat of the kitchen.

Mária nodded at her when she arrived and placed a tray of eggs on the table. Then she added a huge bowl and a large whisk. She mimed breaking the eggs on the side of the bowl and whisking them.

'How many?' Kirsty asked.

Mária shrugged and returned to cutting bread.

Kirsty decided to do them all.

By the time the boarders trooped in at half past seven,

breakfast was laid out on the long counter that separated the kitchen from the dining room. It was a strange meal, so different to the porridge and toast they usually ate in Scotland. There were plates piled high with slices of bread and butter to which the pupils could add scrambled eggs, sausages, some strong-smelling cooked meat or cream cheese. There was also a bowl of fresh tomatoes that Kirsty had quartered earlier as one of her tasks.

The dining room was quieter than the night before, some of the girls clearly still half asleep. Matron was the last to enter. Kirsty wondered if she'd decided to have a lie-in. She greeted Kirsty warmly, asked if she'd slept well, then joined one of the tables as before.

This time, as they were tidying up, a pupil around Kirsty's age stayed behind. She helped clear the tables and stack the plates. Kirsty smiled her thanks and the girl grinned back. She had dark, bobbed hair and intense brown eyes. 'Anna,' she said, pointing at herself. Kirsty gave a similar introduction. They tried on each other's names, each stumbling a little over the unfamiliar pronunciation and both laughed at their own mistakes. Then Anna looked at her watch and waved goodbye.

As Kirsty returned to the kitchen to help Mária start preparing lunch, she wondered if she'd made her first friend.

# 7

Over the next few weeks, Kirsty's life fell into a routine: the early mornings; the gruelling hours spent in the kitchen; the nightly Hungarian lessons with Matron. Mária seemed to grudgingly approve of her work although she made it clear that Kirsty was to be tolerated not befriended. Kirsty had no idea why she was so offhand. Perhaps she'd have rather worked with a fellow Hungarian, or maybe she was resentful at having to mime her instructions. Whatever it was, Kirsty tried not to let Mária's attitude rankle. At least Matron was kind and Anna seemed keen to get to know her. She stayed behind after most meals now to help.

One evening, as they cleared tables together, Anna suddenly put a finger to her lips – Mária was still banging around in the kitchen – then slumped over the table, yawning and rubbing her eyes exaggeratedly.

'*Oysgematert*,' she said, winking at Kirsty.

Kirsty raised an eyebrow.

'*Oysgematert*,' Anna said again, then pulled out the sounds in an exaggerated fashion: '*Oys-guh-mott-turt*.'

'*Oys-guh-mott-turt*,' said Kirsty and Anna laughed. It didn't sound Hungarian. Perhaps it was her own Jewish language. It obviously meant something like 'exhausted'.

Since this was clearly a game, Kirsty decided to teach her

the Glaswegian equivalent. Checking Mária was still out of sight, she threw herself onto the ground and crawled along on her belly, stopping to pretend to wipe her brow every so often. '*Wabbit*,' she said.

Anna tried to repeat the word, but it came out as '*vabbit*'. They both giggled at her attempt.

After Mária stomped out of the kitchen to go back to her room, they carried on teaching each other slang. When Anna pretended to talk rubbish, then stagger around bumping into tables, Kirsty learnt that *mishegas* and *schlemiel* meant 'craziness' and 'fool' respectively. By dint of a similar mime, she taught Anna *bletheration* and *eejit* in Glaswegian. It was fun, getting their tongues round each other's language. Kirsty didn't know why Anna had singled her out for friendship. Perhaps she'd discover that later, when they were able to communicate better. For the time being at least, she was content to have an ally her own age. She couldn't remember when she'd last laughed as much.

But the smile died on Anna's face when the door to the kitchen banged open. Kirsty glanced through the hatch, expecting to see Mária or Miss Mathison, but the figure was male: tall, about their age and wearing casual clothes. At first he seemed to be making for the larder, but then he caught sight of them watching him, and stopped in his tracks.

Anna said something to him and he scowled in return. She caught the word '*anya*', which she knew meant 'ma', in his reply. His hair was the same dark brown as Mária's. He had pale skin and a sulky mouth.

Anna's response was much harsher than her usual friendly tone.

The boy turned round and barged out of the kitchen.

Kirsty raised an eyebrow at Anna as his heavy footsteps died away.

'Mária *fia*, Dasco,' said Anna. Mária's son, Dasco.

Kirsty nodded. She wondered why she hadn't come across him before.

Anna shuddered. '*Szörnyű fiú.* Horrible boy.'

Kirsty raised an eyebrow again.

'*Ő org yilkos.* He is a thug.'

Anna gabbled away furiously. At the sight of Kirsty's blank expression she hawked up some saliva and deposited it forcefully onto the floor, before rubbing it in with her shoe. Her eyes were fierce.

How awful. Dasco must have spat at her. Kirsty didn't have the words to express her revulsion so she mimed her disgust, pretending to be sick into her hands.

A ghost of a smile appeared on Anna's white face.

Later that week, Kirsty was on her way to Matron's office when she heard raised voices speaking in English. It wasn't the wireless this time. She'd become used to the sound of the BBC news, and its dismal reports of the war, but these voices were different: louder, more insistent. She dawdled in the corridor and pretended to look at the noticeboard, telling herself she was only showing due concern for her teacher.

'You must leave at once. We have grave concerns for your safety. We must insist on your immediate return to Scotland.' The voice was strident, easily carrying from the room.

Kirsty had to strain to hear Matron's answer. Her tone was quiet but firm. 'I really think you're overexaggerating the concern. As a Gentile, I'm not in any physical danger, and I certainly couldn't leave my girls at this time. Besides, there are still a number of British subjects here in Budapest – as well as other foreigners. None of them seems in a rush to depart.'

Again the authoritative voice: 'It is our moral duty to implore you to reconsider. You may feel safe now but matters could escalate very quickly. Please return to Scotland before it's too late.'

Kirsty felt a stab of fear. If these men thought Matron was in danger, then she must be too.

But Matron's reply was as quietly determined as before. 'If the situation should change, I will deal with it then. I'm very grateful for your concern, but I assure you my mind is made up.'

There followed another short exchange, then the sound of goodbyes. Kirsty kept her eyes glued to the noticeboard as two men swept past her up the corridor. A trace of cologne and pipe smoke trailed after them.

She allowed some time to elapse, then crept down to Matron's room and peered round the door.

Her teacher had her head in her hands; her shoulders were slumped and the harsh overhead light picked out a few threads of grey in her hair.

'Are you all right?'

Matron looked up wearily. 'Kirsty . . . I'm sorry, I forgot about your lesson.'

'That doesn't matter.' Kirsty sat down opposite her, in her usual place. 'I saw the men leave your office and was worried about you.' It wasn't really a lie. She *was* deeply concerned for Matron, and the men did seem threatening.

'I've just had another visit from the school governors, demanding I return home for my own safety.'

Kirsty fiddled with the hem of her skirt. 'I see.'

'Of course, I said no,' Matron replied.

Kirsty's heart hammered against her chest wall. 'Do you really think we're safe here?'

Matron sighed. 'I think we're as safe as anywhere in Europe. As I told you, Regent Horthy will hold the Germans at bay; he's confident that Hitler will respect Hungary's neutrality. And he's banned the Arrow Cross too.'

'Arrow Cross?'

'A fascist party. Sometimes called the Nyilas.' Matron's eyes narrowed. 'You might have seen their emblem around. It's a cross made of arrows, an ancient symbol of the Magyar tribes who settled in Hungary. They want to restore a pure Hungarian race.' She pressed her fingers against the space between her eyebrows. 'They particularly hate the Jews.'

'Why?'

Matron sighed. 'It's complicated. Hungary's a very poor country, but many Jewish families are quite rich and powerful. People are starting to blame the Jews for their plight. The Arrow Cross are determined to eradicate them.'

'But we have so many Jewish children at the school.'

'And it's our responsibility to look after those poor lambs. How on earth could I desert my post when these little ones depend on me so much?' Matron stared out of the window for a few seconds. 'But of course, you're free to go, Kirsty. I would try to arrange safe passage for your return to Scotland.'

In her mind, Kirsty saw the little line of girls in the dining room, their eyes lighting up at the sight of a meal she'd helped make for them, a meal which made their tummies fuller and their bodies stronger. Perhaps taking their minds off their troubles for a while.

'I'd hate to leave the little ones too,' she said.

Matron smiled. 'You've been a wonderful addition to the school, dear. But you must return if you want to. We have no claim over you. Much as we'd hate to lose you, we could always advertise for a new assistant cook.'

Kirsty imagined returning to the house in Beckford Street – assuming she could pay the rent – trying to blink away the sight of Da at every turn. Or attempting to persuade Maggie to take her back and dreading what Archie would do next. Or taking up her job at the baths again and seeing the miners troop in each Friday night, trying to avoid her eye. Or imposing herself on Aunt Ruth and enduring her chilly ways for the next few years. 'No thanks,' she said. 'There's nothing for me in Hamilton. You and the girls are my family now.'

'Then we'll remain here together. Two Scottish refugees in Central Europe.'

'Do you miss your old home?' Kirsty had never asked Matron about where she grew up.

Her expression softened. 'Sometimes I dream of Dunscore, where I was born. My father was a farmer. We lived out in the country. I still miss the soft hills and thatched crofts; the clumps of snowdrops in spring, the fiery bracken in autumn. I miss the sound of the greylags calling to each other in the mornings, or the bleating of the sheep in the fields. Or the swoop and glide of ospreys in summer. When I was a child I yearned for the hustle and bustle of Glasgow; now I live in a big city, I hanker for the peace of countryside. Budapest is so busy. You don't get much wildlife in Vörösmarty Street.'

Kirsty laughed.

'Sometimes, on a Sunday afternoon, when many of the girls are on home visits, I wander down to Lipótváros, then walk along beside the Danube, watching the swans and mallards on the river. Even a short time away from the busyness of the school seems to restore me for the week ahead.' Poor Matron. She worked so hard. After a while Kirsty realised the reason she was often late to meals was not down to bad time-keeping or wanting a lie-in before breakfast, it was because she was sorting out disputes between the girls or writing reports for the mission, or popping down to the food markets to buy the household groceries. She had so many responsibilities.

'And will you still take the pupils to Lake Balaton next summer?'

Matron's face brightened. 'Aye. It's so beautiful there. You'd love it. We'll definitely have to persuade Mária to release you for a few weeks.'

'That would be wonderful. The only thing I miss about Hamilton is swimming.'

'Ah yes, swimming. You'll be able to do lots of that at the lake. And perhaps you could teach some of the girls too.'

Kirsty felt the sharp shock of cold water on her skin, its silkiness as it wrapped itself around her, the freedom in her limbs as she swam. 'Yes, please!' she said. Cooking was her job now but swimming was her passion, and she'd never given up hope of becoming a swimming teacher one day. Perhaps the trip to the lake would bring her one step closer.

Matron reached for her notebook. 'That's decided then. We're both staying, and we're going to Lake Balaton next summer.'

As Kirsty prepared to be tested on her latest list of Hungarian words, she became aware the pounding of blood in her ears had stopped, replaced by a mellow calm. Matron was confident that Hungary was safe, and Kirsty trusted her. Everything would be all right.

# 8

Spring 1940

The balmy days of autumn gradually hardened into the piercing cold of November and December, and soon it was a new year. More and more Jewish children were applying to join the school; the lines etched on Matron's forehead deepened and new grey hairs appeared on her head amidst the brown. Each week, it seemed, another pupil's father left the country for work – or even both parents – leaving a bewildered daughter behind at the school. Sometimes, at night, Kirsty heard the screams and sobs of a girl having nightmares, followed by the closing of a door then the soft pad of Matron's slippers and her soothing tones as she settled the child. In the morning, Matron's eyes would be red rimmed with exhaustion.

Kirsty often joined her teacher in listening to the BBC news. Last October the first German plane had been shot down over Humbie in East Lothian – only about sixty miles from Hamilton, where she used to live. And food rationing in Britain was announced in January. Once again she reassured herself she was doing the right thing, staying on in Budapest.

In early March, Mária took to her bed with a cold for a few days, and Matron asked Kirsty to accompany her to the early-morning market at Csepel.

'You'll have to be up at five,' she said. 'You can get a basic breakfast ready for the girls the night before, then perform the finishing touches when we're back. There'll be plenty of time.'

Kirsty set her alarm, and was downstairs, dressed in her serge coat, mittens and woollen hat, just before the hour. Matron appeared soon after, wearing a huge knapsack and handed her a similar, but smaller one. 'Here you are.'

Matron helped Kirsty secure the knapsack on her shoulders, then they set off through shadowy, quiet streets. The air was icy. A sharp wind tugged at Matron's headscarf and she stopped for a moment to fasten it more tightly. Kirsty stamped her feet in her thin boots to keep warm while she waited.

As they neared the market, she could see the stall holders setting out crates of produce in the early-morning light. The air was laced with the earthy odour of vegetables and the sweeter scent of fruit. Shoppers with net bags or wicker baskets were already hovering, eyeing up boxes crammed with apples or potatoes, or trays overflowing with spinach.

'We'll go to the butcher's first,' said Matron, leading Kirsty into a small shop to one side of the market. 'Mr Sereda knows me well. I'll see if I can get a little beef for you to make goulash tonight. You'll have to eke it out with plenty of onions and carrots but it will be so warming and nourishing for the girls in this weather.'

Kirsty nodded. She'd made goulash lots of times by now. Mária had also taught her to cook *halászlé*, a kind of fish stew; cabbage leaves stuffed with beef and *meggyleves* – a soup made from sour cherries. Apparently Mária's speciality was *Jókai bableves*, a bean soup that contained pork, but Matron had discouraged her from offering it. The Jewish children were forbidden by their religion from eating the meat and Matron didn't think it was fair to have it on the menu.

Kirsty had grown used to going up to bed with her clothes smelling of paprika and fried onions. But she loved being in the kitchen – the chopping, stirring, mixing and serving; Mária's curt approval; the girls' cries of delight when they saw their favourite food; Matron beaming at her from across the dining hall. No matter that her hands were scarred and chapped and her back often ached from leaning over the kitchen table for hours, it made her feel good inside to be helping. And although the terrible loss of Da still gnawed at her, particularly when she was alone, increasingly she felt accepted.

The bell above the butcher's shop rang as Matron opened the door. Mr Sereda glanced round at them as he chopped meat at the long blood-stained counter that ran along the back of the room, then returned to his work. They waited a few moments, then Matron called out to him. Kirsty sensed a reluctance in the way he slowly turned round. Matron pointed at a joint of beef in the front of the display cabinet and said something in Hungarian. Kirsty's understanding of the language had come on in leaps and bounds over the last few months, mainly due to Matron's diligent teaching and Anna's friendship, but Matron's exchange with the butcher was too fast and complicated to follow. What wasn't difficult to understand, however, were the butcher's expressions which ranged from surly to downright belligerent. Yet Matron persisted and eventually emerged from the shop with a joint of beef and a red face. 'I don't know what was the matter with him,' she said, her expression perturbed. 'He's normally so friendly.'

It was the same at the fruiterer's, where the shop assistant silently took the coins Matron offered her and passed over a large bag of apples, her eyes averted. They bought some more vegetables from the stallholders, who were civil enough, but Kirsty noticed people staring as they made their way around the market.

Matron was pensive as they walked home under the brightening sky. 'I didn't imagine the hostility just then, did I?' she asked Kirsty after a while.

'I don't think you did, no.'

Worry lines played around Matron's mouth. 'Public opinion is turning against us because of our Jewish pupils. I'm afraid Budapest is no longer the tolerant city I thought it was.'

'Are the girls in danger?' asked Kirsty, the old feelings of alarm resurfacing. 'Or are we?'

'I don't think so,' Matron replied. 'But we can't be too careful now. Please don't ever go to the market without me. And don't mention the school to outsiders. I've read a few Budapest newspapers lately and there've been several editorials criticising the work of the Scottish Mission, claiming we're harbouring Jews. Better safe than sorry.'

'All right.' Kirsty gripped the straps of her rucksack more tightly.

They returned to a scene of consternation. One of the girls' mothers was pacing up and down the hall, the tears running down her face, as a clearly ill-at-ease teacher hovered beside her.

Kirsty couldn't follow the woman's words, but it was obvious she was extremely distressed. She could barely speak for sobs, and her fingers constantly plucked at her hair and clothes.

Matron laid a hand on her arm, and the woman sagged against her. Matron stood stock-still, murmuring soothingly in her ear.

Kirsty gently picked up the rucksack from where it had been hastily deposited, then headed towards the kitchen to unpack its contents, alongside those of her own bag. But Matron stopped her.

'Kirsty – could you please bring some food for this dear lady? Perhaps some of the meat and apples we bought? And I do believe there is some of that delicious soup left we had for lunch yesterday. Could you pop it in a flask? And some milk too.'

It was on the tip of Kirsty's tongue to point out there wouldn't be enough supplies left for the girls' breakfasts if she gave all that food away, but something in Matron's expression deterred her. 'Of course,' she said, hurrying off to the kitchen.

She returned with the food, neatly packed into a basket, and Matron handed it over to the woman with a smile. The woman pressed a hanky to her face and nodded her thanks.

Matron came into the kitchen half an hour later, just as Kirsty was buttering bread and decanting into bowls some blackberry jam that they'd made last autumn. She and Anna had spent an afternoon picking the ripe fruit from the school garden one sunny Saturday afternoon and had returned, giggling, with purple-stained mouths.

Matron pulled out a chair and slumped at the table. 'I think this justifies using some of our precious tea, Kirsty. May I trouble you to make me a cup?' Kirsty reached for the small packet of Lipton's at the back of the larder. Most Hungarians drank fruit or herbal tea, but they'd managed to bring some British tea with them in September when they'd come across. They were eking it out, only using it on special occasions. The last time had been Christmas.

She filled the kettle and set it to boil on the range.

'Thank you for giving that poor woman the food I asked for,' said Matron. She massaged her forehead. 'She was in a terrible state.'

Kirsty reached up to the cupboard to retrieve a cup and saucer then rummaged in the drawer for a spoon. 'She looked really upset. What was the matter?'

'Her husband, the only breadwinner, has been forced to join a labour unit to fight the Russians. She's on her own with four bairns, no government help, and at the mercy of thugs who've broken into her house and stolen her food.'

'How awful.' The kettle was shrieking now. Kirsty warmed the pot, added a sprinkling of tea, then poured in hot water. There wasn't much milk left, after giving some to the woman. She wished she'd known, then she could have bought some when they were out, although they were due a delivery soon. She tipped a small amount into the teacup she'd put out earlier.

'I think she'd reached the end of her tether.'

'Poor thing.' Kirsty poured the tea into Matron's cup and handed it over. Then she joined her at the table. 'There's something I don't understand though.'

'Oh?'

'If Hungary is neutral in this war, why are men being asked to fight?'

Matron took a sip of tea, the steam clouding her glasses, which she then removed and polished on her jumper. 'Even after all this time, I still struggle with Hungarian politics, but this is what I know.' She replaced the glasses. 'The Hungarians lost a lot of land after the Great War but recently Hitler let them have some of it back. Now he's called in the debt, demanding Horthy provide him with soldiers to help him fight. He wants vast numbers of men. The anti-Jewish laws have prohibited Jews from entering the regular army so Horthy's forced them into these labour battalions.' Her mouth twisted. 'I have a feeling the Jewish men won't be as well treated as Hungarian soldiers.'

'I see.'

'The families certainly aren't being provided for financially, which is why Mrs Elek is so distraught. The poor thing said she'd be better off dead. I think she was close to doing away with herself and her wee bairns.'

Kirsty swallowed. She'd known desperation too but she'd always had support – first Maggie and now Matron. By all accounts this wretched woman had nothing. 'I'm glad we were able to help her.'

'Aye. I know it leaves us short, Kirsty, but we're well fed here compared to her.' She stood up. 'Come on. I'll help you with the breakfasts.'

Over the ensuing days, Kirsty noticed that some food items were going missing. There were far fewer potatoes in the crate, even though she hadn't used any lately, and when she went to the larder for cream cheese she could have sworn the stock was depleted. Then some more apples disappeared, and worst of all, the precious packet of Lipton's tea. At first Kirsty assumed Matron had taken more food to give to the woman, but when she mentioned it, she assured her she'd have checked with her first. It was strange.

Mária had recovered from her cold now and was back in the kitchen. As if to make up for lost time, she set about energetically cleaning the range after breakfast, while Kirsty tidied away the meal. As she did so she asked the cook about the missing food.

Mária shrugged and kept on cleaning.

Kirsty explained about the items they'd given to the distraught woman and Mária raised her eyes to the ceiling. 'That Matron is too generous,' she said. 'She'll have us left with nothing if we're not careful.'

She also mentioned it to Erzsébet and Célia, the local girls who came in to wash up in the evenings, but they vehemently denied all knowledge. Kirsty was inclined to believe them. They'd risk losing their jobs if they were caught stealing, and anyway they earned enough to buy their own food. Besides, the food disappeared in the day, not during the evenings when they were there.

All was fine for a while, then the following week a chicken carcass that Kirsty had earmarked for soup went missing from the larder. Mária must have heard her cry of annoyance.

'What's the matter?' she asked.

'Now the chicken has disappeared. How am I supposed to make soup?'

Mária avoided her eyes. 'You will have to make bean soup instead. I'll show you how.'

Perhaps it was Kirsty's imagination, but Mária seemed to

take extra care with her instructions about the soup and was gentler with her usual criticism when Kirsty failed to chop the onions finely enough, even offering to redo them herself.

Kirsty was grateful for the extra help, but it still didn't solve the puzzle of the missing food. She mentioned it when she next went to Matron for her Hungarian lesson. They were progressing on to the past tense now, but Kirsty was still managing to keep up and it was clear her teacher was pleased with her.

Matron frowned when Kirsty told her about the thefts.

'I have no idea what's happening,' she said, 'but we need to be extra vigilant. I might invest in some locks for the larder. I'll always help people in genuine need but I won't tolerate stealing. That food is for my girls and their teachers. We must make every effort to protect it.' And she drew out her grammar book with a determined expression.

# 9

As Kirsty's Hungarian improved, so her friendship with Anna deepened. Once her language skills were up to it, she'd asked Anna why she had initially befriended her. Anna told her she didn't trust Mária, or Dasco her son. They were sly and mean. A few of the girls had reported they felt uncomfortable around Dasco; he had a habit of jumping out at them, leering and laughing, when they rounded a corner. And Mária often made the girls eat the fattier cuts of meat at mealtimes, only bringing out the leaner slices when the pupils were leaving the dining room, no doubt keeping them for herself. When Kirsty arrived at the school, Anna was worried she'd be at the mercy of the pair and had decided to hang around after meals to check Kirsty was all right. It was typically kind of her. But then she'd discovered how much she enjoyed Kirsty's company. What had started as an act of support had soon become a mutual affection.

They were in Kirsty's room one Sunday afternoon in early April, a sudden shower lashing the window. Anna was teaching her the rules of *Ulti*, a Hungarian card game. Anna was the same age as Kirsty – fifteen now – and due to leave school the following year.

'What will you do then?' Kirsty asked her.

'My father owns a watchmaking business,' Anna replied, shuffling the cards in her hand. 'It was always the plan that I'd go to work for him – my older brother Endre does so already – but times are very difficult for Jews just now.' She dealt Kirsty seven cards, face down. 'We're lucky *Abba*'s business hasn't been shut down yet.'

'I'm sorry,' Kirsty said. Matron had told her about the restrictions that had been imposed on Jewish stores. Last week a grocer had been told he could no longer stock any vegetables or meats, nor sugar, flour, milk or butter. To prove the point, soldiers ransacked the place and threw all the prohibited goods out into the courtyard behind his shop, making a terrible mess. They threatened to return the following week to check no rules were being infringed. Other businesses had their shop fronts regularly sullied with graffiti; many closed altogether. And things were worse elsewhere in Europe. Over in Germany, Austria and the Sudetenland, nearly eighteen months ago, Jewish shops were ransacked, their glass windows smashed. It had been called *Kristallnacht*, crystal night, because of the constant sound of broken glass. If Anna's father's business was still operating he was indeed lucky.

'Do you like watches?' Kirsty asked her.

Anna shrugged. 'Watchmaking is something to do until I get married and have a family.'

Kirsty giggled. 'Do you have anyone in mind?'

'Of course not.' Anna dealt her own hand then stacked some more cards on the bed. 'We really need three players.' She grabbed Kirsty's alarm clock from her bedside table and placed it in front of the third pile of cards. 'There we are. The clock is our extra player. It even has a face!'

Kirsty pretended to shake hands with the alarm clock. 'Welcome to our game, Mr Clock!'

Anna laughed. 'Now. Have a look at your cards . . . be careful not to show them to me . . . then we'll start the auction.'

The game was complicated and demanded all of Kirsty's concentration for the next hour. The rules were strange and even with her improved language skills, it was hard to follow. Sometimes she'd played rummy or cheat with Da, but *Ulti* was much harder. And Hungarian cards were different too. There were no queens for a start, but two sorts of knaves – known as *Felső* and *Alsó*. Apparently they were based on the William Tell legend – even though that was Swiss. Very confusing.

As Anna collected up the cards afterwards and pushed them back into the packet, Kirsty glanced out of the window. 'It's stopped raining now. We could go into the garden.'

'All right.' Anna picked up her cardigan from where she'd discarded it on the bed.

Matron encouraged them to walk on Sunday afternoons. When Kirsty had first come to the school, she'd taken her sightseeing in Budapest. They'd visited the magnificent Parliament building; walked across the Chain Bridge that divided the two parts of the city, and staggered up the hill to Buda Castle. But lately, she'd warned the girls not to leave the school. 'Too many people are opposing what we do here,' she said sadly. 'I don't think any of us is safe any more.' She still went to the market early each morning, but often returned pale and tight lipped. And the supplies were dwindling too. She hardly ever brought back meat, and even the vegetables were old and rubbery. Kirsty and Mária had their work cut out trying to make the meals palatable.

'Tell me more about your family,' Kirsty said as they wandered round the garden in the watery spring sunshine. The recent shower had drenched the plants and shiny droplets of rainwater still nestled in some of the leaves. The air smelled damp and fragrant. Last month, she and Matron had planted some herbs. Little stalks of marjoram were already poking through the soil and, further down the path, feathery clumps of dill. Another attempt to make the food taste more interesting. There were plans to grow potatoes and carrots later too. Anything to shore themselves up against the possibility of more deprivations.

Anna pulled some blossom off a flowering cherry tree that stood in the corner of the garden. 'Well, there's my parents of course. *Abba* and Endre work in the shop and Mama looks after us all.'

'Do you have any other brothers and sisters?'

Anna paused, her fingers crushing the cherry petals. 'No, I don't,' she replied in a small voice.

Kirsty glanced at her. As an only child she'd always felt an outsider. Most families in Hamilton had three or four bairns, sometimes more, and she'd envied her friends their relationships with their siblings, even the ones who claimed to hate each other. It must be wonderful to be part of a big noisy family. It was often so quiet with just her and Da in the house – and the distant memories of Ma. Thank goodness she'd left Beckford Street. Living on her own would have been unbearable. At least at the school she had plenty of company: surly Mária, warm, motherly Matron, and now, wonderfully, a friend of her own age. Dear, sweet Anna.

'What's Endre like?'

Anna smiled. 'He's a lot like *Abba*, really. Kind, thoughtful. A bit shy.'

'Do you get on?'

'We used to fight a bit when we were younger, but since . . . well, over the last few years we've grown a lot closer. I look up to him now. And he's very protective of me. If he thinks our parents are being too strict he always comes to my defence. He used to protect me when we were both at junior school too.' She stared into the middle distance. 'At one time, an older girl used to bully me. She'd waylay me in the toilets and yank my hair, or deliberately spill sauce down my back at lunchtime.'

'Why?' There were bullies at her school back in Hamilton, probably in all schools, but they'd mercifully left Kirsty alone, probably thinking having a dead mother was suffering enough.

Anna shrugged. 'I was good at sport – always in the school teams – and quite academic too. Sometimes people are just jealous . . . or else she hated me for being Jewish. I don't know. At any rate, I eventually told Endre about it. He'd found me in tears at home time. The next day he sat next to me at lunch, then scowled and put his arm round me as the girl came past. He grabbed her hand and told her if she ever bullied me again he'd inform the headmaster.' Anna grinned at the recollection. 'After that she kept well away.'

Kirsty pushed aside an overhanging bough as they walked under a rose arch, triggering an avalanche of raindrops. 'You're lucky to have an older brother to look after you.' She held the branch back until Anna had gone through, then let it go.

Anna dropped the crushed cherry blossom petals to the ground. 'Why don't you come over next Sunday afternoon? I'm sure my family would love to meet you. You could sample some of Mama's cooking.'

85

Kirsty smiled at her friend. Her face was more animated now, the brown eyes lit up with anticipation. She'd looked so wan earlier that Kirsty was worried she was sickening for something. Perhaps she was just tired. The extra boarders at the school meant it was noisier at night, with more little ones to settle. Poor Matron looked exhausted as she went from dormitory to dormitory, taking hot drinks to pupils who couldn't sleep and soothing those who'd had nightmares. Kirsty's Hungarian lessons had started to be more sporadic and she didn't like to burden her teacher with another demand on her time. There were dark purple shadows under Matron's eyes each morning as it was, and her hair was lank. The noisy nights made it harder to sleep for everyone, and Kirsty and Mária had their work cut out with extra mouths to feed. The war news wasn't good either. Earlier that month, Germany had invaded Norway and Denmark, countries that were only just across the North Sea from Scotland. Kirsty feared for her homeland. She might be living in Budapest but she was still a Scot at heart. Perhaps a visit to Anna's house would cheer her up. 'I'd love that,' she said.

Anna's brother Endre was waiting for them on the corner of Vörösmarty utca. Matron was much happier to let Kirsty and Anna go knowing they had a young man to protect them on the journey. Although Anna could have attended the school as a day pupil, her parents had felt it safer for her, a Jewish girl, to board.

'Good afternoon.' Endre bowed his head as Anna introduced Kirsty. He had the same colour hair and dark eyes as his sister. Anna had told her he was seventeen. They feared he'd be drafted into service within the next few months. More and more of the pupils' fathers were being compelled to join the labour units, or sent to work camps up in the north, another huge cause of anxiety at the school. It was fortunate that Anna's father was quite elderly, much older than her mother apparently, so hadn't been conscripted.

Endre smiled at her, and Kirsty felt a rush of blood to her face. She busied herself smoothing down her coat and checking her hair.

'Did you see that policeman?' asked Anna as they turned into Andrássy út and headed towards the Jewish quarter.

'No, I didn't.' In truth she was too busy darting surreptitious glances at Endre when she thought he wasn't looking, to notice anyone else.

'He was watching us,' Anna said. She bit her lip.

'Ah yes. Matron told me about that. She said the authorities are concerned about the school as we have so many Jewish girls. They've offered to put a guard at the corner of the road. He's protecting us really.'

'I see.' Anna smiled thinly. 'Good for him.'

Endre frowned but said nothing. He led them onto Erzsébet körút, past high cream and brown buildings with arched windows, intricate metal balconies and elaborate stone carvings. He pointed out the brand-new Híradó cinema, and for a second Kirsty imagined sitting with him in the dark, without Anna, watching a romantic film, then blushed at the thought. That was a ridiculous fantasy. And anyway, Jews weren't allowed to go to the cinema now.

Finally, they turned down a street containing several shops at ground level, with towering five-storey apartments above.

He stopped in front of one of them. 'Here we are,' he said. 'This is our family business. We've had to close the shop, but we still make watches behind closed doors. There are workshops on the first floor, and we live above them.' Kirsty looked up at the rest of the building with its numerous windows draped with elaborate net curtains. For a second she wondered whether one was Endre's bedroom, and felt her cheeks flush at the thought.

There was a rattling sound and the door to the shop flew open. 'Kirsty. Welcome.' An older, plumper version of Anna held out her arms.

Kirsty glanced at her friend who smiled and nodded, and Kirsty allowed herself to be hugged. It was comforting to feel Mrs Bellak's arms around her and inhale the smell of fresh-baked bread that clung to her jumper. A figure appeared beside her – a slightly stooped man with a kind face and short grey beard – and proffered his hand for Kirsty to shake. As he smiled, a slew of lines fanned out from his eyes. '*Helló*, Kirsty.' Neither he nor his son wore skull caps.

The couple ushered Kirsty inside and Anna and Endre followed her through the shop, up several flights of stairs and into a small room containing two armchairs and a sofa, all covered in some silky, flowery material. A polished wooden table stood in the corner, topped with a plate of pastries. On the windowsill, in front of one of the cream net curtains Kirsty had seen earlier, there was a large shiny candle holder, presumably made of some kind of metal. It looked very old.

Mrs Bellak handed Kirsty a plate and an embroidered napkin. An image flashed into her mind of Da, with his mine-grimed fingers, chomping on a hunk of bread from an old, chipped plate. She wondered what he'd have thought of her in this fancy house eating with *knabs*.

'Anna tells me you work in the kitchen at the school,' Mrs Bellak said.

'Yes, I do.' Kirsty wondered if she disapproved of her daughter mixing with domestics.

'Well, you'll have to tell me what you think of these *rugelach*.' She offered the plate of pastries to Kirsty. Kirsty didn't recognise the word '*rugelach*' although clearly Mrs Bellak was referring to the little rolled pastry delicacies which seemed to be filled with stewed apricots.

She took one and bit into it. There was an explosion of sweetness, then the tang of fruit laced with honey. 'Very good,' she said, then wondered if she should have emptied her mouth before speaking.

Mrs Bellak smiled and offered some to the others. Then she went out to the kitchen and returned with a tray of glasses which contained a black, spicy tea. Again Kirsty was served first.

Anna's parents asked her about her work at the school and told her how delighted they were with Anna's progress under Matron's care. The conversation felt a little stilted, and Kirsty was very conscious of Endre sitting there silently munching *rugelach* and occasionally sipping his tea. She glanced round the room during a lull in the conversation and noticed a small silver-framed photo on the table that had been partly obscured by the plate of pastries earlier. The picture featured a small child, maybe five or six, with dark curly hair and a winsome smile. Kirsty wondered who she was and resolved to ask Anna later.

After Kirsty had accepted, and eaten, another pastry, but

declined a further cup of tea, Mrs Bellak suggested she and Anna went up to Anna's bedroom.

Kirsty followed Anna up the stairs with some relief. They played *Ulti* for a while, this time Anna's gold watch deputising for the third player, then Anna showed Kirsty her collection of her mother's old fashion magazines. They leafed through them for a bit, marvelling at the silk dresses and extravagant hats. Kirsty couldn't ever imagine wearing clothes like those.

'I could tell my parents liked you,' Anna said as she tried to coax Kirsty's unruly auburn hair into a style resembling that of Vivien Leigh in one of the photographs.

'I hope so,' Kirsty replied, wincing as a hairclip nearly pierced her scalp. 'They're very polite, aren't they?'

Anna laughed. 'It's just their way. They were trying to make you feel welcome.'

'The pastries were delicious. I must talk to Mária about them. See if we can make some at the school – provided we have enough ingredients.'

'That would be nice. Although we usually only have *rugelach* at festivals or holidays. Mama must have been saving up the butter and sugar.'

'Then I'm very honoured.' Kirsty couldn't remember the last time anyone had done something that special for her. Maggie had tried to tempt her with nourishing food after Da had died, but she'd never felt really welcome at the house because of Archie. She wondered fleetingly how he was behaving. Especially with not being able to fight in the war. She hoped he wasn't taking his frustrations out on Maggie.

She suddenly remembered the little photo on the table downstairs and asked Anna who it was.

'My older sister, Róza,' Anna said. 'She died five years ago.' She gnawed at a bit of loose skin beside her thumbnail. 'My parents never talk about her.'

'I'm so sorry,' Kirsty replied. 'That's terrible.'

Anna stood up. 'It is.'

She led Kirsty back downstairs and they said goodbye to her parents before Endre returned to walk them home.

Kirsty was dying to ask Anna more about Róza – or to see if Endre would be more forthcoming about his other sister, but both seemed lost in thought and she didn't like to interrupt them.

But as they turned into Wesselényi utca, they stopped short in horror. An elderly lady, dressed in a black coat with a dark headscarf, was surrounded by a group of thugs with steel-toed boots. They had close-cropped hair and menacing expressions.

One of them drew his arm back then hurled it forward. A stone ricocheted off the woman's coat. 'You filthy Jew!' he shouted.

When she put her arm up to defend herself, another youth pushed her into the gutter. She caught her foot on the kerb and crashed onto the cobbles, her basket falling with her and apples and potatoes flying down the road. Kirsty winced in horror.

'Stay here,' Endre yelled and rushed towards the woman. 'How dare you?' he shouted to the young men – around the same age as himself – 'Picking on a defenceless old lady?'

Kirsty and Anna watched, appalled, as the thugs then turned on Endre, kicking him in the ribs and stomach. He went down like a stone, rolling over to his side, gasping for breath. The boys laughed and ran off.

Ignoring Endre's instructions, Kirsty dashed over to the woman who was sitting up by now, feebly trying to retrieve the contents of her basket. 'Let me,' said Kirsty and ran down the road to scoop up the fallen items. 'The apples are a bit bruised but they'll still be edible, and the potatoes will be fine.' She tipped them into the woman's basket, then helped her to her feet. 'Is there anyone I can fetch for you?'

The woman shook her head. 'I'm nearly home,' she said. 'My daughter's there. She'll look after me. Is your friend all right? He was only trying to defend me.'

'I think so,' Kirsty replied. Anna had gone straight over to Endre. He was still lying on the ground, but he was conscious and taking slow, painful breaths.

Kirsty checked the old lady was steady on her feet, and watched her walk down the road until she reached her house. Then she turned back to Endre. Anna was talking to him quietly.

'Bloody keelie scum!' Kirsty said.

'Sorry?' Anna's face was pale, her eyes wide with shock.

Kirsty translated the Glaswegian phrase into Hungarian. The boys were remorseless thugs.

Endre was silent, apart from the rasping breaths. Gradually his body relaxed, his breathing became easier and he struggled to sit up.

'How are you feeling now?' Kirsty asked him.

'Better.' His dark hair stuck to his forehead and he winced with the effort of moving. Kirsty and Anna supported him. Despite her anxiety, Kirsty felt an electric pulse go through her body as she tucked her hand under his armpit to help pull him up from the ground. He smiled bleakly at her.

'Can you stand?'

He nodded, then grimaced again as they hauled him upright.

'What do you want to do now?' Anna asked, her face still pasty. 'Shall we take you back home?'

Endre shook his head. 'I don't want to worry *Abba* and Mama. Let's carry on to Vörösmarty Street. I think I can walk all right.' He took a few steps to demonstrate.

'You'll be black and blue by the morning,' said Kirsty.

'I know. Thankfully there's no bleeding, though. I'll tell our parents that I tripped on the kerb. It's not really a lie. I'll just omit the fact I was helped on my way.' His mouth twisted.

'Who were they?' asked Kirsty. 'Did you know them?'

'No,' replied Endre. 'But I suspect they're Arrow Cross.'

'I thought Regent Horthy had banned the fascists.'

'He has.' Endre was panting with the effort of both speaking and walking. 'But they still operate. Lucky for me they're illegal, otherwise they might have done a lot more damage.'

'But why attack you? And that poor woman?'

Endre sighed. 'They hang around the Jewish quarter, looking for people to pick on. Usually it's just spitting or shoving. I obviously provoked them.'

'What else could you have done?' asked Anna. 'You couldn't have let them torment that old lady and just stand by. I'm sure Kirsty and I would have intervened if you hadn't acted first.'

'I'm glad you didn't. Much better it was me that copped it than you. I'm supposed to be protecting you.'

'You did,' said Kirsty. 'You protected that woman too. But surely you're not going to let them get away with it? You need to report the attack to the authorities.'

'No point.' Endre stopped to rub his back. 'No one would listen. Our people aren't exactly popular right now.'

'But I thought Jews are coming into Hungary from other countries because they think they'll be safer here.'

'They are. Officially,' Endre replied. 'Our country is still neutral in this war but strength of feeling against Jews is rising. There've been demonstrations, articles in newspapers . . . and essentially Horthy is anti-Semitic. He might not have legalised the Arrow Cross but he's still drafting Jewish men into labour units and passing dozens of regulations limiting our lives.'

Anna shivered and Endre glanced at her anxiously. 'You're safe at the school,' he said. 'But I don't think you should go home for a while. I'll lie low too. See if all this blows over.'

But it was evident from his expression that he didn't think that was likely.

Later, Anna came into the kitchen, just as Kirsty was boiling eggs in a huge saucepan. A kind local smallholder had dropped some off; it would be such a treat for the girls. Kirsty planned to hard-boil them and serve them quartered with some salt and pepper – and the customary paprika, of course. Delicious. And healthy too.

Anna poured herself a glass of water then came and sat at the table. 'Poor Endre,' she said.

Kirsty prodded at the saucepan, set the timer, then joined her friend. 'Yes, I can't believe those dobbers attacked him like that. Sometimes there are fights in Glasgow – usually youths who've had too much to drink and picked on each other – but to beat him up because he's *Jewish*. And that old lady. That's horrible.'

Anna sighed. 'It happens,' she said. 'Nobody seems to like us these days.'

'Well *I* like you,' Kirsty replied.

Anna wrapped her hands round her glass and gave Kirsty a sideways look. 'And do you like Endre too?'

'Of course. He's your brother. And he's kind and gentle.' She felt her cheeks flush with heat.

'Would you like him if he wasn't my brother?' Anna's mouth curved up at the edges and there was a teasing expression in her eyes.

The flush travelled up Kirsty's neck. 'Yes, I would. He's a nice young man.'

'*A nice young man?*' she imitated Kirsty's voice. 'You sound like my mother.' She gave her that speculative look again. 'Anything else?'

Kirsty stood up and went back to check on the pan. She didn't want Anna to see her blush and if she stayed near the stove, she could always blame her red face on the heat coming off the now-bubbling water. She didn't know what to say, so she remained silent and pretended to be busy – looking at the timer and prodding the eggs.

'He likes you,' Anna said.

Kirsty spun round. 'How do you know that?'

'I could tell by the way he looked at you.'

'Oh.' Kirsty grabbed a baking tray from the top of the stove and started to fan her face with it. 'That's nice.'

Anna laughed. 'My lovely brother and my dear friend. What a gorgeous couple you'd make.'

'Anna, stop it. We can't think like that. There's a war on.'

The teasing look vanished. 'Yes, you're right. As soon as Endre turns eighteen he'll made to join the labour service.'

Kirsty dropped the baking tray on the counter with a clatter. 'Matron told me about those.' She didn't add Matron's misgivings that Jewish men were being badly treated in the labour battalions. She blinked away the image of Anna's shy, sensitive brother being shorn of his lovely brown hair, forced to march for mile after mile, beaten as he dug a trench, attacked by Russians . . .

'Mama and *Abba* are worried sick.' Anna fiddled with her watch. 'All we can do is hope the war will end before Endre has to go away.'

'Please God it does,' Kirsty replied, her stomach suddenly knotted with anxiety.

The timer rang shrilly, making both of them jump. Kirsty's actions became automatic. She grabbed a cloth and took the heavy pan off the stove, then tipped out the water, leaving the eggs behind. Next, she refilled the pan with cold water. 'I'll cool the eggs down, then peel off the shells,' she told Anna.

'I'll help you.'

They spent the next half hour preparing the eggs until the skin under their fingernails was sore from prising off the hard shells and they had a pile of discarded fragments, like thin bits of broken porcelain. Kirsty worked mechanically, still brooding over Anna's comments. It was true that she liked Endre and it was exciting to think he might like her too. But what would happen if he had to join a labour unit?

# 10

Despite her conflicting thoughts about Endre, Kirsty normally slept well, exhausted by the early starts and the long hours in the kitchen. But one late April morning she woke suddenly. She didn't know if she'd been disturbed by a noise or a vivid dream but she lay still for a while, her throat dry and her heart pounding. After a few minutes trying unsuccessfully to get back to sleep, she decided to go down to the kitchen for a glass of water. She sat up in bed, swung her legs over the frame and stood up, then retrieved her dressing gown from the back of the door. It was chilly on the dark, silent landing and she drew the belt tightly around her as she crept downstairs in the gloom, careful not to tread on a creaking floorboard or trip on bit of loose carpet in case she woke someone up. She tiptoed along the corridor towards the kitchen, noting with a frown that there was a light on. Strange. She was sure she'd turned it off before she went to bed – and Mária had gone up before her. Perhaps someone else was awake and looking for refreshment. But the figure that greeted her as she entered the room wasn't Matron, or Mária, or any of the girls, but Dasco, his back towards her, sitting at the table with a large hunk of bread and a plate of cold beef in front of him. The very beef she'd cooked and served earlier, intending to use the leftovers for cold cuts the next day. How dare he!

Without thinking of her own safety, she marched into the kitchen and confronted him. 'What do you think you're doing? That food belongs to the school. What on earth makes you think you're entitled to it?'

Dasco jumped, then narrowed his eyes and glowered at her. 'My mother is the cook here and I'll eat what I want. The school has plenty.'

'Did your mother give you permission to eat this food?'

'Of course.' He avoided her eyes. 'But even if she hadn't, I'm still entitled to it.'

'On what grounds?' Kirsty had a fair idea Dasco was chancing his luck. She wondered if he'd done this before. Perhaps that was why the food had gone missing lately. And now she thought about it, that time he'd come into the kitchen when she and Anna were alone in the dining room, he must have been intending to raid the larder. It was only their presence that had stopped him. Doubtless he'd been more successful since.

He ignored her.

'I'll thank you to stop raiding our supplies,' she said, determined to provoke a response from him. 'Surely you're given food at the hotel?' Dasco worked long hours at the Corinthia hotel in Erzsébet körút, which explained why he was rarely around, although he still came back to his room at the school each evening. Thankfully his bedroom was in another part of the building to Kirsty's which meant their paths seldom crossed. She wondered how he'd broken into the larder which they now kept locked. Perhaps he'd got the key from Mária.

He grabbed a piece of bread, shoved it in his mouth and spoke while eating. 'I don't work there any more.'

'Oh?'

'They dispensed with my services.' His tone was angry.

'Well, I'm sorry to hear that but it doesn't give you the right to steal our food.'

'St-eal?' he drew out the word, glaring at her. 'That's a very strong accusation.'

'We only have enough provisions here to feed the girls and the staff,' Kirsty replied. 'I know times are hard, but you should have asked permission first.'

'How do you know I didn't?'

'I don't but I'll check with your mother when I see her later on.' Kirsty was sure that if Mária had known about the food she'd have mentioned it to Kirsty.

'You bloody sneak!' Dasco was on his feet now. He loomed over her menacingly.

Kirsty took a step back. 'All right,' she said, suddenly aware of how vulnerable she was in her dressing gown and night-dress. 'Take the food with you, but don't come back.'

Dasco grabbed at the last of the bread and meat and shoved it into his pocket. 'I'll do what I want,' he said.

'Then I'll make sure Matron hears about this.'

'I'm not scared of a dried-up spinster.'

'Then I'll call the police.'

He marched up to her, hawked up some saliva, and spat on the ground. A bready globule landed on the linoleum. 'They're far too busy to listen to the likes of you.'

Kirsty swallowed. He was probably right, although she remembered the officer watching the school the day they went to Anna's house. 'We'll see,' she said.

Dasco spat once more, leered at her, then left the kitchen by the back door.

Kirsty tidied the table then returned to her room, suddenly light headed.

She didn't go back to sleep that night, her mind endlessly revisiting her alarming encounter with Mária's son. By five, still awake, she decided she might as well get dressed and start preparing the breakfasts. As she entered the kitchen her stomach spasmed, and she had to swallow hard to avoid being sick. But the room was empty, almost as if he'd never been there. She trudged over to the larder, unlocked the door, scooped up two loaves of bread, then took them over to the counter and started slicing. She'd done this so many times before that her actions were automatic.

Eventually, Mária came in. 'You're early,' she said.

Kirsty pushed back a strand of hair. 'I couldn't sleep.'

'That's not like you.'

'There's a lot on my mind.' She returned to the larder to collect a block of butter and started to cut it into small cubes. They'd had to restrict the amount the girls were allowed, supplies had been so limited lately. Then she told Mária about the encounter with Dasco.

Mária didn't look up from quartering tomatoes.

'How did he get the key to the larder?'

Still Mária didn't make eye contact. 'He must have stolen it from my bag when my back was turned.'

'We won't have enough bread for breakfast now, and the beef he ate was earmarked for lunch.'

'I'll buy some more.' Mária finally looked up. 'Are you going to tell Matron?'

Kirsty bided her time. She placed the bread and butter on

the counter, then returned to the larder to fetch a bowl of cream cheese. 'Not on this occasion,' she said eventually. 'But if it happens again I certainly will.' She couldn't afford to further alienate Mária. Technically Matron was Mária's boss, and Mária was Kirsty's, but their shared nationality meant Kirsty and Matron were much closer than Matron was to Mária. It was complicated. Her encounter with Dasco gave Kirsty the moral high ground, but Mária could still make her life very difficult if she wanted to.

Mária grunted. 'He's got out of hand lately. Mixing with the wrong sort. Yobs that roam the streets looking for trouble. And now he's lost his job at the hotel, he has no money. I don't earn enough for food and rent for us both.' She sniffed. 'But he shouldn't have stolen from us.'

'No, he shouldn't.' Kirsty banged a large jar of jam onto the counter. 'I'm sure Matron would find him some jobs here if he wants. Assuming she can trust him.' She was relieved Mária had confided in her. She must really be worried about her son to have suspended her usual belligerence.

'I'll talk to him tonight,' Mária said, her lips a firm line.

Kirsty nodded and carried on with her preparations.


Kirsty told Anna about Dasco's visit when they were tidying up later after breakfast. They were on their own, Mária having gone to the shops to replenish a few items they'd run out of.

'That doesn't surprise me. He's a nasty piece of work,' Anna said as she swept breadcrumbs off the counter and into her outstretched hand.

'Yes. Made me feel a bit sorry for Mária, having such a lout for a son.'

Anna walked over to the bin and deposited the bread-crumbs. She gave Kirsty a sideways look. 'Makes you appreciate a *nice young man* like Endre even more.'

Kirsty grinned. She was still worried about Endre having to join a labour battalion, but perhaps they could get to know each other better in whatever time remained.

'He dropped in a note to say he'll collect me later,' Anna said. 'He also asked if you'd be around.'

Kirsty picked up a jug of milk and took it into the larder to hide the blush that was travelling up her neck. 'I might be.'

When she came out, Anna shot her another searching glance. 'I could finish up here if you wanted to go and change or anything.'

'All right. Thanks.' Kirsty took off her chef's hat and apron, then sped upstairs to her room.

By the time Endre appeared in the kitchen, Kirsty was dressed in a tweed skirt and blue blouse, which Matron had once told her matched her eyes. She'd splashed cold water on her face and blotted it with a towel. Thankfully her complexion was now calmer and less shiny.

'Hello, Kirsty.' Endre's smile triggered a surge of warmth in her body.

'Hello.' She willed herself not to blush again.

'Anna tells me she'll be busy for a while. I wondered if you'd like to go for a walk until she's ready.'

'A walk outside? Is it safe?' Kirsty had a vivid flashback to Endre lying on the pavement, struggling for breath, after the drubbing by the Arrow Cross thugs. Thugs like Dasco. She knew Endre was taking a risk coming to collect Anna and walk her back to their home, but she sensed he wouldn't want Kirsty to see him so vulnerable again.

'I thought we could look round the school garden. I've never seen it.'

That was a good idea. The garden was private; there was little danger of running into anyone threatening there.

'All right.'

They said goodbye to Anna, who smiled at them knowingly, then made their way outside.

It was warm in the spring sunshine, the air lightly scented by newly budding lilac trees. At first Kirsty felt awkward on her own with Endre, wondering if Dasco was watching from an upstairs window or whether Matron would come out and tell her off for being on her own with a young man. But nobody appeared and after a while she relaxed.

'Are you enjoying being in Hungary?' Endre asked her, as they strolled past a flower bed vivid with tulips.

'Yes, I am. The school feels like home now.' She told him about Matron offering her a post at the school after Da had died. She wondered if Anna had already mentioned it, but if so he didn't let on. He just listened carefully, his brown eyes full of sympathy.

'And Anna isn't too much of a nuisance in the kitchen?'

She laughed. 'Of course not! I love working with her. She's more like a sister to me now.' Did that make Endre like a brother? That didn't seem right.

'Anna loves working with you too.' His whole face lit up as he smiled. 'How are you finding all that cooking?'

'It's nice to be doing something useful, and I don't mind the long hours, only . . .' Endre had such a considerate manner that Kirsty instinctively trusted him.

'Yes?' His tone was gentle.

'. . . I don't want to be a cook all my life. When I was in Scotland I dreamt of one day being a swimming teacher.'

Something flickered in Endre's eyes. Kirsty couldn't tell what. Then he composed himself. 'Why's that?'

Kirsty told him about Da being a lifeguard at the Hamilton baths as well as teaching her to swim in the pool. 'I was happy being a cleaner there, but I always hoped I'd become a swimming instructor one day.'

Endre nodded but didn't ask any more questions. She wondered if she'd said too much, so she moved the subject on to watchmaking and his father's business. They'd walked round the whole of the small garden by then and were sitting on a bench beside the rose arch.

'Like you, I have big dreams,' he said. 'But this terrible war is making everything so difficult.' He frowned, lost in his own thoughts.

'Big dreams?' she prompted.

His face brightened. '*Abba* will pass on the business in time. He's already changed the name to *Bellak and Son*. I don't want to lose *Abba* of course, but I'd love to expand the business to jewellery-making one day.'

'He must be delighted you've inherited his skill.'

'I love making watches. It's fascinating. I love the intricacy, the delicate mechanisms, the satisfaction in bringing something broken back to life.'

Kirsty glanced down at Endre's fingers. They were long and

tapering, the nails clean and neatly cut. She could imagine him handling the miniature tools, painstakingly teasing out a damaged part, or easing a new component into place. She shuddered to think of those gentle hands clawing at the earth as he was forced to clear mines, his nails encrusted with dirt, his fingers roughened with calluses.

'You must have to be very patient,' she said.

Endre smiled. 'That's what I like about it. The calmness of the workshop. The careful movements. The sense of achievement with a job well done.'

'And your father is training you?'

'Yes. It's a long apprenticeship – and *Abba* is a hard taskmaster. I've got a few years to go yet before I can start designing jewellery.' The frown returned. 'As long as my training doesn't get interrupted.'

Kirsty nodded. It was sometimes hard to reassure the girls at the school, when they became anxious about the war and the plight of their fathers, but they were children, and under the protection of the Scottish Mission. Endre was seventeen – almost an adult. And working in a Jewish business made him especially vulnerable., even if it was one of the few remaining. They must be in constant fear there'd be a repeat of *Kristallnacht* in Budapest. Or worse.

'Endre.' Anna was at the door, tapping her watch. 'We really need to go.'

'Coming.' Endre flashed her a warm smile, squeezed Kirsty's hand briefly, then followed his sister inside. Kirsty returned to the kitchen, her fingers tingling from the pressure of his.

# 11

Endre popped over to the school often after that and they spent many hours talking or strolling in the garden, finding time between her long days in the kitchen, and his work as a watchmaker. Anna seemed pleased her friend and her brother were getting to know each other, although she was careful to point out from time to time that as soon as Endre was older he'd be made to join a labour unit. All they could do was live in the moment.

Everyone was being much more cautious these days. Pupils were no longer allowed to go on daily walks, and Matron made sure she went to the markets at different times of day, to avoid anyone lying in wait, intent on punishing her for harbouring Jewish girls at the school. The fear and tension in the streets was palpable.

The war news had been grim too lately. In May, Winston Churchill took over from Neville Chamberlain as Prime Minister, and Matron said she felt sure he'd *give Hitler a doing*. But later that month Belgium surrendered, soon followed by France. In mid-July, Hitler ordered Britain to join them but Churchill refused. Kirsty and Matron listened with dismay to the BBC news in August, announcing that the RAF had lost sixty-eight aircraft in a huge battle with the Luftwaffe over the Channel. Matron reassured her again that they'd made the right decision coming to Hungary, but both of them were worried for friends back home.

Kirsty was in two minds about going to Lake Balaton now. She'd miss Endre's company, but she was also keen to swim again, and it would be good to get away from the increasing tensions in the city. She just wished Endre could have come with them, but his father couldn't spare him – even if Matron had allowed him to go.

The principal had arranged for builders to create an air raid shelter on the premises and someone needed to stay behind to supervise and cook for them. It was decided that Mária would help her buy and pack up the provisions, but remain in Budapest for the builders, whilst Kirsty went on to Balaton. She just hoped that wasn't an open invitation for Dasco to help himself to more food while his mother looked the other way, but decided she couldn't be responsible for everything and at least, away from the school, she'd be able to feed the girls properly.

So, one stiflingly hot August day, they set off in a coach for Balatonszemes, to the rented villa on the lake where they were to stay. Kirsty sat next to Anna on the red leather seat as the coach rumbled out of Budapest and headed south-west, past fields bleached blond from weeks of drought, with occasional flashes of silver birch and poplar trees. In the small villages they drove through the houses were very different to those in Budapest. No towering buildings or wide streets. Here the dwellings were much smaller – one or two-storey homes covered in cream plaster and with strange, pointed roofs, like witches' hats. The land, mainly arable, was flat almost as far as the eye could see. In places it looked almost marshy.

'I can't wait to swim again,' said Kirsty, turning back towards Anna after looking out of the window for a while. 'Can you?'

Anna laid her head back against the rest, biting her lip. Kirsty wondered if she was worried about her parents and Endre. But Anna's response seemed to suggest it was something else that concerned her.

'I'm not keen on swimming,' she said. 'I think I'll just paddle, or maybe go out in a boat. It'll be nice to feel the breeze on our faces though.'

Kirsty nodded. 'Why don't you like swimming?'

Anna's shoulders were hunched and she licked her lips nervously. 'I'm frightened of water,' she said. 'I was in two minds whether to go to the lake. I stayed at home last year. But I wanted to spend more time with you.'

Kirsty was pleased Anna had chosen her company but amazed that she didn't swim. 'Didn't you ever go to the baths when you were younger?'

Anna shook her head. 'My parents wouldn't let us. Neither Endre nor I like swimming.'

Kirsty found Anna's admission really strange. Perhaps she'd been lucky having a father who encouraged swimming. But even if you didn't swim for pleasure surely it was a means of keeping yourself safe in water? No wonder Anna only wanted to paddle. An idea played around her mind. Perhaps Anna would let her give her some lessons. It would be a lovely way to spend time together and help her friend at the same time. Content with the thought, she closed her eyes and gave in to the exhaustion that had plagued them all for so long.

\* \* \*

The rented villa was a low, single-storey building with arched windows and carved gables in the Hungarian style, and a well in the garden. There were three dormitories for the girls, and single rooms for Kirsty and Matron. The kitchen was small but well equipped and Kirsty set about unpacking the provisions, before making tea for everybody. They spent the first evening playing *Capitaly*, which Kirsty soon realised was very similar to Monopoly, and taking turns to ride the three bicycles that belonged to the house. As they walked beside the lake in the dusk, watching the low sun gilding the water and backlighting the weeping willows near the water's edge, Kirsty felt a warm glow of anticipation. As though she was coming home.

The next morning, after Kirsty had prepared and served breakfast, Matron suggested a swim. The girls ran down to the lake in their black costumes and plunged in, laughing. Most of them stayed in the shallows, splashing each other and jumping the low waves, but Kirsty swam further out, revelling in the long-missed joy of immersing herself in water and the satisfaction of her muscles tensing and relaxing. At first she swam breaststroke, the morning sun on her forehead, the water trailing through the slight gaps between her fingers, but after a while she flipped over onto her back, and lay starfish-like, sculling gently as she squinted up at the bright blue sky with the faintest wisps of cloud, like whisked egg whites. She was far out now, the other girls' cries mingling with the shrieking of gulls and the soft slap of the waves. The water was cooler here, but nowhere near the icy grip of the Clyde. She thought back to that day when, raw with grief and fury, she'd bashed at the water until her muscles were screaming and her body exhausted. Anything to exorcise the anger that consumed her. So much had changed since those terrible early days after Da's death. She still wasn't whole, but Hungary was healing her.

Behind her, the vast expanse of water seeped like ink into the blue horizon; in front of her, tiny figures ducked and bobbed in puddles of light. She tried to distinguish Anna from the other girls, but failed to make out her friend amongst the group of bathers. Perhaps Kirsty was being unsociable, swimming so far out; she didn't want to alarm Matron – although Matron knew she was a good swimmer. It was probably time to return.

As she neared the shore, she finally spotted Anna sitting by herself on the grassy bank, watching the other girls with a pensive expression. Kirsty swam until her knees scraped the bottom, then stood, water droplets cascading down her costume, and headed over to her friend.

'Are you all right?'

Anna smiled wanly and shrugged. 'I suppose so.'

Kirsty tipped her head to one side and squeezed her wet hair between her fingers, releasing a thin trickle of water. She sat down next to Anna, conscious of the rigidity of her friend's body and the bleakness of her expression. 'Did you decide not to go in?'

Anna frowned at the ripples slowly wrinkling the surface of the lake. 'I told you, I don't like swimming.'

Kirsty found it hard to imagine anyone not enjoying the water. But Anna clearly had her reasons. Yesterday, on the coach, she'd sensed her reluctance to talk about swimming and she felt it here again today.

'Why's that?'

There was a silence and Kirsty wondered if her Scottish bluntness had been too much for her. But finally Anna spoke, in a low voice that she had to strain to hear. 'My older sister Róza drowned five years ago,' she said.

Kirsty recoiled in shock. 'That's terrible.' She put her arm round Anna. 'You poor things.'

Anna chewed at a fingernail.

'Are you able to tell me what happened?' Kirsty didn't want to pry, and she certainly didn't want to open up old wounds, but she sensed Anna wanted to talk. She could always say no after all.

But Kirsty's instincts were right. Anna looked down at the ground as she spoke, as if any glimpse of sympathy would weaken her resolve to tell her story. 'My parents had just bought a puppy. Miksa.' She paused as though to rekindle the memory of her pet. 'The three of us were taking him for a walk by the Danube one day. Endre had thrown a stick into the river, then Miksa jumped in after it. But the current was strong and he got into difficulties. Róza adored that sweet dog . . .' Her voice became husky. She gave a little cough and swallowed hard. 'She jumped in after him, but she wasn't a strong swimmer. The current soon overpowered her. Miksa scrambled onto the bank further down the river. But we never saw Róza alive again.' She turned to Kirsty with tear-glazed eyes.

'How awful,' Kirsty said, rubbing Anna's arm. 'I'm so sorry.'

Anna nodded. 'From then on, my mother couldn't bear to look at Miksa. She took the puppy to the pound for rehoming. And neither Endre nor I have swum since.'

Kirsty gazed out over the lake, barely registering its mirrored blue surface, or the still-frolicking swimmers. So that explained Anna's determination not to go into the water. It must be so painful for her to be at the lake, after her sister's accident. No wonder she didn't want to swim. But water was healing as well as dangerous.

'What an appalling thing to happen,' she said. 'I can understand you never wanting to swim again.'

Anna wiped her cheeks with the back of her hand. 'Thank you.'

How could Kirsty put into words what she was thinking? If she was ever to encourage Anna to swim, she needed to gain her friend's trust. And although she was now fluent in Hungarian, she still lacked the linguistic subtleties to convey nuances of emotion. She tried to speak as gently as possible, to reassure rather than to alarm. 'After my mother died, I found swimming helped me. It gave me something to work at, to keep my mind busy. I've barely swum since my father's accident, but I found going in the lake just now a great comfort.' It was true. The water connected her with Da. Learning to swim had been his gift to her, all those hours spent helping her improve her strokes until swimming had become as natural as breathing.

'I can swim a little,' Anna replied in a flat voice. 'My parents made sure we all had lessons when we were younger. Róza too.'

'Even strong swimmers can get into difficulties,' Kirsty said.

'Yes.' Anna's neck and shoulders were stiff with tension.

'But the more we practise, the more we improve our chances of safety.'

Anna fiddled with a strand of hair for a while, then looked up, as though she'd come to a decision. 'Will you teach me?'

'Of course, but won't your parents mind?'

112

'They don't need to know.' She rubbed her forehead. 'I think they couldn't bear to take us swimming, knowing what happened to Róza, but you're right – in some ways they're just risking me getting into difficulties myself. The best thing I can do is to make sure I'm safe.'

'Come on then.' Kirsty pulled Anna up and they walked towards the lake, hand in hand, until their feet were enveloped in the sun-warmed water. Then they continued through the shallows until the lake became deeper and chillier, clenching their thighs and hips. Anna's face was pale but she kept on walking. The water was lapping their waists now. The hot sun still warmed their heads and shoulders but their lower bodies were encased in cold. Once they were submerged up to their chests, Kirsty stopped.

'All right?'

Anna nodded.

'Now,' said Kirsty, letting go of Anna's hand. 'Push off from the bottom and start swimming.'

Anna darted her a frightened look but did as she was told, propelling herself through the water in a rapid, panicky doggy-paddle.

'Hmmm. I wonder if you're better swimming breaststroke. It might be easier.'

Anna frowned. 'I never learned breaststroke,' she said.

'I'll hold you up so you don't have to worry about staying afloat.' She supported Anna under her arms until Anna was horizontal, her legs drifting out behind her. 'All right, now try those legs. Bend . . . kick round . . . and squeeze.'

Anna followed her instructions.

'Good.'

They practised for a few minutes.

'Now, if you stand up again, I'll show you how to do the arms.' Kirsty let Anna go and stood in front of her, pushing her arms forwards then scooping them round. 'You try.'

Anna tried to follow suit, but her arms were too rigid and the movement looked awkward.

Kirsty tried to think of something to help. 'I know. Imagine a pudding basin.'

'Really?'

'Yes. The huge one back at the school that we use to make cakes with.' Kirsty visualised the glazed earthenware bowl that Mária sometimes heaved down from the shelf to fill with sugar, eggs and flour.

Anna shrugged. 'All right.'

Kirsty showed Anna the movement again. 'So . . . you push your arms into the bowl like this.' She made the gesture. 'Then you scoop them round the side of the bowl like this.' She made her arms follow the curved sides of the imagined bowl.

'Oh, I see.' Anna mimicked the movement perfectly.

'You've got it! Now do it in water.'

Anna stepped back a few paces, then swam towards Kirsty, her arms performing a near-perfect breaststroke, her legs trailing behind her.

'Hey! Well done.'

Anna beamed.

'Now do the legs and arms together.'

'All right.'

Anna swam away from her, executing the stroke impressively well.

114

Kirsty felt a surge of emotion. 'Anna, that's wonderful. You're swimming. Really swimming.'

Anna blinked back the tears. 'Yes, I am, aren't I?' She squeezed Kirsty's hand. 'Thank you.'

They waded out of the water and onto the little stretch of grass that bordered the lake, their bodies glowing. They'd decided to have a picnic on the shore that day, and Matron had already laid out the checked cloth and weighed it down with the packets of sandwiches Kirsty and Anna had made earlier and the little bags of cherries they'd managed to buy at the local store. Provisions were much more plentiful out of the city. It must be all the farms – and the sparser population. The other girls joined them and they sat in the sun eating their lunch and chatting. Afterwards, lulled by the midday heat, some of the pupils slept and some talked quietly while Kirsty and Anna packed away. Anna's movements were languid, her expression tranquil. Kirsty was relieved. Perhaps water really could work magic.

Over the next few balmy days, their lives fell into a routine. Each morning, Anna would be up early to help Kirsty serve and clear the breakfast and do some of the lunchtime preparation. Then they had a few hours at the lake before serving the midday meal. With only a small group of girls at the villa, and with Anna's help – and Matron's too at times – Kirsty's chores were quickly performed, leaving her plenty of leisure time.

They swam regularly over the next few weeks, each session bringing new improvements in Anna's skill and confidence; her expression became more relaxed, her speech more animated.

She really did have an aptitude for swimming and her rapid progress amazed Kirsty. By the end of their time at the lake Anna was swimming happily alongside Kirsty, her strokes matching hers for style and speed. Anna told her she was a good teacher but Kirsty suspected it was more than that: Anna was a natural.

On the last but one morning of the holidays, Kirsty was lugging the picnic stuff down to the lake when she heard screaming. She dropped the bag of sandwiches and sprinted towards the shore. One of the smaller girls had swum too far out. She was about fifteen metres away from the bank, gasping for air, coughing and spluttering. Her face was red, her eyes wild with fright. The other girls were standing helplessly near the water's edge.

'I'm coming.' Kirsty quickly undid her shoes, and ran into the lake in her blouse and shorts.

She splashed through the shallows as fast as she could, then launched herself into the water and swam a rapid front crawl towards the girl. But as she did so, another figure appeared, swimming towards the child from the other direction. A swimmer who performed a perfect, fast breaststroke. A stroke Kirsty had taught her.

'Anna!'

Either Anna didn't hear or she was too intent on reaching the girl. As Kirsty watched, she swam up to her, cupped her hand under her chin to lift her head out of the water, then towed her in jerky but powerful movements towards the shore.

Kirsty swam up to them and helped Anna drag the child onto the beach, where she lay, panting and coughing, her little chest heaving with the effort of taking in air. Matron had arrived too by then, with an armful of towels, which she draped round the little girl, murmuring to her soothingly.

'It's all right, Léna. You're safe now.'

Léna nodded, her breaths starting to slow, her skin returning to its normal colour.

'Thank goodness you were there, Anna. You probably saved her life.'

Anna's expression was a mixture of shock, concern and pride. 'I couldn't save Róza but at least I've rescued one little girl.'

The girls helped Matron take Léna back inside and Kirsty set about making hot cocoa.

Everyone was subdued after the incident on the lake. It was a stark reminder of how powerful water could be and how easily there could have been a tragedy. But in spite of that, Kirsty was amazed at Anna's courage. She'd come so far after witnessing her own sister drowning. And in a strange way, she thought, saving Léna would help her own recovery.

The holiday drew to a close all too quickly. On the last day, Anna and Matron insisted on preparing dinner themselves so that Kirsty could have one last dip in the lake.

She left the shore behind in rapid strokes, conscious that this would be her last swim for a while, and determined to make the most of it. The water wrapped itself around her, viscous yet fluid and she felt again the sense of freedom. The last few months had been hard: Da's death . . . the still-painful grief . . . the difficult days with Maggie . . . the terrifying journey to Budapest just after war broke out . . . learning to adapt to her new role as cook's assistant . . . Léna's near-drowning. But there were positives too – such as her friendships with

Endre and Anna. She flipped onto her back as before and lay looking upwards, just sculling her arms gently to keep afloat. The sky was an intense cloudless blue; there was no drone of planes or whistling of bombs to break the stillness, just the far-off cries of bathers enjoying the lake, and bairns playing on its shore.

Please let the war end soon, she thought. Then Endre won't be forced into a labour unit and we can spend more time together. She tried to picture them walking round the lake, the sunlight dappling their bodies as they luxuriated in the warmth and peace. But for some reason the vision refused to appear. She swam back towards the bank then waded out of the water, wrapping her arms around her body at the sudden chill.

# Part Two

# 12

Kirsty drew the small wooden box from under her bed, lifted the lid, and removed the pile of letters. Loneliness and loss so often overwhelmed her these days; the letters were her only comfort. She smoothed the first one out on her lap and started to read it to herself, even though she knew the words off by heart:

> *Dearest Kirsty,*
>
> *We've just stopped for a breather after being on the road for hours, so I thought I'd write a few lines. It's much colder here, and I'm glad of the warm scarf you knitted me. I'm wearing it now and trying to imagine it's your arms wrapped round my neck. I miss you! The men here are friendly and we are making the most of things but we are all wondering what the next few weeks will bring . . .*

It had been written last year, when Endre was en route to the Ukraine. She smiled as she remembered working on the scarf each evening before he'd left, while she and Matron listened to the wireless in her small office. The war news had worsened. They were alarmed to hear of bombing raids on London night after night. Events were concerning closer to home in Budapest too. In November 1940 Hungary had joined the Axis powers, fighting with the Germans. They'd realised with dismay that their adopted country was now at war with their country of birth.

Now Kirsty no longer needed Hungarian lessons, Matron taught her to knit instead. Counting stiches kept her mind busy and the repetitive clacking of the needles was soothing in the face of so many worries. There was no wool to be had in the shops so she'd unravelled an old jumper that Da had once given her and used the wool from that. Perhaps the spirit of Da would watch over Endre and keep him safe. It was lovely to think something she'd once worn was now next to Endre's skin. As if a little part of her had gone with him.

They'd grown closer over the months until one day, when they'd sat in the school garden as usual, the spring sun on their faces and the scent of plum blossom in the air, he told her he was falling in love with her. She confessed she loved him back. In truth she'd loved him since the day they'd first met. Their friendship had deepened over time, their feelings burgeoning and blossoming. But they couldn't tell anyone about this thrilling new development. It was illegal for Jews and non-Jews to form relationships. They were a couple in private and friends in public.

Her face suffused with heat as she recalled that wonderful moment when he first kissed her: the nearness of him, the heady smell of his sun-warmed skin. At first the kiss felt awkward, noses bumping, the strangeness of his face so close, but then his mouth moved against hers and she started to enjoy it, delicious feelings running through her body. There'd been many more stolen kisses after that. They'd agreed to live in the moment, enjoy the precious times of togetherness while they could, not knowing what the future would bring.

But all too soon the day they'd dreaded came round: Endre's eighteenth birthday. He was conscripted into a forced labour unit and, soon after, sent to the Eastern Front alongside the Hungarian Second Army. Thank God for his letters. It was lucky she always came downstairs early, and could intercept the post. He couldn't tell her much, or the censor would intervene, but she was cheered to read how much he loved her, how much he missed her. And she'd written back to assure him of the strength of her own feelings.

Kirsty pulled out the next letter. Endre and his fellow labourers had arrived and were setting up camp. Then the next, informing her that fighting was fierce but her letters kept him cheerful. Then another, asking her to knit him some warm socks. But as time went by the letters became more and more vague. Then silence.

She was worried sick that something had happened to him. Or had he gone cold on her because her own letters were always full of bad news? She wished she'd written about how lovely the roses in the school garden were that summer instead of pouring out her fears for the girls, who were so anxious about their fathers being away and their mothers having to find jobs to support the family. Many had had nightmares after they discovered that ten thousand Jews had been shot dead in Galicia. Lots of the children were thin and anxious these days and the numbers of boarders had increased as the other Jewish parents sought somewhere safe for their daughters to be educated. Disturbing reports filtered through from refugees who'd fled from countries now occupied by the Germans. They said that Hungarian Jews now had to wear a yellow star on their outer clothing, making them even more vulnerable to attack by those who hated their people. Matron was exhausted trying to offer her pupils as much support and comfort as she could.

Kirsty hadn't heard from Endre for months now. Were events too terrible for him to relate? Had he lost interest in her and wanted to sever the relationship? Had he met someone else, although goodness knows how or where? Or, the most awful of all, had he been killed?

She shuddered as the dreadful options pulsed through her brain. *Please let Endre come home safe,* she pleaded with God. *Please let us have a future together.*

Mária and Kirsty were working flat out to cater for all the extra mouths. After turning sixteen, Anna had left the school but came back so often to help in the kitchen that Matron took her on as permanent staff. Matron had insisted that now she and Kirsty were both older they should call her Jean. It sounded strange after so many years of addressing her with her formal title, but eventually they got used to it, and it seemed to put their relationship on a more equal footing.

One spring day, Anna failed to arrive to help prepare the breakfasts.

'Lazy girl,' muttered Mária, hacking at a loaf of bread. 'Probably still in bed.'

'I doubt it,' Kirsty replied, filling the huge urn with water and setting it to boil. 'She's never been late before and she's certainly not lazy.' She reached up to the cupboard for some teacups. How dare Mária make assumptions like that? Anna worked harder than she did. Despite Anna's obvious concerns about her parents and brother, she was a welcome addition to the kitchen staff – a quick learner who soon knew instinctively what needed doing without being told. There must be some reason why she was late.

They served and cleared the breakfast, but still Anna did not appear. Kirsty kept thinking about the time she'd waited for Da at the pit and he'd failed to emerge. Her stomach tightened.

'I don't suppose we'll get a break at all now,' Mária grumbled as she started collecting the lunchtime ingredients from the larder. They'd planned to make *csirkepaprikás*, a chicken dish garnished with soured cream. Mária usually complained about it as some of the strict Jewish girls couldn't eat meat and dairy together so they had to serve the cream separately. Increasingly Mária seemed resentful of the deference Matron – Jean – insisted they showed their Jewish pupils. 'Why can't we give them *Gyulai*?' she'd fume. 'You know why,' Jean would reply. 'It contains pork. There are plenty of other dishes that won't give offence.' Mária wouldn't respond – they'd had this conversation many times – but it would be evident from her pronounced sniffing and dour expression that she wasn't happy. At times like these, Jean usually ignored her.

Mária had become increasingly bad tempered over the last few months. Jean seemed to think she was worried about Dasco, who'd become more and more wild, staying out late with his yobbish friends. They'd barely seen him around the school lately, which was a mercy, but Kirsty was always on her guard.

She took three chickens out of the larder and placed them

on a board on the table. She and Mária had spent an hour plucking them yesterday, pulling at the brown feathers and piling them up in a tawny tower until only pink puckered skin remained. Then they'd removed the innards and extremities which they boiled for hours on the stove, together with some leftover vegetables, to make stock.

She deftly cut the chickens into pieces and dropped them into the huge pot she'd already heaved onto the range. Then she lit the ring and waited until the chicken started to cook. Soon the kitchen was filled with a rich meaty aroma. Just as she was chopping the onions at the kitchen table, Anna walked in.

Kirsty wiped her eyes with the back of her hand. She never could stop herself from crying whenever she cut an onion. 'Anna! Are you all right?'

Anna drew out a chair and slumped at the table. 'No, I'm not. It's Endre.'

Kirsty put down her knife, her heart rate accelerating. 'What about him?'

Anna's eyes were red rimmed, her face white. 'He's in hospital. At the Dániel Bíró in Buda.'

'Oh no.' Kirsty reached for the chair to steady herself as her legs almost gave way. She pictured his head wrapped in a blood-soaked bandage, or his arm in a sling, or, worse still, missing a limb or an eye. Whatever happened she'd still love him. Perhaps she could help nurse him back to health. And at least now he was away from the war. Whatever his injuries, he would recover, surely? They'd assumed he was still in the Soviet Union but the news was sketchy at best.

'He doesn't seem to have been physically hurt.' Anna put her head in her hands. 'He has some sort of combat fatigue. My parents are visiting him now.'

Kirsty sat down next to Anna. Her fingers curled over the edge of the table; she felt she had to hang on for fear of falling. 'Will you go too?' It was a risk travelling all that way.

Anna nodded. 'I will later on. You'll come with me, won't you?' Her expression was weary but warm.

'Of course.' Kirsty tried to tell herself that at least Endre was alive. Combat fatigue was curable, wasn't it? And being in hospital meant he'd be away from the fighting for a while. That was a blessing.

She wiped away the tears pricking the back of her eyes and Anna looked at her sharply.

'Onions always make me cry,' Kirsty said.

Anna nodded. Thank goodness she seemed to believe it was from chopping the vegetables. Not the real reason.

'Kirsty! What on earth are you doing?' Mária rushed towards the stove, her face reddening with annoyance. A smell of singed chicken skin tainted the air.

'I'm sorry.' Kirsty leapt up. 'I'll see to it.' She could always cut off the burnt bits. It would take a while but the chicken would probably taste all right. She'd just have to make sure the sauce was extra flavoursome.

Mária banged the pan on the counter and started prodding at the chicken pieces. 'You two. Anna disappears for hours then even when she does show up, she doesn't help. And, Kirsty – I leave you for five minutes and you burn the dinner.'

'I'm sorry,' Kirsty said again. 'Anna had some bad news. I'll sort it out. I promise.'

'You'd better.' Mária stomped off to the pantry and returned

127

with a dish of paprika and the bowl of chicken stock they'd made yesterday. She thumped them down on the table. 'Right, Anna, you make the sauce and, Kirsty, you make good the chicken.'

'Of course.' Kirsty stood up to retrieve a knife from the cutlery drawer and set about rescuing the burnt meat.

After the meal, mercifully still edible, was cooked and served, and the kitchen tidied, Anna and Kirsty set off to visit Endre. 'At least he's among our own people,' Anna said. 'I'm sure the doctors and nurses will look after him well.' The Dániel Bíró was Budapest's only Orthodox Jewish hospital, which was why Endre must have been taken there, despite it being so far from his home.

The girls made their way north from the school then took the tram across the Margit Bridge, followed by the cogwheel railway up Castle Hill. It was dusk now, the sinking sun bathing the Buda hills in an apricot light and gilding the rails. If Kirsty hadn't been so focussed on Endre, she'd have enjoyed the rare trip across the river and the chance to visit another part of the city. Her whole body tingled at the prospect of seeing him again. They couldn't be affectionate publicly, but perhaps he'd hold her hand, or kiss her goodbye. A blush travelled up her neck at the thought.

They walked along Városmajor Street towards the hospital. After about ten minutes Anna stopped in front of a three-storey building. Endre was in the sanitorium which lay next door, behind a yellow stone wall. It took them a while to locate his room, by which time Kirsty's stomach was churning, both from the antiseptic smell on the corridors and the anticipation of seeing Endre again. He was at the far end of a ward with around sixteen beds, his nearest the window. But despite having a view of the twilit rooftops and occasional glimpses of the pewter-coloured river beyond, Endre was sitting in a chair with his back to the outside world. Anna and Kirsty walked up the ward, past men with wan faces and haunted eyes, surrounded by little groups of disconsolate visitors. Low murmurs filled the room, interspersed with the clack-clack of a nurse's heels as she hurried to and fro checking on patients and responding to relatives' questions.

'Hello, dear.' Anna approached Endre and gave him a hug. He held on to her briefly but showed no signs of recognition. 'Look who I've brought with me.'

Kirsty had hung back to let Anna greet her brother first, but now she stepped forward. 'Hello, Endre.' She tried to smile but it was hard not to flinch in shock. He looked so different to the Endre she'd known. His face was haggard, with sunken cheeks and a grey pallor to his skin. His clothes were baggy on his thin frame, much thinner than when she'd last seen him.

At the sight of her, Endre shrank back in his chair, his white-knuckled hands gripping the arms, his eyes wide and staring.

'It's all right, dear.' Anna hastened forward again and put an arm round him but he shrugged it off, the look of terror still vividly etched on his face. Anna bit her lip. 'I'm sorry, Kirsty, I don't think he recognises either of us.' She looked round for the nurse but she was busy talking to some visitors further down the ward. 'Perhaps if we sit down . . .'

They perched on the bed, watching, appalled, as Endre seemed to collapse into himself. The frightened expression was replaced by one of sadness. Then he moaned quietly as the tears ran down his face.

Kirsty fought against a rising tide of emotions: fear, revulsion, shock, anxiety . . . She had no idea he'd be this bad. When she'd heard he was suffering from 'combat fatigue' she thought he'd be tired or anxious. But this was far, far worse. They'd had no warning about what to expect. There'd been no time for Anna to go home before they'd left for the hospital so she hadn't had a chance to ask her parents how their visit had gone. Eventually, the nurse appeared, alerted by Anna's frantic glances.

She drew them aside, out of Endre's hearing, and looked at them sympathetically. 'It's early days,' she said. 'And he's on a lot of medication. But Doctor Angyal is hopeful there'll be some progress.'

'I see,' Anna whispered, lines of worry playing around her mouth. 'Is there anything we can do?'

The nurse smiled kindly. 'Just be patient,' she said. 'He's obviously had a terrible time. Minds don't heal overnight. Keep coming to see him and eventually you should see bits of him returning.'

'Will he ever make a full recovery?'

'We have no way of knowing, but as I say, the doctor is hopeful. Your brother is very young still. Time is on his side.'

Anna nodded, her face still pale. 'Thank you.'

They stayed with Endre for another half hour, talking to him quietly while he avoided their eyes and repeatedly pulled at the hairs on the back of his hands. The hands that had once held Kirsty's so warmly. She tried to suppress her instinctive

130

urge to pull back from him, and instead to demonstrate the patience the nurse had advised, but it was hard to watch him so evidently distressed. He was so far from the strong youth who'd fearlessly tackled the Arrow Cross keelies threatening an old lady the day she'd first met him. And far from the boy she'd fallen in love with. Now he seemed frightened of his own shadow. But maybe he was still in there, deep down. As the nurse said, they just had to be patient. At length he seemed a bit calmer and his eyes started to droop.

'I think we should go now,' Anna said. 'He's obviously tired.'

Kirsty agreed and they returned to the school through the now-darkened city, both lost in their own disturbing thoughts.

# 13

Anna appeared at work the next morning with lank hair and puffy skin.

'Any news?' Kirsty greeted her.

Anna's voice was laced with misery. 'My parents were able to speak to the doctor yesterday. Endre was found cowering in a ditch sobbing hysterically. The Hungarians had put the labour divisions in the front of the army so they caught the full force of the fighting. They were tortured, beaten and starved.' Her eyes brimmed with unshed tears. 'Endre was never cut out for warfare. He's a watchmaker. He creates beautiful things out of intricate parts. He hates violence.' She picked up a handful of tomatoes and started sawing at them. 'Thank God the new defence minister is more humane. He ordered that the slaves in the labour battalions be treated the same as the soldiers. Endre was brought back to Budapest when the army retreated and then taken to the Dániel Bíró hosptial. Now all we can do is hope.' The tomato slices were piled on a plate. 'And keep busy.'

Kirsty put her arm round her friend. 'We'll visit him often. Try our best to coax him back to the old Endre. He's in there somewhere. I'm sure it's just a matter of time.' She was trying to convince herself as much as Anna. She tried to recapture the boy she knew, his eyes clear and untroubled, his expression full of optimism, but all she could see was a frightened man, plucking at the hairs on the back of his hand.

Jean came in just as they were clearing away. Kirsty had filled her in on Endre the night before. 'You are much in my prayers,' she assured Anna with a sad smile. 'Visit your brother whenever you need to. We'll try not to overtax you here.' There was a snort from the larder where Mária was checking their stock, moving tins around on the shelves and muttering to herself.

'That's very kind,' said Anna.

'And I know Kirsty will give you a great deal of support.'

Kirsty squeezed her friend's arm. 'Anna's always been so good to me. It's the least I can do.' She hadn't confided in Jean about her relationship with Endre. It would only have caused her anxiety and Jean had enough to deal with. As far as she was concerned, she was just friends with Anna's brother. And anyway, there was nothing settled between them. Things were too fragile with the war. 'We'll do our best to get him well.' The words were heartfelt. She never had the chance to mend Da – it was too late for him. She'd do all she could to help mend Endre.

'That's good to hear.' Jean brushed a crumb off the table. 'Kirsty, I was wondering if you might come with me to the municipality office this afternoon. We need to check that our papers are in order.' All foreigners were required to have their papers checked regularly, never more so than in wartime.

'Of course,' said Kirsty, although visiting the authorities always made her anxious. There was always a risk something minor would be found out of place on her documents and she'd be sent away. She couldn't bear to leave the school . . . or

Anna . . . or her brother. She swallowed. 'What time are you going?'

Jean glanced at her watch. 'About half an hour?' she said. 'Apart from anything else, it will be a good test of your language skills.' Except with each other, when they still spoke English, Kirsty's conversations were now entirely conducted in Hungarian. Jean had drilled her well in the more formal constructions; Anna had enlightened her with colloquial expressions – even the odd swear word, much to Kirsty's amusement. As Jean had predicted, she'd even begun to dream in Hungarian now.

She checked the kitchen was tidy, then disappeared off to her room to change, emerging several minutes later in one of the smarter skirts and blouses she'd bought in Vörösmarty tér with the money she'd saved from her small salary.

Jean was waiting for her in the hall. The midday sun, glinting through the windows, picked out the white strands in her hair and illuminated the spidery red veins on her cheeks. She's aged so much in the last few years, Kirsty thought. The worry about the Jewish girls and the responsibility for looking after them in these troubled times had taken its toll. Kirsty couldn't believe how naïve she'd been back in the summer of 1940, convincing herself that all would be well. Her friendship with Anna was just beginning then, cemented during those idyllic weeks at Lake Balaton, and Endre was a whole and healthy young man. So much had changed. Regent Horthy had managed to keep the country stable, but war was licking at its fringes – as Endre's terrible experience confirmed. She just hoped there wouldn't be worse to come.

They set off southwest on foot towards the office. Jean had

explained to her when they'd first arrived that Budapest had twenty-three districts, each with its own local government. The nearest municipality office to the school was in Városház utca, a couple of kilometres away.

It was a mild spring day, white clouds chasing each other across the sky and a light breeze ruffling the leaves of the plane trees on Teréz körút. Both of them carried baskets in case the queues at the Városháza park market had died down enough for them to get a few provisions. It was becoming harder to track down the basics these days and Jean was constantly trying to procure bread, cabbage, beans, maize, flour and sugar. Kirsty and Mária were having to be more and more inventive with their limited food stocks.

Jean pointed out the Dohány Street synagogue in the distance, the gold on its onion-shaped domes gleaming in the sun.

'I fear for our Jewish pupils,' she said, 'the fate of their people is worsening by the day across Europe.'

Kirsty nodded. More and more Polish and Slovak Jews were pouring into the country to seek refuge. But life was hard in Budapest too. There were many sanctions now. So far Anna's father was still able to work – one of a dwindling few who were – but Anna was getting more and more nervous that his watchmaking business would be closed down. The family had enough problems worrying about Endre.

They turned into Terézváros. 'I had a visit from a former pupil yesterday,' Jean continued. 'Do you remember Ilona?'

Kirsty conjured up an image of a slight girl with dark frizzy hair and a shy smile. 'I do,' she replied. 'She didn't like her bread buttered. I always put some plain slices on a plate for her.'

Jean smiled briefly. 'So you did. That was kind of you. Anyway, last month her father was dragged out of the house, placed in the back of a lorry and sent to a work camp. No one would tell them where he was going. She and her brothers and sisters were distraught, hearing his terrified screams. Since then her poor mother has taken on a job distributing newspapers in attempt to earn some money. Ilona is the eldest, but the whole family help. They all have to get up very early in the morning – even the little ones. Ilona is very worried about her mother's health. And she misses her father desperately.'

'Poor girl. It must be terrible for her and her family.' Kirsty knew what it was to miss a father. She no longer felt the raw agony of grief, and her days were too busy and exhausting to dwell on her loss, but it was at night, as she clutched Da's old handkerchief, that she allowed the memories to flood in, probing her mind for the underlying hurt like a tongue seeking out a sore tooth. She wondered what he would have made of her new life in Hungary, the country that had become so dear to her now. Would he have been proud of her? She hoped so. Jean had lost her parents at a young age too. Both trying to help others struggling with loss – perhaps more so because they had known suffering themselves.

They joined the end of the long queue in Városház utca, people standing patiently in front of grand old buildings painted in pastel shades, their roofs reddy-orange against a still-bright sky. 'It's a terrible situation for these poor families,' Jean went on, lowering her voice now others could overhear. 'Many of them are fearful of being rounded up and taken God knows where while their men are at work camps. They have no idea exactly where their husbands, brothers and sons are, or how they're being treated. And if the women and children have to leave their homes, the families might never be reunited.'

'It's insufferable,' replied Kirsty. She'd been angry when she discovered that some Jews had been forced to go into hiding and heard rumours that some of their young men had had to form smuggling bands, bringing food supplies from across the Romanian border at great risk to their own lives. 'What have they ever done to deserve this?'

Jean nodded. 'All we can do is look after the girls as best we can. Provide a sanctuary for them.'

The queue moved slowly. Most of the people seemed to be non-nationals, like themselves, judging by the babble of different languages. She wondered if there were any Scots like her and Jean.

'Well, this is a long wait,' said an educated-sounding voice behind them. Kirsty looked round to see a tall gentleman in a Homburg hat, which he raised politely in their direction.

'Indeed,' said Jean. 'Unfortunately, we can't do much about it.'

'Sadly not,' said the man. Kirsty judged him to be in his early thirties. He had a cultured air about him. She'd have called him a knab if he'd turned up in Hamilton, but there was a compassion about his eyes that made her think he mightn't be as arrogant as some of his sort.

'Is that an English accent I detect?' he asked them in perfect Hungarian.

'We're both from Scotland originally,' Jean said. 'But we consider ourselves locals now.'

'And what brought you to Budapest?' The man smiled again. Jean looked around to check no one was in earshot.

'I'm matron of a school on Vörösmarty Street,' she said quietly. 'And Kirsty is one of our cooks.'

'What worthwhile jobs,' the man said.

'Thank you,' said Jean. 'And what do you do?'

'I'm from near Stockholm,' said the man, 'but I'm thinking of moving to Budapest as I come here so regularly on business.' He held out a hand. 'Raoul Wallenberg.'

They shook hands with their new acquaintance. 'So as a Swede I assume you're neutral in this war,' Jean said.

'Indeed I am.'

The queue shuffled forward and Mr Wallenberg bent down to pick up his briefcase. He turned back to Jean. 'What kind of school do you work at?'

Jean lowered her voice still further. 'It's a girls' school,' she said. 'Many of our pupils are Jewish.'

He raised an eyebrow. 'What are two Scottish women doing working at a school for Jews?'

Was this a loaded question? Kirsty glanced at Jean to see how she would respond. They both knew all too well how public opinion had turned against Jews over the last few years – and some people were very suspicious about the school. She thought back to that day at the market when shopkeepers had slighted them because of where they worked. Was this man luring them into a trap? Was he trying to find out about their work with the Jewish population in order to report them to the authorities?

But Jean didn't seem perturbed. In normal circumstances she was very careful whom she confided in but there was something about this man that she clearly trusted. She was usually a good judge of character. She knew instinctively which tradesmen were reliable and who needed a careful eye. She could often predict which girls would be troublesome within a few minutes of meeting them. If Jean felt happy talking to this man, then that was good enough for Kirsty. She looked up the line to the official who was stamping papers. His eyes were flinty, his mouth a grim line. In contrast, Mr Wallenberg looked genuinely kind and sympathetic.

Jean told him the story of Archduchess Maria Dorothea and how the Scottish Mission to the Jews of Hungary came about.

He laughed at the account of one of the missionaries being kicked by a camel. Then his expression grew serious again. 'And how are things at the school now?'

Jean grimaced. 'Very difficult. Many of the girls' parents have been forced to join labour battalions against their will. The girls are terrified, and with good reason. We're getting reports that Jewish labourers are being very badly treated.'

'That's putting it mildly,' said Kirsty, thinking of Endre.

Mr Wallenberg turned to her. 'What do you know?' he asked.

She darted another glance at Jean, who nodded.

'The commanders protect Hungarian soldiers but put Jewish men at the front of the army so they're the ones the Russians attack first. They're effectively human sacrifices.' She could hear the bitterness in her own voice.

Kirsty felt Mr Wallenberg's sharp blue eyes upon her. 'How do you know this?'

'My friend's brother was forced to join up in 1941. He was so traumatised he's now in hospital, having lost his mind.' Her poor darling boy.

'And he's Jewish?'

Kirsty nodded.

Mr Wallenberg shook his head. 'Terrible,' he said.

Kirsty swallowed, her throat suddenly tight. She wondered if she'd said too much but Jean hadn't interrupted her.

'And do the Arrow Cross give you any trouble?'

An image of Dasco shot into Kirsty's mind. A while ago, Jean had told her she'd suspected he'd joined those thugs. It explained his hatred of the Jews and accounted for Mária's concern about the company her son kept. She shuddered.

Again the piercing look.

'We're very careful about letting the girls out of the confines of the school these days,' Jean said. 'And the local police have been good about protecting us.'

'I see.'

They were nearing the front of the queue now and would soon need to stop talking. Mr Wallenberg raised his hat to them again. 'I'm so pleased to have made your acquaintance,' he said, then in a quieter tone: 'Thank you for speaking to me. I won't forget what you said.'

The next few minutes were taken up by paperwork. Mercifully everything was in order. Kirsty and Jean were free to go, and the official beckoned Mr Wallenberg forward.

Knowing he'd be preoccupied for a while they smiled their goodbyes and walked off down the street.

'He was a braw gadgie,' Kirsty said as they trudged back to the school.

Jean laughed. 'I haven't heard that phrase for a while. But yes, he was nice. I wouldn't have spoken to him otherwise but I trusted him instinctively. I think he was really interested in our work with our Jewish pupils.'

'It's good to know not all people are against them.'

Jean firmed her lips. 'I think they're going to need a lot of support in the coming months.'

Thankfully a few of the stalls were still open at the market and only a handful of shoppers remained. Kirsty couldn't face another queue. They managed to get some potatoes and carrots and even a few sour cherries. 'So good for the girls to have fresh fruit and vegetables,' Jean said, inspecting the produce in her basket.

'Especially these early cherries,' added Kirsty. 'I could make *meggyleves*.' When Mária had first taught her to make the cherry soup she'd thought it very strange but by now it had become a favourite. She was already anticipating the glorious sweet-sour aroma infusing the kitchen. Hopefully there was a little cinnamon left over from Christmas so she could follow the recipe properly.

Jean broke into her thoughts. 'And how is Endre?' she asked.

Kirsty and Anna had been to see him a few times since that first shocking visit to the hospital. Kirsty shrugged. 'A little better, I suppose. He's no longer quite so agitated but he's heavily sedated these days.' She summoned up Endre's face from when she'd last visited. He never looked at her any more. It was as though he was fixing his attention on someone just behind her, but when she turned round there was no one there. Occasionally, when they walked down the ward, and before he'd caught sight of them, they'd watch him pulling at the hairs on the back of his hand, rocking backwards and forwards in his chair, his face a troubled mask of absorption. Then he'd recognise them. On a good day there might be a slight smile, the ghost of the wide grin Endre gave in the past, but on a bad day there was barely any acknowledgement. It was as if they were never really there. He certainly gave no sign of he and Kirsty having a relationship, and there was no mention of his affection for her. The man who'd declared his love for her that day in the school garden, who'd kissed her so tenderly, felt like another person now.

'And what do the doctors say?' Jean asked gently.

Kirsty sighed. 'They say that technically he could still recover, but the more time that elapses, the less likely it becomes.'

Jean frowned and was silent for a few moments. 'Why don't you invite him along to Lake Balaton this summer? Swimming might help.'

'Or it could make things worse,' said Kirsty, remembering Róza, and the way the family was still haunted by her drowning.

'It's a risk,' Jean agreed. 'But it doesn't seem to me that languishing in hospital stuffed full of drugs is going to improve things. Perhaps a change of scene, some fresh air and exercise will make a difference.'

Hope flickered in Kirsty's chest. 'All right,' she said, 'I'll talk to Anna.'

# 14

The next evening, Kirsty was alone in the kitchen, Mária having taken to her bed with a headache. She quite enjoyed having the place to herself. It was always so busy with Mária, and sometimes Anna, clattering pans, chopping, stirring and pounding for hours on end. Then there were the girls and staff filing past the hatch, chatting about their lessons or grumbling at the dwindling food supplies. Often the babble in the dining room was almost unbearable: the scraping of chairs and tables, along with the clatter of cutlery on plates and the chink of glasses. Some days it was hard to think clearly. Although to be honest, all her mind did now was to fret about Endre. He was still no better, despite the many weeks in hospital.

She unlocked the larder and drew out a precious joint of cooked lamb. Jean had got up at three o'clock that morning to buy it from the market, bringing it into the kitchen with a flourish. They hadn't seen meat for weeks. Mária's eyes had lit up with rare enthusiasm and she and Kirsty had spent a long time discussing the best way to cook it, both to preserve its flavour and make it stretch as far as possible. In the end they'd decided to pot-roast it with onions and carrots. For hours the kitchen had been filled with a wonderful savoury aroma. Kirsty planned to slice the now-cooled meat thinly and serve it with potatoes and paprika sauce. She couldn't wait to see the pupils' faces. It would be such a treat for them.

She'd just delved into the cupboard for the wooden block they used to cut meat on, when she heard a noise at the back door. 'Who's that?' she asked. It was too late for a delivery, and neither Jean nor Anna would come in through the back door.

A tall figure slid in. He was wearing black trousers, a green shirt with a distinctive cross insignia and stripes on the sleeve, and a black tie. Ice inched up Kirsty's spine. It was a uniform she dreaded ever since she'd heard that the fascist group had gained more and more power in Budapest: Arrow Cross. Although he still lived at the school, and she glimpsed him from time to time – usually before walking in the opposite direction – their paths hadn't crossed in a long while. But there was no doubt that it was Dasco. Jean had been right. Mária's son was now a member of the Nyilas.

'Hello, Dasco,' she said, closing the drawer. She tried to keep her voice level. It was important he didn't realise how scared she was. Bullies always sensed a victim.

'Ki-rr-sty.' Dasco drew out the word, his lip curling. 'How nice to see you.'

'What do you want?' Kirsty asked.

He approached her, trailing the stench of beer and cheap cigarettes. 'I seem to remember you weren't very welcoming the last time I was in this kitchen.'

Kirsty tried not to flinch. 'That was a long time ago. A lot has happened since then.'

'Yes,' he said, pulling out a chair and sitting down at the table. 'I'm older and stronger now.' He had indeed filled out since their last encounter, and was even more cock-sure. His gaze travelled up and down her body in a way that made her want to pick him up and hurl him out of the door. She tried to keep her eyes fixed on his face and not pull her cardigan tighter around her as she was longing to. 'And the Nyilas have a lot more power in Budapest now that Horthy has seen sense and joined the Germans. The Nazis want to rid the world of Jewish scum – and so do we.'

'But you're still not legalised.' The words were out of her mouth before she had time to think.

Dasco scowled. 'Don't underestimate us, little girl,' he said. 'We'll have our time. Just you see. Nobody likes the Jews.' He spat on the table, a watery globule appearing on its wooden surface. 'People like you, and your precious matron, cooking for those kikes, protecting them . . .' he spat again, 'are traitors to Hungary. You won't get away with it, you know.'

Kirsty glared at him. When he'd threatened her before she'd stood up to him and he'd backed off. For all his bravado and bluster he'd been a coward underneath. But something told her she'd not be able to intimidate him so easily now. Her stomach clenched and nausea rose in her throat. Even if Mária were here, she probably wouldn't offer Kirsty any protection, although he might be more restrained in front of his mother. If Jean or Anna appeared there'd be strength in numbers, but there was no way of summoning them. She had to deal with this on her own.

Dasco lurched across the table for the cooked lamb. He tore a piece off the end and crammed it into his mouth. 'Delicious,' he pronounced. 'How kind of you to provide some food for me.'

White-hot anger flared in Kirsty's chest. How dare he? That

food was for the girls. Those Jewish pupils Dasco had been so disparaging of. It wasn't their fault they'd been caught up in all this hatred. It was people like him who were scum, stealing what wasn't theirs, bullying those who couldn't defend themselves. Anna had told her that marauding groups of Nyilas youths were ever more present on the streets, harassing and attacking Jewish people, just as those men had that day Endre had walked her and Anna back to the school. In fact she'd been sure Dasco had been there then. He and his kind were vermin, terrorising the innocent. It should be her spitting on him.

'Leave that!' she said.

'Oh? And what are you going to do?' Dasco's face was red with annoyance now, his eyes blazing, meat juice running down his chin.

He stood up, his fingers fumbling on his belt. 'I think little girls like you need to be taught a lesson.'

He strode towards her and shoved her chest with one fleshy palm, pinning her against the cupboard, then unbuttoned his fly with the other hand. Why on earth had she provoked him? Why hadn't she offered him the meat, allowed him to eat his fill and then leave? It was foolish to take him on; she was going to pay for it now. There was no point screaming, it would only antagonise him. Better to submit to his brutality and hope he'd eventually leave, than oppose him and risk an even worse fate. But even as she considered that, another thought occurred to her.

She reached back to one side of the cupboard, feeling the smooth surface of the drawer with her palm. He was so close she could smell his yeasty breath and the animal reek of his sweat. Her fingers scrabbled until they reached a handle. He made a grab for her blouse, tearing it apart and groping for her breasts. She pulled the drawer open. Please let it be there. He thrust his pelvis towards her. But just as he moved his hand down, ready to wrench up her skirt, she found what she'd been looking for. She slid her hand silently out of the drawer, round the side of her body then pushed the knife's point against his chest. His eyes opened wide in shock. 'You bitch!' he exclaimed. 'You bloody bitch!'

Kirsty jerked the knife enough to puncture the skin but not inflict a serious injury. 'Leave my kitchen now,' she commanded. 'Or that knife will be ten centimetres deep.'

Dasco's mouth twisted in fury, but he backed off. 'You might have won this battle but I'll win the war. From now on, you'd better be looking over your shoulder.'

Kirsty advanced towards him, the knife still outstretched. Thankfully it was a carver with a good sharp point. She had no doubt it could inflict a lot of damage if necessary.

Dasco spat at her. She let the saliva dribble down her chin without wiping it away. It was vital she didn't let herself be distracted, however revolted she felt. Eventually he turned his back and left the way he came. She stood by the door, her fingers still gripping the knife, until she heard his footsteps die away. Then she ran to the sink and vomited again and again until her body was empty.

She couldn't face going to her room. She was too much in shock, her heart racing, sweat coating her body. Fortunately, when she'd stumbled down the corridor, she discovered Jean was still in her office. She took one look at Kirsty's face and drew her in, gently settling her into a chair.

'What on earth's happened?'

It was an effort to speak. 'Dasco,' she whispered.

There was a sharp intake of breath and Jean's mouth hardened. 'What did he do?'

'He attacked me in the kitchen . . . I think he intended to rape me but I fought him off.'

'The bastard,' Jean said. Even in her shocked state, Kirsty registered the force of the word. She'd never heard Jean use language like that before. 'I'll get him removed from the school immediately.' She put her arms round her. 'You poor wee bairn. What a brute.' She held her tight, rubbing her back and murmuring soothing words.

The softness of Jean's jumper against Kirsty's skin, and her usual faint scent of cold cream were comforting. 'Do you need a doctor?' Jean asked.

Kirsty shook her head. 'I sent him packing before he did anything. If he'd persisted it would have been him needing a doctor.'

Kirsty felt Jean chuckle. 'That's my girl,' she said.

'He's joined the Arrow Cross,' Kirsty told her, shivering as she remembered the distinctive green shirt.

Jean tightened her embrace. 'I suspected as much. He's been heading that way for a long time. Delinquents like Dasco always find their own kind. I'm concerned about Mária's behaviour too. She's become more and more hostile towards the girls.' She gave Kirsty one last hug then sat back down in her chair. 'I'll give her a severe talking-to; tell her exactly what her son has been up to, and why he has to go. She'll be lucky not to be dismissed as well.'

Kirsty wiped a hand across her forehead. It came away

slippery with sweat. She still felt wobbly. 'I don't think she has any control over him now.'

'Hmmm. You're probably right. The Arrow Cross are becoming far too powerful and the authorities less and less able to do anything about them.' There was no longer a police officer at the corner of Vörösmarty Street. They'd been abandoned to their fate.

'We'll get a lock put on your bedroom door until Dasco is evicted. And you must promise me you'll never be on your own in the kitchen. Make sure Anna or I are with you.'

'Jean – you have enough to do.'

'Yes, but right now you're my priority. To think we've been housing that nasty piece of work under our roof. I'll speak to Dr Molnár about this. Make sure he gets him sent away and told never to come back. The most important thing is keeping you safe.'

Kirsty nodded. She wondered what Dasco had meant when he'd warned her to keep looking over her shoulder. She'd certainly make sure she was never on her own again. She'd never felt so vulnerable in the school before. The enemy was always outside. Now, with Dasco having joined the fascists, it was within.

Jean stood up. 'Come with me,' she said. 'I'll heat up some milk for you. In fact, we'll both have a cup. And I'll make up a bed in my room. You can sleep with me until we have the lock in place.'

Kirsty followed her gratefully back to the kitchen.

# 15

Summer 1943

Kirsty went with Anna many more times to see Endre, but there was little change, apart from him seeming to get thinner each day. He'd almost started to blend in with his surroundings now, motionless for hours at a time, his face as pale as the dull, distempered walls of the hospital. It was hard to remember the bright eyes and lively expression of the boy she first met. With his withdrawn behaviour and disturbed mind, he couldn't be more different to the savage Dasco. It didn't seem fair that the Dasco, at seventeen, was still free when Endre, only two years older, had already been to hell and back.

The staff seemed relieved when Anna asked if they could take Endre out for a few weeks. 'As long as he takes his tablets, he should be able to cope,' the doctor said, writing out a prescription. 'The change of scene and fresh air should do him good. But it's very important he stays medicated. I can't guarantee his behaviour otherwise.'

Despite the war, they still managed to visit Lake Balaton again each summer. With Kirsty's help, Anna's swimming came on well. She'd quickly mastered breaststroke and had since added front crawl and backstroke to her repertoire. It wouldn't be long before she'd be beating her in races. Kirsty loved being able to use the skills Da had taught her, and to spend several blissful weeks at the lake was a treat that sustained her all year round. Taking Endre was a risk, but it was hard to see how he'd ever improve at the hospital.

It was decided they'd pick him up en route to Lake Balaton, and the nurses agreed to have him ready. As they drew up outside the building, a stooped, tentative figure appeared, leaning on the arm of an orderly.

'I'll get him,' said Anna, rushing along the aisle and down the steps. She helped Endre onto the coach as though he was an old man. He froze with alarm when he saw all the passengers – there were twelve girls going on the holiday this year – but Anna spoke to him quietly and eventually he slumped into a seat.

Kirsty thought it would be best to leave the two siblings alone so she didn't go up to join them, much as she wanted to. Instead she watched from a few seats back. Anna continued to talk to Endre, holding his hand to stop him fidgeting. Then he looked out of the window for a while, before finally laying his head back on the padded leather and closing his eyes. Anna threw a glance back at Kirsty and mimed a thumbs-up sign, which Kirsty returned. So far so good.

She looked out of the window herself now, half registering the flash of fields and woods; the proud parades of poplars; the distant, tree-studded hills; the occasional farm building. It was hard to imagine they were at war. Even though Endre was still so unwell, many of his comrades were dying on the Eastern Front. The Germans had been beaten at Stalingrad and now the Russians had recaptured more towns. It looked as if the tide was turning. Although Jean was hopeful that Budapest would remain protected, seeing how the war had traumatised poor Endre brought it home to Kirsty that none of them was safe. It was four years now since the conflict had started. The Great War had been over in that time – perhaps this war would follow suit. She allowed herself to dream of a time when Endre was whole again, when the anti-Jewish laws were revoked, when they could stroll by the Danube hand in hand, when she could watch Jean turn on her wireless without her stomach contracting in fear . . .

She tried to banish Dasco, and her still-vivid encounter with him two months ago in the kitchen, from her mind. Jean and Dr Molnár had tried to get him evicted but they'd had a visit from an Arrow Cross leader one night, insisting Kirsty's allegations were false and that Dasco was to stay. When the principal protested, he'd been informed that the school would be vulnerable to attack if he didn't obey orders. He'd reluctantly capitulated. Since then, to her intense relief, Kirsty had only seen Dasco in the distance and the revenge he'd hinted at hadn't happened, although it was disturbing to know he was still at the school. She had to take a deep breath and will herself to be calm every time she entered the kitchen, and she never went in alone. At least the lock had been installed on her bedroom door.

But now she needed to concentrate on getting Endre well. And try to get some much-needed rest herself.

With a hiss of brakes, the coach finally drew up at the villa where they were to spend the summer. Up ahead of Kirsty, Anna was gently waking Endre. He jerked upright and looked around, wild eyed, for a few seconds, then slowly relaxed and followed Anna down the aisle like a sleepwalker.

As the only male of the party, Endre had a room to himself. Jean put Anna and Kirsty next door, so they could be on hand if needed.

Once they'd all unpacked, and Kirsty had assembled a makeshift tea, she, Endre and Anna wandered down to the lake. The sun was sinking now, spangling the water and making silhouettes of the reeds. They sat on the shore watching two swans glide over the rippled surface. It was still warm, the heat of the day lingering in the air and soothing their limbs until they felt languid and peaceful. Kirsty glanced at Endre. He was leaning back, his head against a rock, his eyes closed. For so long he'd swung between drugged apathy and intense agitation, but this evening he just looked relaxed. Kirsty smiled at Anna and Anna nodded back. Another good sign.

They stayed beside the lake until it was nearly dark, then Kirsty reluctantly left to heat the milk and put out the cups for bedtime drinks. It was good to have a break from Mária's strict regimes and petty rules. More like a holiday for her too. Especially away from Dasco. She was secure here. The pupils drank quietly, sleepy from the journey and the mellow evening spent by the lake. Kirsty knew she'd have to be up early the next morning to visit the local market but for now everyone seemed satisfied.

She awoke in the night to the sound of screaming. Anna was already on her feet, a ghost in her white nightdress.

Kirsty sat up, her heart beating rapidly. 'Endre?'

Anna nodded, her face a tense mask. 'Come with me. It might need two of us.'

They dashed into Endre's room without knocking. He was

still in bed, his forehead glistening with sweat, his hair sticking up as though he'd run his hands through it again and again. But it was the sound that came from his mouth that stopped Kirsty in her tracks. He was howling like a wounded animal in pain.

Anna rushed to his side and put an arm round him, but he threw her off with an expression Kirsty had never seen on his face before. A look of pure hatred mingled with terror.

Anna backed off. 'Endre. It's me, Anna. It's all right. You're at Lake Balaton.'

Endre stopped howling but continued to stare, panting, his eyes wild and unfocussed. The room was filled with the primitive stench of fear.

Kirsty stayed in the doorway, uncertain what to do.

Anna took a step forward again. 'Endre,' she whispered. 'It's all right. You're safe.' She picked up a bottle of tablets on his bedside. 'Kirsty, could you get some water?'

Kirsty ran to the kitchen as quietly as she could. It wouldn't do to wake everyone up – assuming they'd managed to sleep through the noise.

She returned a few minutes later with a filled glass.

Anna took it, then handed Endre the tablets. But he swiped at them, knocking them out of her hand, then grabbed the glass and hurled it onto the floor.

Anna shot Kirsty a desperate glance.

Endre was trying to get out of bed now, despite the shards of glass everywhere.

Kirsty hastened to help Anna hold him down but he was too strong for them both. His arms were muscled from months of labouring and he threw them off easily, then sprang out of bed and straight onto a piece of broken grass. In his agitated state he failed to notice the pain, even though his blood was now staining the floor.

'What's going on?' Jean appeared at the door, her face filled with concern.

At the sight of this new intruder, Endre bent down, picked up the largest piece of glass and brandished it towards them. 'Stay back,' he said. 'I'm armed.'

Kirsty felt rather than saw Jean take a deep breath. Her gaze was fixed on Endre clutching the broken glass, his knuckles white and his eyes wide with intended threat. If he attacked any of them, its sharp, jagged edges could cause a serious injury. How on earth would they calm him down? And why on earth had they risked taking him away when he was clearly such a danger – to himself as well as them? Kirsty's heart pounded faster with each terrible thought.

# 16

'Bellak. Put down your arms. That's an order!' Kirsty had never heard that tone in Jean's voice before. So strident and authoritative. Even when reprimanding a naughty pupil – although they were more troubled than naughty these days – her voice remained firm but quiet. Now she sounded like an army major.

To the girls' amazement, Endre obeyed, dropping the shard of glass to the floor with a clatter.

'Now sit down,' Jean commanded.

Again, Endre did as he was told.

Without turning round, Jean asked Kirsty to get another glass of water.

Kirsty did so and returned to find Jean talking more gently to Endre, who was now sitting on the bed shaking.

Jean held out her hand for the glass, which Kirsty passed to her. Anna tipped two more tablets from the glass jar and handed them over as well. 'Take these please, Mr Bellak,' Jean ordered.

Endre took the glass in one hand and scooped up the tablets with the other. He popped them into his mouth, sipped some water, then tipped his head back. But he gagged instead of swallowing, his cheeks reddening, his eyes bulging. The tablets shot out.

'Calm down,' said Jean, retrieving the sodden tablets from the bedspread where they'd fallen and placing them on her palm. She put her hand on Endre's shoulder. 'Take some deep breaths. Do it with me.' She took a long draught of air herself, then exhaled through her mouth, looking at Endre the whole time. Endre copied her and Kirsty saw the rise and fall of his chest under his nightshirt. 'That's right,' Jean said. 'Now just take one tablet.' She handed it over to Endre. 'Slowly. There's no rush. Keep breathing.'

Endre placed the tablet in his mouth and took another sip of water. As he tipped his head back as before, Jean spoke soothingly to him. The tablet went down.

'Well done. Now the next one.' She handed over the second tablet and Endre followed the same procedure. When it got stuck in his throat and he started to gag again, she told him to take more water, and that shifted it.

Then Endre's shoulders slumped and he started crying. Huge, wracking sobs that shook his whole body and were somehow more awful than the screaming.

He let Anna comfort him this time. She drew a chair up to his bed and stroked his hair until his sobs became quieter and his breaths more even. At one point he allowed her to prise a sliver of glass from his foot and press her thumb against the puncture hole until it stopped bleeding.

Kirsty and Jean stood quietly until Endre fell asleep, then helped Anna collect up the broken glass.

'Thank you, Jean. You were wonderful,' Anna said when they'd tiptoed into the corridor and were murmuring to each other, further down the passageway.

'How did you know what to do?' Kirsty asked.

Jean shrugged. 'My father once had a very nervous sheep. We called him Custard. Papa tried all sorts of ways to calm his behaviour, but strangely I found that being firm with him seemed to help. After a while he was much more docile.' She shrugged and smiled. 'I just applied the same principle to Endre.'

Anna smiled wanly back, but her tone was full of regret. 'I should have checked he took his tablets last night,' she said. 'I put them out for him but didn't insist he swallowed them in front of me. We'd had such a lovely evening; I didn't want to spoil it by being a bossy sister. And he seems to have trouble swallowing sometimes. I don't know if you've noticed.'

Come to think of it, Kirsty hadn't seen Endre eat anything at supper last night. She'd have to keep an eye on him.

Jean squeezed Anna's hand. 'It's going to take us a while to work out how to handle things,' she said. 'He might be away from the front, but he's still in a battle.

'If anything, I blame myself for encouraging you to bring him here. But the doctor wouldn't have allowed him to go if he'd been seriously worried. We just need to make sure he takes those tablets.'

Anna nodded. 'I'll be much more careful from now on.'

'I think he'll sleep for a good while,' Jean said. She looked at her watch. 'And we need to go back to bed too. I'll see you in the morning.'

They returned to their room, both still shaken. It took Kirsty a long time to get back to sleep, and when she did she dreamt of terrified creatures howling in the darkness.

As Jean had predicted, Endre didn't disturb them again. Kirsty tiptoed to the kitchen early the next morning to get breakfast ready, leaving a pale-faced Anna still asleep. Endre limped into the dining room just as they were clearing away, the cut on his foot obviously hurting. He looked vacant and his hands shook as he took the cup of black tea Kirsty offered him, although he refused anything to eat. He thanked her briefly then stumbled across to a table to sit down, gripping the cup tightly. Kirsty left him alone, just darting little glances in his direction while she piled up dishes and took bowls of butter and jam into the larder.

Eventually she drew out a chair and sat down next to him. Anna had joined him by now and was talking to him quietly but Endre didn't reply. He stared straight ahead, his eyes leaden.

Girls' voices floated down the corridor. They were going out in a boat that morning and Jean had instructed them to collect bathing costumes and towels before meeting her outside the villa.

'That foot might need a good soak. Do you want to come to the lake?' Kirsty asked. 'You could wash it there.' It was a long shot but worth a try.

Endre's eyes flickered with interest.

'We could just paddle if you'd rather.'

Endre shrugged. 'All right.'

Anna smiled. 'I'll come with you to get your swimming things. Shall we meet you outside, Kirsty?'

Kirsty nodded and rushed off to retrieve her own costume.

The lake looked different in the morning sunshine: a huge sheet of milky green, spreading to purple hills that loomed, shadowy, on the horizon. Kirsty, Anna and Endre sat on a grassy bank watching the girls as they waded out to take turns in a small rowing boat. Some strode ahead, furrowing the water with their legs; others jumped and splashed, sending tiny droplets arcing through the bright air. Shrieks and laughter drifted back to them. It wasn't only Endre that needed healing. With their fathers absent, the Jewish girls had witnessed their mothers' grief and fear. The day pupils often had to care for younger siblings as well as trying to focus on their own schoolwork. And all with a war going on that each day seemed to bring new acts of hatred against their people. Jean was constantly dealing with the girls' squabbles and tantrums. It wasn't surprising considering the stress they were under, and Kirsty could see that Jean tried not to be too hard on them. At least the holiday would give boarders a reprieve.

The hot sun beat down on their heads, picking out strands of gold in Anna and Endre's hair. Liquid warmth seeped into Kirsty's skin and oozed through her mind and body until she felt herself relaxing. It was hard to imagine that the peaceful young man next to her had been a frightened animal the night before. They still didn't know exactly what he'd seen on the battlefield. Only that Endre and his comrades had taken the full force of the Russian attack. The doctor had warned them he might never speak of the full extent of the horror. All they could do was to try to tame it, to dilute the memories, and help him to find some peace. Jean had been right; in spite of the risks – and last night's events had made those risks all too evident – time at the lake could bring healing for them all.

Anna stood up. 'I'm going in,' she said. 'Want to join me?'

Kirsty looked at Endre, who nodded. 'It's too hot to sit on the bank any longer,' he said.

They walked over sun-scorched grass to the edge of the lake, where gentle waves formed lacy patterns on the shore.

'Let's paddle,' Kirsty suggested. They stood in the shallows as the warm water made eddies round their ankles and a slight undertow sucked at the soles of their feet. Jean was further out with the girls, up to her waist in water, smiling as her pupils took it in turns to row the boat round in circles. 'It's so good for them just to be silly,' Kirsty said.

Anna smiled. 'Yes, it's as if they'd forgotten how to play when they're at school. It's coming back to them now.'

Endre was looking out to the far shore, his eyes shielded against the sun. Kirsty couldn't resist glancing at his strong shoulders and muscular chest, a few dark hairs sprinkled across the front. He was no longer the slight young man frowning at the bench of his father's watchmaking shop; all that physical work had hardened his body, even though it had weakened his mind. She caught a glimpse of another line of hairs running from his chest to his belly button, then down into his trunks. She swallowed and turned away, conscious of the sudden flush to her face.

'I'm going to swim,' she told Anna, not daring to look at her or Endre in case they noticed her reddened face. She waded quickly into the deeper water before she could hear a reply, launched herself off and swam towards the horizon until her burning cheeks had calmed and she'd put some distance between herself and the others. Then she turned onto her back and frowned up at the sky. Normally she relished the chance to swim outside. Back in Scotland it was what took her down to the Clyde again and again; the joy of swimming in the open air, despite the cold; the wonder of looking up at the scudding clouds and wheeling birds; the sense of peace when her head was submerged and she could hear her own thoughts and the sound of the water. Indoor baths were practical, and Hamilton always had a special place in her heart for the hours she spent there with Da. Pools nourished her body, but wild water nourished her soul.

Yet it was harder to concentrate today, her mind was too full of Endre. She still loved him deeply but affection was mingled with pity now. It was difficult to know how he felt with his mind so damaged. Could they ever have a future together? Last night she'd been frightened of him but his calmness this morning reminded her of the boy she'd first met. So many conflicting emotions. She took a deep breath and struck out for shore. Better to focus on physical things: her work in the kitchen, supporting Jean with the girls, and helping Anna to mend Endre. Anything else was beyond her control.

Later, Anna volunteered to go back and start lunch, leaving Kirsty and Endre alone.

'Do you want to swim?' she asked him.

'Not yet,' Endre replied. 'But maybe a walk?'

Kirsty looked at the lakeside path that followed the curve of the water, meandering past towering willows and dark green shrubs. It looked cool and inviting. But was it wise to go with Endre alone? In spite of his mellowness today, was she entirely safe with him?

'I'll go and ask Jean,' she said. She discarded the towel she'd draped round herself after her swim and waded back into the lake.

Jean wrinkled her forehead. 'I'm not sure that's a good idea,' she said. 'Endre is still a very unpredictable young man. I think it would be irresponsible of me to let you accompany him on your own.'

'I understand.' Jean's response confirmed Kirsty's own feelings, tempted as she was to risk her safety for the prospect of being on her own with Endre.

'Why don't you just stay on the bank where I can see you?' Jean suggested.

'All right.'

She reported Jean's advice to Endre who shrugged. 'I don't blame her,' he said. 'Perhaps it was a silly idea.'

'Not silly,' said Kirsty, sitting down on the bank in the hope he would join her. 'It would have been nice. But you are still recovering and Jean has to take care of her employees.'

'I'm sorry about last night,' Endre said, easing himself onto the grass.

Kirsty plucked a blade of grass and chewed at it. 'What do you remember?'

Endre wrapped his arms around his chest and frowned. 'I remember waking up suddenly from a nightmare. I was back at Uryv, fighting. When you and Anna ran in, I was sure you were going to attack me.'

'It seemed as if you couldn't see us. You were responding to something inside your head.'

Endre stared out at the lake, then blinked rapidly.

'Can you talk about it?' Kirsty tried to keep her voice as gentle as possible.

'Not yet, no.' A tic pulled at the corner of his eye.

Of course. It was too soon. Perhaps a different tactic. 'I've noticed you never eat much.'

'No. Sometimes I feel hungry but I just can't swallow.'

What terrible event had occurred to produce such a strong physical reaction? Kirsty felt she'd pushed Endre as far as she could. He would talk when he was ready. But somehow she needed to get him to eat.

Endre turned to her, his brown eyes full of despair. 'Do you think I'll ever get better?'

'Yes, I do.' She searched for something comforting to say. 'I was in a terrible state when my father died. Maggie teaching me to cook and Jean bringing me to Budapest helped me to cope again.' She plucked another piece of grass. 'I don't know where I'd be if it wasn't for them.'

'How long did you take to recover?'

Kirsty thought for a minute. 'I don't think you do ever recover from something as awful as that. But you find ways. Cooking saved me. And swimming.' She gazed out at the lake where three of the girls were tugging the rowing boat ashore and laughing, the others swimming alongside. 'I think swimming could save you too.'

Endre smiled. 'Maybe. I certainly feel calmer with you. It's much easier to talk too.' He moved a little closer, and in spite of herself, desire curled low in Kirsty's body. She hadn't felt that for a long time.

'It's wonderful being here at the lake, but you know I will have to go back to the hospital.'

Kirsty nodded. He seemed a different man to last night, the words flowing, his expression peaceful. Perhaps that was down to her. He certainly seemed to think so.

'I'm afraid I can't promise you much. I'm still a patient at the Dániel Bíró, and technically still part of a labour unit. I've no idea what the future will bring.'

Kirsty ran her fingers across the grass. 'None of us does.'

'All I can offer is the hope that we can be together in better times. When the war is over and the anti-Jewish laws are revoked.' He fashioned a loop from a blade of grass, tied the ends together, then offered it to her.

'A ring?'

Endre smiled. 'A friendship ring for now. But maybe one day it'll be different.'

Despite his cautious words, Kirsty felt a rush of joy. She slipped the grassy loop onto her finger. 'That's good enough for me,' she said.

'Kirsty?' Jean was out of the water now and already dressed. 'I think lunch is ready.'

'All right.' Kirsty stood up.

'I'll come back with you,' Endre said.

She was acutely aware of his tall figure beside her as they returned to the villa.


Jean helped Endre to take his tablets that evening, in the same way as before, and he was able to swallow them both down. As a result, there was no disturbance from his room all night.

Kirsty was up early the next morning and wandered outside for some fresh air. The garden was peaceful in the early light: the sun filtering through the trees, a slight mist rising from the grass as the heat evaporated the dew. A few wild strawberries nestled at the base of the old disused well. She picked one and ate it, the luscious fruit a burst of sour sweetness in her mouth. She'd forgotten how intense they tasted. She picked the rest and popped them into her pocket, then returned to the kitchen.

When Endre came in for breakfast, she made him his usual cup of black tea and placed it in front of him. He smiled his thanks, then lingered in the dining room while Kirsty cleared away. The girls left early, eager to get on with the day, but Endre stayed behind, sipping his tea slowly. Kirsty felt him watching her as she moved around the room, collecting and stacking plates, retrieving cutlery, scraping leftover food into the bin – not that there was much these days. Supplies had been so scarce back in Budapest, they knew not to waste any. Once they were on their own, she put her hand in her pocket, gently scooped out the delicate wild strawberries she'd picked earlier, and offered them to Endre. He gave her a surprised look, then took the berries wordlessly, his fingers brushing her palm. Kirsty went back into the kitchen; it was important that Endre didn't feel she was watching him. She busied herself washing and drying the breakfast things then putting them away, deliberately taking her time, before returning to the dining room.

But when she got there, Endre was gone, leaving his teacup behind. And the strawberries had vanished.

Endre continued to sleep well. Their days were spent at the lake: paddling, boating, picnicking, walking. Their limbs turned brown from the sun and each morning more and more freckles appeared on Kirsty's face, much to her dismay. But Anna assured her they suited her, and after a while she stopped worrying – it was the price she paid for being in the fresh air, enjoying the warmth on her skin and revelling in the chance to be out of the kitchen for long stretches of time.

Endre grew bolder about going in the water. Like Anna,

he'd spent his youth traumatised by Róza's death. But now he was happy to wade out, watching Anna and Kirsty in their underwater swimming competitions. Jean had told them of the fishermen's legend that there was an entire village hidden in the lake's depths and that at one time the bell tower of the village could be seen sticking out of the water. A few years ago, divers had found relics and tools in the mud at the bottom of the lake, and, near a place called Örvényes, they'd brought the wreckage of a whole ship to the surface. The girls searched and searched but to their disappointment, couldn't spot any treasures. What they did find though was another world: of green, shadowy depths and rocks covered in furry aquatic moss; of shoals of silvery fish that trailed light in their path; of weed like thick ribbon and stultified gardens with strange, contorted plants. When their lungs were bursting they'd kick upwards, towards strands of sunlight that combed the water, and burst onto the surface in a fountain of bubbles. Kirsty had never known such clear water: the Clyde was murky, polluted by years of mining and shipbuilding, but this underwater world was sparkling and new. Endre and Anna shared her joy at the discovery and each day they became fitter and bolder, their ability to stay under water increasing as their lungs strengthened. As before, Anna impressed Kirsty with her swimming ability. She really was becoming very good indeed. And the war seemed a million miles away.

Kirsty continued to tempt Endre with food. Provisions were still more plentiful away from the city, farmers keen to sell their produce. Sometimes, after she'd cleared the breakfast things, or prepared a picnic lunch, she would stay on in the kitchen, trying to invent little treats: some lemon posset she made when their neighbour brought them some cream; a cheese soufflé when she'd got some eggs at the market; more wild strawberries; a summer vegetable soup. Endre always stayed behind in the dining room now and each time she would present him with the day's delicacy, then disappear into the kitchen while he ate. The food was always consumed, and he began to look healthier, less haunted as a result. They managed a few snatched kisses on the rare occasions they were alone. The grass ring was faded now, and she didn't want to draw attention to it, so she kept it in her pocket – a bit like Da's old hanky which she still reached for whenever she felt sad. She had two mementos now, of the two men in her life who loved her.

All too soon the last day arrived. They spent it at the lake, which still sparkled in the late August sun, then picnicked on the shore with the last of the provisions. Kirsty had managed to buy some cold cooked beef, a few tomatoes, a local fried bread called *lángos* and a handful of ripe peaches. They lay on blankets afterwards, toasting their bodies one last time, their tummies full, their minds lazily vacant. Then Kirsty, Anna and Jean cleared up and they all returned to the villa to pack.

Endre came into the kitchen just as Kirsty was loading the equipment she'd brought from the school into large crates.

'Here,' he said. 'I'll give you a hand.'

'Thanks.'

He picked up some of the larger utensils – the big ladle, an outsize colander, and the huge pan she used for jam making – and stacked them neatly.

'That's a great help,' Kirsty said.

Endre smiled. 'It's nothing compared to what you've done for me.'

Kirsty looked enquiringly at him.

'All that lovely food you cooked. You've made me want to eat again.'

'You hardly ate a thing when you first came.'

Endre sat down, his face suddenly grave. 'Terrible things happen in war,' he said.

Kirsty stopped packing and joined him at the table 'The doctor at the hospital told us you'd been through some awful experiences.'

'The Hungarian soldiers were very cruel to us Jews . . . but the worst thing . . .' His fingers curled into a fist which he ground into the table. 'The worst thing was what they made us eat.' His expression turned inward, as though he was replaying some appalling scene in his head.

'Endre?'

His hands were scrabbling at his mouth now, as if to hold back the words – or stem a rising tide of nausea.

'Just breathe in and out,' Kirsty said, remembering how Jean had got him to take the tablets on the first night. 'Slowly.' She turned to face him and started to inhale and exhale, signalling to him to follow suit.

After a few breaths, his pallor began to fade. He looked straight ahead and spoke in a monotone. 'One day we refused to fight. We were exhausted, so weary we could no longer put one foot in front of another. We Jews had been placed at the head of the army – *unimportant flesh* they called us. When we refused to act as a shield any longer they . . .' He swallowed, and rammed his hand against his lips, sweat greasing his forehead.

Kirsty squeezed his arm. 'It's all right. Take your time.'

Tears ran down Endre's face, strangled sobs coming from

169

his throat. He took a deep breath and turned to face her, locking his eyes onto hers. When he spoke, his voice was a cracked whisper. 'They ripped up pages from our holy books that they'd looted from synagogues, and stuffed them into our mouths.'

'My God.' It was inhumane. Brutal. No wonder poor Endre couldn't eat.

Endre was properly crying now, his shoulders shuddering, deep primitive noises combining with his sobs.

'It's all right. It's all right.' She wrapped her arms around him, and he laid his head on her shoulder.

They stayed like that for a long time, until his shaking stopped and he was quiet and still.

Then she gently pulled away and wiped his face with her sleeve. 'It's all right,' she said again. 'I'm so glad you told me.'

He gave her a watery smile. 'I am too.'


The journey back was much quieter than the journey out. Then the girls had been full of anticipation and excitement. Now they were rested, but feeling the first pinpricks of anxiety as to what the new term would bring.

Nevertheless, Lake Balaton had restored them as usual. As Kirsty looked out of the window in drowsy contentment, she allowed herself to nourish a little spark of hope that Endre would recover. Perhaps, somehow, they could have a future together. A future when a Jew was allowed to have a relationship with a Gentile, when war was only a distant memory, when Endre could go back to being a peaceful watchmaker.

Inside her pocket, she slipped the grass ring onto her finger and kept it there for the remainder of the journey.

## 17

The coach driver dropped Endre back at the hospital, as agreed with the medical staff. They'd said a proper goodbye the night before, so Kirsty just smiled and waved as he got off, but inside she felt bereft. Her only consolation was that he'd asked her to visit him as soon as possible.

Once the coach returned them to Vörösmarty Street, Dr Molnár met them at the door.

'Welcome back,' he said as the girls struggled in with their cases and bags. They looked tanned and happy – very different to the pinched, white-faced group of pupils who'd left Budapest several weeks ago. The principal went straight up to Jean. 'You have a visitor,' he said.

'Oh?' Jean put down her case and pushed back a wisp of hair that had escaped its clip. Even she looked more relaxed after the break, although the lines of worry on her forehead had never quite disappeared. 'Who's that?'

'A man named Carl Lutz. Apparently, he's the Vice-Consul of the Swiss legation to Budapest. Seems like a good chap.'

'What does he want with us?'

'He heard about us through his Red Cross contacts. He says he'd like to chat to you about the work of the school. Nothing to fear, I promise.' Dr Molnár picked up Jean's case. 'Why don't I take this to your room while you go and talk to Mr Lutz? I've shown him to your office.'

'Thank you,' said Jean and smoothed her hair again. 'I'll go there straight away.' She set off down the corridor.

Kirsty and Anna supervised the girls with their luggage then Kirsty popped into the kitchen to check Mária had something ready for them to eat.

'I can manage here, if you unpack the supplies,' Mária said, reaching for the kettle. She'd already laid some bread and jam on the counter, along with a big bowl of cherries.

'I'll help you,' Anna told Kirsty and the two of them returned to the coach to ferry the equipment and surplus food to the kitchen.

By the time the girls had finished their supper, Jean had still not emerged from her office. 'Do you think I should offer them some coffee?' Kirsty asked.

Mária nodded. She didn't ask them about their time away. No doubt she'd had a much grimmer experience trying to keep an eye on her brute of a son. Thankfully Dasco was nowhere to be seen.

Kirsty knocked on Jean's door. She wondered what was keeping them deep in conversation for so long. As she waited for a reply a few words drifted out: 'Jews ... Zionist ... Palestine.'

'Come in,' Jean called out eventually.

Kirsty entered the room. A slight man with combed-back dark hair and round glasses sat in front of Jean's desk. He stopped talking when she came in.

Jean introduced them: 'This is my cook and fellow Scot, Kirsty McClean,' she said.

Mr Lutz shook her hand. 'Pleased to meet you. We foreigners need to stick together.'

'Pleased to meet you too,' Kirsty replied.

'What made you decide to stay in Budapest?' Mr Lutz asked. His remark was addressed to them both.

Jean massaged her forehead. 'The Scottish Mission wanted us both to return back in thirty-nine,' she said. 'But I couldn't leave my girls . . .'

'And I couldn't leave Jean!' Kirsty added.

Mr Lutz laughed. 'You are brave women,' he said, then frowned. 'I think the time is coming when you'll need to be braver still.'

Kirsty's chest tightened.

'We'll do all we can to help you,' Jean said.

Kirsty wondered what Jean meant but she didn't feel it was her place to stay any longer. She offered them some refreshments and both agreed to some black coffee which she brought them a few minutes later, finding them deep in conversation again. Then she left to help Mária clear the supper things.

Half an hour later, Kirsty heard the front door open and shut. She and Mária were still in the kitchen, preparing tomorrow's breakfast, when Jean came in. She looked pensive.

'Would you like something to eat?' Kirsty offered.

'Maybe just some bread, if there's any left.'

'Of course.' Kirsty cut a slice and placed it in front of Jean, together with a knife and a pot of jam.

'I had an interesting conversation with Mr Lutz,' Jean said, dipping the knife into the jam and spearing some sugary fruit.

173

'He seemed to know a lot about what's going on,' Kirsty replied. She and Jean still spoke English to each other when they were on their own. Mária was busy in the larder.

'He spent some time in Palestine when he was younger,' Jean said. 'He's very keen to support any Jews who want to go there.'

'And how will he do that?' Kirsty asked. Immediately her thoughts went to Anna and her parents. And Endre.

Jean took a bite of bread. 'With great difficulty, I suspect. The Nazis will make things incredibly hard for him. He thinks it's best that those Jews elsewhere in Europe who've avoided deportation or worse stay in hiding.'

Kirsty nodded. She assumed Endre was safe in the hospital, and Anna was protected by the school – as much as she could be – but their parents might need to 'disappear' soon.

'It would be a dangerous path though,' Jean continued. 'The Arrow Cross are getting more and more militant, particularly against Jews and their supporters.'

There was a sudden crash from the larder.

'Are you all right, Mária?' Jean called out in Hungarian.

Mária emerged, clutching a tin of treacle and scowling. 'It bounced,' she said, indicating a dent on the side.

'Still edible then,' replied Jean. 'We can't afford to lose any more food. It's hard enough tracking down supplies as it is.'

Mária grunted and disappeared back into the larder.

Jean stood up and yawned. 'Thanks for the bread and jam, Kirsty,' she said. 'I think I'll have an early night.'

Kirsty stood up too. 'I'll just finish off in here, then I'll turn in as well.' Dasco still hadn't made an appearance since they'd arrived, but she was keen to go up to her bedroom and lock the door. Now she was back at the school her heart had started to thump again, in a way that it hadn't in all the weeks at Balaton.

Jean squeezed her hand. 'Thank you for all your hard work at the lake. The girls had a wonderful time.'

Kirsty thought back to the sun-filled days, the joy of swimming, the picnics, the precious time spent with Endre . . .'So did I,' she said.

Two weeks later, Kirsty was slicing some cheese, ready for breakfast, when Anna came flying into the kitchen, wild eyed with shock.

'What's the matter?' She laid down her knife and rushed over to her friend. Mária tutted and raised her eyes to the ceiling, but Kirsty ignored her. Anna gripped the table with one hand, white skin taut over her knuckles, and put her other hand to her chest from which came a rattling sound as though she was struggling to breathe. 'Sit down,' said Kirsty. 'I'll get you some water.' She hastened to the cupboard, seized a glass and plunged it under the tap, then set it in front of her friend. Anna took a sip but her face was still bleached with fear.

Kirsty sat down and put an arm round her. 'Anna. You're worrying me now. Tell me what's wrong.'

Anna took another sip, then looked at Kirsty bleakly. 'It's Endre.'

Kirsty's heart started to thrum. 'What's happened? Has there been another incident? He was doing so well.'

Anna nodded. 'He was. That's the problem.'

All sorts of terrible scenarios flashed through Kirsty's mind:

a deranged Endre holding a shard of glass to a nurse's throat; Endre escaping from the hospital, the doctors in pursuit; Endre dead in his bed of a sudden heart attack . . . Her pulse rate accelerated with each awful thought.

Anna took another juddering breath. 'The authorities reviewed Endre's case. They said he'd made so much progress he was fit enough to return to his labour unit.' She took a gulp of water and continued in a voice that cracked with emotion. 'He's been sent back to the front . . . and this time I know he'll be killed.'

Kirsty was too appalled to reply. She saw Endre, bronzed and happy, sitting on the grass beside the lake watching her swim. Whatever had they done? Encouraging him to go into the water, feeding him delicacies. The good food and the weeks at the lake had healed him. That and their growing closeness. But she never dreamt he'd be discharged from hospital. She imagined he'd see out the war still having treatment, or be sent home to convalesce, or allowed to live a peaceful life somewhere. Her fingers shook as she took Anna's hand.

All their efforts in patching Endre up had only served to ensure he'd be exposed to yet more brutality. Instead of doing him a good turn, they'd made things infinitely worse. And now there was nothing they could do. Her fingers scrabbled for the grass ring in her pocket.

A fortnight after that, a letter arrived.

*My dearest Kirsty,*
    *I'm sorry there was no time to say a proper goodbye. I never dreamt I'd be sent back so soon . . .*

Kirsty swallowed down a surge of guilt. Did Endre think it was her fault? Anna seemed to blame her too. She'd been much cooler with her lately.

*Some of the men from my last stint are with me; most, sadly, are not.*

Did that mean they'd been killed? Something terrible must have happened to lose so many men.

Then came a strange sentence:

*Whenever we have enough time to think, I find myself remembering the stories I read as a boy, particularly that of poor Mordechai and all the troubles he had with Haman. I think of you too of course. I miss you so much . . .*

What did the reference to 'Mordechai' mean? And who was 'Haman'? Some of the boys at school back in Hamilton had read Biggles books, but she didn't recall any stories with these names in.

She asked Anna about it as they were slumped at a dining-room table after serving and clearing breakfast.

Anna paled. 'Mordechai and Haman are from the Book of Esther, in the Bible,' she said. 'Mordechai was a Jew, living in Persia. The king's top official was a man named Haman who hated the Jews. Mordechai refused to bow down to him. In revenge, Haman made his life an absolute misery and plotted to kill all the Jews in the Empire.'

'So what does that mean?'

'It means that Endre is being badly treated by a man who hates Jews,' Anna replied, her eyes blazing.

Kirsty's heart plummeted. Poor Endre. He obviously couldn't tell them what was going on, because of the censor, but he'd used code knowing that Kirsty would ask Anna to explain the references. Things must be truly terrible. Perhaps worse than before.

'Why on earth did we take him to Balaton?' Anna said. 'Why did you give him all that good food and encourage him to go into the lake? If it wasn't for that he'd be still in hospital, away from the war!'

'I thought I was doing the right thing,' Kirsty replied, tears prickling at Anna's harsh tone. 'How was I to know he'd be sent back? I thought he'd stay in hospital. It was awful to see Endre like that . . . so broken.'

'Better broken in hospital than mangled on the battlefield.'

'I'm so sorry. I love him too. I wouldn't have hurt him for anything.'

'But you did. And you hurt my parents as well.' The colour was high in her cheeks.

Mr and Mrs Bellak flashed into her mind. Mrs Bellak's lively warmth, her husband's more diffident personality. Endre took after him; Anna was more emotional, like her mother. The whole family would be devastated that Endre had returned to the front. Perhaps Anna's parents blamed her too.

'That was never my intention, Anna. I had no idea this would happen.'

But Anna wouldn't listen. She pushed her chair back from the table and strode out of the room.

# 18

Autumn 1943

It didn't take Jean long to discover the fracture in Kirsty and Anna's friendship.

'Give her time,' Jean said, her forehead creased with sympathy. 'Anna and Endre are very close. Anna's still in shock.' They were sitting in Jean's office, each with a cup of hot water. Coffee was just for special occasions now, and, although tasteless, the water at least staved off the hunger for a while.

'I know,' Kirsty replied. 'But I'm in shock too. I honestly never meant this to happen.'

'Of course you didn't. And Anna knows that deep down.'

'Then why can't she be more understanding?'

Jean sighed. 'Think of it from Anna's point of view. She lost her sister in a terrible accident and she's worried sick about her parents, given the way the Jews are being treated now. Endre going back is the last straw.'

Kirsty thought back to those awful days after she'd lost Da. Her emotions had been all over the place. She ran her hands through her hair. 'I know. But she's blaming the wrong person. It's the authorities she should be accusing, or Regent Horthy, or the army . . .'

Jean came over, wrapped her arms round her and dropped a kiss on her head. 'Why don't you take Anna swimming?'

'*Swimming?* How will that help?'

'You said she's become very good at it. It will give her something else to focus on, and going back to being teacher and pupil again might bring you closer.'

Kirsty shrugged. 'Maybe.' After Da died, she'd gone down to the Clyde and swum until her body was exhausted. It had calmed her mind then; it might help Anna now. It was worth a try.

'Try the swimming baths in Szőnyi út,' Jean said. 'You'll need to be careful on the roads of course, but as it's so close, I think it's worth the risk.'

'Thanks, Jean.' Kirsty hugged her back and went off to find Anna.

The October weather was mild, a mellow sun peering through the still-leafy chestnut trees and the air yet carrying a little warmth. Kirsty and Anna hurried along the road, constantly on the lookout for anyone who might pose a threat. Kirsty thought sadly how Endre would have walked them there in times gone by.

As an elderly lady, a shopping bag hanging limply from her arm, approached, Anna stepped into the road to let her pass, rather than move closer to Kirsty as she usually would. She did the same for a harassed-looking mother chivvying two children a few yards later. Kirsty didn't comment, but it hurt to think Anna wanted to keep her distance – physically as well as metaphorically.

She told Anna a little more about the Hamilton baths back

in Scotland and Anna briefly replied. The conversation was stilted but at least they were talking. Sometimes, when they were together in the kitchen, there was no conversation at all. Anna always made sure she did a separate task to Kirsty instead of working alongside her. But when Kirsty repeated her conviction that Anna had the makings of an excellent swimmer, she was rewarded with a wan smile.

As they turned into Szőnyi út, a gust of wind sent some old newspaper pages skittering across the pavements. Normally there'd have been a road sweeper brushing the rubbish into piles, but the street was empty. The windows of some of the houses were boarded up, old bits of cardboard nailed haphazardly across the glass. Weeds sprouted from cracks in the brickwork, and the paint on several front doors was peeling off.

The baths were halfway down the road, a yellow stone building which must have once looked imposing but now reflected the general decay of the rest of the street with its patchy stucco, and moss-streaked roof. Anna pushed open the door and Kirsty followed.

The smell of chlorine instantly transported Kirsty to the last time she'd been to an indoor baths, the day of the mining accident. She hadn't visited a swimming pool all the time she'd been in Budapest; not wanting to risk making herself vulnerable. That's why the annual visits to Lake Balaton were so precious. She'd told Anna ages ago about Da's death, there was no point alluding to it again, but it was still hard to blank out the horror. She still thought about Da every day, of course, and sometimes had nightmares about that terrible time at the pit, but the memories were softer now, and balanced by thoughts of happier times. It was only occasionally, like today, that a smell or a sight took her instantly back to the past.

Anna approached the reception desk. 'Two to swim please,' she said, rooting in her bag for coins.

'Papers?' The receptionist wore round glasses and her hair was swept back into a tight bun. Kirsty thought of Maggie, sitting by the kiosk at the Hamilton pool in one of her fluffy jumpers with a scarf round her neck, and wondered fleetingly how she was. They'd corresponded for a while but the letters petered out after the war intensified.

Anna delved into her bag again and handed over her documents.

'*Zsidó*?' said the woman. Jewish?

Anna nodded.

'I'm sorry,' the woman said. 'Jews are not allowed to swim here.'

'Why not?' Kirsty asked.

The woman sniffed. 'Management orders. Do you have your papers, miss?'

Kirsty passed hers across and the woman glanced at them. 'You may swim, but not your friend.' Her mouth was a firm line.

Kirsty grabbed her documents back. 'I'm not going on my own. Come on, Anna, if you're not welcome here, we'll swim elsewhere.'

Anna nodded, her expression rigid.

'I'm so sorry,' Kirsty said as they let the doors bang behind them and set off back down the road. 'It's ridiculous. Just because you're Jewish.'

Anna's didn't reply. Her face had a pinched look again.

'It's not fair!' said Kirsty. She swung her bag so violently it hit the wall and she bent down to brush off the scuff marks. 'They'll let young Jewish men die for their country but they won't allow you to use their facilities.'

Anna gave a sharp intake of breath, and Kirsty realised she was thinking of Endre. 'I'm sorry,' she said. 'I shouldn't have said that.'

They walked on in silence. Kirsty could have kicked herself. Anna had been thawing a little but inadvertently reminding her of Endre was the worst thing she could have done.

They were nearly back at the school now, and Kirsty was desperate to say something to placate her. An idea darted into her mind. 'I'm sorry you can't swim at the baths, Anna, but what about the river?'

Anna turned a wary face towards her.

'I swam in the Clyde all the time when I was younger,' Kirsty said. 'It was much colder than the Danube will be.'

Anna bit her lip and frowned.

Again, Kirsty was furious with herself. Of course. Anna's sister drowned in the Danube. She apologised for the second time. 'That was tactless of me. Perhaps we should just leave it.'

'No,' Anna drew a long juddering breath. 'I need to swim.'

'Good.' Kirsty smiled. 'We'll go tomorrow.'


'How was the swimming?' Jean asked when they got back. Anna had rushed off to change, so Kirsty and Jean were on their own in the dining room.

Kirsty explained about Anna being refused entry to the baths. 'That's awful,' Jean said. 'But perhaps we should have

183

expected it. The penalties against Jews are getting harsher and harsher.'

'I know. Anna didn't say much. In fact I think I was more angry than she was.'

'Is she still distant with you?'

Kirsty drove her nails into her palm. 'Yes.'

'I've been at the school for eleven years. I've constantly seen girls fall out and make up. Friendships shatter and re-form.' Jean massaged the space between her eyebrows. There were deep clefts there now. 'Someone once told me that friendships are for one of three things: a reason, a season or for life. Perhaps you and Anna just need a break. She needs time to work through all that's happened.'

Kirsty nodded. Her friendship with Maggie had been for a reason: getting her through the first traumatic days after Da's death. She'd assumed she'd be friends with Anna for life, though. They got on so well, despite hardly being able to communicate at the beginning. They shared a similar sense of humour, a passion for swimming, a love for Endre. She'd thought they were kindred spirits. But maybe their closeness was just for a season. Perhaps she should try to make friends elsewhere, even though there was no one who seemed to understand her like Anna. But Jean was right. She needed to be patient. Thank God for dear, wise Jean.

She was certainly a friend for life.

The next day was a Sunday and they usually had a few hours to themselves after they'd served lunch. Anna was still quiet but helped Kirsty to clear away as quickly as possible to leave more time for swimming.

184

They'd told Jean earlier what they were intending to do. Even though they were both eighteen and no longer needed her permission to leave the school, with the streets becoming increasingly unsafe, they'd got into the habit of letting her know when they were going out and when she could expect them back. 'Just avoid Andrássy Avenue,' Jean had warned them. 'Those Arrow Cross yobs tend to hang around there, picking on anyone remotely Jewish-looking. Take the back roads instead.' It was good advice. Kirsty remembered how youths had pushed an old lady into the gutter that time, and how Endre had tried to rescue her – getting beaten up himself in the process. She blinked away the frightening thought that he would likely be experiencing far worse now that he was back with his unit. Again she felt for the ring.

They stayed south of the main boulevard, finding their way down to the river through a warren of little streets, towards the Chain Bridge with its squat towers, metal lattices and the stone lions either end – supposedly similar to those in Trafalgar Square in London. Jean had once told her the bridge was designed by an Englishman but built by a Scotsman. 'Typical,' she'd said, her eyes twinkling behind her glasses. 'The English do all the nesh stuff but the Scots put in the hard graft!'

The sun shone from a clear autumn sky, creating bursts of light on the river's green surface. A few children were already in the water, shrieking and splashing, while their mothers sat on the bank chatting. It was still mild for October. Kirsty had mixed feelings about the swim. She longed to be in the water but she worried how Anna would cope. It was hard to tell how she was feeling; her expression was inscrutable.

They discarded their dresses, having already put their

costumes on underneath, then Kirsty plunged into the river and Anna followed slowly. It was only about three feet deep near the bank, so Kirsty swam out towards the centre until her feet could no longer touch the bottom. Anna caught her up, her face a mask of determination, and Kirsty smiled her encouragement, although the smile wasn't returned. As they continued to swim side by side the water became colder and the colour changed to a darker green. It was often referred to as the *blue* Danube, but in truth it was more green than blue.

'Shall we swim all the way across?' Kirsty asked, treading water so that she could speak. The current was quite strong here, trying to tug them downstream, but they'd swum at an angle to allow for the undertow.

Anna nodded then struck out for the far bank.

Kirsty followed in her wake as they swam from Pest towards Buda. Soon the children's cries were faint sounds, hardly distinguishable above the slap of water on their legs and the ragged sound of their breaths. Despite her worries about Endre, and Anna's aloofness, it felt wonderful to be in the water. She hoped it would sluice the anxieties from their minds and invigorate them for the week ahead. 'So much better to be outside than in a stuffy swimming baths,' she shouted.

Anna nodded.

'It's the baths' loss,' said Kirsty.

Anna nodded again.

They swam across the river in wide languid strokes until they were twenty metres from the far bank.

'Race you!' Kirsty called and they increased their stroke speed, intent on swimming as fast as possible. Anna won by a hand's length.

'I can't believe you beat me.' Kirsty's words were staccato, her breath ragged.

Anna didn't reply but her expression was triumphant.

Even though Kirsty had swum her hardest, she was pleased Anna had won. She'd been so hurt for her when the receptionist at the Szőnyi Street baths had refused her entry yesterday, just because she was Jewish. But they'd had the last laugh. Out here in the Danube, the still-warm sun on their backs and the wonderful views of the city before and behind them, it was a much better experience than swimming in an indoor pool. Thank God Anna had forced herself to go in, in spite of the disturbing memories of Róza.

'Are you all right to swim back?' Kirsty asked as they stood in the shallows on the Buda side, getting their breath back from their race. 'We could always use the bridge.' She looked up at the Chain Bridge, its struts gleaming in the sun. There were Hungarian soldiers, in brown-green uniforms and carrying rifles, at each end. She hoped Anna had enough energy to keep going. It might be awkward, not to mention scary, if they had to walk past the soldiers in just their bathing costumes.

'I'm fine,' Anna replied. 'How about an underwater competition?'

'You're on.'

They waited as a couple of barges chugged past them, furrowing the water and trailing the smell of diesel. Then they both took deep breaths and launched themselves into the grey glow under the surface of the river. Normally Kirsty would have plunged downwards to see what lay on the bottom, or swum slowly to check for fish or eels, but today she was focussed on beating Anna so she propelled her body forwards as strongly as she could, willing herself to swim as fast as possible. She carried on until her chest was burning and her lungs were screaming, then kicked upwards and surfaced in a shower of bubbles.

She trod water until Anna came up a few metres behind her. 'One all!'

Anna wiped her face with the palm of her hand. 'Now race you to the bank.'

They set off once again.

Later, they walked back through the cooling streets, their wet hair hanging in damp tendrils, their bodies still glowing from the exercise. But just as they'd turned into Alkotmány utca, they heard a buzzing sound over towards Buda, like a swarm of angry bees. Kirsty looked up. There was a line of planes in the distance, flying like a dark arrow towards them.

Her stomach lurched.

Within seconds the planes became larger, screaming across the sky and swooping low over the parliament building. A series of black objects fell from their underbellies.

'We're being bombed!' Anna was frozen with fear. There was a thunder of explosions and the pavement throbbed under their feet.

All too late, the sirens wailed like banshees.

Kirsty grabbed Anna's hand. Up ahead people were screaming and running. The girls followed them, their feet pounding on the stone, their chests taut.

'Where can we take shelter?' Her words came out strangely high pitched.

'I don't know,' Anna shouted, above the sound of booms and blasts. 'Best make for the school.'

They ran on as bombs rained down in the distance and the air was filled with the crashing of falling masonry, and the acrid smell of burning.

Electrical charges of fear ran up and down Kirsty's body. Anna was panting beside her. There was no need to take the back roads; the greatest danger came from the sky not the street. Terror made them fast. They sped across Teréz körút, along Vörösmarty utca and up to the school. Kirsty fumbled with the door, her fingers greasy with sweat, then it flew open and they were inside.

'Thank God,' said Jean. 'The shelter is already full. Go to the cellar.'

Anna and Kirsty stumbled down the steps into the basement, threw themselves onto two battered armchairs and sat breathing heavily with exhaustion and relief. Several teachers and some of the older girls were already there, their expressions full of fear as the bombs continued to drop, their sounds muffled by the thick walls of the building and the groans from ancient pipes.

'Surely that's not the Allies?' Kirsty asked once she'd recovered her breath. She couldn't believe she and Jean could be bombed by their own people. Britain had declared war on Hungary at the end of 1941 but there'd been no attacks so far.

'No,' one of the teachers replied. 'It's the Russians. It's their reprisal for the Germans forcing us to fight with them. They caught us napping.' That explained why the sirens hadn't warned them.

Kirsty wiped a dribble of sweat from her forehead. It was

terrifying how close the war had come. She and Anna could easily have been killed. And the school could have been destroyed if it had sustained a direct hit. The Russians were ruthless. And Endre was much closer to them than they were. After that initial communication, soon after he'd been sent back, his letters had dried up again. They had no idea where he was or what he was going through. Although the continued absence of news at least gave them hope.

The pupils and staff waited until the all-clear sounded then stumbled back to their beds, weak with weariness and fear.

# 19

Winter 1943

One mid-December morning, Kirsty popped into Jean's office with a cup of thin soup, to find her on the floor, her leather suitcase in tatters on the ground in front of her, and a pair of strong scissors in her hand.

'What are you doing?' Kirsty hastily put the cup on the table.

Jean sat back on her heels. 'I'm trying to make some soles for the girls' shoes. Leather is really expensive now, and their poor feet are getting so cold. I thought the soles might make good Christmas presents. For the staff too.'

'But it's your suitcase! Won't you regret cutting it?'

Jean gave her a sad smile. 'I'm not going anywhere, am I? At least not for the foreseeable. If we manage a trip to Lake Balaton next year, which I'm afraid might not be possible, I can always take my things in a knapsack.'

Kirsty nodded. The news about Balaton was a disappointment but not surprising. Rumours were flying around that the Germans were preparing to invade Hungary, that Horthy could no longer hold them at bay. Resistance would be impossible; the Germans were too powerful. The Russians had left them alone since the sudden attack in October, but they could

191

easily be supplanted by a new menace. She'd longed to be back in the cool waters of the lake, sleeping and eating at the little villa which had become a haven from the outside world. But doubtless Jean was right. They were unlikely to have that respite this year. They'd just have to sit it out at the school and hope against hope that the war would be over soon. Surely it couldn't go on much longer?

She gently took the scissors from Jean. 'Why don't you have your soup? I'll carry on here for a while.' Jean had already marked out the patterns. All Kirsty had to do was to cut round them, and her fingers were probably stronger, thanks to all the years spent in the kitchen preparing food. Day after day her hands had pounded herbs in a pestle and mortar, stirred stews, hacked at joints of meat and sliced huge piles of vegetables. Cutting up a few bits of leather would be easy.

'All right, dear. Thank you.' Jean staggered to her feet and sat down at the desk. She'd grown very gaunt lately, and her face was always pasty. Kirsty wondered if she was eating properly. She was always so busy serving at mealtimes, it was hard to check whether Jean was present. But from her increasingly emaciated figure, it seemed not.

'There's some bread left over from breakfast,' Kirsty said. 'Why don't I pop to the kitchen and get you some?'

'That would be kind, thank you,' Jean said faintly.

By the time Kirsty returned, Jean was leaning back in the chair, as if asleep. Kirsty set the plate of bread down quietly on the desk in front of her and Jean's eyes snapped open.

'Sorry. Did I wake you?'

'No. I was just resting.' Jean took a sip of soup. 'I was thinking about Christmas. What we can do to make it special for the girls.' Christmas was always a big event at the school, even though the Jewish pupils didn't celebrate it at home. Their parents seemed happy for them to go along with a Christian tradition on this occasion. 'I've saved a few items from the benevolence parcel.' A few months ago, the Women's Jewish Committee had sent over some goods, and the extra food items had been a welcome addition to Kirsty and Mária's larder. It had been shrewd of Jean to keep a few things back. 'There are some books I can give the older girls and a few toys for the younger ones. I think that will be enough.'

'I think that's more than enough in the circumstances.' Kirsty pushed the plate of bread nearer Jean and was pleased to see her take some. 'I'll talk to Mária about what sort of lunch we can rustle up. Leave it with me.'

Jean smiled. 'You're a good girl.'

On Christmas Day, the girls were delighted with their presents and particularly grateful for the new leather soles, which Jean helped them glue onto their shoes. Mária and Kirsty were able to procure enough meat to serve the chicken dish, *csirkepaprikás*, for lunch, and Jean insisted that all the girls help afterwards to give the cooks a break.

When everyone was busy sleeping off their meal, or occupied with their presents – depending on their age – Jean beckoned Kirsty into her office. 'It's three o'clock in England. I thought you'd like to hear the dear King's speech with me,' she said, twiddling the dial on the wireless. There was a scribble of static, then the national anthem being played. Kirsty had been in Budapest for four years now, and Britain seemed increasingly remote, but at times like this the memories came flooding back: sitting with Da at the kitchen table listening to the wireless after she'd tried, and usually failed, to concoct a Christmas lunch. Da singing along to the national anthem, then nursing 'a wee dram' of whisky as the sun went down. How surprised Da would be if he knew how skilled a cook she'd become. She'd love to serve him her *csirkepaprikás* and watch his eyes light up with pleasure at how good it tasted.

Da always attempted to make Christmas special too. One year he'd given her his very own guide on swimming, a notebook in which he'd written down everything he'd told her. She wished she'd brought it to Budapest. It might have been useful when she'd taught Anna to swim. Although in truth, she knew most of it off by heart.

The King was speaking now. His theme was families; how hard it was for parents and children to be separated 'at home and abroad.' In the school were many Christian girls whose fathers were away fighting with the Hungarian army, as well as the Jewish pupils whose fathers were in labour units. The fear and worry was clearly affecting the pupils. Little Léna wet the bed each night, appearing, tearful, each morning, with a urine-soaked sheet in her arms; Luca refused to eat at mealtimes, but was hiding food in her locker; Zoé spent lesson times writing letters to her father – letters that would never be sent or received.

King George was right, children deserved to be given as good a Christmas as possible. Kirsty swallowed down a lump in her throat at the thought of how Jean had cut up her own suitcase to provide precious gifts.

When the speech finished, she remained with Jean, mulling over the speech and the emotions it had triggered. It was hard to fathom what Jean was thinking from her wistful, sad expression. When the King had mentioned how people's thoughts were in distant places and their hearts with the ones they loved, Kirsty's mind went immediately to Endre. Was he even alive? The possibility of his death nagged at her constantly. The grass ring was almost disintegrated now, yellow and brittle with age. She hoped it wasn't a bad omen.

They were all vulnerable. British and American forces were already making their way through Italy. Much as she wanted the Allies to win the war, in Hungary they were the enemy. Her fear at the time of the Russian attacks that they could be bombed by their own people was becoming increasingly possible.

'Do you think we were right to stay here?' Kirsty asked eventually.

Jean took off her glasses and rubbed her eyes. 'I could never have abandoned the girls. It's what God told me to do and I wouldn't have had any peace if I'd failed to answer my calling. If these children need me in days of sunshine, how much more do they need me in days of darkness?' She put the glasses back on. 'But I've often wondered if I did the right thing bringing you to Hungary.'

Kirsty reached across the table and put her hand on Jean's, noting with concern the slack skin and bony fingers. 'You weren't to know what would happen,' she said. In truth, her feelings were mixed. She was grateful for the cookery skills, and, of course, if she hadn't come to Budapest, she'd never have met Anna . . . or Endre. Although she might have been safer back in Hamilton. But she needed to reassure Jean, who was looking so anxious. She smiled at her. 'You've been like a mother to me for all these years.'

Jean returned her smile. 'They were good years, early on, weren't they? Despite the deprivations and the worry. Budapest felt like a sanctuary.'

'Yes, it did. And who knows what we might have encountered if we'd stayed in Scotland?'

'Thank you, dear. You've reassured me. I do worry about you.'

'You've no need to,' Kirsty said. 'Meeting you was one of the best things that could have happened to me.'

'Let's pray for the war to end very soon,' said Jean. Kirsty dutifully closed her eyes and bowed her head as Jean prayed out loud. But she failed to hear Jean's prayer, as all she could hear were the words going round and round in her head: please keep us all safe. Especially Endre.

# 20

January 1944

Jean and Kirsty listened to each new announcement on Jean's wireless with mounting trepidation. 'The Germans are losing, aren't they?' Kirsty asked, when they heard they'd been forced to withdraw from Leningrad. They were sitting in Jean's office one freezing day, huddled in blankets to keep warm.

'It would seem so,' Jean replied. 'So many of their cities have been bombed.'

They both felt conflicted. Deep down they were glad the Allies were doing so well, but what did that mean for Hungary . . . for their poor pupils . . . for them . . .?

'Any news about Endre?' Jean added.

As usual, the corners of Kirsty's vision blurred with fear at the mention of his name. 'Nothing,' she said.

Jean wrapped her arms round her, and she felt the comfort of wool on her skin, easing a little of her dread.

But in March everything changed. There'd been rumours for a while that Horthy might make peace with the Allies. Prime Minister Kállay had already withdrawn the remnants of the Hungarian army and only a small number of poorly armed troops remained. Where did this leave Endre? They still hadn't heard from him.

At four o'clock on the morning of 19 March, Kirsty woke with a start, her heart drumming. From outside her window came a deafening roaring and rumbling, interspersed with loud creaks and clangs, and the menacing beat of hundreds of jackboots on the streets. Terror gripped her body. She jumped out of bed and tweaked the curtain. People in dressing gowns or coats over their pyjamas were flooding down Vörösmarty Street towards Andrássy Avenue, from where the noise was coming. As she let the curtain go, she became aware of other, indoor, sounds: screams . . . doors banging . . . pounding feet in the corridors.

A loud knock on her door caused her heart rate to accelerate further. She opened it with trembling fingers, then sagged with relief at the sight of Anna standing in the corridor with a shocked face and tangled hair. There was an uneasy truce between them now. They hadn't returned to the warm friendship they'd once enjoyed, but Anna had sought out her company more and more lately.

'They're here,' Anna whispered.

Kirsty put a hand to her chest. The news they'd been dreading for four and a half long years. Hitler must have grown impatient for Hungary to commit and decided to force the issue.

'Jean's asked us all to assemble in the senior dormitory. Come on.'

Kirsty grabbed her dressing gown from the hook on the door and followed Anna along the corridor on suddenly hollow legs.

\* \* \*

The dormitory was already packed with girls and staff, most in a dishevelled state of dress, with white faces and fear-filled eyes. Jean, who was talking quietly to the school principal, looked composed if shaken. Once she'd checked everyone was there, she clapped her hands to get their attention.

'This is the day we hoped and prayed would never happen,' she began, 'but sadly I was informed earlier this morning that the Germans are in Budapest, taking control of our city. No one is to leave the school without my permission. It isn't safe to be on the streets at this time. Other than that, I am confident nothing need change. You girls will continue your schooling here. We are under the protection of the Church of Scotland, and on account of that no one can do us any harm. Now . . .' she took a deep breath and drew herself upright. 'I suggest we sing a psalm to compose ourselves and ask God for help. How about "The Lord's My Shepherd"?'

She began the first verse in a quiet, melodious voice, still with a Scottish lilt even after all these years.

*The Lord's my Shepherd, I'll not want . . .*

The girls joined in, hoarse and shaky at first, their dry mouths making singing difficult. But after a while sweet, high voices started to soar. The pounding in Kirsty's ears receded as she blinked back the tears.

# 21

The girls returned to bed a lot calmer, but Kirsty couldn't sleep. She hadn't felt so frightened since the night of the mine accident when she'd stood waiting at the pit, terrified that Da had been killed. With due reason, it turned out. She tossed and turned for a couple of hours, her mind racing, then wearily stumbled down to breakfast.

Just as she and Anna were laying the tables, and Mária was cutting up slices of bread, Jean appeared. 'Can you and Anna manage by yourselves?' she asked Mária.

Mária shrugged. 'I suppose so.'

'I'd like to take Kirsty food shopping with me. I think it will be safer to go in pairs now and I'm worried about securing enough provisions to feed the girls.' Despite her confident words earlier that morning, the violet shadows under her eyes and her unkempt hair told a different story.

'Of course,' Kirsty said, running to get the knapsack they used for food purchases. Her chest had tightened again but if Jean was prepared to take her life in her hands then so was she.

They set off down Vörösmarty Street towards the market, cautiously making their way along the back roads to avoid the Germans, although their tanks rumbled ominously in the distance. The sun struggled to appear through a pearl-coloured sky; a chill wind buffeted their faces and numbed their ears.

An empty paper bag cartwheeled briskly down the road before coming to rest, deflated, in the gutter.

Normally, the marketplace was full of noise – stall holders shouting their wares, customers haggling, friends stopping to exchange news. But today it was silent. Some of the stands were still wrapped in tarpaulin, their owners clearly too scared to venture out. The few traders who'd shown up were bleak-faced statues making no effort to sell their produce.

'We can't return empty handed,' Jean said. She pointed to a stall at the back of the market in front of which a small line had formed. 'I'll queue for bread; can you try to get some vegetables?'

'Of course.' Kirsty looked round. Their usual supplier, Mr Kovacs, wasn't in his customary spot in the corner; only a few papery onion skins and some Brussels sprout leaves in a ragged pile offered evidence that there was usually a vegetable stall there. She was half tempted to pick them up; perhaps she could coax some kind of soup out of them, if she washed the grit out first. But then she saw a woman walking towards her, a small cabbage poking out of the top of her shopping basket.

'Where did you get that?' she asked.

The woman pointed to a stall at the far side of the square. Kirsty could just make out some green, leafy objects perched on a trestle table. There didn't seem to be any other vegetables.

'Thank you,' she said, and hurried off.

There were about five ancient cabbages left, their outer leaves yellow and wilting – doubtless the fresher ones had already been snapped up. The man seemed happy to let her buy him out. As she made her way back to Jean with the earthy-smelling vegetables, she started to think what she could cook

201

with them. The tougher leaves could be made into soup with a little stock and some onions. She could stuff the more tender leaves, although what she'd stuff them with was anyone's guess. Thankfully, Jean announced she'd managed to track down some milk as well as a few loaves of bread. By grating some of the bread into warm milk and adding paprika Kirsty reckoned she could make a filling of sorts for the cabbage leaves. Not very appetising but at least it would have some nutritional value.

Back at the school, they found the corridors empty. Not a sound came from the classrooms.

Jean handed her basket to Kirsty. 'I'll go and see Dr Molnár,' she said. 'Find out what's going on.'

Kirsty nodded and went off to the kitchen where she unpacked the provisions and started to follow her plan for an improvised lunch. Mária was nowhere to be seen.

Jean joined her just as she'd finished stuffing the cabbage leaves and was placing them on a tray ready to go into the oven. She'd sprinkled some of the breadcrumbs over the top to give the concoction a bit more texture.

'Do we have any coffee left?' Jean asked, slumping at the table and massaging her forehead.

'A little,' Kirsty replied. They'd been saving the few grains at the bottom of the jar for an emergency. From Jean's expression it looked as though they'd reached it. She filled the kettle and set it on the stove.

'The government has just issued an edict saying all Jews in Hungary must wear the Star of David,' Jean said.

'How awful.' Kirsty imagined the poor Jewish girls running round the playground with stars emblazoned on their coats, and thought of Anna's indignation. 'I can't believe it's come to this.' She took down two cups and spooned a small amount of coffee into each.

'Apparently the new government has given in to all the Germans' demands. The stars have to be in place by the end of the week. Identity papers will be regularly checked in the streets and any Jew over six years old found not wearing the star will be immediately arrested and processed for transportation. No one knows where.'

Kirsty poured boiling water into the cups and added a dash of milk. 'Those over six years old? So that's all our pupils. Even the little ones.' She tried to keep her hand from shaking.

Jean nodded, her face pinched with anxiety. 'We have no choice,' she said. 'I'd better find some yellow thread.'

Two days later, Kirsty sat next to Jean at the table, a pile of yellow stars in front of them. Each was about the size of her palm, edged with black, and shaped from two interlocking triangles.

'I'll tell the girls this is a badge of honour,' Jean said, as she tacked yet another star with neat stitches onto the front of a small serge coat. 'They should wear them with pride not shame.'

Kirsty let out a length of cotton from the reel and cut it with her kitchen scissors. It was important to sew the stars on closely. Apparently, if they were deemed to be loosely attached (defined by whether a pencil could be inserted between the stitches) the wearer could be sentenced to six months in prison. 'It's so cruel of the Germans to make the girls wear these,' she said. 'They've done nothing to deserve it.'

'No,' Jean replied. 'They haven't. Nor have their mothers.

203

Nor their poor fathers at the labour camps . . .' She put down her sewing to pull out a pristine white handkerchief from inside her cuff. Then she took off her glasses and dabbed at her eyes.

Kirsty put an arm around her shoulders. 'We were both orphaned young,' she said. 'We know how hard it is to be separated from parents. Let's make those girls' lives the happiest we can.'

Jean gave her a faint smile. 'I wonder if we should start by sewing stars on everyone's coats. Even though many of us aren't Jewish, it would be a way of supporting them. We must show those poor girls that we're on their side.'

'I agree it would be fairer,' Kirsty said. 'And I want to support them. But if we have to undergo the same restrictions as the Jews, we won't be able to get food for the girls as easily, or run any errands for them.'

'Aye, you've got a point. But I don't know what else we can do.' Jean wrinkled her forehead.

Kirsty picked up Jean's sewing basket. 'May I?'

'Of course.'

Kirsty rummaged in the basket and produced a small card of metal press studs. 'How about we sew on temporary fastenings?' she said. 'Then we can show solidarity with the girls, but remove the stars so we can get around more freely.'

Jean's smile was wider now. 'I had no idea, when Reverend Murray introduced me to a wee skelf of a lassie at Queen's Park in Glasgow, that she'd become the strong, capable girl you are today,' she said. 'But how I thank God that He did.'

Worse was to come. The next day, Jean didn't appear for breakfast. When Kirsty brought a tray into her office, she found her sitting, ashen faced, at her desk, her ear pressed close to the wireless. She beckoned to Kirsty to join her.

Kirsty set the breakfast tray down and pulled up a chair. 'What is it?'

Jean looked at her through glazed eyes. 'Kállay's fled Hungary.'

They'd known for a long time that the Prime Minister had been holding out against the Nazis in protecting the Jews. Jean had once confided in Kirsty that she suspected Kállay was secretly negotiating with the Allies too, especially now the war was going badly for the Germans. But if he'd left the country, all attempts at moderation had gone with him. That was bad news indeed.

'Who's replacing him?' Kirsty asked.

'Döme Sztójay.' Jean chewed on a fingernail.

'Who's he?'

'The Hungarian ambassador to Germany. And much more supportive of the German cause,' Jean replied. 'Some people think he's even a Nazi sympathiser.'

Each revelation had Kirsty's stomach contracting more and more. But the next piece of news was worst of all.

'Rumour has it he'll legalise the Arrow Cross Party.'

As she recalled Dasco's pockmarked face and beery breath, bile rose in her throat. 'That's terrible,' she said. 'They're thugs.'

Jean nodded, her expression full of anxiety. 'I fear for our girls,' she said. 'I fear for us all.'

## 22

After a troubled night, punctured by nightmares about Dasco, Kirsty trudged wearily down to the dining room and started preparing breakfast. There was still a little bread left from their trip to the market, although it was far from fresh. Toasting might make it more palatable. She was just foraging in the larder for anything else she could offer the girls, when the door opened. She was expecting to see Mária, who seemed to arrive later each morning. She'd become more and more grudging in the kitchen lately. She just hacked at the bread rather than cut it into even slices; if she spilled some milk she often failed to wipe it up; and sometimes she wandered off as soon as the meal was finished, leaving Kirsty and Anna to clear away.

But it was Jean who'd entered. 'What can I do to help?' she asked.

'That's kind,' Kirsty replied. 'Perhaps you could put out some teacups.'

Jean nodded and went over to the cupboard. 'How are you managing in the kitchen these days?' she asked, reaching up to grasp a pair of cups in each hand.

'Well enough,' Kirsty replied. 'It's hard to find food, as you know, but of course there are fewer mouths to feed.' Some of the girls had failed to return to the school after they'd gone home to visit their parents, despite being advised to the contrary. Jean had been to their homes only to find them deserted. They'd hoped against hope they'd managed to safely escape Hungary or that they'd found a safe house. The alternatives were too awful to contemplate. 'And Anna helps.' She'd suggested Anna had a lie-in that morning, after yesterday's shocking news, but that was because she'd expected Mária to be helping her. It didn't need three people to prepare breakfast, but it was too much to manage on her own. Thank goodness Jean had popped in.

'How are you getting on with Anna these days?' Jean asked.

Kirsty shrugged. 'We're not as close as we were.'

'Such difficult times. Everybody responds differently.'

'I know. We're both so worried about Endre.'

'Still no news?'

Kirsty shook her head.

Jean took the cups over to the tables and positioned one by each place setting. 'I think we might have to dismiss Mária,' she said. The morning sun picked out silver strands in her white hair; it had lost all its colour now.

'Oh?' It was true that Mária was becoming increasingly sloppy in her ways but surely a telling-off would be enough? It seemed a little harsh to discharge her altogether, although it would be a huge relief to have Dasco out of the way. She'd barely seen him lately. The Arrow Cross must be occupying most of his time, but she still feared bumping into him.

'The Germans have announced that Hungarian Aryans are no longer allowed to be employed in an establishment where there are Jews living.' Anxiety tugged at the corners of Jean's eyes. 'That excludes you and me of course, as we're still British citizens, but I'm afraid it affects Mária.' She pushed back a strand of hair that had dropped onto her forehead. 'I've not been impressed by her work lately. And I certainly don't approve of her son and his appalling behaviour. Yet I don't want to be the one to put her out of work.'

'But you didn't make the rules,' Kirsty said. 'You can't blame yourself for a German decree.'

'I know,' Jean said, wrapping her hands tightly round one of the cups until her knuckles turned white. 'I'll speak to her later today. Can you and Anna manage on your own – perhaps if I help when I can?'

'We can cope between us,' Kirsty reassured her. 'You've got enough to do.'

'Thanks.' Jean patted her hand and got up from the table, steadying herself on the back of the chair as she did so.

Kirsty glanced at her. Her expression was bleak and she looked shaken. 'Are you all right?'

'Yes, I'm fine,' Jean said. But as she left the kitchen Kirsty couldn't help thinking that she walked like an old woman with her bent back and slow gait.

March turned into April. Crocuses and daffodils flowered in the garden and the magnolia trees sprouted fat buds. Normally Kirsty felt more hopeful when spring came. But not this year. This year Budapest felt frightening. Everyone seemed to be holding their breath, wondering what the Germans would do. They'd taken over a building in Andrássy Avenue, just at the top of their road, to use as their headquarters. She'd been past it once and had seen guards with rifles outside, and the black swastika on a huge flag hanging down from the roof. Even worse, now the Arrow Cross were legalised, they'd established headquarters in the same street. They were becoming more violent each day, with the police powerless – or unwilling – to stop them. As a result, Jean had forbidden them from going anywhere near Andrássy Avenue. They had to use a much more roundabout route. But they couldn't avoid the Arrow Cross completely. Their loud rallies, slogan-chanting and threats against Jews and Roma people could be heard from the school. Some of the girls sat at their desks with their hands rammed over their ears to avoid hearing the incessant shouts of *Zsidók kifelé!* Jews out!

One mild morning in late April, there was a thundering on the front door. Kirsty had been about to go to her room to tidy herself up before starting the lunch preparations. Her chest tightened. She didn't know anyone who would knock that loudly. No other staff were around so she hurried down the hall, her shoes clicking on the tiled floor, and opened the door. Without waiting for an invitation, two men in grey-green uniform strode in. Germans. Gestapo officers by the looks of it. Her chest squeezed further, smothering her breath. Both men were tall, dominating the space in the narrow entryway. The sun, pouring through the side window, illuminated the barrels of the guns that hung by their sides.

One of the men came up to her, bringing with him the smell of hair oil and eau de cologne. Kirsty instinctively shrank back.

'Get me Jean Mathison,' he said, his voice a low growl.

Kirsty didn't understand German but she recognised the name of her dear friend.

'Of course,' she muttered and hastened back down the corridor towards Jean's office.

She was sitting at her desk, a pile of documents in front of her, a pen in her hand and her forehead creased. At the sight of Kirsty's face, her pen dropped onto the floor.

'What's the matter?'

Kirsty's mouth was almost too dry to speak. 'Two Gestapo officers are asking to see you.' Her voice came out small and reedy.

'I see.' Jean stood up. 'I'm not intimidated by these people. They're only following orders.'

Kirsty tried to take on Jean's calmness but she couldn't suppress the rush of adrenaline that flooded her body. It was impossible to feel sorry for the men. They were too powerful looking, too menacing with their towering figures and huge shoulders. They could do so much harm to the school and the poor girls.

Jean followed her down the corridor towards the officers. She spoke to them confidently in a guttural language that Kirsty imagined was German. Kirsty looked at Jean's mild, helpful expression. Surely the men could see the goodness that shone out of her? Jean wasn't a threat to anyone.

One of the men barked something back and Jean shrugged a reply. She turned to Kirsty. 'I've been asked to pack a bag. They've given me fifteen minutes.'

'Pack a bag. Why?'

'They're taking me to their headquarters for questioning. Probably won't take long. Doubtless the bag's just a precaution. Can you show the men to my office?' Jean gave her a brave smile and disappeared off to her room.

Kirsty felt weak at the thought of staying with the men but

she nodded her agreement and tried to smile back through lips that were suddenly rigid.

She led the men down to Jean's office, conscious of their boots pounding on the wooden floor.

What was she to do with them for fifteen minutes? Should she offer them a drink? Some refreshments? Yet they barely had enough for the girls – why should she waste their precious food on the enemy?

But the Gestapo had other plans. As soon as they were in the office they started rummaging through Jean's things. The taller of the men, with close-cropped blond hair and chilly blue eyes, started to pick up papers from her desk, scanning each one quickly, then throwing it on the floor. Kirsty's heart heaved as she saw the discarded sheets of Jean's neat copper-plate writing in an untidy pile. What on earth was he looking for? Surely laundry lists and pupils' reports were of no interest to the Third Reich? Jean was an innocent middle-aged woman – no threat to anyone. What on earth did they suspect? His companion was pulling volumes out of the bookcase, flipping through the pages, then thrusting them aside. As time went on, he became more and more agitated, tearing out leaves and bending spines, hurling books across the floor in fury.

Kirsty hardly dared move in case she brought his anger on herself but inside she was outraged on Jean's behalf. How dare they invade her office and treat her belongings in this despicable way? How dare they destroy her precious books and papers? But behind that thought came a more horrifying one still: if they could do that to Jean's possessions, what on earth could they do to Jean?

Clearly they didn't find what they were looking for, as one of the officers asked Kirsty in English to show her to Jean's room.

Kirsty debated whether to give him false directions, but what would that accomplish? It wouldn't do to provoke them and their reprisals might be worse as a result. 'Follow me,' she said and the two men clattered up the stairs behind her.

Jean's door was closed so Kirsty knocked on it quietly, but one of the Germans pushed past her and shoved it open, revealing Jean, a small bag on her bed, pulling open a bedside drawer.

'Carry on packing,' said one of the men, still speaking English. 'We will search your room.' He jerked open the wardrobe door and pulled out a handful of clothes on hangers, some of which slid to the floor in a poignant pile. Next he banged the back of the wardrobe several times with his flat palm, then, seemingly satisfied, started to open and empty drawers.

'Ah, there's my Bible. I was looking for it,' said Jean, holding out her hand as the officer plucked a small leather-bound volume from one of the drawers.

'You won't need it where you're going,' the man said and hurled it to the floor.

Jean gave him a sharp look but said nothing.

Kirsty felt a furious stab of indignation, but she knew she'd be no match for the men's strength and violence.

'Have you finished packing?' the shorter of the two men asked.

Jean nodded.

'Then come with us.'

They led her back down the stairs and into the hall where a small group of girls and a couple of teachers had gathered.

Kirsty caught sight of Anna, her forehead creased with concern.

'Don't worry about me,' Jean told them. 'I'm sure I'll be back soon. I've done nothing wrong.'

One of the men opened the front door and pushed Jean through it.

She stood in front of the school in her patched winter coat, carrying her battered holdall, and gazed into the distance where the blue hills of Buda rose up gently from the far side of the Danube.

'I will lift my eyes unto the hills,' she said. 'From whence cometh my help.'

One of the men grabbed her by the upper arm and thrust her towards a waiting car.

# 23

For a second nobody moved, then some of the smaller girls started crying, and ashen-faced staff rushed to comfort them. Little Léna was sobbing loudly, her face streaked with tears.

'She'll be back soon, just you see,' Miss Laski told her. Léna stood quivering as the teacher dabbed at her face with a hanky. But Kirsty glimpsed the look that was exchanged between Miss Árvay and her colleague Miss Nagy, and her deeply worried expression had her heart plummeting once more. How on earth would they cope without their beloved matron – the woman who'd become a second mother to her and whose kindness and love she treasured so much?

'Come on,' said Anna. 'We need to start getting lunch ready.'

'Yes. I suppose we have to carry on,' Kirsty replied, running her hands through her hair.

'No doubt about it,' said Anna. 'Jean would expect it.'

They walked wearily down to the dining room.

All through lunch, Kirsty listened for Jean's return, but the front door remained shut. She and Anna cleared away the lunch things and started preparing supper. Each meal tested her ingenuity to the limit now. There was no meat, only a few old vegetables, but they still had a sack of rice in the larder.

'We could make some sort of vegetable stew,' she told Anna. 'There won't be much to go round, but we could bulk it out with rice.'

'Perfect.' Anna gave her a feeble smile. 'I'll start peeling carrots.'

Despite the meagre rations they'd lived off lately, the girls didn't seem to have much appetite. It was frustrating to scrape their precious food from the plates into the bin, but there was nothing to be done. Anna had barely touched her supper either.

As they laid the tables for the next morning's breakfast, still alert to any sign of Jean's return, Anna told Kirsty she intended to go into the Jewish quarter that evening.

'Is that wise?' asked Kirsty. 'It's so dangerous to be out on the streets now.'

'I know . . . but I'm worried about my parents. I haven't been home for ages. They usually write once a week but there's been no letter recently.' Her voice wavered.

Kirsty put a hand on Anna's arm. 'I'll come with you.'

'There's no need.' Anna's expression was pensive. As though she was wondering whether to trust her.

'It'll be safer with two of us,' Kirsty insisted. 'But let's wait until tomorrow. Jean might be back this evening and we can ask her advice. And it would probably be less dangerous in daylight. It's not as if Endre is around to protect you.' She swallowed. 'You haven't had a letter?' It was a forlorn hope. Anna would have told her if she'd heard, and Kirsty would have done the same.

'No.' Anna's face was rigid. 'All of my family feel so distant now. And poor Jean's gone too . . .'

Kirsty bit back the retort that at least she had some family. 'I'm sure Jean will be back soon, just as she promised.'

'Yes.' Anna took a shuddering breath. 'I think we need to keep busy. Let's tidy up Jean's office. It would be awful for her to come back and find it in the terrible state the Germans left it in, and it might keep our minds off the worry.'

'Good idea.'

The office was in complete disarray, books and papers on the floor where the Germans had thrown them; the desk piled with a mess of pens and notebooks; and an overturned glass trailing water which had leaked into some letters, making smudgy puddles of Jean's beautiful writing.

'We won't read anything,' Kirsty said. 'We don't want to be nosey. We'll just set it to rights for when she returns.' She was determined not to say 'if' but the longer Jean was away the more anxiety she felt. She tried to stay occupied, picking up books, piecing together the pages that had been ripped out, and putting them back in the bookcase while Anna stacked the papers in a neat pile and wiped the desk. But Kirsty couldn't forget the image of the two men ransacking the office. The room still smelled of them – a lingering trace of cologne and hair oil – and she felt their unwarranted aggression in the cracked spines and jagged pages of the books.

Upstairs, Jean's bedroom was almost as bad as the office. Clothes were strewn around the bed, the drawers half open, more books on the floor. Worst of all was the sight of Jean's precious Bible lying discarded. Kirsty picked it up and leafed through it, noting with a pang the many passages that had been underlined with Jean's treasured fountain pen. Her faith was so important to her, so much a part of everything she did.

How would she manage without it? Her eyes alighted on one verse that Jean had underlined:

> *Like a sheep being led to the slaughter or a lamb that is silent*
> *before her shearers he did not open his mouth.*

What had Jean ever done to deserve this treatment? She'd been a caring matron to the girls, a loyal member of staff to the school, a surrogate mother to her. She blinked back the memory of Jean's dignified manner as she submitted to the Germans, *like a sheep to the slaughter*, and tried not to think of what might be happening to her. Was she being held at the German headquarters in Andrássy Avenue? She debated with herself whether she and Anna could walk past there. But if Jean was in danger then so were they.

# 24

Concern for Jean haunted Kirsty all night. Everything had happened so quickly, she hadn't even said a proper goodbye. She tried not to contemplate never being hugged by Jean again, inhaling the faint scent of the cold cream she put on her face; she'd eked out the pot until there was virtually nothing left. With Jean gone, the world seemed even more precarious than ever. It was almost unbearable to think of her in a prison cell, maybe even being tortured.

Kirsty tossed and turned in bed, alert to the slightest sound. She kept thinking of how much Jean meant to her. She'd rescued her from Hamilton when her life seemed so bleak she hadn't known what to do. She'd nurtured her like a mother, responding to her every need. And over the years she'd adapted the way she handled her to accommodate each stage of her life. At first she'd been cossetting and maternal, but lately she'd been treating her as an adult and friend – asking her to accompany her to the market, involving her in key decisions. Comforting her when Anna gave her the cold shoulder. She couldn't imagine how she'd cope without her.

Even if she hadn't already been awake, the sound of distant bombing would have disturbed her. Now that Budapest was occupied by Germans, Allied pilots had started to bombard the city. She thought back to that day when the Russian planes had dropped bombs and she and Anna had only just escaped. What if a stray bomb hit the school? The chaos inside her head – the feverish anxieties about Jean – gave way to the chaos outside her head: the relentless sounds of war. She lay on her back in the darkness, listening for the roar of shells, her muscles tense in case the air siren summoned everyone out of bed and into the cellar. But this time there was no insistent wailing. Thankfully the bombing must have been too far away. She twitched back a small corner of the curtain and saw the inky sky punctured with bursts of light. Somewhere in the city, people's homes – and maybe even their lives – were being destroyed. She couldn't believe she'd escaped from the bombing of Britain only to be subjected to the bombing of Budapest – and by her own people. Why on earth had she imagined Hungary would be peaceful? Now they were under attack from the Allies on one side and the Germans and Arrow Cross on the other. She just hoped the Americans and the British would win soon. A picture flashed into her mind of Jamie Pattison and some of the other boys she'd been at school with. Barely men, with gangly limbs and breaking voices. They'd be nineteen by now and probably in the army. She imagined them in their smart green uniforms arriving in Budapest and marching up to defend the school. Please come quickly, she thought. Her heartbeat increased with each awful blast until she abandoned all attempt to sleep.

By the next morning, Jean had still not appeared. Kirsty was up early, having decided there was no point in lying in bed any longer, but she found Anna already in the kitchen, putting out plates and glasses.

'Couldn't you sleep either?'

219

Anna shook her head. 'The bombing kept me awake. That and the worry about Jean.'

'Me too. Come on, I'll give you a hand.'

Breakfast was a subdued affair. It was clear from their haunted expressions that many of the girls, and most of the staff, had suffered the same sleepless nights as Kirsty and Anna. People spoke in low voices, or stared into silence, darting glances at the door every so often in the hope of seeing Jean arrive. Kirsty imagined her standing in the doorway in her patched winter coat, looking weary but relieved. 'I'm back,' she would say. 'See. I told you I wouldn't be long.' But she didn't appear.

Two days later, Dr Molnár knocked on Kirsty's door as she and Anna were sitting cross-legged on the bed, playing a rather lacklustre game of *Capitaly*. They'd spent more time together lately. The challenges of living at the school had brought them closer, but Anna was still reserved at times. 'I've managed to track Jean down. She's in Fõ utca prison, in Buda,' he said.

Anna jumped off the bed, scattering game pieces all over the floor.

'*Prison*?' Kirsty's stomach swooped and her heart rate accelerated. 'Oh no!'

'Poor, poor Jean,' said Anna, clapping her hand to her mouth in horror. 'But I suppose at least we know where she is. Can we visit her?'

Dr Molnár shook his head.

Kirsty couldn't bear to think how devasted Jean must be to have been put in prison. She always put others before herself. How on earth could she have been accused of any crime?

But it seemed there wasn't just one crime. There were many. The principal counted them off on his fingers. 'One: working amongst the Jews . . . two: crying when she saw the girls wearing their yellow stars . . . three: dismissing her Aryan cook . . . four: listening to news broadcasts on the BBC . . . five: entertaining many British visitors . . . six: being active in politics . . . seven: visiting British prisoners of war . . . and eight: sending parcels to the British prisoners.'

'But most of those are preposterous,' Anna declared.

Dr Molnár's voice was thick with indignation. 'Of course she works among the Jews – it's been her vocation since 1932 to be in the Scottish Mission which was established for the purpose of bringing Jews into the Christian church.'

'And she wept when she saw the girls wearing yellow stars because she hated them having to bear that stigma.' Jean's tear-stained face as they'd sat sewing swam into Kirsty's mind. She'd been so dismayed on their behalf.

Anna joined in. 'She had to dismiss Mária once the law was passed that Aryans were no longer permitted to work for Jews.' Mária and Dasco had moved out a few days ago. Neither of them was missed, although Kirsty still braced herself at every corner out of habit, expecting to run into Dasco. She desperately hoped he wouldn't take revenge for their eviction.

'She needed to listen to the wireless to get word of the air-raid warnings since she was responsible for a house full of children,' added Kirsty, remembering all those evenings in Jean's office spent listening to the BBC news. 'And of course she had British visitors since she's British herself.'

'And she did indeed have written permission from the Hungarian government to visit British prisoners of war and send them parcels,' Dr Molnár declared. 'As far as I can see the only inaccurate accusation is that she took part in politics.' His eyes blazed. 'She was far too busy!'

The following day Dr Molnár called Anna and Kirsty into his office. He must have been holding his head in his hands – there were white marks on his forehead where his fingers had pressed in.

'I'm extremely worried about Jean,' he said. 'She just seems to have vanished. I've been in touch with the Swiss legation again but they have no news.' He drew his eyebrows together. 'I've heard that no one who disappears in this fashion ever comes back.'

Kirsty's chest tightened and she felt Anna's sharp intake of breath beside her. It was horrific. What on earth was poor Jean going through? If she was even alive.

# 25

Kirsty swallowed down a rush of bile and tried to take in the principal's next words.

'As things seem to be more serious than we first thought, we'll need to evacuate the girls. We can't risk the Gestapo coming back and seizing them. I've contacted the parents of those pupils who have homes to go to. They'll be collecting their daughters this morning. As for the rest . . .' He ran his hands through his hair then picked up a sheet of paper in front of him. 'I have a list of people who are sympathetic to the school and its values. If I call them, would you two assist me in placing the children?'

'Of course,' Kirsty replied. There was a pain in her stomach, a twisting agony of misery. What would Jean say if she knew her beloved school was being disbanded? Though she'd want the children safe at all costs.

'You can stay with me at my parents' apartment,' Anna said, in response to her unspoken question. Kirsty felt some of the tension leave her shoulders. Their priority was to the girls but it was a relief to know that she and Anna would still be together, and that there was somewhere they could go. Whether or not they'd be safe was another matter.

They spent the morning going backwards and forwards to Dr Molnár's office, while he telephoned their contacts and they allocated the girls to their new families. They concocted a makeshift lunch out of what remained in the larder, then locked away the more valuable equipment. Who knew when they would be back there again?

Little Léna was the last child to go. They'd found a family for her on the outskirts of Budapest and a middle-aged couple with kind, weathered faces came to collect her around four p.m. She hugged Kirsty and Anna. 'Matron will be all right, won't she?' she asked.

'I'm sure she will,' Kirsty replied, blinking to stop Léna seeing her tears. 'Be good, be happy – and we'll see you soon.'

Léna's own eyes were brimming now. She gave them a sad little wave and disappeared with her new family. The man carried her bag and the lady had an arm round her as they walked down the road.

Anna gave Kirsty a sympathetic smile. 'I hate goodbyes,' she said.

'Me too.' There'd been too many: Ma, Da, Maggie, Endre, Jean . . . and now poor little Léna.

Anna put her hand to the wall as if no longer able to stand up by herself. She wiped her forehead with the back of her hand.

'Are you all right?'

'I think so. There's so much to take in. Jean's disappearance. The girls going. The closure of the school . . .'

Kirsty looked round the empty hallway, seeing the ghost of herself just over four and a half years ago, exhausted after the arduous journey, terrified she'd made the wrong decision and alarmed by the governors' instruction to return. But the school had welcomed her, given her a role and a purpose. The thought that the corridors might never again ring with the sound of running footsteps and girlish laughter brought a lump to her throat.

'Do you think the girls will be safe?' Anna asked.

'I think they'll be safer than they would here, with the school so vulnerable.'

They'd done their best to find hosts at such short notice, but there were no guarantees. The new families would have to hide the girls' Jewish identities, arrange forged papers for them, keep up their morale in these frightening times, fend off the children's anxious enquiries about their parents. It was all so precarious.

'Kirsty . . .' Anna swallowed. 'I owe you an apology. I've not been the same with you since Endre was sent back.'

Kirsty nodded. 'I never meant that to happen.'

'I know. I was so angry, I needed someone to blame.'

'I was only trying to make him well.'

'Of course you were. We both were. I shouldn't have taken it out on you.'

Kirsty's heart heaved with sadness. 'I've missed you!'

'I've missed you too. With Jean gone and the school disbanded, we need to be strong for each other.'

Kirsty gave Anna a warm hug. 'Indeed we do.'

# 26

When Anna and Kirsty arrived at Anna's parents' flat, they found her mother packing. The pristine elegance of Mr and Mrs Bellak's apartment had been replaced by a muted chaos: the floor covered with piles of clothes and papers, an old battered suitcase beside them; ornaments shrouded in newspaper and tied up with string, wobbly towers of books, and an assortment of framed photographs scattered over a rug, including, Kirsty noted with a stab of sadness, the one of Róza. Mr Bellak stood surveying the scene, his hair in a rumpled peak, as though he'd run his hands through it again and again.

'What's going on?' Anna asked.

'Haven't you heard?' There were dark shadows under Mrs Bellak's eyes and two vertical lines between her eyebrows that Kirsty was sure hadn't been there before.

'Heard what?' Anna's voice was tight with anxiety.

'The mayor has asked us to move. There was a notice on the town hall.'

'The *mayor*?'

'No doubt under German instruction,' Mr Bellak replied bitterly. 'We've been given five days to find a place and move in.'

'Why?' Anna asked.

Mr Bellak sighed. 'Because we're Jews. Apparently we need to be identified.'

226

Anna took off her coat and hurled it onto an armchair. 'Because we're Jews, *Abba*'s business is under threat . . . because we're Jews, Endre has been sent to a war he doesn't believe in . . . because we're Jews we can't walk the streets freely . . . or shop when we want to . . . or go to the cinema or the theatre . . . it's just not fair.'

'None of it is fair,' her father replied, looking at her steadily. 'But we're better off than most of our people. It's over five years since those Jewish businesses were smashed in Germany; all over Europe Jews have been rounded up and taken goodness knows where, suffered the most extreme violence – or worse. If all that happens is that we have to live somewhere else for a few months before we can return, we won't have suffered so greatly.'

'Where will we live?' Anna's voice was quieter now and her shoulders slumped in resignation.

'We have to find a yellow-star house,' Mr Bellak said. 'It's what they're calling houses with a Star of David on the front, designated for Jews.'

'It's ridiculous,' Mrs Bellak added. 'There are more than two hundred thousand of us in the city – and we've got to be crammed into around two thousand houses.'

'That's one hundred people to a house!' Kirsty glanced round the Bellaks' sitting room. It was a comfortable size, about twice as big as the small lounge she and Da had in Beckford Street, but to share it with so many others . . . they'd be jammed in like sardines. It was inhuman.

'Can't you just put a yellow star on our apartment?' Anna asked.

'It's not one of the designated houses,' Mr Bellak replied,

rubbing at his forehead. 'Even if it were, we'd have to share it with so many others.'

'I don't know which would be worse,' Anna's mother added. 'Seeing our apartment full of strangers . . . the place where you and Endre grew up . . .' *And Róza,* Kirsty said to herself. They still never mentioned her name. '. . . or abandoning most of our possessions and moving to a strange part of the city. It's not what we anticipated at our age.'

'The war isn't what anyone anticipated,' Mr Bellak said, coming over and putting his arm round his wife.

'Except Adolf Hitler,' Anna snorted.

'And the Arrow Cross seem to be revelling in it too,' Kirsty couldn't help adding.

Anna gave her a sharp look. 'Do you think our belongings will be safe?'

Kirsty looked at the gleaming candlestick still adorning the windowsill. It must be worth a fair bit.

Mr Bellak shrugged. 'We can only hope and pray,' he said. 'At times like these, people are more important than possessions.'

Anna gave him a weak smile. 'Do you know where our yellow-star house is?'

'We're going to try for one in Zoltán utca. It's a nice area and it's near the Danube.'

For a second Kirsty imagined popping down to the river with Anna for a swim each day, letting the water wash away their fears and worries – at least for a few blessed hours of reprieve. But of course this would be out of the question. It was far too dangerous. And Jews had so many restrictions now that Anna would never be allowed to go.

'Perhaps it won't be so bad,' Mrs Bellak added. 'And we'll all be together.' Her smile included Kirsty.

Kirsty bit back the comment that she wasn't Jewish and had no obligation to go with them. But where else could she go? Jean's experience proved no one was safe at the school. And there was no way she could get transport back to England with a war on, even assuming she could find somewhere to live. No, Anna was her friend – even more so now their relationship had been repaired – and the Bellaks had been kind to her. She would throw in her lot with theirs, whatever it involved.

She picked up a sheet of newspaper. 'Now, what else needs wrapping up?'

Three days later, the four of them walked down Zoltán utca. They couldn't move fast. Not only were they carrying cases containing the few possessions they were allowed, but they were also wearing several layers of clothes. Kirsty had a chemise, a blouse and two jumpers on under her serge coat. The sun pounded down until her fringe clung to her forehead and a rivulet of sweat ran down the side of her face. Anna and her parents looked similarly hot and tired. Mrs Bellak stopped every few metres to put down her suitcase and wipe her hands on her coat, until her husband insisted he carry her luggage for a while. Eventually they came to a tall, light-coloured building with large windows and a row of plane trees in front, their new leaves bright in the sunshine. A yellow star had been attached to the front door.

'Here we are,' Mr Bellak announced, setting down both cases with a grunt of relief. He pulled a piece of paper from his pocket and knocked on the door.

'I'm sure we can make a home here,' Mrs Bellak said, in a strangely high voice, gazing up at the building.

Anna frowned and said nothing.

But Mr Bellak appeared all too soon, shaking his head. 'It's already full,' he told them. 'Apparently there might be some accommodation in Vadász utca.' He picked up the cases again. 'Come on. We'll need to hurry.'

The rest of them followed him down the road in a weary line, their feet shuffling, their backs stooped with exhaustion. Away from the river the air was thicker; there was no cooling breeze on their faces and they had to stop several times to transfer cases from one aching hand to another, with Mr Bellak constantly urging them on. But when they eventually got to Vadász utca, it was the same story. All the rooms had already been taken.

'We should have packed more quickly,' Mrs Bellak said, making no effort to blink back the tears. 'I didn't realise how quickly the houses would fill up.' Her husband put his arm around her shoulders, his mouth a grim line.

'What do we do now?' asked Anna.

Mr Bellak looked down at his feet. 'Apparently there are some yellow-star houses in the Magdolna Quarter,' he mumbled.

'The Magdolna Quarter! That's a dump!' said Anna.

'I'm afraid beggars can't be choosers, my dear. We'll just have to make the best of things.'

They picked up their bags again and trudged on. At one point Kirsty thought Mrs Bellak would crumple onto the pavement, she looked so exhausted, but somehow she kept going.

The sun was low in the sky by the time they reached Salé-trom utca. The street was full of grey, dilapidated houses with grimy windows and bits of plaster missing from the walls. There was a smell of rotting vegetables and the gutters were choked with debris.

Mr Bellak knocked at the door, spoke to one of the inhabitants, then returned to the bedraggled group standing on the pavement. They were too done-in even to talk.

'They have some spaces,' he said, 'but only for two people.' His forehead was creased with worry. 'There might be more next door.'

'Right,' said Anna. 'You and mother go on in. Kirsty and I will try our luck with the neighbours.'

Mrs Bellak threw them an anxious glance. 'We'll stay out here until you're settled.'

'No, don't risk it,' Anna insisted. 'We've already lost two houses by being too late. You must take this one. Otherwise I don't know what we'll do. We'll let you know when we've found something.'

She watched her parents enter the house, then her body sagged. 'Oh Kirsty,' she said. 'How has it come to this?'

Kirsty gave her a hug. Another family was walking towards them along the pavement, craning their necks to look up at the house Anna's parents had just disappeared into.

'Come on, Anna. You want to be near your parents, don't you?' She threw an anxious glance at the advancing family.

They dragged themselves along the street to the next house and Kirsty knocked at the door.

A thin-looking woman in a black headscarf and a shabby dress of indeterminate colour answered. 'Yes?'

'Is there any space in the house?' Kirsty asked.

The woman widened the door to let them in, then jerked her head upwards. 'In the attic,' she said, 'follow me.'

Relief surged through Kirsty as they followed the woman up several flights of stairs, their weary hands gripping the rails and their feet beating a tired tattoo on the wooden steps. Eventually they reached the top floor and the woman opened the door to reveal a small, airless room into which were packed about a dozen beds. It smelled of bad food and poor digestion. There was a tiny window, smeared with condensation. Each bed was piled with a muddle of clothes and possessions; clearly there were no cupboards or drawers in which to put their things. A bed by the far wall was occupied by an elderly woman who lay on her back, staring listlessly up at the ceiling. Nearby, two small children were jumping on the mattresses while their mother looked on wearily, making no effort to stop them.

The woman pointed to two empty beds, side by side, in the middle of the room. 'You can have these,' she said, sniffing.

'Thank you,' Kirsty replied.

The woman departed, leaving Kirsty and Anna to contemplate their new surroundings and the roommates they'd be sharing with.

Anna strode over to one of the central beds and dropped her bag on the mattress.

'Why don't you go and tell your parents we're next door?' Kirsty said. 'I know it's awful, but at least we're close to your family.'

Anna nodded. 'All right. Thanks.'

* * *

While Anna went next door, Kirsty opened their cases and piled their belongings neatly at the end of their beds. It occurred to her that she'd never shared a room with anyone before – apart from once with Anna at Lake Balaton. She'd had her own room in Beckford Street, at Maggie's and also at the school. Now she'd be sharing with eleven people. She wondered again if she'd made the right decision in going with Anna and her family. But what other choice did she have? She could have stayed on at the school, where a skeleton staff remained, but that would mean being separated from her best friend, and anyway, the school was still vulnerable. If the Gestapo could arrest Jean they could arrest anybody, and as the only other British staff member she could be next. On the other hand, staying in a yellow-star house was equally precarious – especially as the bold yellow star on the door so obviously advertised its Jewish inhabitants. They were easy pickings for the Arrow Cross and the Germans, and the whole city was under bombardment by the Allies. Nowhere was safe.

She picked up a photo of Anna's that she'd unpacked, showing her with her parents and Endre in a smiling group. How happy and hopeful they looked. Those cheerful figures had no idea that one of them would lose his mind and the others their home in this terrible war. She wondered, as she did so often, what Endre was doing. Once again a memory sidled in. His brown eyes full of tenderness as he held her hand and kissed her . . . the smell of his skin . . . the way her body tingled whenever they were together. There was still no news, and she had no idea how a letter would get to them at the Magdolna quarter. She just prayed he was safe. She no longer daydreamed about a shared future; these days you could only live in the present. All she could do was to desperately hope he was still alive. That golden time at Balaton seemed so long ago now, and the grass ring he gave her had long since disintegrated.

She looked up as Anna re-entered the room.

'Everything all right?'

Anna shrugged. 'They're in a room with forty other people. Mother is crying and *Abba* is looking bewildered. But they're relieved we're not far away.'

Kirsty squeezed her hand. 'Let's be thankful for that,' she said.

As they got to know their fellow attic-dwellers better, so their stories emerged. The elderly lady was called Margit. Her husband had been killed in the Great War after being conscripted into the Austro-Hungarian army. 'János gave his life for his country,' she said, her eyes filled with bitterness, 'and this is how they treat us, locking us away like prisoners.' They'd been a young married couple when war had broken out in 1914 and János had died before they'd had a chance to have children. She'd been a widow for thirty years.

The weary mother was called Évi. Her husband, Tomaj, had been drafted into a labour battalion months ago. She hadn't heard from him since. Despite the difficult conditions in the yellow-star house, she was trying to keep her fear and distress hidden from the children, Szalók and Tünde. Szalók was particularly boisterous. His favourite activity was to complete circuits of the room by jumping once on each person's mattress, like a manic frog, shooting people's belongings everywhere, triggering indignant shouts – and, occasionally, a slap on the back of his leg – from the residents. His sister might have been more docile if left to herself, but her brother's behaviour emboldened her, and she followed him on his circuit round the room.

'Why don't we see if we can amuse them?' Anna whispered to Kirsty. 'What did we used to do with the little ones at the school?'

'"Bújj, bújj zöld ág"?' Kirsty summoned up a memory of Jean standing in the middle of the hall, with a group of six-and seven-year-olds doing the actions. It involved two children facing each other, pretending to form a gate. The children decided between themselves who would be an angel and which a devil. They'd sing a song until each of the other children was standing behind one of the gatekeepers, at which point it would be revealed who was the angel and who the devil. The ones standing behind the angel won.

'We can't do "Bújj, bújj zöld ág" with just two of them,' Anna said, 'and I doubt if the rest of our roommates would want to play.' She glanced round the room at the other residents who sat talking quietly, reading or lying on their beds with their eyes closed. None of them looked like they were eager to participate in a children's game. 'And anyway, I'm not sure singing a song about who goes to heaven and who goes to hell when we're all awaiting our fate is a good idea.'

'No.' Kirsty frowned. 'You're probably right.'

'What about swimming?' Anna whispered.

'Swimming? In here?'

'Yes. I know we can't go to the baths or the river, but we could teach the children to swim on mattresses.' She jumped onto her own mattress, lay face down and beat her legs up and down for a few seconds, then started curving each arm

235

forwards, pushing it into the ticking of the mattress at the end of each stroke. The children watched, intrigued.

'Can you swim?' Kirsty asked them. They shook their heads. Poor things. It was unlikely their mother had ever taken them to Lake Balaton, and they were too young to swim in the Danube. Like Anna, they would have been forbidden to go to the public baths.

'All right,' Kirsty said. 'Szalók, your turn first. Copy Anna.'

The boy lay down on Kirsty's mattress and imitated Anna's front crawl. Kirsty watched, then straightened his legs a little before guiding his arms closer to his head. 'That's it. Well done.'

'I want a go.' Tünde jumped up and down with frustration.

'Swap over,' Anna said. At first Szalók protested but they talked him round, promising he could have another turn soon.

Tünde took his place, and again Kirsty helped her form the stroke, noticing with a pang the thinness of her limbs.

The impromptu swimming lesson lasted an hour before the children tired.

'That worked well,' Anna said. 'We could make their lessons a regular thing.'

'Yes, let's. But I think they need some fresh air too.'

'We could take them to the City Park later on.' The Jews were allowed out between two and five for medical appointments and shopping. The afternoon was deemed preferable – by then most Hungarian housewives had returned home for the day so wouldn't have to mix with 'undesirables'.

'How can we do that?' Jewish children were not permitted to play outside.

'Let's borrow a couple of shopping baskets and pretend the

children are accompanying us to the market,' Anna said. 'It's a risk but it will be worth it to give them a treat.'

Kirsty smiled. 'Good idea.'

It felt wonderful to be out in the fresh air with the soft spring breeze on their faces. The girls allowed the children to run ahead along the pavement, provided they promised to stop when they came to a road. Kirsty was conscious of people's curiosity as they glanced at the yellow star on Anna and the children's coats, then registered the lack of adornment on her own. Kirsty had spent so much time with Jewish people she almost felt one of them, and yet by rights she was entitled to live as a free person, with no identifying stigma.

They came to the park and the children sped off, playing some complicated game of their own. Anna and Kirsty followed like two indulgent parents.

'They'll sleep well tonight,' Kirsty said, watching as Szalók emerged from under a tree with a battered football in his hands. Some child must have kicked it there and given up trying to find it. Szalók dribbled the ball along the grass while his sister ran after him.

Anna frowned. 'It's all wrong for children to be cooped up. When we were little our parents took us to the park to play every day.'

'With me it was always swimming,' Kirsty admitted. 'In the Clyde in summer and the Hamilton baths in winter.' She smiled at the memory of Da sitting on the pool side shouting encouragement as she thrashed up and down the pool, or watching from the riverbank as she swam in the muddy water.

'Of course,' said Anna. 'You and your swimming.'

'You're a pretty good swimmer yourself these days.'

Anna flushed pink. 'Thank you. I do love it. And I'm really grateful to you for teaching me, but I can't imagine when we'll have the chance to go into the water again.'

'Maybe not for a while. But we're still getting some exercise. Keeps our muscles supple.'

Both girls stopped as Tünde came running towards them, her face white, tears running down her cheeks.

'Tünde, what's the matter?' Kirsty knelt down on the ground, holding out her arms, and the little girl flew into them, gripping her tight.

'It's Szalók,' she sobbed.

Kirsty looked over her shoulder to where Szalók was standing, frozen in horror. In front of him stood a German soldier wearing a metal helmet, a rifle at his side and an embroidered eagle with a swastika above his breast pocket. To Kirsty's consternation, Szalók's precious football was trapped under the soldier's steel-capped jackboot.

Anna ran towards him without hesitating.

Kirsty picked up Tünde and followed suit.

'Ah, what have we here?' the soldier asked in heavily accented Hungarian.

Szalók bit his lip and didn't reply.

'Jews – in the park?' His gaze took in the yellow stars that Anna and the children wore.

'We were going shopping,' Anna muttered, holding up her basket.

'I see. But your baskets are empty.'

'We are on our way to the market,' Kirsty said, hoping against hope that the soldier's knowledge of Budapest's geography was

238

poor. You wouldn't normally go through the City Park to the market.

'Then run along, all of you,' the solider said. He took his foot off the football, flicked it up, then swung his leg back and kicked it hard. The ball flew over the grass, travelled for what seemed like an age, then landed with a cracking sound in the middle of a holly hedge. 'Ha,' he said. 'Football is for men, not little boys.'

Szalók scowled at him but Anna grabbed his hand before he could say a word. The four of them hastened across the park as fast as they could.

# 27

Over the next few days and weeks, they learned to get up early in order to use the tiny bathroom at the end of the first floor landing. Otherwise the queue built up and people could wait for ages, only to find what limited hot water there was had run out. They'd not been allowed to bring a wireless, so all contact with outside was effectively cut off, although sometimes rumours got through. The news seemed positive: the Allies had taken Rome . . . the British and Canadians had landed in Normandy and were starting to win back towns in Northern France . . . a German submarine had been sunk in the Bay of Biscay by British aircraft.

Each revelation gave Kirsty new hope although she learned to keep it to herself. Hungary was still part of the Axis powers, at least nominally. But to her fellow roommates, the rest of the world had almost ceased to matter. The house was their whole existence now, and the biggest battles were against disease, starvation and despair.

Jews were only allowed out for three hours a day, but as an Aryan, Kirsty had greater freedom. She would go down to the market first thing, and bring back as much food as she could with the limited money people were able to give her. She and Anna helped to make big cauldrons of soup in the scruffy downstairs kitchen and their housemates queued with tin bowls to receive a couple of ladlefuls each. But it was never enough.

Next door, Anna's parents were faring even worse. After a few weeks Mrs Bellak developed a fever. Anna answered an urgent summons from her father and rushed next door to visit them.

She returned visibly wracked with worry. 'She has a terrible headache and can't keep anything down. There's no one with medical knowledge in the house, and I doubt if any doctor will come out.'

Kirsty stood up. 'I'll go to the chemist,' she said. 'See what they can offer.'

But the chemist shook his head at her list of symptoms; she didn't mention the patient was Jewish. 'Might be typhus,' he said. He turned to the racks of pills and medicines in brown glass bottles lined up behind him and took down a small jar. 'Here, aspirin. That should help with the headache. Give her two tablets every four hours.'

Kirsty took the medication. 'Anything else?'

The chemist grimaced and shrugged. 'We've run out of all other medication. Try prayer.' He turned to his next customer.

Mrs Bellak grew worse. She developed a rash . . . then a hacking cough . . . then her breathing grew ragged. Anna muttered the *Mi Shebeirach*, the Jewish prayer for healing, each evening but still her mother deteriorated. Kirsty could barely imagine fastidious Mrs Bellak, the woman who wouldn't serve rugelach without an embroidered napkin on the plate, lying in her own filth in a disease-ridden room crammed with forty other people.

Finally, came the news they feared: she'd passed away during the night. Anna was beside herself. All Kirsty could do was hug her friend and remind her she still had a father and brother who loved her. Kirsty had been too young to remember much about Ma's death, but she still felt the loss of Da, and her own experience of bereavement meant she could be a genuine comfort to Anna. But there was only so much she could do to help assuage her grief.

'It hurts so much here,' Anna said, her hand on her chest. 'Just like when Róza died. I'd forgotten the pain of losing someone could be so physical.'

Kirsty put her arm round her. 'There's no way round grief,' she said. 'You just have to go through it. I wish I could take the pain away, but I can't. All I can do is to be here for whenever you need me.'

Anna hugged her back. 'Thank you,' she said, her voice laden with sadness.

Kirsty thought of Maggie sitting with her at the kitchen table, helping her plan Da's funeral. That was when she'd told her about 'Gresford'. It was such a powerful tune. Perfect for the service. The funeral had helped a little – all those people crammed into the church to honour Da. So much respect for him. So much sympathy for her.

'Will you have a funeral for your mother?' she asked Anna.

Anna frowned. 'I don't know.' She shuddered. 'Her body was taken away in a funeral cart early this morning. They round up the corpses of those who've died during the night and burn them in deep pits.' She made a series of rapid gulps, gagged, then turned away and retched into her hands.

Kirsty rubbed her back in an attempt to comfort her. 'How awful.' At least her parents had had proper burials. There must be something they could do to mark Mrs Bellak's passing. 'Why don't you hold a little service for your mother? It might help.'

Anna raised a blotchy face. 'We don't have a rabbi.'

'Maybe there's someone in the house next door, where your father is.'

'I could ask. But what about Endre?'

Kirsty's heart contracted at the mention of his name. 'Maybe afterwards . . . when he's back . . . we could hold a memorial service for your mother then, with Endre present.' She didn't like to say 'if he's back' – she needed to hold on to hope as much as Anna, but it was months now since they'd heard from him and despair seeped further into her bones with every day that passed.

Kirsty was right. There was a *chazan*, a cantor, at the yellow-star house next door. Apparently his job was to lead the congregation in worship. Kirsty realised with a jolt that although everyone shared a common weariness these days, with their white faces, hollow eyes, and threadbare clothes, many of them had been prominent members of the community before the war: schoolteachers, business owners, lawyers, ministers – cooks like her and Anna. Suffering might have taken away their individuality but it hadn't diminished their spirits.

They gave Mrs Bellak the best tribute they could. The cantor sang some beautiful songs for her, and Anna and her father both made little speeches. They wore black armbands which someone had made for them by tearing up an old shawl.

'Thank you,' Anna said as they made their way back to their own house. 'That did help.'

Kirsty squeezed her hand.

# 28

The summer had been stifling that year. Inside their attic room the air was hot and putrid, and so thick you could almost cut it. The intense heat made the children listless, and although being subdued made them less challenging to deal with, Kirsty was concerned by the sight of their pallid, almost transparent faces each morning. She and Anna had set up a school of sorts, teaching them basic subjects in the morning, and encouraging some swimming practice in the afternoons. Sometimes Tünde helped Kirsty prepare and serve the scant meals it was taking all her ingenuity to concoct from the meagre ingredients she hunted down each day. In some ways life at the yellow-star house had become a poor imitation of their time in Vörösmarty Street – helping children, buying food, cooking, clearing away. She'd never appreciated before how carefree those early years in Budapest had been, despite the war raging in Europe. Now their very existence was on a knife-edge. Sometimes Kirsty felt she was holding her breath just to get through the day.

Anna still grieved the loss of her mother, although the initial shock had faded. She often visited her father next door and Kirsty was glad they both found solace in each other's company and their shared bereavement.

244

Eventually the air became cooler and sleep more possible. In the mornings the room would be filled with an amber light, the colour of the whisky Da permitted himself at Christmas. Autumn had come at last.

One crisp morning, Kirsty took the yellow star off her coat – she still kept it on indoors to show solidarity with the Jewish occupants of the house – and went down to the market as usual. The sun was gilding the rooftops of the buildings, disguising their shabbiness with molten gold, and the sky was streaked with pink. Her breaths formed tiny clouds in the sharp air. As usual, she felt the surge of guilt that she could enjoy such relative freedom whilst the others were left in the cramped attic. Since the football incident they'd taken the children out a few times, just for a brisk walk round the streets, but they hadn't dared return to the City Park.

The trees were losing their leaves, and her feet crunched over the papery debris. It wasn't all that long until the year would turn again and it would be 1945, the sixth year of the war. Surely it would end soon?

She went into the city for food, but she also went to pick up news. From the road sweeper at the corner of Salétrom utca and József utca she learnt that more Messerschmitts had been shot down and several German submarines had now been sunk. From an elderly lady walking her dog she discovered the Americans had beaten back the Germans just outside Haaren. A housewife with a bulging shopping bag told her that Athens had been liberated. There were rumours too that Hungary had signed a ceasefire with the Soviets and would soon declare war on Germany. With each new insight, Kirsty felt a little more hopeful. Perhaps Endre would be sent home, and peace would reign once more in Budapest. Dare she allow herself to dream of the future? She fantasised about him coming back whole and healthy, hugging her joyfully, his strong arms around her, a broad smile lighting up his face. Perhaps he'd even design a beautiful ring to replace the grass one he'd given her so long ago now. The thought filled her with warmth. She kept that little spark of hope, like a treasured gift at the back of her mind, taking it out to savour whenever she needed cheer.

But one glance at the market traders' faces had her heart plummeting. Normally they'd be calling out to each other, chatting to customers or rearranging their displays. But not today. Today they stood mutely by their stalls, staring at the ground or darting fearful glances up and down the street.

Kirsty approached her favourite vegetable seller, a whiskery old gentleman, who wrapped up a few rubbery carrots in newspaper for her and tipped them into her basket. 'What's the matter?' she asked him. 'Why is everyone looking so glum?'

The vendor grimaced. 'Horthy's been forced out of office,' he muttered. 'There are rumours that Szálasi's replaced him.'

Kirsty gasped. Ferenc Szálasi was the Arrow Cross leader. That meant the Nyilas would soon be in power. Dasco's scarred face and predatory leer loomed in front of her and bile rose in her throat. The German occupation of Budapest was bad enough but the Arrow Cross would take persecution to a whole new level.

Thrusting some coins into the trader's hand, she rushed back to Salétrom utca as quickly as she could.

Anna's jaw clenched at the news. 'Sometimes I think the Nyilas hate us more than the Nazis do,' she said. 'They'll stop at nothing to get rid of us. And their methods are barbaric.'

Kirsty remembered the Arrow Cross men who'd set upon Endre that time. 'Bloody keelie scum,' she said again.

'We'll have to be on our guard even more from now on. I'll go and warn *Abba*.' Anna sped off down the stairs.

It turned out they were right to be wary. Three nights later, Kirsty woke to the sound of shouts and gunfire outside. She sat up in bed, her heart racing. The other women were coming to as well. Only Tünde and Szalók remained asleep, their hair tousled on their pillows, Tünde's little fingers still clutching her ragged teddy bear.

Anna stood up and made her way across to the tiny window, cupping her hands to see into the darkness outside. When she turned back, her face was creased with fear. 'Arrow Cross,' she hissed.

Blood pounded in Kirsty's ears. She swallowed. 'Are they coming in?'

'Not yet,' Anna replied. Her hand shot out to steady herself against the wall. 'Oh no!'

'What? What's happened?'

'They've gone next door.'

Kirsty hurried to the window to join Anna. She put an arm round her friend, conscious of her shaking shoulders.

Both girls watched in silence as burly Arrow Cross members, in long trench coats no doubt intended to resemble those worn by the Germans, barked orders at a clearly terrified stream of residents stumbling out of the neighbouring house. The house Anna's parents had moved into, and where Mrs Bellak had died. 'All you filthy sons of Abraham, all you Israelites, all you dirty Jewish pigs – females and children

247

included – march downstairs! Hands high. Yellow star displayed. Stragglers will be shot. Resisters will be shot. Every vile Jew who is not down here in three minutes will be shot. Long live Szálasi!'

Anna's eyes darted from one dishevelled figure to another, obviously searching for her father. Kirsty winced as one of the Nyilas men used the butt of his rifle to force an old woman into line.

There was a sharp intake of breath next to her and Anna leant forward. '*Abba*,' she mouthed, placing her palm against the window as though to reach out to him.

Kirsty eased her friend closer, trying to communicate reassurance through the press of her fingers.

Anna's father was standing on the pavement, looking bewildered. He was wearing slippers and pyjamas with a coat hanging around his shoulders. The yellow star was clearly visible on his chest. Kirsty's heart heaved with pity for him, such a dejected figure. Apart from at the funeral, she hadn't seen him since his wife had died, sensing Anna needed to spend time with her father alone, but she was shocked by how much he'd changed. He was painfully thin and stooped, and his hair was much sparser than she remembered.

As they watched, Mr Bellak wandered towards the house next door where the girls were staying, peering up at the roof as though to catch a glimpse of them.

An Arrow Cross thug marched up to him. '*Állj vissza a sorba*,' he thundered. *Get back in line*.

Kirsty held her breath, silently willing Mr Bellak to do as he was told. But to her dismay, he failed to move. Waves of terror were radiating from Anna. 'Come on, *Abba*,' she whispered.

Something about the man was familiar. Kirsty strained to see his face. The figure was about Dasco's height and had similar mannerisms, spitting at Anna's father – his grotesque trademark. Kirsty's skin began to crawl. Even if her brain couldn't fully discern her former tormentor, her body was recoiling in horror.

Anna jumped beside her as Dasco – or whoever it was – slammed his fist into Mr Bellak's chest. He went down like a stone.

'*Abba*!' Before anyone could stop her, Anna rushed out of the room.

Kirsty grabbed her coat and followed her as she hurtled down the several flights of stairs, slipping and sliding on the wooden steps.

The sound of a gunshot reverberated upwards.

By the time she got outside, Mr Bellak was lying in a crumpled heap on the pavement, blood oozing from a bullet wound at the side of his head. Anna was kneeling beside him, stroking his hair, tears streaming down her cheeks.

'Come away, Anna.' Kirsty tried to pull her up gently but Anna remained locked in place, her whole body shaking.

Kirsty felt helpless. When Mrs Bellak had died, at least there'd been some warning – she'd been ill for a while. But the death of Anna's father was such a terrible shock. Just like Da's had been she thought grimly, a sudden vision of herself crying her heart out at Maggie's kitchen table transporting her back to those first awful days of grief.

'*Állj fel*!' demanded an imperious male voice. *Stand up*. Kirsty turned round, alarm coursing through her. In front of them was an Arrow Cross man, his chest straining against a dark green shirt and black tie with the menacing Arrow Cross symbol, a set of crossed arrows, glistening on his armband. The figure was stockier than she remembered, the features hardened into manhood, the eyes as mocking as ever. Her earlier suspicions had been correct. It was Dasco.

'Fancy seeing our little Scottish girl,' he said, leering at her. 'My mother's skivvy.'

A tiny part of Kirsty bristled. She'd been far more than that. For the last few months she and Anna had managed the cooking on their own, and even when Mária had been there, Kirsty had been far more than an assistant. But there was no point arguing about it now. She was no longer facing him in the school kitchen, with a drawer of knives close to hand. And he was no longer a member of an illegal party. The Nyilas were the ruling power in Hungary, with all the authority and entitlements that entailed. And he had a rifle hanging from his shoulder that she had no doubt he would use at the slightest provocation.

She was aware of Anna quivering beside her, clearly incapable of speech or any sensible action. Kirsty sensed that what she said or did in the next few minutes might determine their fate.

'Dasco.' She tried to keep her voice low and steady, despite the weight on her chest and the air being slowly squeezed from her lungs. 'As you yourself have just declared, I am a British citizen, not one of the Jewish people. And my friend here is newly bereaved. Please let us go back inside.' She wasn't prepared to desert Anna on the basis of being a Gentile, and she certainly had no intention of letting her down at such a terrible point in her life. But maybe, if there was any shred of

250

compassion in Dasco's thuggish heart, she could appeal to him. She didn't know if it was he who'd killed Anna's father, but if it was, there might be a sliver of guilt deep down . . . or perhaps she could implore him to be lenient for his mother's sake.

But Dasco strode up to her, his looming presence causing her skin to crawl once more, until she had to ram her palms into her side to stop herself pushing him away.

'You are not one of the Jewish people, you say?' His mouth was mocking, yet his cold eyes bored into hers. 'So what is this?' His fleshy fingers reached out to grasp the front of Kirsty's coat.

Oh no. Adrenaline surged. In her haste to get down the stairs earlier, she'd neglected to unfasten the yellow star. Jean's attempt to show solidarity with the Jewish girls – which she'd readily agreed to at the time – was going to prove her downfall. Her apparent Jewishness was emblazoned on her chest for all to see. She tried to keep her expression rigid rather than betray any evidence of the fear that pounded through her body.

Dasco rubbed his thumb across the surface of the star. 'Hmmm. It's not very well attached is it? I thought there were rules about that.'

Kirsty bowed her head and stared at the ground. Dasco was right. The sewing had to be even and tight. There were no such stitches on her star. Only press studs that fastened it from the back. She didn't trust her voice enough to speak. And anyway, what could she say? There was no explanation that would satisfy him. Despite the cold day, dribbles of sweat ran down her spine.

Dasco jerked the star with his fingers. It came away easily.

'Hmmm. I see your sewing is as poor as your cooking,' he said, his face up close to hers. A waft of sour breath hit her.

*Don't flinch, don't flinch*, she told herself. She ignored the jibe about the cooking. She knew different: the girls' clear enjoyment of her food over all the years proved him wrong. But it wasn't worth pointing it out.

He turned the star over and saw the press stud. 'Ha! So a hypocrite as well. You are a Jew when it suits you and a Gentile when it doesn't.' He rammed the star back onto her chest, his finger boring into the fabric far more deeply than was needed to secure it, and her body recoiled. Then, for good measure, he spat in her face. She let the slime trickle down her cheek, despite it taking all her resolve not to wipe it away – or even to spit back. It would only make things worse and she had to protect poor Anna at all costs. She didn't dare look at her friend, but she was conscious of her uneven breaths, and swaying body. Poor, poor Anna.

Dasco took a step back, removed his rifle from his shoulder, and fired a shot into the air, causing a ripple of shock through the crowd of residents on the pavement. 'Crawl back inside your homes, you miserable vermin,' he said, including Kirsty and Anna in his glare. Then he shouted up to the residents watching from the windows of the second house. 'You're all going on a train journey. You have ten minutes to pack. One bag only. Go!'

Kirsty grabbed Anna's hand and pulled her back into the house.

## 29

Anna was still too numb with shock to function. Kirsty helped her onto the bed before grabbing both their bags and piling in their possessions – blouses, skirts, woollen stockings, nightwear. They hadn't taken much to Salétrom Street in the first place but this time they were allowed even less. When they'd left the Bellaks' apartment it had been spring; now it was well into autumn. She picked up Anna's warmest jumper and added one of her own. Just as before, they'd need to wear extra clothes in order to smuggle a few more belongings. She felt a bolt of anger at the way the Germans and the Nyilas were proscribing their lives – where they could live, where they should go, what they could take with them. All for a war they wanted no part in. It was always innocent people who suffered. She added Anna's photo of her parents and Endre, realising with a jolt that her friend was now a fellow orphan.

All around them the other occupants of the attic – their roommates of six months – were packing too. Choked with sadness, Kirsty watched Szalók and Tünde's mother assemble their meagre belongings while her children stood watching forlornly. The elderly lady, Margit, was picking things up and putting them down in a daze. Kirsty quickly helped her to bundle them into her bag.

Another shot rang out outside. Kirsty darted a glance out of the window to see Dasco with his rifle in the air, surrounded by leering cronies as they watched the occupants pour out of the Salétrom Street houses and onto the pavement.

'Anna, we have to go.' Kirsty picked up her friend's bag, along with her own, and gestured to her to leave the room. Anna did so, walking like an automaton, then stepped listlessly down the stairs. They joined the other prisoners on the street, trying to avert their eyes from Mr Bellak's body.

Like vicious sheepdogs, the Arrow Cross men herded them into line with bellowed orders, reinforced by frequent uses of their rifle butts to prod and poke any stragglers.

When they were finally satisfied, the command was given for them to march. They obediently followed the Arrow Cross guard at the front, in an untidy line, chivvied on by other Nyilas members walking alongside them. All had their rifles cocked, although it was unnecessary: the bedraggled prisoners were too scared and weary to protest.

Kirsty walked with Anna, carrying both bags, and talking in a low voice to keep her friend going. Up ahead were Évi, Szalók and Tünde, the children silent and fearful. For once Kirsty missed their normal exuberance. It wasn't natural for children to be this quiet. Margit was behind them. Normally Kirsty would have helped her along, but all her efforts were concentrated on encouraging Anna to put one foot after another. If she deserted her, Anna wouldn't be able to continue. But she turned as gunfire rang out. A crumpled heap of clothes lay writhing at the end of the line. It was Margit. She must have stumbled and fallen. Presumably one of the Arrow Cross men had shot her rather than help her up. As Kirsty watched, the guard lowered his rifle again and fired. The body was instantly still. Kirsty felt saddened about the elderly woman's death, but not surprised or shocked by it. In normal circumstances it would have been a tragedy, but now it seemed commonplace. She wondered if she'd lost all compassion to feel so little grief for a fellow human being, but deep down she knew she had to concentrate all her energies on keeping Anna safe. In the view of the Arrow Cross, people were dispensable, and the elderly and frail the most dispensable of all. It was easier for the men to kill someone frail than try to keep them walking. Kirsty took a last look at the crumpled figure before turning away. Maybe it was better like this. Margit may never have survived a train ride, wherever it was going, and perhaps now she'd been reunited with her beloved husband.

They kept walking.

## 30

They made their way east out of Salétrom utca, towards the Kerepesi cemetery. For a terrible second, Kirsty wondered if the guards were going to shoot them all there and pile them into a mass grave, but Dasco had told them they'd be going on a train. He'd no reason to lie, although she doubted he needed a reason. It was almost a relief when Jozsefvaros station loomed into view. Kirsty had never been there before – she and Jean had come in to Keleti all those years ago – but it was obvious this was where they were headed. A dirty black plume rose over a row of dilapidated buildings, merging with the dark clouds overhead, and soon Kirsty smelled the smoke from the steam train that stood, snorting, on the rails.

It was a wretched scene: elderly men in shabby coats, exhausted and frightened; weary white-faced women in headscarves; anxious children sitting on battered cases. Everyone wore a yellow star. Kirsty fingered hers thoughtfully. There didn't seem any point in taking it off now. Dasco knew she wasn't Jewish. He could have released her. This was revenge for her rejection of him last year. And anyway, how could she abandon Anna at this terrible time? Jean's own Aryan status hadn't saved her. There was still no news, and Kirsty and Anna continued to fear the worst. She wondered, with a new rush of anxiety, if their own deaths were about to be added to Jean's.

Men in long coats, accompanied by fierce-looking Alsatians, were patrolling the area, the dogs barking and straining on their leashes. Elsewhere, guards stood on truck roofs, long rifles pointing at the disconsolate groups of people. There was nowhere to hide. Escape was impossible. Dread and anger tightened like a band across Kirsty's chest. Anna trembled beside her, probably as much from shock as the cold that penetrated their very bones.

'All right?'

Anna shrugged. A sore at the corner of her mouth was livid against her pale skin and her hair was lank.

Kirsty put an arm round her. 'We'll be all right.' She tried to inject as much confidence into her words as possible, despite the despair that had solidified into something hard and unyielding in her gut.

A ripple passed through the crowd as a car drove onto the platform, a Swedish flag flying from its bonnet. As Kirsty swivelled to look, the car stopped and two men emerged. They opened the boot and took out a collapsible table which they erected on the platform. Something about one of the men's gestures was familiar, but Kirsty couldn't think where from.

The train doors opened and the guards began pushing people forwards. Kirsty and Anna found themselves caught up in the throng surging towards the train, their faces thrust up against serge coats, their feet stumbling against bulging bags. Kirsty couldn't see Évi, Szalók and Tünde anywhere. Perhaps they were already on board.

They were shoved into a carriage, little more than a box car, with a domed roof and a dusty floor. The barred windows were high up, too high to see out. More and more people were packed in until the space became filled with the rank odour of sweat and putrid breath. Kirsty stood on tiptoe to gulp a mouthful of cleaner air. Anna was rigid beside her, her pale lips pressed into a thin line, her eyes dull. Jean's words of five years ago, when they'd made that mad train journey across Europe at the start of the war, came back to her: *we're two orphans on a train*, she'd said. And here she was again with another orphan, facing another fearful ride. But that time they'd been journeying towards hope and purpose. Today the destination could be much more dangerous.

'Does anyone know where we're going?' a man asked.

A woman with a grizzling toddler clamped to her side replied. 'I think we're headed north.'

'North? So Poland then?' the man asked.

The woman shuddered and buried her face in her child's hair.

Kirsty's already racing heartbeat increased. There'd been rumours of terrible things happening to those Jews who'd been taken to Poland. She glanced at Anna but she had her eyes closed now and Kirsty didn't like to drag her away from whatever place her mind had taken her to. She wondered bleakly if Poland would be their final resting place. They were only nineteen; they'd barely leave a whisper of their existence on the surface of the earth. Where were her dreams of marrying Endre now? Or being a swimming teacher? She always thought she'd be buried alongside her parents, not in a remote Polish cemetery – if they were even accorded that.

More and more people piled into their carriage. Sharp elbows and bulky luggage bored into Kirsty's back and shoulders. Babies cried, toddlers wailed; weary mothers trying to placate them. Most older people stood silently, their faces masks of exhaustion, their bodies limp with resignation. The air thickened with fear.

Kirsty braced herself against the expected lurch of the train which would signal the start of their journey. But none came. A disturbance sounded outside on the platform, the shout of a man's voice and an answering gabble from the guards.

Anna was instantly alert. 'What's happening?'

'I've no idea,' Kirsty replied.

Their train door burst open and someone shouted, 'Is anyone here Swedish?' A man in a long coat and a Homberg hat made his way down the carriage, thrusting papers into people's hands. 'If you have a pass, or if you've lost one, you can get off the train. You have the full protection of the King of Sweden and the Swiss republic.'

'I'm sorry, my dear.' The man had stopped in front of an elderly woman in a mud-splattered coat who was begging him for a pass. 'I can only take the young.'

The blood leached from the woman's face as she slumped back against the wall.

Some of the passengers started to get off, easing the press of people. As the man approached Anna and Kirsty, Kirsty had a sudden recollection: Városház utca. The local municipality offices. In a long queue with Jean. A conversation about their work at the school. A man with compassionate brown eyes. The same brown eyes that were staring into hers right now.

'Ah,' he said. 'I remember you. The school cook.' He thrust a paper into Kirsty's hands. 'You're originally from Sweden, aren't you? Here is your pass.' He turned to Anna. 'And this is your sister. Here is your pass too.' He handed another

259

document to Anna. 'You can both get off the train. You are exempt from deportation. Come to the Swedish embassy tomorrow and we'll take your photos and get them mounted on the passes.'

Kirsty felt her knees buckle as she thanked the man profusely. She remembered his name now. He'd introduced himself as Raoul Wallenberg that day in the queue. Although Scotland was a lot closer to Sweden than Hungary was, with her auburn hair and green eyes she looked more Celtic than Nordic, and Anna had dark hair and brown eyes. It didn't matter though; if these passes would save them, they would happily both be Swedish.

The man flashed them a smile then moved off down the train.

Kirsty glanced down at the pass. It was a sheet of paper with the words *Schutz-Pass* printed on top. There was a blank rectangle on the top right of the page, presumably space for a photograph. Further down the page it read *Schweden. Svédország*, the words separated by the emblem of three crowns. Did this mean they'd be given immunity by Sweden, a neutral country? A hastily scribbled signature – Wallenberg's no doubt – appeared at the bottom. It certainly looked authentic – or it would do as soon as they had their photos included.

'We're free?' whispered Anna.

'So it would seem.' Kirsty could hardly believe it.

Flooded with relief and gratitude they staggered off the train, along with a number of other passengers, all clutching the same pieces of paper. But as Kirsty anxiously scanned the platform for Évi, Szalók and Tünde, a whistle blew and the train lurched off with a loud hiss, more plumes of smoke and the bone-crushing scraping of metal against metal, carrying the rest of the travellers to their unknown fate.

They stood on the platform as an icy wind circled round and a few flakes of sleet fell from the bleak and bloated sky. The low winter sun was just the faintest smudge of brightness now behind glowering clouds. Kirsty put her arm round Anna, who still looked numb and dazed, as though the recent succession of events was too much for her to process.

'What now?' Anna murmured.

'I suppose we need to find somewhere new to live. The attic room is clearly no longer safe – not that it ever was.' Kirsty had always been uneasy about the yellow star on the front of the Salétrom Street building. It effectively made them sitting ducks. She shivered at the memory of Dasco's thick, fleshy fingers probing her body. They'd have to make sure their next accommodation was a lot safer.

As if on cue, Raoul Wallenberg appeared again, driving along the platform in his black limousine, the Swedish flag still fluttering on the bonnet.

He wound down the window. 'Are you all right?'

Kirsty nodded. 'We're so grateful to you for the passes. You saved our lives.'

Mr Wallenberg smiled. 'Not at all. I'm so pleased I could help.' His expression turned serious. 'I'm just sorry I couldn't save everyone.'

Kirsty's chest tightened. 'Did you see a woman with two small children – a boy and a girl of around seven and six?'

'I'm sorry. The train was so full. As I said, I couldn't get to everyone.'

'Of course. We were in a yellow-star house with the family. They must still be on the train. Let's hope they will be well looked after where they're going.'

His forehead creased and he looked down at the track, then turned back to Kirsty and Anna. 'Where are you girls going to stay tonight?'

'We've no idea,' Kirsty replied. They were still coming to terms with the fact they wouldn't be trying to sleep in a stuffy box on a train heading off to God knew where.

'Get in the car. I'll take you to the Glass House.'

'The *glass house*?' Kirsty didn't want to seem ungrateful but this sounded even more vulnerable than the yellow-star apartment.

'Yes. There are many, many Jews there already. You'll see.'

Anna glanced at Kirsty who shrugged. All her instincts told her Raoul Wallenberg could be trusted. Jean had confided in him, that was good enough for her. He'd snatched them from the jaws of death. What did they have to lose?

They lay their heads back against the car's padded seats as their Swedish rescuer drove them rapidly through the darkening streets.

# 31

As Mr Wallenberg headed north-west through the city, he told them more about the Glass House.

'It's owned by the Weiss family,' he said. 'Lajos Kozma, the famous architect, drew up the plans.' He glanced at them through the rear-view mirror. Kirsty hadn't a clue who Lajos Kozma was, and she doubted if Anna did either, but she tried to arrange her features in a suitably impressed expression, despite her exhaustion. Outside the window, shadowy buildings and the occasional tree flashed past. The car was warm and her limbs started to thaw even though her mind was still frozen with the shock of recent events. 'The reason it's called the Glass House is because it was built to create and sell glass for the building industry.' Mr Wallenberg stopped to navigate a junction, then continued. 'But since October it's been a safe haven for Jews wishing to escape deportation.'

'How does Mr Weiss manage to keep them hidden?' Anna asked.

Mr Wallenberg laughed. 'I think a fair amount of bribery has gone on. German and Hungarian officials must have looked the other way. Somehow or other, Weiss has managed to have the building declared an annexe of the Swiss consulate.'

Kirsty tried to concentrate on Mr Wallenberg's words,

despite desperately wanting to close her eyes and sleep away the fear and worry. He must have sensed they'd had enough as he fell silent for the next few minutes.

At length the car drew up in Vadász utca, outside a yellowy-brown building. It appeared to be only one storey high, although Kirsty imagined it must have several floors inside in order to house all the people. She looked down the wide street, realising with a jolt it was where she and Anna had been with Anna's parents, in an earlier attempt to find a yellow-star house. She didn't mention it to Anna, not wanting to bring back bad memories.

Mr Wallenberg sprang out of his seat and helped them with their luggage. 'Come on in,' he said. 'I don't live here, but my friend Carl Lutz, the Swiss Vice-Consul, has been very involved.'

'Mr Lutz,' Kirsty exclaimed. 'He came to see Jean once at the school.' She recalled a slight man, with combed-back dark hair and round glasses, earnestly talking to Jean. The two of them had been united in their work to help the Jews. And now it seemed as though Mr Lutz would help her and Anna. Such a miraculous coincidence. Although Jean would have called it divine providence.

The outside of the building had been nondescript, but the inside was a revelation. Mr Wallenberg led them into a bright hallway with a high ceiling. There was a large reception desk manned by a clerk in a dark suit.

'Is Mrs Tibor around?' Mr Wallenberg asked.

'Of course. I'll go and find her.' The clerk hurried off.

Kirsty looked round the hall while they waited. Colourful glass panels filled the wall along the stairway leading to a second level. It was like being inside a boiled sweet – not that she'd seen one of those for a long time.

The clerk returned with a middle-aged woman with greying hair and friendly brown eyes. She smiled at Anna and Kirsty as Mr Wallenberg introduced them, then bid them goodbye. Kirsty again thanked their rescuer.

Mrs Tibor ushered them into a large cobbled courtyard filled with people huddled together on benches made from planks of wood perched on bricks. Long tables, also on bricks, formed a grid across the courtyard. Some of the more elderly occupants, wrapped in blankets, sat on chairs and younger ones were on boxes that, from the description on the outside, were full of glass. Four women stood in a makeshift kitchen at one side of the courtyard frying dough, which was collected and handed round by youths of around Kirsty and Anna's age. A warm yeasty smell permeated the air. Despite the trauma of the last few hours, Kirsty realised she was hungry, and eagerly accepted a piece of bread when it was offered to them. It looked and tasted a bit like the bannock that Maggie had taught her to make all those years ago – except without the currants.

'Perhaps we could help with the cooking,' Anna whispered to Kirsty.

Kirsty squeezed her hand. 'Good idea. It might help to keep busy.' Maggie's advice travelled back to her through time and space: *Nothing can bring our loved ones back, but it helps to keep occupied.* And they'd be doing their bit to support people too.

'How many people are living here?' Kirsty asked Mrs Tibor.

'Over two thousand people in the Glass House – and in the Hungarian Football Federation headquarters next door.'

Kirsty couldn't imagine that many people in a building.

Accommodation at their yellow-star home had been cramped, and that housed only a few hundred.

'And how do you get in enough provisions?'

'There's a man who owns a big food warehouse in the city. He's known as Uncle Slomo.' Mrs Tibor chuckled. 'He's been very generous. Somehow or other we manage to cook and serve three meals a day.'

She pointed out Carl Lutz, who was standing at the back of the courtyard talking intently to another man. The Swiss Vice-Consul was indeed the slight bespectacled figure Kirsty remembered.

'I'll show you to your dormitory,' Mrs Tibor said. 'Most of the couples and older people sleep in the lower level of the house, but the young people sleep here, in the football head-quarters.' She led them down to the basement and through a makeshift tunnel that had clearly been made by knocking through a wall. Then she stopped and put a finger to her lips. 'We have to maintain the illusion that the building is uninhab-ited,' she said, 'so it's vital to be as quiet as possible.'

They both nodded.

'We knocked through the wall a few weeks ago to accom-modate all the extra people. Most of them are young like you. I think you'll feel at home here.'

As they went closer, Kirsty realised that, despite the lack of noise, the room was packed: youths in their late teens or early twenties sat reading, talking in hushed voices or lay on their backs staring up at the ceiling.

'We allow these residents to go over to the Glass House in the evenings, in small groups, to wash and use the facilities, but all movement has to be undertaken as carefully as possible.

If the gendarmes, or, worse still, the Arrow Cross, suspect the headquarters are occupied then we're done for.'

Kirsty glanced at Anna whose face was devoid of colour in the gloom.

'There's a little space over here,' Mrs Tibor said, pointing to a double mattress in the corner of the room.

'Thank you.' They picked up their bags and followed her.

'I'm afraid you'll have to share though.'

'Oh, we don't mind sharing,' Anna replied.

'I mean with others. Two girls are already using this bed. There'll be four of you now.'

'Of course,' said Kirsty. 'You've been very kind.' She really was grateful. Between them, Raoul Wallenberg and Carl Lutz had saved them from being deported. And Mrs Tibor had gone out of her way to show them around when she must have been busy. Only being able to occupy a quarter of a mattress was the least of their problems.

'I'll bid you goodnight now.' Mrs Tibor smiled and went back the way she'd come.

Kirsty had barely had time to speak to Anna – the events of the last few hours had happened so quickly – but now she hugged her as they got ready for bed. 'I'm so sorry about your father.'

Tears brimmed in Anna's eyes and she blinked rapidly. 'Poor *Abba*. Such a terrible way to die.'

Kirsty squeezed her friend's shoulders. 'At least it was quick. He wouldn't have suffered.'

'Bloody Arrow Cross.'

'They're inhuman.' They'd been treated worse than animals; shot at, herded into line, prodded with weapons.

Anna wiped her cheeks with the back of her hand. 'How can I get word to Endre?'

'I don't know.' It had been over a year since they'd heard from him. Recently Kirsty had been tortured by the thought he might be dead too. Poor Anna, all her family possibly wiped out. And Jean gone too. She was going to need Kirsty more than ever.

'Shall we hold a service for your father, like we did for your mother?'

Anna's expression brightened a fraction. 'I'd like that.'

'There must be someone here who can help. I'll ask around in the morning.'

Anna nodded. 'Thank you,' she whispered.

The two girls, Elza and Vera, didn't look too keen at having to share their bed, and insisted on sleeping top to toe, with Anna and Kirsty's heads at the foot of the bed. It was strange to be so intimate with people they'd barely met. Within hours Kirsty had become familiar with Elza's body odour and the strange snuffling sounds Vera made. She knew how Anna's breath smelled and the fact Elza ground her teeth when she was deeply asleep. Even if her mind hadn't been endlessly racing through the events of the day and trying to imagine what the future might hold, Kirsty would still have still struggled with insomnia. It was impossible to lie on your back with three other bodies alongside, and if anyone wanted to turn over they had to signal the fact to their fellow occupants so that they could all turn together. If she thought life in the yellow-star house was hard, this was far worse. But at least they were safe. And alive.

She sensed Anna was still awake too. Poor girl. Kirsty remembered trying to sleep in Maggie's daughter's bedroom the night Da died, and knew only too well that the endless film of her father's death and the forced march to the train would be spooling through her mind. Thank God Maggie had taught her to cook. Learning recipes had helped keep her busy and, for a few precious hours at least, given her something else to think about. She kneaded her stomach to stave off the gnaw of hunger. In spite of the bread she'd had earlier it was still empty. She willed her mind away from all the buttery treats Maggie had helped her bake. She and Archie were hardly wealthy but there were always ample supplies of butter, sugar, eggs and flour. So different to the scant provisions over the last few years. But cooking had been therapy during those first raw weeks of grief. It had given her a job at the school too – where physical work had continued to be a balm, and gentle Jean had taken over from kind Maggie in offering her support.

Now it was her turn to provide that same support to Anna. She decided to offer their services to Mrs Tibor in the morning, as well as finding out who could help lead a funeral service for Mr Bellak.

Mrs Tibor was indeed grateful for two extra pairs of hands and Kirsty and Anna were kept busy distributing apples to the children and elderly, then collecting and washing the dirty plates. There were several other youths of about their age helping, along with three other women doing the cooking. Once again the smell of fried dough threaded through the courtyard. Kirsty was amazed how they managed to feed so many people.

She remarked on this to Mrs Tibor.

'In the beginning some of our wealthier residents gave us money,' she said. 'We managed to buy some food ration vouchers, but I'm worried that supplies in the city are running out. It's going to be tough to feed so many over the winter.'

'I can imagine,' Kirsty replied. She told Mrs Tibor about her role as cook at the school. She'd struggled so much to find food for the last few months. And that was for a relatively small group of people. She had no idea how the cooks at the Glass House managed to feed nearly two thousand residents.

After the meal they returned to their sleeping quarters. As before, young people were sitting on their beds playing cards, reading, or talking quietly. A small group of teenage girls was even doing a jigsaw. Another was having a competition as to who could catch and kill the most lice from their clothing.

Elza and Vera weren't there so she and Anna had the mattress to themselves. Kirsty had eventually tracked down another cantor, who agreed to lead a simple service for Anna's father. It seemed to help a little, but Anna was clearly still in shock. She spent hours staring into space now, as if failing to register what was going on in the room. Her mind was too taken up with grief. At least Kirsty hadn't seen her father die; it would be an image Anna would have to live with for a long time. Kirsty saw again the bewildered figure on the pavement, still wearing his dressing gown and slippers . . . the crumpled body . . . the trail of blood . . . then heard once more the sickening thump to the head. It was vividly imprinted on *her* mind, goodness knows what it was doing to Anna's.

'Come on, Anna,' she said. 'Let's go for a swim.'

Anna snapped out of her miserable reverie. 'A swim? Are

270

you mad? It's far too cold and dangerous to leave the house – and anyway, where would we go?'

'We don't need to go anywhere,' Kirsty replied. 'We'll just practise on the mattress, like when we taught Tünde and Szalók.'

'But that was only to keep them occupied.'

'Exactly. But we need to keep busy too. It will give us some exercise. And besides, all good swimmers need to train.'

'Train for what?'

Kirsty drew Anna down onto the mattress. 'Mr Wallenberg saved our lives yesterday. We owe it to him, and to ourselves, to think about the future. The war could end soon. We have to try to build a life for ourselves and I think that life should include swimming.'

'What's the point?' Anna's fingers crept to her mouth. 'My parents are dead, my brother is who knows where. How can I think about the future? I don't have one.'

Kirsty took Anna's fingers in hers and gently stopped her probing the sore.

'Life is incredibly hard for you. I know a little of what that's like. You must feel there's no point in going on. But you have to try. We have to live our lives for ourselves, not for other people, even if they are – were – family.'

Anna looked at her bleakly and Kirsty wondered if she'd been too harsh. No one had spoken to her like this when she'd become an orphan, but the last few years had made her a lot more self-reliant. She'd learnt the hard way that people can only do so much to help; ultimately you needed to find your own sense of purpose. It was important to persuade Anna she needed to keep going for her own sake.

'Come on. We'll start with front crawl.' She lay prone on the bed and performed the stroke. It felt good to stretch and move her body again after the cramped night. She willed her mind to leave the stuffy room behind and transport her back to Lake Balaton, the morning sun beating down on her head, her limbs moving effortlessly through the warm water . . .

There was a sigh then a body plumped down alongside hers. She turned her head to see Anna join her in their strange swim, her legs and arms synchronised as Kirsty had taught her. Gradually she picked up speed and energy and her expression became determined. By the time they finished she was pummelling the mattress for all she was worth.

## 32

Winter 1944

The drifts of fog outside the windows dispersed, to be replaced by swirling ice patterns frozen onto the panes each morning. Despite the packed accommodation, the air in the rooms was chilly. For once Kirsty and Anna were grateful for their close sleeping companions and their welcome body heat. All they could do was to keep going and hope for spring.

Towards the middle of the new month they celebrated Hannukah. Someone in the camp had managed to collect some nutshells, and by placing a wick in them and pouring in oil, they were able to create some makeshift candles. Kirsty and Anna helped Mrs Tibor make *tócsni* or potato pancakes which they fried in the kitchen, ready for the celebration meal.

'You two have been such a help,' she said. 'Your cookery knowledge is excellent – you always seem to know exactly what to do.'

'Kirsty was well taught at the school,' Anna replied. 'And she passed her knowledge on to me.'

Kirsty smiled. It felt good to be useful and the busyness helped the hours pass more quickly.

Anna insisted they still practised 'swimming' when they could, keeping their bodies strong despite the lack of food, and taking their minds to happier places. Whenever they had the bed to themselves, she'd start 'training', flailing her legs and punching the air with her arms, driving herself to exhaustion. Kirsty remembered how she'd swum in the Clyde after Da's death, punishing her body to push back the pain of grief. It had helped her then, she was sure it was helping Anna now.

Kirsty used their swimming practice to daydream about Endre – reliving his kisses and the way they made her feel. Sometimes she had to bury her face in the mattress to stop Anna seeing the way her cheeks flushed with remembered desire – or turned white whenever she felt consumed with fear about his survival.

But Anna was more interested in exercise. She became fanatical, spending hours running silently on the spot and executing star jumps, squats, leg swings, sit-ups, her expression rigid with determination. Often others joined in. Exercise gave their minds and bodies freedom, despite their enforced captivity.

But there were still long hours to fill. 'Do you remember when we played *Capitaly* at the school?' Kirsty asked Anna one day as they lay on the mattress trying to occupy another hour before leaving to help prepare dinner. 'I wonder what happened to the game.'

'We had a set at home,' Anna replied. '*Abba* used to love playing it.' Her eyes clouded with sadness. 'We obviously couldn't take it with us when we left for the yellow-star house, but now it feels like one more link with *Abba* gone.'

'I could fetch it,' Kirsty said. 'It would be a good diversion and I'm sure there are loads of people here who'd like to borrow it.'

Anna's fingers flew to her mouth. The sore was still there, a little less livid now. 'But won't it be dangerous going back?'

'I'll keep away from the main roads.' She didn't like to emphasise her Aryan status to Anna, when she and her fellow Jews were suffering so much, but in truth it allowed her much greater freedom. She had far more licence to be out and about in Budapest than she normally afforded herself. Dasco hadn't appeared again. It would be unlucky to bump into him, although perhaps it was inevitable at some point – he couldn't be living that far away.

Anna unclipped a chain from round her neck and detached two brass keys, which she handed over to Kirsty. 'The larger one unlocks the back door and the other is for the apartment itself.' She swallowed. 'Be very careful, won't you?'

Kirsty gave her friend a quick hug. 'Of course.'

She felt a stab of guilt as she slipped out of the Glass House's front door into the white sheen of a winter morning and inhaled the icy air. It felt so good to be outside after many long weeks cooped up in the football headquarters. Admittedly, there were the daily stints in the courtyard to cook and serve meals but there they were so occupied with preparing the food they barely had time to notice their surroundings. Now, for the first time in ages, she could enjoy a brief sense of freedom, even if it was tempered by the knowledge that her housemates couldn't share that privilege. At least she could check on the apartment for Anna, and bring back a new means of entertainment.

All along Vadász utca, the trees were strung with glistening spiders' threads, and the grass verges stiff with silver frost. She

275

made her way south, parallel with the river, towards what had been the Jewish quarter. Vera had lent her a headscarf and she pulled it tighter as a group of Arrow Cross members, in their familiar uniform, loomed into view. She was surprised to see a couple of women in their midst, dressed in black skirts and dark green shirts. Of course, her own sex could hate and maim too, but most of the females in her life were gentle, nurturing types. She wondered what had happened to these women fighters to make them throw in their lot with the fascists.

She kept her head down as the group passed, but to her relief they left her alone. Perhaps it had been foolish to leave the relative safety of the Glass House just for a board game, but with her auburn hair covered, and her yellow star left behind, she just looked like a Hungarian housewife out shopping. She'd even taken a bag along too. If anyone searched her, after she'd collected the game, she'd intended to say she'd bought it for her children for Christmas.

There was a clot of German soldiers on Arany János utca, tall figures in their grey-green uniforms and metal helmets, carrying huge rifles. But somehow they looked less intimidating than the Arrow Cross, possibly because of the violence she'd witnessed. The attack on the old woman, the shooting of Anna's father, Dasco's attempt to rape her, had all been Nyilas led.

The soldiers stood aside to let her pass, and although she was conscious of cold blue eyes following her down the road, she wasn't challenged.

Budapest life had continued while they'd been immured in the Glass House, and the yellow-star dwelling before that. Here were people walking into shops and pausing to chat in

276

broad daylight. A woman in a fur coat, a little dog trotting behind her, stopped just ahead of Kirsty for the dog to relieve itself on the lamppost. A wraith of steam rose from the puddle of urine and disappeared into the cold air. The woman sniffed and walked on.

Kirsty passed a jeweller's shop with the door and window boarded up and wondered what had happened to its owners. Were they huddled in a safe house, clutching the few meagre possessions they'd managed to take with them, waiting in fear for the knock on the door? The long walk to Austria and an uncertain future? Jean's earnest, sweet face appeared before her, and she swallowed. No one who'd left the city under German guard ever seemed to return.

As Kirsty turned into the street where Anna and her family had lived, with its broad pavements and tall apartment buildings, she was anxious that their shop too might have been boarded up, but she needn't have worried. The watchmaker's looked much as before except a man Kirsty didn't recognise stood behind the counter. Kirsty felt a sharp pang for the Bellaks. Even though the parents weren't alive to witness it, someone else was clearly profiting from their hard work building up and running their business. She walked past the open doorway of the shop, ignoring the temptation to glance in, and skirted round behind the building, where Anna had told her the rear entrance could be found. Apparently they liked to welcome visitors in through the shop they were so proud of, as they'd done with Kirsty, but the family themselves used the back way.

Kirsty delved into her pocket for one of the keys, counted four doors down from the corner, then located the black door that Anna had described. The paint was peeling off in parts, and the bottom of the wood was scratched as though an animal had sharpened its claws on it, but the key fitted and soon Kirsty was inside and climbing the mud-streaked steps to the next floor.

Mercifully no one was around. The stairwell smelled musty and there was a cobweb stretched, hammock like, across one of the corners. Anna's house-proud mother would have been appalled.

She found the door to the Bellaks' apartment and let herself in with the second key. As she did so, she heard a faint banging. She tiptoed in, her heart fluttering violently, wondering if it had been a mad idea to come after all. The hallway was empty, just a few old coats, now covered in dust, drooping on the stand. She made her way to the parlour, where Anna's mother had served her *rugelach* all those years ago. She saw again the doily-covered plate, the sugary pastries, Mrs Bellak's wrinkled hands as she'd offered Kirsty the refreshments. The flowery chairs were the same but the candlestick was missing from the windowsill. She wondered if they'd hidden it for safe-keeping, or if it had been stolen.

Another slight noise turned her unease into foreboding. Had she disturbed an intruder in the act of burglary? Or was it a mouse or a rat? She tiptoed into the kitchen. The winter sun, slanting through the window, illuminated a smear of jam and a few breadcrumbs on the table. That was strange. Kirsty was sure she'd seen poor Mrs Bellak, who'd been such an immaculate housewife, wipe it before they left. She fetched a cloth from the sink and cleaned the surface of the table. It was strange that the cloth was damp, rather than bone dry as it should have been. Her stomach lurched at this new concern. She grabbed a knife from the cutlery drawer to arm herself.

Anna had told her that the *Capitaly* box was in Endre's old bedroom. She opened the door and stood on the threshold brandishing the knife, her senses sharpening. *There was some-one in the room.* The bedspread was pulled up but instead of being flat and smooth, it was lumpy. Someone was hidden under the covers and lying as still as possible. A chill rippled down her spine.

'Who is it?' she said.

The bedspread slowly moved and, like a primeval hump-backed creature emerging from the swamp, an old man appeared, his thinning hair plastered to his head, his eyes buried deep in their sockets, loose skin drooping either side of his face. He looked even more terrified of her than she of him.

The knife slipped from her hand and clattered to the floor. 'Endre,' she said.

## 33

Endre paled when he saw her. He was dressed in a ragged red jumper and the lower half of his face was flecked with stubble. With his gaunt features and slow movements, he seemed decades older than the young man she'd last seen when they'd dropped him back at the hospital after the trip to Lake Balaton. A world ago now.

'What happened to you? Why are you here?' Kirsty perched on the end of the bed, causing Endre to draw his knees up and shrink against the headboard. She didn't dare move any closer. He looked at her through haunted eyes.

'Can I get you anything? A drink, perhaps?' Anxiety tightened her throat. Had he reverted to the terrified man in the hospital, unable to recognise people, his mind still trapped in a battlefield?

Endre dipped his head then slowly raised it.

She hurried off to the kitchen to fetch a glass and fill it from the tap. At least the water supply hadn't been cut off. She wondered how long Endre had been camping out in his old home. On return, she carefully placed the glass on his bedside table, sensing he wouldn't take it from her hand.

He picked it up and took a sip.

Silence built up in the room. Endre plucked at the hairs on

the back of his hand, a gesture she remembered all too well from his time in the hospital.

Kirsty looked away, anxious not to put him under pressure. She'd never been in his room before. On her few visits while he'd lived there she'd sat in the parlour with Mr and Mrs Bellak, or on Anna's bed playing and chatting. Endre's bedroom was furnished for the boy he'd once been. A couple of model biplanes hung suspended from the ceiling. Kirsty imagined him making them with his father, gluing the pieces together on the table, their foreheads furrowed in concentration. School textbooks were lined up in a small brown bookcase in the corner, next to a similar-coloured wardrobe. *Mathematics is Fun* read one. And *Exercises in English* said another. Kirsty wondered what his favourite subject at school had been, what he was best at. There were so many things she didn't know about him.

Finally he cleared his throat. 'I ran away.' His voice was hoarse, as though he hadn't spoken for a long time.

'From your battalion?' Anna had told her that Endre had been put back into a labour unit after he'd left hospital. They hadn't had any news since. What on earth had gone on?

Endre nodded. 'I couldn't . . . couldn't . . .' He clawed at the bedspread with work-roughened hands. His nails were bitten to the quick.

Kirsty wrapped his hands in hers. What terrible scenes were playing behind his eyes? He'd seemed so much calmer after the summer at Lake Balaton, but it was too brief a respite. It had been cruel to send such a troubled young man back to the carnage of the war. And this time there'd be no healing swims or a chance to sit on the bank and talk gently, the sun warming his body and soothing his mind. Her heart ached for those days and the comfort they'd found in each other.

Endre took another sip of water.

Kirsty watched his Adam's apple shift as the liquid slid down his throat. 'What happened?' She felt the threat of tears behind her lids and she willed them back.

'A copper mine in Yugoslavia,' Endre whispered.

An image slid in: labyrinthine tunnels, a low roof, darkness . . . She shivered. Another man risking his life in the bowels of the earth.

'The overseer . . .' Endre released her hands to roll up the sleeve of his shirt, revealing angry red weals slashed across his arms.

Kirsty sucked air through her teeth in sympathy, then bent to kiss them, her lips brushing the raw uneven skin.

'Worse on my back . . . Twenty lashings.' He grimaced. 'I dropped a sack of sand.'

Kirsty braced herself to see the wounds but Endre didn't show them. Perhaps he was embarrassed, or sparing her feelings.

'So how did you get back here?'

Endre looked into the middle distance, his eyes glazed. When he spoke, his voice was flat but the words tumbled out more coherently. 'When the Russians came last September, we knew the Germans had to retreat. They disbanded our battalion and marched us all towards Hungary. One night there was a terrible storm. Thunder . . . lightning.' He swallowed. 'A small group of us managed to get away under cover of darkness. We were soaked to the bone, and scared witless . . . but we were free. The weather camouflaged our escape. We hid in the forest for three days until we were

282

certain they were no longer searching for us, then slowly made the long trek back to Budapest. I've been lying low here ever since.'

'But what have you done for food?'

The ghost of a smile appeared on Endre's face and Kirsty was briefly reminded of the young man she'd fallen in love with. 'You know what Mama's like,' he said. 'The cupboards were full of jam and pickles and bottled fruit. A feast after living on whatever we could salvage from the forest. I've had plenty.'

There was no inkling he was aware of his parents' deaths. Should Kirsty tell him about his mother's last illness and the murder of his father? She decided the terrible news would be better coming from Anna. She hadn't known Mr and Mrs Bellak that well. But it wasn't fair to keep him in ignorance. She needed to get him across to the Glass House.

'Come with me,' she said. 'Anna and I are living somewhere safe, with lots of other Jews. You'll be welcome there. No questions asked.' People were turning up in Vadász Street all the time. The place was bursting at the seams but one more wouldn't make any difference. 'It's too risky here. The Arrow Cross are constantly prowling round. They could mount a raid and find you any day. If they do, they won't show any mercy.' Rumours were abounding in the Glass House about Jews from the ghetto being rounded up and shot. The Nyilas' methods were no secret. She'd once called them *bloody keelie scum*. In truth they were ruthless murderers. Endre had suffered enough.

But he shook his head, clearly terrified at the prospect. 'I'm not going anywhere. They can round me up if they want to. I can't face any more.' He still hadn't asked about his parents. Perhaps he already knew, deep down – or maybe someone had told him. Whatever it was, it was clearly a subject he wasn't willing to raise. But surely he should be reunited with Anna? And if Endre came to the Glass House, she could nurse him back to health like last time. But she'd make sure that he stayed in hiding. There was no way she'd let him go on being used as forced labour in such terrible conditions.

'Endre, please? You must want to see Anna.'

Endre's expression was wistful now. 'Maybe in a few weeks,' he said. 'But not yet. I just need to hunker down here for a bit. I don't feel I can leave the apartment. But give her my love.'

Kirsty squeezed his hand. 'May I come back again? I could try to bring some more food?'

'I have plenty of food,' Endre replied. 'But yes, do come back.' He twined his fingers with hers. 'Another time, another place,' he said.

A slight tremor ran through her. Perhaps there was still hope.

It was only when she approached the Glass House again, Endre's haggard expression having hounded her for the whole journey back, that she realised she'd forgotten the *Capitaly* set.

It was rare that Anna smiled these days, but her face lit up at the news that Endre was alive, safe, and living in their old apartment.

'When can I see him?' For once her eyes blazed brighter than the sore that still festered at the side of her mouth.

Kirsty explained his refusal to leave the building, despite her persistence and warnings about the dangers.

'Then I'll go to him.'

'It's not safe, Anna. You know that.'

'But you got there and back without any trouble.'

'I was safe because I didn't have a yellow star on my coat. I was dressed like a Hungarian housewife. There was no need for anyone to challenge me.'

Anna's fingers strayed to her mouth. Her shoulders slumped. 'I know. You're right of course. I just want to see my brother. Especially after . . .' The tears bulged.

'I know.' Kirsty put an arm round her. 'I'm sure you'll see Endre soon. In the meantime, I can take him a letter from you when I next go.'

'Thank you. I'll see if anyone has any paper.' But as Anna stood up, there was a deafening noise of explosions and the rapid tattoo of machine-gun fire. She rocked on her feet. 'What was that?'

Kirsty looked around. There were so many possible causes of attack: Allied bombing, German shells, Arrow Cross raids . . . Sometimes she just thought it was a question of who would get them first.

Each part of the building had its own allocated runner, who was in charge of warning his or her section in the event of crisis. When Samuel, their runner, entered the basement, with a flushed face and an urgent expression, everyone fell silent. 'No one talk,' he rasped. 'Not even a whisper. Nyilas and Nazi soldiers have beaten up the guards. They're in the courtyard now. Don't even breathe.' Someone blew out a candle and Samuel's eyes turned white in the darkness.

Kirsty held her breath. She and Anna had survived the Arrow Cross raid on their yellow-star house, had been rescued from deportation on the train at the last moment by Raoul Wallenberg, had been protected for weeks in the Glass House. Had their luck now run out? And behind those thoughts lay a deeper, more disturbing one: had someone seen her visit Endre and followed her back? Perhaps a Nyilas guard, maybe even Dasco. Had she inadvertently led an attacker to their refuge? And all for a silly board game that she hadn't even managed to bring back.

The room was thick with dread and fear. Next to her, Anna scratched at her sore. Kirsty didn't even dare reach out a hand to restrain her. Around them, people stood or sat like statues. All they could hear was shouting coming from the courtyard. Urgent messages crashed through Kirsty's brain: *Don't let them go any further, don't let them come in here.* She wasn't even sure who she was begging.

An hour passed. Maybe two. Around her, people were silently flexing their limbs, shooting warning glances at anyone whose joints creaked or whose feet inadvertently scuffed the floor. Kirsty's stomach growled with hunger and she clapped her palm to her belly to stifle the noise. Terror and lack of food was making her feel weak. She drove her nails into her hands to keep herself alert.

At long last, the door opened. Kirsty took a deep breath and braced herself for the attack. Adrenaline surged through her. She caught sight of Anna's terrified expression and suspected that hers mirrored it. But the voice was Samuel's. 'It's over,' he said. 'At least for now. The soldiers have gone.'

The whole room let out a collective sigh of relief.

Details emerged the following morning: the men had forced their way through the front gates but only advanced into the courtyard by a few metres. They never got anywhere near the entrance to the girls' basement. Mr Weiss and some other members of the committee had rushed down to negotiate with them. They had some money put by for badly needed food but used it all up persuading the soldiers not to proceed. The bribe was successful, although it cost them dearly.

The reprieve was short lived. At the end of December came the news that the Russian and Romanian armies had reached the outskirts of Budapest and were surrounding the city. The Germans were mercifully on the retreat but now they were under siege from new enemies. And very soon the food supplies began to dry up. They lived on thin pea soup, runny as water, and mouldy bread. The days were long and cold. Candles were rationed so they sat in darkness most of the time, their only light the flares from explosions as bombs were dropped on the city.

Rumours swirled through the Glass House: *they were about to be executed*; *the Americans were sending paratroopers into the courtyard to rescue them*; *the water main just outside the building was poisoned* . . . And still Endre hadn't arrived.

One morning, Anna sat up in bed and announced she was going to see him.

'You can't,' Kirsty said. 'Now that the Russians have encircled Budapest, the Arrow Cross are trying to exterminate any witnesses against them. They're shooting anyone they catch. It's far too dangerous.'

Anna shrugged. 'Dangerous? Just by staying here we could be killed by an Allied bomb, a Russian tank, a parting shot from the Germans, or the Nyilas, still hell-bent on annihilating all of my people. No one and nowhere is safe. I've lost both my parents. I'm no longer prepared to save my own skin by sacrificing the chance to see my only living relative.' Kirsty was concerned about her plan, but relieved to see some of the old Anna returning. Her face was still white, but her eyes had more life in them than there'd been for weeks. She reminded herself that she'd made it to the apartment and back without any problems. Perhaps they'd get away with it.

'All right,' said Kirsty. 'But I'm coming with you.'

Anna flashed her a brittle smile. 'Thank you.'

The night before, Kirsty had talked Anna through the route she'd taken a few weeks ago, avoiding the main roads. It was incredibly risky. Jews were no longer allowed on the streets. She could be shot or deported on site. They needed to be quick. And canny.

They were by the front door by five to ten, both carrying baskets as though going shopping. At ten o'clock they stepped out into a sharp winter morning. The sky was dark and threatening but, despite the cold and the vicious snow-laden wind that swirled round them, it felt good to be out in the fresh air.

'I'm glad you're with me,' said Anna. Her skin was translucent in the watery sunlight and her breath came out in clouds. She was thin as a rake but her muscles were strong, thanks to all the exercise.

Kirsty took her arm. 'Come on. Think how wonderful it will be to see Endre again.'

The streets were busy but not overcrowded. People looked anxious and defeated, their features care worn, their shoulders hunched. Kirsty recognised the same expression on Anna's face, and possibly her own too: a kind of stoical resignation. Life was about as bad as it could be, but somehow they would get through it. It was almost 1945 now, surely the war couldn't go on much longer? Despite the gloom and misery, there was always hope. Kirsty tried to imagine a new Budapest – without yellow stars, or curfews, or lack of food, or the terrible stomach-grinding fear. But it was impossible to summon such a paradise.

Signs of bomb damage were all around them. They skirted around huge piles of bricks that must have once been buildings, and passed blown-apart homes, like huge, denuded dolls' houses, with the outer walls missing yet some of the rooms strangely intact. Kirsty pointed up at a bedroom with cheerful sprigged wallpaper, a dark wood dressing table and clothes draped over a chair, despite the rest of the house being in ruins.

They had to zigzag to avoid the streams of sewer water that ran down the pavements, and once they crossed the road to avoid walking past a pile of dead bodies. Kirsty chatted loudly to Anna to stop her focussing on the tangled pile of white limbs and the putrid stench of corpses that filled the air. The streets were eerie without the usual constant tram noise, the vehicles having been stopped to save power.

The further they travelled, the more Anna's pace slowed and Kirsty was worried they weren't going fast enough. The dangers increased with every minute they were on the streets. But at the sight of the Bellaks' old apartment, she seemed to regain some energy. Thank God it was still intact. They used the back entrance as before and climbed up the stairs, stopping every so often to take a breath.

Anna called through the letter box before using her key, and Endre was waiting for her in the hall. Kirsty stepped back as the siblings embraced. For a second her heart twisted. Over the years she'd often wished she'd had a brother or sister. Someone to cling to when Da had died. Someone to share the burden of grief and the decisions about the future. But then again, if she'd had a sibling in Scotland, she might never have met Jean, or gone to Budapest. Or met Anna. Or Endre.

She busied herself in the kitchen while Anna led Endre into the parlour and gently broke the news of their parents' death.

Endre must have suspected it though, as when they both emerged he was pale but composed. And although he looked lean, he was not skeletal. Mrs Bellak's provisions must still be holding up.

Kirsty glanced at her watch. She was anxious about the journey. The sooner they set off, the sooner they'd be safely back in the Glass House.

'I think we should go,' she said.

Endre had barely looked at her since their arrival. Understandably all his concentration had been on Anna. But now he did, his brown eyes lingering searchingly on her face. She swallowed down the memory of his lips on hers.

'Please come with us,' Anna begged him. 'We need each other more than ever now.'

Endre glanced at her then turned back to Kirsty.

'We have to get back,' she said. 'But you could follow on later. You know where the Glass House is and we could get a space ready for you.'

This time Endre didn't turn her down straight away. 'I'll think about it,' he said.

Anna gave him one last hug, then they left.

# 34

'We need to hurry,' Kirsty said as they retraced their steps back to the Glass House, over pavements glazed with ice and frozen puddles that cracked under their feet. The snow was coming down more strongly now. This time Kirsty took them a different route, to avoid the corpses. Unlike her last journey to the Bellaks' apartment, there were hardly any Germans on the street now. But the fear was still palpable. The Russians were poised to invade Budapest. It could happen at any time. The enemy was different but the sense of apprehension was the same.

'I ought to feel safe now many of the Germans have gone,' Anna said. 'But the Russians could be worse.'

Kirsty shuddered. 'I've heard they rape women,' she said. It didn't bear thinking about but they had to press on. 'Come on, we're nearly there. Let's avoid the streets and go across the park.'

They struck off diagonally, intending to walk across the grass, now stretching like a white blanket before them, but at the entrance their luck ran out.

'What are you doing here? I put you on a train. You should be in Poland by now.' His eyes bored into Kirsty's. The one person she dreaded above all. And surrounded by a group of similarly leering men in the familiar green and black Arrow Cross uniform.

Dasco. Why did it always have to be him?

Her heart started to race until her whole body pounded with its pulse.

Beside her, Anna took a sharp breath.

'Hello, Dasco,' Kirsty said. 'We decided not to proceed with our journey.'

Dasco's expression darkened.

'How is your mother these days?' It was all she could think of. Reminding Dasco of the person who connected them, the woman she'd worked with for all those years. An attempt to make Dasco see her as someone other than a potential victim. Not that the tactic had worked before. Kirsty suspected that violence, or the threat of violence, was all Dasco and his kind understood. And this time he had all the cards.

'She's a lot better now she's not working with Jewish scum,' he replied, hawking up some phlegm and spitting at Anna's face. Typical Dasco.

A trail of slime ran down Anna's cheek. She wiped it with the back of her hand. Her eyes were blazing but thankfully she said nothing. Doubtless that would have made things worse.

'Please send Mária my best wishes,' Kirsty replied, hoping to divert attention back to her.

'Bloody hell, Dasco,' called one of his mates. 'We're not at a cocktail party.'

Dasco blinked and seemed to collect himself. 'This tart used to work for my mother,' he said, nodding towards Kirsty. 'She's a kike-lover.'

One of his companions shrugged. 'Kikes. Kike-lovers. They're both the same.' He turned to Dasco. 'You know what to do.'

Dasco nodded grimly, his expression full of malice. Then he jerked his head towards a straggly line of people standing by the railings at the side of the park. In her shock at encountering Dasco, Kirsty hadn't noticed them. There were men with livid bruises wearing baggy jackets; women in coats and headscarves; children wearing knitted hats and mittens. Their faces were white and fearful. Some were openly crying. All of them wore yellow stars.

Anna and Kirsty were shoved into the line.

Dasco took his place at the rear and another of his mates moved to the front. Others stood along the line scrutinising the miserable assembly.

'Now march,' said the leader. The line shuffled forwards.

'Where are we going?' Kirsty asked a woman clutching the hand of a little boy in a bulky green coat. He trotted silently along beside her, his gaze fixed on the ground.

The woman darted a glance at her. Although she couldn't have been more than thirty, there were lines of weariness and suffering etched onto her sallow skin, her brown eyes dull and despairing.

'The rumour is we're going to the Danube,' she muttered.

'The *Danube*?'

'Haven't you heard? They line up Jews and shoot them. Our bodies will fall into the river so there's no need to bury us.' The words spooled out of her mouth dispassionately, as though she'd distanced herself from the full horror they conveyed.

Kirsty stopped so suddenly that the man behind her banged into her. The air was sucked out of her body until she was literally gasping to breathe.

'I'm sorry. I thought you'd have known.' The woman clutched at her sleeve.

Kirsty put her hand to her chest which burned with the effort of speaking. 'We've been hiding in the Glass House on Vadász utca. News doesn't always filter through.' Or had they just shut their minds to the atrocities, refusing to admit that Jean was most likely dead? As, probably, were Évi, Szalók and Tünde. Along with Anna's parents. Was it essential to their own survival that they denied their compassion for others? Either way it scarcely mattered. They'd be dead themselves soon: mere bodies in the Danube, along with all the others. No chance to carry on Jean's work at the school, or to achieve their swimming ambitions, or for Kirsty to be buried in the same country as her parents. If the heaven that Jean had so fervently believed in existed, maybe they would meet again one day. Either way, any hopes or dreams for the future were about to be cut off with a gunshot . . . the tumble into the water . . . then oblivion. She thought of the occasions she and Anna had swum in the river, little realising it would be their graveyard. She shut her eyes for a second, trying to summon up those blissful times: their bodies swathed in silky water, their limbs moving freely, the sunlight causing stars of light to burst on the waves. Perhaps if she told herself it was just another swim, it would make the prospect easier to deal with. It was no good protesting that she was a Gentile – Dasco knew that and wouldn't make an exception for her. In fact he'd delight in seeing her die – a just punishment in his view. And anyway, she couldn't leave Anna.

An idea half-formed in Kirsty's mind. It was mad and probably futile, but they were desperate. They had nothing to lose.

They might as well die trying to survive than passively submit to their fate. And somewhere behind that lurked the determination not to let Dasco win.

'Anna,' she whispered. 'They're going to shoot us by the river. Unless we can find a way to escape this will be the end.'

Anna's face was blank.

A spark of anger flared in Kirsty's stomach, travelling along her nerves until her whole body seethed with fury. 'We can't give up like this,' she hissed. 'We have to fight.'

'How?'

Kirsty grabbed Anna's hand. 'Listen.' She outlined her idea, adding in details as they came to her.

Interest flared in Anna's eyes. 'All right. Anything to thwart that bastard.'

Kirsty smiled grimly. 'We literally have nothing to lose.'

They marched on in silence. Kirsty tried to assume an expression of abject terror for the benefit of the guards, but inside she was cementing her scheme.

Every so often she glanced at Anna. Her features still gave little away but there was a new energy to her gait.

There was no guarantee either of them would survive. But at least they'd go down fighting.

They were marched down to the embankment through the freezing streets, grim-faced Nyilas members striding alongside, their fingers resting on pistols attached to their belts. From time to time they removed them and used the butts to shove people into line. The icy air was filled with angry shouts and orders. There were no passers-by. If anyone had ventured out they must have returned home or darted into the shadows before they were seen. Many Hungarians had turned against the Jews, and those who sympathised weren't prepared to risk their own lives.

When they got to the quay, several men were waiting for them, one or two brushing something into the water. The metallic stench of blood mingled with the earthy smell of the river. Kirsty swallowed down the acid that had pooled in her mouth. They must be cleaning up after a previous execution. The site was away from the busy road and out of view of the traffic. It had been chosen deliberately so that no one would be around to witness the killings – or attempt to rescue them.

'Take off your shoes,' their commander barked.

'Our *shoes*?' Anna whispered.

Kirsty shrugged. 'Shoe leather is expensive. The bastards might get some money for them.' As she bent down to unlace her black brogues, a faint memory stirred of trying them on in the shop in front of Jean, and Jean contributing some of her own money when they turned out to be more than Kirsty could afford. She thought, too, of the Christmas when Jean had cut up her own suitcase to patch the girls' shoes.

All around her people were taking off their footwear, lining them up on the path, then standing forlornly in bare or stockinged feet. Her heart heaved when she saw two tiny pairs of children's boots nestling alongside a woman's court shoes, and she tried to banish the image of a doting mother lacing them up on her children's little feet that morning. The same mother who was now standing on the embankment, her face bleached with fear, holding on tightly to the hands of her small son and daughter. Kirsty looked away, her breath catching in her chest.

The guards pushed them towards the river, its icy water swirling below them.

'Think of it as just another swim,' she whispered to Anna.

Anna nodded, her lips mauve with cold and terror. Kirsty doubted if she could have spoken even if she'd wanted to. Her own heart was beating wildly in her chest.

They stood in a terrified line, facing the river, a guard with a pistol standing behind each of them, so close she could smell gun oil and the reek of sweat. The commander stood at the far left, his mouth hardening as he surveyed the row. Somewhere further down a woman retched violently, watery orange vomit pooling in front of her.

Dasco was walking down the line, tying people's hands together. She heard stifled cries as the ropes bit into their wrists. When he got to Anna and Kirsty, she pleaded with him with her eyes. 'Please help us. For your mother's sake,' she murmured. He scowled and pulled the rope tight, skewering her with pain. *But he didn't tie the knot.* As he moved on, she glanced at Anna and gave her a subtle wink. 'We still have a chance,' she whispered, keeping her arms in position so the rope didn't drop off.

Anna nodded back, almost imperceptibly.

'Remember. Jump in when I say.'

Anna nodded again.

The commander gave the first order. A shot rang out in the cold air and two bodies tumbled into the river. Kirsty tried to suppress the shudders of revulsion and hysteria. *Keep calm, keep calm*, she told herself. She didn't dare look at Anna again but the lack of movement beside her suggested that she was either frozen with fear or poised to jump. Hopefully the latter. She was going to need to move on cue or they wouldn't stand a chance.

Fear gouged her throat as the guards came closer and closer and the line of bodies grew smaller and smaller. Three sounds were repeated: the commander's shout, the crack of gunfire, the deathly splash. She willed herself not to be sick.

When the woman next to Anna was shot, Kirsty knew she couldn't delay.

'Now,' she shouted. She jerked their wrists to discard the loose rope and pushed Anna hard in the back.

Both girls plunged into the freezing water.

# 35

The limb-numbing cold that seized her already-frozen body was too savage to allow conscious thought. Anna, beside her, was already floating on her front as they'd planned. Kirsty took a deep breath and followed suit, forcing her body to relax, her arms and legs to drift out. Normally she'd have swum for all she was worth, in order to keep warm and put as much distance as possible from the Arrow Cross men on the bank. But she fought the urge; they needed to convince the guards they were dead. Her heavy, waterlogged clothing made it harder to float against the drag of gravity, but spreading her body into a starfish shape helped. That and grim determination.

The current was mercifully strong and she was twenty metres downstream before she needed to take a breath. She inched her head up until her nostrils were just above the surface and snatched some air. As she did so she glimpsed a tangle of lifeless bodies and saturated clothes. Bullets shrieked past her. She dipped her head again, reimmersing herself in the world of silence. Tendrils of blood unfurled and billowed and writhed through the water as the *Blue Danube* turned red.

She let the current carry her down towards the Elizabeth Bridge, through drifts of leaves and twigs, conscious that Anna was still beside her. Incredibly, the plan seemed to be working. She'd been worried that Anna was too much in shock to follow her instructions, but some primitive urge to survive must have kicked in. Thank God for all those hours spent swimming. There must be more strength in their muscles than she'd imagined – that and sheer terror propelling them forwards. When she came up to take another breath, it was much quieter. No shouts, no bullets. Just the faint lap of waves and the cluck of a distant flock of geese.

She risked a look around. There was no one on the bank, and no sign of any guards. Thankfully, none of the Arrow Cross had come after them, seemingly satisfied they were dead. If the water hadn't been so glacial, and the situation so desperate, it would almost have been peaceful on the river. *I'm alive*, she told herself. *We've survived*. Anna was still face down next to her. Kirsty swam closer and nudged Anna's arm. Anna looked up.

'I think we're safe,' Kirsty mumbled through numb lips.

Anna started swimming alongside her, clearly too stunned and cold to reply, but at least she was reacting.

As they rounded a bend Kirsty glimpsed a dock up ahead, on the Buda side of the river, behind which was some sort of boathouse.

'We can scramble out up there,' she said, lifting her water-logged arm out of the river to point. She was still wearing her coat, and felt its weight pulling her down. It was tempting to struggle out of it and consign it to the river in order to free up her body, but she knew she'd regret that later.

Again Anna followed her, her tired limbs forcing their way through the water, her expression rigid with the dogged intent to keep going.

But when they neared the dock, Kirsty took in two disturbing facts. First, that the structure was about a foot high, and would demand another huge effort to push themselves onto it. Secondly, and more appallingly, there were corpses stuck on the guy-wires that connected the dock to the shore – the bodies of people who, like them, had been lined up on the river bank, now with patchy white skin, glassy eyes and slack mouths. She swallowed down the heave of nausea. It was essential that they focussed on getting out of the river.

She swam up to the dock, slapped her palms onto the wood, then pushed down for all she was worth. At first she only succeeded in raising herself a few inches above the surface before her arms gave way. Treading water, she struggled out of her sodden coat and tossed it onto the dock. Then she tried to hoist herself again. This time she managed to push up as far as her waist, then haul her knee onto the platform and scramble up. She reached down to Anna, gave one almighty tug and pulled her onto the dock too. They both collapsed on the wooden boards, panting, exhausted.

But they couldn't stay there for long. They were too exposed, too vulnerable.

'Come on,' Kirsty said. 'Let's go into the boathouse.' It was a risk – they didn't know who could be in there, but it was shelter of a kind and probably their best bet. They staggered across the dock and into the large wooden shed, which probably belonged to a rowing club. It smelled of mould and fish, and was crammed full of boats, oars and life jackets but, to Kirsty's immense relief, it was empty.

'Quick,' she said. 'Let's get out of our wet clothes.' She went over to the wall, grabbed hold of a strut to balance herself, and peeled off her blouse, jumper, skirt and stockings. She wrung them out as best she could, releasing a stream of river water across the floor. Looking round the boat house, she spied a couple of sacks hanging from a low rafter. She pulled them down, ripped a hole in the top and sides of one and threw it to Anna before doing the same for herself. Then she took off her underwear and pulled the sack over her head to create a make-shift tunic. Anna did likewise. Kirsty picked up their wet clothes and strung them across the rafters.

'Is that a fire?' Anna asked, pointing to a cylindrical metal object in the corner.

Kirsty followed her gaze. 'Yes, it's a paraffin heater.' She searched round for matches, eventually locating some on a dusty shelf at the back. Then she went over to the heater, opened the hatch, turned up the wick and lit it. The heater flared into life, releasing the distinctive chemical smell. Kirsty held out her hands, revelling in the delicious heat.

'Come on, Anna. Let's warm ourselves up.'

They sat on the floor in front of the heater, their knees drawn up to their chests and their arms wrapped round them until the warmth seeped into their bones.

'Thank God for the snow,' Anna said. 'It must have been too cold for the rowers to go out on the river.'

Or too clogged with dead bodies, Kirsty thought.

They must have eventually dropped off to sleep, exhaustion affording them merciful oblivion. Kirsty woke a few hours later, conscious that the heater had gone out. Her breath was white vapour in the chilly boathouse and her limbs were stiff. She glanced across at Anna who was lying on her back staring up at the ceiling.

She propped herself up on one elbow. 'Did you sleep?'

'I think I must have done, briefly.' Anna's features sagged from exhaustion.

Kirsty stood up and stumbled over to relight the fire. Their clothes from last night were still damp, but not as wet as before. She turned them over so that they dried evenly.

'I doubt if anyone will come in here for a while. It's still freezing. But we'll need to get out before daylight. We can't risk being seen. And we no longer have our papers. We'll just have to hope no one stops us.' Anna's papers were a sodden mass, too fragmented to be of any use, and Kirsty's had disappeared altogether. They must have come out of her pocket in the water.

'Where will we go?' Anna sounded as if she didn't care either way and a part of Kirsty felt the same. It would be so easy to give in to despair, to wish they'd never survived. But they had. And somehow they needed to keep going.

'I don't think it's safe to go back to the Glass House,' Kirsty said. 'I know our things are there, but that's not important now. Perhaps we can collect them later. Elza and Vera might look after them for us.' She thought of the photo of Anna's parents and Endre that she'd so treasured, and saw again their happy faces as they stood in a group smiling into the camera, full of hope. Like her, all Anna would have of her parents would be the memories: the mental snapshots of family gatherings, days out, festivals . . . and the more mundane images: eating breakfast together, clustering round the radio listening to music, walking down the road on a spring morning . . . Life was just a series of little cameos, and when people died you immortalised them in the bank of recollections you kept in your mind and in your heart. Some days, if it wasn't too painful, you could take out a memory, dust it down and smile at it. Otherwise you just had to plod through the pain, hoping the next day would be better, while trying to make something of the diminished life you had left.

But now all they could do was to concentrate on staying safe. 'There's a rumour the Germans will blow up all the bridges,' she continued. 'It's too much of a risk to cross over to Pest now.' Back in November, German troops carrying out a military exercise at the Margit Bridge attached explosives they could detonate if they needed to destroy the bridge later on. But a boat passing beneath the bridge had accidentally set off one of the fuses, causing a violent explosion. Most of the bridge collapsed into the Danube and over six hundred soldiers, some German, some Hungarian, as well as some Jewish forced labourers, lost their lives. More corpses in the river. Anna and Kirsty had been so lucky not to have been added to the tally that morning.

She stood up and searched around the boathouse, before retrieving some more sacking. 'We'll stand out a mile without any shoes. I'll try to make some from these.' She sat down and started tearing the sack into pieces, trying them against her feet, then remodelling until she had something resembling a shoe. Anna did likewise. 'Do you know anywhere in Buda we could go to?' Kirsty asked as she tore and shaped the sacking.

Anna's fingers crept to the sore at the corner of her mouth, picking at it while staring into the distance. 'There's the tunnels I suppose.'

'Tunnels?'

The fingers stopped. 'There are miles and miles of tunnels under Budapest. From when people mined for limestone,' Anna explained. 'They're used to store beer now.'

Kirsty had a sudden flashback to Da's colliery. The narrow shafts. The dripping walls. The miners' blackened skin. The smell of coaldust. The sound of trucks being hauled along bumpy surfaces. A feeling of dread settled deep in her bones. Would she be able to cope with going underground? There were so many terrible memories. But then again, they couldn't risk staying in the boathouse for fear of being discovered. A tunnel might be warmer too, although she had no idea where they'd get food.

Anna darted a glance at her. 'There are some caves by Buda Castle – about a mile from here,' she said. 'We once went there when we were small . . .' A sob caught in her throat. She took a deep breath. 'I think I can find the way.'

'All right. It might be worth a try.'

Anna nodded. 'There was talk of a hospital being built over there.'

'A hospital?' Perhaps they could get themselves admitted on the grounds of their ordeal in the Danube. It was quite possible they were suffering from hypothermia. Kirsty tried not to fantasise about a comfortable bed, clean white sheets, hot food. Someone else to look after them. Someone who would make decisions on their behalf. Whenever she'd suffered a crisis in her life before, an adult had been there for her: Da when Ma had died; Maggie when she'd lost Da, then later Jean . . . But she'd been so young then. She and Anna were nineteen now. Adults themselves. And having to make adult decisions.

She stood up again and went over to check on their clothes. They weren't completely dry but they would do. They couldn't wait any longer. 'Come on,' she said. 'Let's get dressed.'

The streets were still full of compacted snow and their 'shoes' offered them little protection as they hobbled along on painful feet. Once Kirsty cried out as she stubbed her toe on a cobble and bolts of pain shot up her leg. White flakes swirled through the icy dark air and their damp clothes began to stiffen on their bodies. Anna stopped several times to catch her breath, her palm to the wall, while Kirsty glanced anxiously around for Arrow Cross men. In the distance she caught sight of a dead horse on its side in the snow. She wondered if it would do for food but concluded it could have been there for weeks. Eating rancid meat, even assuming they were able to cook it, could make them very ill. But the problem of food was one that end-lessly revolved in her mind as Anna led her to the caves. They wound their way upwards, towards the hills of Buda that sloped up to the skyline.

Kirsty had a sudden vision of Jean standing outside the school, looking over towards the hills on the other side of the river. '*I will lift my eyes unto the hills,*' she murmured. '*From whence cometh my help.*'

Anna stopped. 'What did you say?'

'Only a line from the Psalms. It's what Jean said when she was arrested.' Kirsty tried to summon Jean's kind face, her calm expression, her gentle ways. If this terrible war ever ended, she'd try to find out what had happened to her. Maybe even visit her family in Dunscore. The Germans and the Arrow Cross between them had taken almost everyone she and Anna

306

held dear. Thank God for their friendship. She swallowed down the thought that it might be all they had left.

They limped on along the icy paths. The wind clawed their faces as if trying to remove their skin. Every time Kirsty breathed in, freezing needles pierced her nostrils; every time she breathed out her breath created clouds in the thin air. Above the boarded-up shops, wooden signs creaked and rattled.

They passed a young woman of around their own age, in a bulky coat and headscarf, grimacing to see her way ahead through the swirling snow. She shot a glance in their direction but didn't speak to them, or seem to notice their strange foot-wear. Mercifully, they didn't see any soldiers.

Their lips were blue with cold and they were both shivering uncontrollably by the time Anna led them along a windy cob-bled street in the shadow of the castle, and down some stone steps flanked by metal railings. A tunnel stretched ahead with whitewashed, damp walls either side. It was damp underfoot too, but at least the snow hadn't penetrated underground. Kirsty was aware of a musty smell, mixed with something chemical. It was warmer than outside though, and a huge relief to be away from the icy blasts.

'Thank God you remembered where to go,' she said to Anna. 'We'll be safer here.'

Anna nodded. 'What do you think we should do now?'

Kirsty shrugged. 'Follow the tunnel, I suppose.'

As they hobbled along the track, leaving little lumps of impacted snow behind them, their bodies started to thaw in the milder temperature. But the further they got from the entrance, the darker it became, and Kirsty wondered if they'd made the right decision. What if it was a trap and someone was lying in wait for them with a revolver? But if it was, it was a trap they had chosen themselves – no one else knew they were coming. She was sure they hadn't been followed. And what were the alternatives? Chance their luck at the boathouse and almost certainly be discovered? Or stay on the streets and die of cold and hunger? No, it was better they continue, even though she had to force herself to keep going, to suppress the fear that dogged her at every step.

They limped along the path, feeling their way through the increasing darkness by touching the wall as they went. As they did so, Kirsty became aware of a low sound, a little like the sighing of the wind, but more undulating. She stopped to listen.

'That sounds like people talking,' Anna said.

Kirsty strained her ears and the sounds separated. Some were deep and rumbling, others higher pitched, more soothing. 'I think you're right.' There was something about the timbre of the speech, if it was speech, that made her think it was Hungarians talking. Jean had once given her a complicated lesson on poetic metre, which Kirsty hadn't understood at all, but she'd been listening to Hungarian for long enough now to know its cadences. The noises that floated back to her lacked the harsher guttural sounds of German. They were softer, more melodic. She was sure the voices belonged to Budapest citizens. A bubble of hope rose in her chest as they walked on.

It wasn't only the sound of voices that became more pronounced as they continued through the tunnel. The smell became stronger too. An undeniably human stench. Kirsty's stomach churned and she sensed Anna's footsteps slow beside her. What were they about to encounter?

The tunnel twisted several times until at last they came to a cave opening on the right-hand side. This was the source of the noise and the smell. To her amazement the cave was crammed with people lying on makeshift beds, their faces glowing yellow in the flickering lights from candles and lanterns placed on some of the rocky outcrops. The ceiling was low and the brown walls dripped with water.

The girls hovered at the entrance, uncertain what to do. Kirsty was relieved to find warmth and company and, hopefully, food and shelter, but no one was inviting them in.

After a few minutes they were approached by a tall woman, her hair pulled back tightly and a formidable frown across her forehead.

'What do you want?' she demanded, scrutinising them through small dark eyes.

They'd discussed their story on the way, deciding it wasn't safe to tell people about their near escape from the Arrow Cross. You never knew who might be sympathetic to their cause – or prepared to turn them in when they discovered Anna was Jewish.

'We're both orphans,' Kirsty said, sticking to the account they'd concocted. 'Our parents were killed in the bombing. We're starving and homeless.'

The woman nodded. 'I'm sorry for your ordeal,' she said, 'but we can't put you up here. We have no space. The hospital was built to accommodate around seventy patients. We have nearly ten times that now. Too many people coming for sanctuary, or because they are related to someone who's had surgery, or who is really ill. We need to keep the beds for the genuine cases.'

'We're desperate,' said Kirsty. 'Is there anything we can do to earn our keep? We were cooks at a girls' boarding school. We could work in the kitchen. Or assist the nurses.'

'Please . . .' Anna said. 'We have to . . . we have to . . .' Her words clotted and faded, her mouth silently opening and closing. Then her eyes rolled upwards in her head. She stretched out her hand to grab on to Kirsty, missed, and crumpled to the floor, unconscious.

36

'Please help.' A strangled sob caught in Kirsty's throat. Surely she couldn't refuse them now? They were exhausted in mind and body. Kirsty looked around. People were starting to wake up, yawning, and searching for their belongings. It was difficult to tell what time of day it was in the darkness, but it must be morning by now.

The woman grunted. 'I'll see if I can fetch someone.' Even her footsteps sounded indignant as she strode off down the tunnel.

Kirsty squatted beside Anna. Should she try to sit her up or leave her on the floor? Jean would have known what to do. She smoothed back a strand of Anna's hair. Her face was ghostly white, her breath shallow and erratic.

'It's all right, Anna,' she whispered. 'Help is coming.' People were staring at them from across the room as they changed out of their nightwear and started to queue up at a small sink in the corner.

'What can I do?' A girl of about their own age approached. She had lank, dark hair and was wearing a dress several sizes too big for her.

'Could you get some water, for when my friend comes round?'

'Of course.' The girl rushed off.

By the time she returned, clutching a small cup, Anna had regained consciousness but was mumbling confusedly.

Even though she instinctively trusted the girl, Kirsty repeated the account of them being homeless orphans. It was more or less true anyway.

'You poor things,' she said. 'There are so many terrible stories coming out of this war.'

Kirsty nodded. 'We were lucky to survive.' But was it luck behind what really happened, she asked herself. In part probably. But also their own swimming skills. Finding the boathouse had been lucky though, and perhaps also the hospital. Provided, of course, that people were willing to help them here.

'I'm Hajna,' said the girl.

'Kirsty.'

They exchanged weak smiles.

The cross woman returned, bringing a nurse with her. It was a relief to see someone in a blue uniform and starched white apron and cap, with a calm expression. The voices in Kirsty's head, all asking her how they were going to cope, what they were going to do, where they would go if they had to leave the caves, started to quieten at the sight of this reassuring figure.

'Can you help me sit her up?' the nurse asked, stooping down to examine Anna.

Hajna supported Anna's back while Kirsty and the nurse eased her into a seated position. Her skin was still sallow, and there were mauve shadows under her eyes, but her pupils were focussed now and she looked a little brighter. The nurse wrapped a blanket round her shoulders then took her pulse, while Hajna held the cup to her lips.

'Welcome back.' Kirsty squeezed Anna's hand. It felt cold and lifeless. She sandwiched it between her palms and rubbed, trying to inject some warmth into her fingers.

'I'll fetch a stretcher,' the nurse told Anna. 'We need to get you to a bed so we can keep you under observation.'

'May I stay?' Kirsty asked. Thankfully the cross woman had disappeared as soon as she'd brought the nurse.

'Of course,' the nurse replied. 'We'll have to talk to you to find out more about what's happened. And I'm sure you could both do with something to eat.'

Kirsty felt like fainting herself with relief. She had a few hours' reprieve at least. That was enough for now.

Anna was loaded onto a bloodstained, foul-smelling stretcher and taken onto one of the crowded medical wards where they were both given some watery soup. Then Kirsty sat by her side, watching anxiously as she drifted in and out of sleep. Eventually a doctor with puffy, red-ringed eyes came to look at Anna. He listened to her heart with a stethoscope, felt her forehead and checked her breathing. 'She'll be fine in a few days,' he said. 'Just needs some bed rest and good food – assuming we can find some.'

Kirsty thanked the doctor before he stumbled off to look at another patient. It was hot and stuffy on the ward, bunk beds crammed together, the air carrying the stench of disease. The room had a domed ceiling, following the curve of the tunnel, and the central space was full of trolleys and equipment. Many of the patients wore bandages. Nurses with weary expressions rushed up and down, attending to those most sick. At times the murmur of voices and occasional cries of pain were drowned out by the sound of Soviet bombardments. With each explosion, the Red Army was getting closer.

As the days wore on, Anna started to recover, in body if not in mind. Her pale face began to regain some colour and she became able to leave her bed and walk around the ward. Kirsty looked after her as best she could and tried to keep her spirits up.

As Anna gained more strength, she also became more angry. 'What's the point of living any more?' she asked one January day, as they stood in the kitchen together chopping up onions for soup. They'd volunteered their services as cooks as soon as Anna was up to it, and their offer was gladly accepted. No one mentioned them leaving the hospital. And even the cross woman they'd seen on the first day grudgingly acknowledged their usefulness. For the time being at least, it seemed their places were secure. 'Everyone I've ever loved is dead or missing,' said Anna. 'How can I have a future when all the dreams I had have been destroyed? *Abba* will never walk me down the aisle; Mama will never knit clothes for her grandchildren; Endre may never be an uncle . . .'

Kirsty felt weighed down with sadness for her. Her own dreams were in tatters too. She squeezed her friend's arm. 'I'm still here.'

'Yes, you are.' Anna wiped her tears with the back of her hand. 'You've been wonderful and I'm so grateful that you're my friend. You're more like a sister to me now. But I wanted to make my parents proud of me. I thought I'd have years to spend with Endre, caring for our parents together when they got old, being at each other's weddings, introducing our children to their cousins. But now I've no one left to share my memories with.'

'You still might. We have no reason to suppose Endre is dead. He could still be hiding out at your old apartment.' She was trying to convince herself as much as Anna. 'And we can still make new memories, and perhaps one day we'll have husbands and children of our own to share them with.'

'It's all so hard to imagine.' Anna scooped a pile of chopped onion into a pan, then rinsed her hands under the tap.

'Listen, Anna.' Kirsty tried to frame the words in her head first so they came out right. 'There are so many different ways to live a life. You grew up anticipating one way – the traditional way, with your family. But we don't just do things to make our parents and our siblings proud. Ultimately we have to live the best life we can for our own sake. Look at all we've been through. We've been rescued from a train, survived the shootings in Salétrom Street, avoided the explosions at the Glass House, recovered from near death in the Danube. And we're still alive. Perhaps there's a reason for that. Jean would have said that God has a purpose for us. We have to make something of our lives in memory of those who weren't given that chance. And we have to show thugs like Dasco that they can't beat us.'

Anna took a deep breath. She pulled back her shoulders and stood taller. 'Yes,' she said. 'You're right.'

The war news continued to worsen as the Russians advanced. One day they were sitting on their mattress, combing each other's hair in an attempt to remove the ever-present lice, when there was an announcement that everyone was needed to help

315

with a large number of injured soldiers who'd just been brought in. Kirsty and Anna jumped up and made their way to the hospital entrance, flattening themselves against the walls as the stretchers were carried through. Kirsty glanced at one of the casualties, clearly unconscious, with a makeshift bandage round his head. The face belonged to a teenage boy with conker-brown hair and sallow skin. His chin was dotted with pimples and the faintest whisper of stubble. Under the thin blanket, his body was slight. Kirsty swallowed. She watched as more and more injured arrived: young men with still childlike features, bearing adult wounds – a severed foot, huge burn marks, an eye bathed in blood. Some were shaking with shock, others either lifeless or thrashing on their stretchers in agony.

Her heart heaved with pity. 'What on earth's happened?' she asked Anna.

Anna's appalled expression doubtless mirrored her own. 'These aren't soldiers, they're children,' she whispered. 'They should be holding pens, not weapons.'

They found out later that high-school pupils had been taken out of their classrooms, given guns and sent direct to the battlefield, with no experience or training. The army was so desperate for troops they were forcing boys to fight. Cannon fodder really. Hundreds of lads had been killed or injured. The tears rolled down Kirsty's cheeks for the young men who would never again see a Budapest sunrise, or swim in the sun-warmed waters of Lake Balaton or make big plans for a long future.

They continued to stay at the Hospital in the Rock as the Soviets encircled Buda. The fighting became louder and more urgent by the day, gunfire and explosions being heard deep underground. Sometimes, if the bombardment was fierce enough, the whole ward shook, the glasses rattling on the trolleys, pill bottles vibrating in the medicine cabinets. Terrified patients screamed and shuddered, reliving their experiences outside.

Leaving the hospital, even briefly to bring in snow to melt for drinking water, was a dangerous mission, and more than once those doing so failed to return. Bodies piled up near the entrance.

More and more casualties were brought in. The medical staff were stretched to breaking point. There was no time to rest at all now, apart from a few snatched hours of sleep each night. Even delousing became a luxury. Kirsty and Anna were rushed off their feet trying to make the scant food rations stretch further and further, as increasingly people came to the tunnels seeking sanctuary. The girls were constantly serving and clearing away soup and drinks, helping with the wounded, washing clothes that needed to be transferred from the dead to the living. And each day they lived in fear that they would be bombed, demolishing the hospital and destroying all of its occupants. But at least that would be quick. Perhaps an even worse outcome was that all food supplies would dry up in the siege and they'd die a lingering death from starvation.

Seeing those young boys with appalling injuries had been harrowing, but the next influx of patients had Kirsty much more conflicted. She was washing a sick woman one morning, trying to use as little water as possible. There was only one shower between six hundred people, and that was the preserve of the walking wounded. Those who couldn't move had makeshift bed baths, although these were few and far between, with water such a precious commodity. She looked up at the sound of urgent voices, and saw a couple of badly injured men being brought in on stretchers. One had an enormous chest wound, a puddle of red spreading across his green shirt. An Arrow Cross shirt. A doctor was attempting to staunch the flow of blood as the man moaned in agony. The other man was grey skinned, his leg bent at an unnatural angle, bone poking through a huge gash in the skin. Kirsty suppressed a surge of bile. She'd seen many casualties by now, with varying degrees of severity, but it didn't get any easier. There was a reason she'd become a cook and not a nurse. The sight of blood still made her want to retch. But this was more than squeamishness. There was something about the first man that had her stomach curling with revulsion. 'I'll be back in a minute,' she told her patient. She put down her sponge and crept closer. As she took in the bloated face and matted brown hair, she realised her instincts had been right. The man with the chest wound was Dasco.

The doctor drew her a short distance away. 'I don't think this one will last long,' he said, jerking his head towards Dasco. 'He's lost a lot of blood.'

'Do you know what happened?' Kirsty asked.

'It's the Arrow Cross's last stand. They've been fighting the Russians hand to hand in the streets. This chap's been stabbed. Can you comfort him while I try to treat his wounds?'

Acid churned in her belly. How could she sit by the man who had brought her so much grief? How could she hold his hand and reassure him all would be well when she hated him so much? She needed time to process the confusing swirl of feelings. 'I won't be long,' she said. The doctor's expression was baffled as she hurried off.

Anna was further down the ward, reading to a patient. She jumped up at Kirsty's approach. 'Are you all right? You look as though you've seen a ghost.'

Kirsty grimaced. 'I think I have.' She told her about Dasco's arrival and his terrible injury. 'The doctor's asked me to look after him. How can I when all I want to do is kill him?' Kirsty balled her hand into a fist. 'Pretty much everything that's gone wrong in our lives is down to Dasco. He nearly raped me, he murdered your father – and doubtless hundreds of other Jews. And if it wasn't for him and his kind, your mother might still be alive.'

Anna's mouth was hard, her eyes seething. 'I know. He accused us of being vermin, but it's Dasco who's the real scum of the earth.' She folded the book on her lap then stared into the middle distance for a few seconds. Different emotions flitted across her face as if she was wrestling with some inner turmoil. 'But what would Jean have done?' she asked at last.

It was a fair question, and one that brought Kirsty's thoughts juddering to a halt, sending them off in a different direction. 'I suppose she'd have said to turn the other cheek.'

Anna's expression was more thoughtful now. 'There's a verse in the Talmud that says, "Whoever destroys a single life is as guilty as though he had destroyed the entire world. And whoever rescues a single life earns as much merit as though he had rescued the entire world".'

Kirsty nodded. Despite his atrocious actions, Dasco was still a human being, Mária's son, the man who'd given them half a chance of survival when they'd been lined up at the Danube. It was ironic that she'd resisted the urge to drive her knife into him that day in the kitchen, only to have him come into the hospital with a stab wound. She took a deep breath. 'You're right, Anna. Much as it costs me, I'll go back and sit with him.'

She returned to the doctor, determined to do all she could to help save Dasco. She had to steel herself to pick up his hand, ignoring the animal reek that came from his body and resisting the temptation to recoil with disgust. She clasped the still-fleshy fingers and tried to blank out the pounding of blood in her ears. The doctor acknowledged her briefly then carried on trying to stem the flow of blood.

Dasco half turned his head towards her. His eyes locked on to hers but he didn't speak.

She told herself that Dasco was just another casualty in this terrible war. Admittedly, a casualty who deserved all he got for his hate-filled attitudes and barbaric behaviour. He and Endre had just been two young men – but one hated violence and the other embraced it. Neither had escaped unscathed.

'You've done some terrible things, Dasco,' she said, 'but I won't leave you on your own.'

'I'm sorry about Jean,' he said.

Her stomach tightened. *Jean?* What about her?' If Dasco had something to do with Jean she'd have to stop herself throttling him with her bare hands.

'I . . . told . . . the . . . Gestapo . . . about . . . her.' Every word was forced out, his chest rising and falling with effort.

Bolts of fury charged up and down her body. 'Where is she now?'

'Put on a train – full of Jews – Poland.'

'Where in Poland?'

'Auschwitz.'

*'Auschwitz?'*

'Prison camp. Very . . . bad . . . place. No one returns.' Dasco's features contracted in a pain-filled grimace. Tears sprang into Kirsty's eyes. Their worst fears were confirmed. Never again would Jean pacify an anxious pupil, or take Kirsty shopping to the market, or listen with her to the wireless. Never again would she brush a fallen strand of hair off her forehead, or kiss Kirsty's cheek, bringing with her the faintest scent of cold cream. And it was all down to Dasco. He must have reported Jean to the Germans in revenge for her beating him off in the kitchen that day. The bloody murderer. For all those months they'd held out the faintest shred of hope that somehow Jean had survived. With a few words, Dasco had crushed that hope.

She wanted to hurl his body from the stretcher, then bash his head on the ground again and again, until his skull cracked open. Or drive a fist into his flabby face, or shout at him until the last words he heard were 'rot in hell'. No reprisal was too extreme for what he'd done. Poor innocent Jean. Had she paid the greatest price for Kirsty's actions that day in the kitchen? Her life sacrificed for Kirsty's?

But gradually the red mist thinned. Would murdering Dasco bring Jean back, satisfying though it might be to punish him? And would Jean condone that? Anna was right – not that she'd known the extent of Dasco's wickedness. Killing him would only make her equally culpable, and Jean would have been horrified. She tried to breathe slowly, in and out, while she considered what to do.

'Forgive me,' Dasco said.

Kirsty dipped her head in silent acknowledgment of his words. She wasn't going to give him absolution, but nor was she going to give him the drubbing he deserved. He'd have another judge soon.

Something flickered in Dasco's eyes and she felt a slight pressure on her fingers. Then there was a spurt of bright red from his mouth and he lay still.

The doctor sighed heavily. 'We've lost him.'

She extricated her hand. Already his features were softening, his mouth slack, his expression unfocussed. The life had gone.

The doctor shrugged. His skin was grey, his eyes sunken in his face. 'We did all we could.'

Like an automaton, Kirsty helped him cover Dasco's body, then wheel the other man into theatre before returning to her own patient. It was hard to know how she felt. Anger still simmered in the pit of her stomach, compounding the grief. But there was calmness too. She'd done the right thing at the end.

Jean would have been proud of her.

## 37

February 1945

The Russians tightened their grip on the city. The hospital was running out of supplies: bread became scarce and patients and staff were reduced to one cup of soup a day each; newborn babies were placed in suitcases as the cots were all occupied; soiled bandages were removed from corpses to bind the living wounded. Everyone was infested with lice. It was so dangerous to go outside that waste couldn't be emptied. Buckets overflowed with excrement, the stench in the hospital almost unbearable. The electricity often went off for hours at a time, plunging people into darkness. Kirsty and Anna stumbled through each day famished and exhausted.

But by the middle of February, something changed.

'Do you hear that?' Kirsty asked as she sat trying to spoon soup into the mouth of a severely ill patient, whilst Anna was winding wool into a ball beside her. The nurses took jumpers from dead patients, washed and unravelled them, then knitted them into new garments. Anna and Kirsty were frequently asked to help.

'What?'

'Silence.'

Anna stopped winding. 'You're right. I haven't heard any explosions for a while.'

'Or gunshots, nor the sound of tanks . . .'

Anna stood up and the ball dropped to the floor. 'I'll go and find out what's happened.'

She returned a few minutes later, looking thunderstruck. 'Budapest has surrendered. Apparently the Arrow Cross government has fallen and Ferenc Szálasi has fled to the West.'

Kirsty slumped in her chair. 'And the Russians?'

'In control.'

'So what does that mean?'

Anna sat down and retrieved the wool. 'No one knows, but effectively the fighting is over.'

'So we're free?'

Anna gave a fragile smile. 'I suppose we are. I hardly dare believe it. We can finally look for Endre.'

Kirsty thought of that time at the mine, when she'd hoped against hope that Da was still alive. All those hours of trying to convince herself, when all the time he was lying dead in a tunnel. She and Anna had endlessly discussed their plans for after the war, but had they just been building castles in the air? Their faint hopes for Jean had been unfounded. In spite of everything, could Endre have survived? There'd been no word of him all the time they'd been in the Hospital in the Rock. Not that he could have known they were there, and it had been too dangerous to go back to Pest to track him down. Anything could have happened in the meantime. He'd been in such a bad way when they'd last seen him, and the fighting on the streets was so fierce. What if he'd gone outside and got caught in the crossfire? What if Dasco had tracked him down, or betrayed him to other Arrow Cross members? Dasco had confessed to betraying Jean, which had ultimately led to her death, but what if he was indirectly responsible for Endre's too? It was a thought that tormented her every waking moment. Often it haunted her dreams too. But at long last she would finally know.

It didn't seem right to speak about their plans in front of a patient, even a barely conscious one, and Kirsty had a feeling this would be a long discussion. 'Let's talk about it later.'

Once they were on their own in the kitchen, washing up after another meagre meal, they fell upon the subject again. 'Where shall we go first?' Kirsty said. 'I still can't believe we can leave.' She looked round the tiny room with its assortment of battered and burnt pans, chipped cups and tarnished cutlery. It was a miracle how they managed to cook for so many.

Anna picked up a grimy tea towel and started drying some spoons. 'I think we should go back to my parents' apartment, in case Endre's still there. It's unlikely, but . . .' She took a short, shaky breath.

Kirsty gently took the spoons from her hands and put them in the drawer. 'Yes, let's go there. It would give us somewhere to live. And even if Endre's not at the apartment, someone might know something.' She blinked away the vision of a neighbour sadly informing them of Endre's death. So many people they loved were no longer with them: Jean . . . Mr and Mrs Bellak . . . Margit . . . Szalók and Tünde . . . the children's mother, Évi . . . *Please let Endre still be alive*, she pleaded for the thousandth time.

Anna picked up a cloth and wiped down the sink. 'How are

we going to get back to Pest?' The Germans had blown up all the bridges so it wouldn't be straightforward. Their belongings were still at the Glass House and they were hoping that Elza and Vera would have kept them safe. 'I've heard there are boats,' Kirsty said. 'We'll see if we can book a passage.'

Although they were desperate to leave, they owed it to the hospital staff who'd been so kind to them to help move the patients and supplies back to Saint John's, the main hospital which had been diverted underground for the duration of the war. They also applied for, and were granted, new papers to replace those lost in the river.

The whole process took another few weeks but by early May, buoyed up by the news that Germany had surrendered and that the war was finally over, they booked their passage back to Pest, and the new life that awaited.

Despite the soft spring air and the bright blossom on the trees, it was hard to avoid the sights of devastation. Budapest was in ruins: buildings destroyed, rubble everywhere, gaping holes where houses had been, mangled pipes and looping wires hanging from walls. A fine grey dust still powdered the air. Anna and Kirsty picked their way through the potholes and cracks in the broken streets, appalled at the slaughter of their beautiful city.

'It's all so awful,' Anna said, wiping her cheeks with the back of her hand as they skirted round a pile of buckled metal and broken bricks.

They made their way down to the Danube and stood on the bank with a large group of people. The last time they were by the river it had been winter. Now May sunshine glinted off the water, and the sky was a kaleidoscope of white clouds. Next to Kirsty, Anna started to shiver.

'Are you all right?'

Anna nodded but her face was grey.

Like her, Anna would be remembering the shoes lined up on the bank, the gut-wrenching sound of gunfire, the bodies tumbling into the water. Her breath caught in her chest. They had to be strong, for those who didn't survive, as much as for themselves.

The crowd surged forward as the boat arrived, a middle-aged man standing at the helm. It was a rickety old vessel, more rust than metal. Kirsty wondered how on earth it would get them all safely to the other side. The man jumped ashore and fastened the boat to a mooring on the bank. Then he started helping people climb aboard: mothers with young babies, older children, then an elderly couple who looked alarmed when the boat lurched as they got on. Kirsty and Anna, possibly the most able bodied despite their ordeals, waited until last.

'Bunch up,' said the man, acknowledging them and gesturing to two children sitting on the middle seat to move closer together. Then he held out his hand. 'Fares please. That's five *pengő* each.'

Kirsty handed over two blue notes. It was a huge amount. The hospital had given them some welfare money when they left, but that was intended to tide them over for the next few weeks. They never dreamt they'd need to give so much to the skipper. They climbed aboard, carrying the scant possessions they'd brought with them, and wedged themselves next to the children. The boat, already low in the water, dropped a couple of inches.

'All right,' said the man. 'Let's go.' He untied the ropes, jumped back on board, then started the engine. The boat chugged forward slowly.

At first Kirsty enjoyed the sun on her skin, the wind ruffling her hair, the space and light around them. But then Anna nudged her and pointed to the side. River water was slopping over the edge of the boat, splashing the people sitting closest to it. The engine started to make a groaning noise. Kirsty glanced at the man. He was frowning.

'What's the matter?' Kirsty asked.

The man wiped his forehead with the back of his hand. 'Too many passengers. The boat's struggling.'

To the girls' alarm, the front of the boat started to tilt, sending more water over the sides. One of the children screamed and her mother shushed her. A red-faced baby began to wail.

People were looking worried now, shuffling around on the seats and rearranging their belongings.

'Are we going to make it?' Kirsty asked.

The man looked even more concerned. 'I shouldn't have allowed so many people to get on. Should have left some in Buda and come back for them. Stupid of me.'

Or greedy, Kirsty thought. 'What are you going to do?' She looked anxiously across to the far bank. It was a long way away.

'I don't know. The boat's just too heavy. We're close to capsizing.'

Kirsty moved closer to Anna and spoke in a low voice. 'Without us on board the boat will float higher in the water. It might just be enough to get them across. We can't let it capsize. Those poor children and babies. We don't know if their mothers can swim.'

'But we can.' Anna's eyes were bright.

'And we've done it before.'

Anna nodded. 'We can leave our things on the boat then collect them later.'

'Yes. We'll keep some clothes on, for modesty's sake.' The hospital had given them spare garments soon after they'd arrived. They'd taken them gratefully, knowing better than to ask where they'd come from. Kirsty took off her cardigan, leaving a grubby blouse underneath, then removed her shoes, a tremor running through her at the memory of the last time she'd done that. Anna followed suit.

They explained to the skipper what they were going to do and he nodded with relief. 'Thank you. We might just make it now.'

'We'll expect a refund,' Anna said as she climbed over the side.

Kirsty followed her into the water, gulping at the initial clench of cold, then relaxing as her muscles eased into their familiar routine. They struck out for the bank, the coolness cloaking their bodies and freeing their minds, sluicing away the horrors of the past. As they sliced across the sparkling water, the warm sun beat down on their heads and shoulders.

There was something wise and timeless about the river and the secrets it held, some happy, some tragic.

But who knew what awaited them on the other side?

## 38

The stairwell of the Bellaks' old apartment was even grimier than the last time Kirsty and Anna had been there, the stairs dusty, the air stagnant.

Thankfully the back door was open, as both Anna's keys to her old home were still at the Glass House where they'd left them that fateful day. It might have been sensible to go there first, but they were both so desperate to see Endre they decided to risk going straight to the apartment.

Anna's eyes were huge with apprehension as she knocked on the door. That too was much scruffier than Kirsty remembered, and she wondered fleetingly when someone had last polished the metalwork, it was so dull and tarnished.

There was a long silence, then the faint sound of footsteps and a blurred shape appeared behind the frosted glass. Kirsty's heart leapt in her chest. Endre was there! Her body tingled with anticipation. Soon she would see his dear face again.

Her pulse raced as someone fiddled with the lock. Hurry up. Hurry up, she willed him.

But the door opened to reveal a middle-aged woman with tightly curled hair and a thin mouth. 'Yes?'

A hard ball of disappointment formed in Kirsty's stomach.

Anna took a step back, her expression full of dismay. 'Who are you?'

The woman sniffed. 'The owner.'

'No you're not,' Anna shouted. 'This is my house, I lived here with my parents and brother. We own the jeweller's shop downstairs.'

'Not any more you don't.' There wasn't a shred of compassion in the woman's expression.

'How dare you?' Kirsty said. 'This property belongs to the Bellak family.'

'Jews?'

Anna nodded.

'They won't be needing it now then, will they?'

'Mr and Mrs Bellak are dead,' Kirsty said. 'But their children are alive and will be coming back to live here.' A bolt of resentment shot through her. Was that appalling woman sitting in Endre and Anna's parents' apartment looking at their silver-framed photographs, eating food from their beautiful plates, reading their leather-bound books?

'Then they'll have to fight me for it,' said the woman, and the door was shut firmly in their faces.

Anna aimed a kick at the wood, then turned to Kirsty with an agonised expression. 'What now?'

'We'll get your home back,' Kirsty assured her. 'But I suspect it will take time. And we don't know what the Russians will do.' Kirsty didn't like to add that the Communists could be just as harsh towards the Jews as the Nazis were. 'In the meantime, let's go back to the Glass House and get our things.'

They made their way wearily back down the stairs and into the street.

\* \* \*

331

Kirsty told Anna a little more of her feelings for Endre on the journey. Now the war was over, surely the anti-Jewish laws would be revoked? If Endre was still alive they'd be planning their future together, and Anna would be a part of that; if not, then she still needed to tell Anna how deeply she loved her brother. She was worried Anna would be hostile, as she was when he'd been sent back to join his unit, but she just gave a weary smile. 'I'd wondered as much.'

'And you don't mind?'

'If Endre is alive, I'd be delighted to see the two of you together.' Her face had a pinched look; weariness and dejection tugged at the corners of her eyes. 'If not, then I'm glad he at least found love.'

Kirsty squeezed her hand and they walked on through the darkening streets above which a flush of pink and orange still lingered on the horizon, the distant hills of Buda turning into silhouettes. *I will lift my eyes unto the hills*, Jean had said. *From whence cometh my help*.

If ever they needed help it was now.

By the time they reached the Glass House, the sky was velvet-black, bats flying low over the roofs of the parliament building. As they walked down Vadász Street, Kirsty saw two flags at the entrance, one a white cross on a red background, the other a red cross edged in white with thinner lines radiating out, all on a blue background.

'The British flag,' Kirsty murmured.

'Alongside the Swiss one,' Anna added. 'It must be some kind of signal to the Russians: keep away.'

Kirsty's heart heaved with an emotion too big to identify.

Her own country's flag. Plucky old Britain who'd helped win the war. Was this a good omen?

Another door. Another anxious wait. This time their knock was answered by an elderly man with a balding head and stooping gait, a pair of heavy-rimmed spectacles perched on his nose.

Kirsty explained they'd once stayed at the Glass House, and told him about their ordeals since. 'We've come to collect our things,' she said. 'But more importantly, to find out if my friend's brother is here. Endre Bellak?'

The man thought for a bit then shook his head. 'I'm sorry, my dears, that doesn't sound familiar.'

Again the tight knot of disappointment, threatening to harden into grief.

Kirsty felt Anna swaying beside her, pale faced in the gathering darkness. 'Please,' she said. 'He's tall and thin with dark hair . . .'

The man shook his head again. The description could have fitted any number of young Jewish men. 'But do come in,' he said, opening the door wide. 'You're welcome to stay as long as you want. And of course, you need to locate your belongings. Can you find the way?'

They followed him into the hallway then continued on their own to their old dormitory in the Hungarian Football Federation headquarters. The room was empty, no sign of Elza or Vera, only a saggy mattress propped up against the wall testament to their shared intimacy for all those months.

Anna looked round the room, her eyes bleak with sadness. At length she pointed to a little pile in the corner. 'Is that our stuff?'

Kirsty went over. Sure enough, there were their clothes, the photo of Anna's family, even the keys to the Bellaks' apartment – not that they were of any use to them now. Maybe one day. She handed the picture to Anna who pressed it to her lips, then passed it back to Kirsty while she wiped her eyes. Kirsty looked at the young, carefree Endre smiling into the camera, and her stomach twisted. *Where was he?*

There was a noise at the door. Kirsty turned round. A young man about Endre's age appeared.

'Samuel,' Anna said.

It was the runner from when the Glass House had been raided by Nyilas and Nazi soldiers. He'd come into the basement to warn them not to move or talk for fear of discovery. Kirsty remembered the hours of fear, the cramps in her motionless legs, the growls of hunger.

Samuel beckoned them forwards. 'Come with me.'

They followed him back to the entrance hall, and into a small office where another young man sat hunched over a typewriter. A man with dark hair and dark eyes. A man whose body was thin and gaunt. A man who jumped up at the sight of them, enveloping Anna in a hug while his arm reached out to draw Kirsty in.

Finally . . . incredibly . . . wonderfully . . .

Endre.

## 39

Kirsty watched Endre as he spoke. He looked familiar yet different. The soft contours of his face were firmer, his jawline tighter. There were dark shadows under his eyes. But he didn't pluck at the hair on the back of his hands, or stare, terrified, into space. He was more the Endre she'd once known than the deranged creature he'd become.

He told them he'd eventually decided to leave his parents' apartment and join them at the Glass House. But he got there only to find Anna and Kirsty had vanished. All anyone could tell him was that they set off to see him at the Bellaks' old home but had never returned. He was horrified to hear of the shootings at the Danube and their narrow escape.

'What a mercy you are good swimmers.' His deep brown eyes were full of compassion.

Kirsty nodded. 'And only this morning we swam back from Buda to Pest.' She explained how they left the boat to prevent it from capsizing.

Endre ran his hands through his hair. '*Baruch Hashem*,' he said. *Thanks be to God*.

Anna hugged Endre again. 'What a miracle we found you.' She told him about their visit to their old apartment and their hostile reception by the new occupant.

'Perhaps I should have stayed there,' Endre replied. 'We might still have our home and all our things.'

Kirsty shook her head. 'I'm sorry about your home but you'd have been in even more danger. We'll fight to get that awful woman out.'

'What have you been doing in the Glass House?' Anna asked.

Endre shrugged. 'After the war ended, I stayed on here to help with the business.' He frowned. 'Arthur Weiss was captured by the Arrow Cross and has never returned.'

Kirsty remembered a man with thinning hair and a pleasant expression. 'Poor man. He helped save so many people.'

'Probably thousands,' Endre said. 'And doubtless lost his own life in the process.' His shoulders slumped with sadness.

'So what now?' Anna asked.

Endre's expression was bleak. 'I'm not sure I want to stay in Budapest.'

A sharp intake of breath from Anna. 'Why not?'

'So many awful memories.'

'But you've got us back now. And what about your work at the Glass House?' Anna asked.

'I was happy to help them out, and it gave me time to search for you, but I trained to be a watchmaker and that's what I want to do. Jewellery design too in time. There are plenty of other people working here. Samuel for instance.'

Samuel had melted away once he'd reunited them but he must still be somewhere in the building.

A thought occurred to her. 'How come Samuel tracked you down when the old man who let us in didn't seem to know you?'

Endre avoided their eyes. 'I changed my name. The man wouldn't have known me as Endre Bellak.'

'What did you change it to?' Anna asked.

'McClean.'

'But that's Kirsty's name!' Anna said.

Endre smiled at her sheepishly. 'I hope you don't mind. After everything, I wanted a new start. Adopting a new name was part of that.'

'But why choose mine?' Kirsty said.

Endre took her hand and a ripple of desire ran through her. 'Do you still have the ring I gave you?'

'It disintegrated.'

'I'll design you a new one.' He threaded his elegant watch-maker's fingers through hers and her body tingled again in response. 'If you still want me, we can get married. Then we can choose to be Bellaks or McCleans!'

Anna laughed. 'That's wonderful.' Then her expression changed. 'But will you be allowed to marry?'

'We'll be allowed to in Scotland,' Endre said.

'*Scotland*?'

Endre's expression was full of hope. 'How would you feel about that?'

Memories flickered in Kirsty's mind: the Scottish hills, alive with heather, the brackish waters of the Clyde, even the once-familiar smell of the Hamilton baths. She let the memories settle. There was none of the usual queasiness she associated with thoughts of her homeland. Endre was offering her a new life and a new hope. She could face going back if he was with her. She'd no longer be the poor little orphan; she'd be a grown woman returning with her fiancé. 'All right. If you're sure you want to make a life there.'

Endre smiled. 'I assume they have jewellers in Scotland?'

'Of course. But what about your father's business?'

The smile faded. 'I'm going to set up Bellak and Son over there. Then I won't be spending every day wondering if the windows will be smashed or slogans daubed on the door.'

'There are keelie scum in Hamilton too you know,' Kirsty said.

'But they're not Nazis. Or Arrow Cross.'

'No.' But what about Anna? She turned to her friend, 'You'll come with us, won't you? You could keep up with your swimming there. I could even be your coach.'

Anna frowned. 'Maybe one day,' she said. 'But I don't feel ready to leave Budapest just yet. It's our last contact with *Abba* and Mama. I need time to mourn them properly. Going to Scotland right now would feel like I'd deserted them.'

Kirsty's heart heaved at the thought of leaving Anna. It would be like losing a limb. Much as she wanted to be with Endre, how could she leave her dearest friend behind? Her own instincts back in 1939 had been to turn her back on the horror of Da's death and start life anew in Hungary. But clearly Anna felt the need to remain closer to her parents by staying.

'I was hoping we'd all go together,' Endre said, his face falling. 'How can I desert you when I've only just got you back?'

'It may not be for long. We can write. And visit.'

Kirsty squeezed Endre's warm, strong fingers. 'We'll help you reclaim the apartment,' she said. 'And you'll keep up with your swimming? You've got too much potential to waste it.'

'Of course,' Anna replied.

'Right then,' Endre said, finally releasing her hand. 'There's a lot to be done.'

A month later, Kirsty, Endre and Anna stood on the platform at Keleti station. It had been a rush to organise Endre's papers, but thankfully everything went smoothly. They had their tickets in their hands, and they'd soon be travelling through Austria, Germany and Belgium en route to Scotland. Kirsty blinked back an image of a *wee skelf of a lassie* stumbling off the train with Jean, frightened and exhausted after their harrowing journey. Perhaps it was as well her former self didn't know of the trials to come. But there were good memories too: the happy times with Jean, meeting Endre, getting to know Anna. Their friendship had floundered when Anna had blamed Kirsty for Endre's return to forced labour, but now they were as close as ever. It would be such a wrench to be parted from her.

'Will you be all right?' she asked Anna, yet again.

Anna nodded, her eyes huge. 'Promise you'll write?'

'Of course. And you'll write back?'

'Definitely.'

'But we don't know how things will turn out with the Russians,' Kirsty said, suddenly frightened for her friend. She thought back to the war when Endre had used a secret language to evade the censor. 'Let's have a code.' What word would work? *Vörösmarty . . . Jean . . . Scotland . . .* None of them felt quite right. Then it came to her. 'If you're ever in trouble, just mention Lake Balaton. I'll know that's a signal for help.' Anna darted her a worried glance but all conversation was abandoned as the train hissed into the station in a cloud of billowing white smoke.

Endre helped Kirsty aboard, and stowed their cases in the overhead rack, then they stood waving out of the window until Anna became a small speck in the distance.

She wiped her eyes as Endre reached for her hand. She leaned against him, reassured by the bulk of his shoulders and the warmth of his coat against her cheeks. 'A new life, and new hope,' she murmured.

# 40

Kirsty sat at Maggie's kitchen table, where she'd learnt to cook all those years ago, nibbling at the end of her pen, a sheet of foolscap paper in front of her. There was so much to write that she hardly knew where to start.

> *Dearest Anna,*
>   *Endre and I have arrived safely in Scotland. It was a long journey but thankfully a lot smoother than the trip Jean and I made back in 1939. I'd forgotten how beautiful Scotland is in the summer. The hills are ablaze with heather, the skies a brilliant blue . . .*

She stared out of the window. There was a greenfinch on Maggie's bird table, pecking at some left-over seeds she'd put out after she and Kirsty had made a seedcake that morning. He darted at the food with his beak, looked around, pecked at some more, then flew away.

She'd written to Maggie before they'd left Budapest and Maggie had been overjoyed to hear from her, having imagined the worst after so many years of silence. She was a widow now. Archie had died of liver disease back in '43, the drink

341

having finally got him. Maggie told them they were welcome to stay as long as they needed. 'No hanky-panky, mind,' she'd said, in her typical forthright fashion when she met them at the bus stop. 'You can bunk up with me, and Endre can have our Susan's old room.' Her face was thinner than Kirsty remembered and her hair more grey than brown, but she was still full of energy – always busy, particularly now she had extra guests.

They'd been there a week now. She'd tried to teach Endre some English on the train, but his attempts at pronunciation had made her laugh. She acted as interpreter whenever he wanted to speak to Maggie. Maggie had waved away their offers to pay for their bed and board. 'Wait until you're on your feet,' she said. She was still working at the baths and had a widow's pension too. She wasn't well off but she assured them she could manage for a bit. Kirsty was relieved; it meant Endre could concentrate on learning the language instead of having to find a job straight away. His plan was to work at a jeweller's until they'd put aside enough money to buy their own business. It might take them years, but he was determined. And there was a wedding to save for too.

Kirsty picked up her pen.

*I have a little piece of news. I went back to the Hamilton baths to see if there was any work available. They agreed to give me a few hours a week on reception, which will help tide us over until Endre can get a job. But the really exciting thing is, they're running swimming classes there now, and they're going to pay for me to train as a coach. I'll have to reimburse them of course, as soon as I start earning, but it's a wonderful opportunity.*

The dream of teaching swimming burned bright again. She loved cooking, but swimming was where her real passion lay. Helping Anna overcome her fears at Balaton, and seeing her skills develop, had made her realise how much she loved teaching. Hamilton was where Da had taught swimming. She'd be honouring his memory by carrying on his work, and Endre was happy for her to pursue the ambition she'd cherished for so long.

Ten days later, a reply arrived from Anna:

> *Dearest Endre and Kirsty,*
>
> *I'm so pleased you've arrived safely and that you are happy living with Kirsty's friend. I'm afraid there's still no news on our old apartment but I'm allowed to stay on at the Glass House for as long as I want.*
>
> *I'm delighted to hear you're going to train as a swimming coach, Kirsty. Last week I plucked up courage to go back to the baths in Szőnyi út, and – guess what – I was actually admitted. There is a Russian trainer there now, and when he saw my times, and realised how good I was, he invited me on to their competition team. It seems you were right all along!*

Kirsty was jubilant. She felt guilty that they'd not managed to reclaim the Bellaks' old apartment as they'd promised. It was as she'd feared: the Russians were almost as hostile to the Jews as the Germans had been. It was a mercy they still allowed Anna to swim. They must have been sufficiently impressed by her talent to overlook their prejudice. Perhaps they'd provide her with accommodation eventually. Kirsty wondered whether her friend would one day find a young man of her own and know the happiness Kirsty now felt.

But she still missed Anna, and the life they'd had at the school. She missed Jean too. Even more so now they were in Scotland. And she had a pilgrimage to make. One she wrote to Anna about a few days later.

*Endre and I went over to Dunscore today . . .*

They'd gone on the bus, bumping and swaying over the narrow roads, past moss-covered walls, rows of copper beeches and streams that glinted in the sunlight as they watched the highland cattle with their shaggy coats and long horns staring at them from the fields, and pheasants strutting in the undergrowth. They'd walked hand in hand from the bus stop, past the old mill, then up towards the browny-orange church situated in a sea of gravestones. This was where Jean had gone as a child, walking with her father and sisters along the road she'd once referred to as *the black brae*, because of the number of black-clad visitors that went up and down it. They'd met with the minister of Craig Church, as arranged by letter a few days previously. Kirsty didn't feel she could cope with meeting Jean's family yet but the minister knew the Mathisons well and promised to pass on the news. The Church of Scotland had informed them of Jean's death in Auschwitz, but no other details. So she told the minister, in a voice thick with sadness, of Jean's selfless care for her pupils and staff, her warm friendship, her quiet dignity in the face of hardship. The tears rolled down her cheeks as she described Jean's arrest and imprisonment, and finally, her deportation to Poland. The minister listened gravely. 'I'll tell the Mathisons they can be proud of their lass.' He wiped his cheek with his thumb. 'She was indeed a martyr.'

The journey home was quiet and sad, she and Endre each lost in their own thoughts. The minister had talked of the village building a memorial to Jean. It would be a fitting tribute to the woman who had given up her life to help others.

The letters from Anna continued. Her swimming was coming on well. She'd won the hundred metres freestyle race at a meet held on Margaret Island. 'A gold medal, can you believe it?' Kirsty told Endre, glowing with pride. Then there were bigger competitions, bigger stakes and bigger prizes.

Kirsty told Anna what was happening in Hamilton. Endre's English had progressed sufficiently for him to apply for, and be offered, a job at a Glasgow jeweller's. He went there on the bus each day. Eventually they'd saved up enough to contemplate renting a small flat, even though Maggie had told them they were welcome to stay as long as they wanted. Kirsty continued to do her coaching training, gaining more and more qualifications along the way. They'd wanted to hold off the wedding until Anna could come across to be bridesmaid, but she said to go ahead without her – the Russians were clamping down on people travelling. And truth be told it was becoming ever harder for Endre and Kirsty to pull away from each other after their lingering goodbyes on the landing each evening, his body pressed against hers, the warmth of his lips, her insides turning liquid, the desire to surrender to him so strong. In the end they had a small ceremony at the church where Da's funeral had been held – with Reverend Murray officiating, Maggie as maid of honour and a traditional blessing to acknowledge Endre's heritage. They were a married couple at last.

Over the next few months, Anna's letters became less

frequent and then stopped altogether. Kirsty and Endre were increasingly worried. In March 1946 they listened on the wireless to Winston Churchill's chilling speech from America: *From Stettin in the Baltic, to Trieste in the Adriatic, an iron curtain has descended across the continent.* The whole of Eastern Europe was under Soviet control. Anna was now behind this 'iron curtain', her beloved country having been taken over by the Communists. Doubtless all letters from the West were intercepted. Anxiety for her friend and her fellow countrymen constantly ravaged Kirsty's thoughts. Endre talked about going back to Hungary to check on her as soon as they could afford it.

Then one day, after weeks without news, Kirsty saw an envelope on the mat with Anna's familiar handwriting on the front. Her breath caught in her throat as she tore it open. Only one sheet of thin blue paper. No address, no name at the bottom, just one word in Anna's immaculate copperplate:

*Balaton.*

# 41

1948: The Empire Pool, Wembley

Kirsty's plan was fraught with danger. She could lose her job, Anna could lose her freedom – possibly even her life – but they'd faced worse. They'd only have one chance. They needed to get everything right.

As Kirsty entered the pool area for the Olympic opening ceremony, along with the other Great Britain coaches, all her senses were heightened. First came the familiar sharpness of chlorine, laced with something earthy, like sweaty gym shoes that have languished too long in a locker. Her stomach twisted with anticipation. She hadn't expected the noise of the crowd: a terrifying, unintelligible roar, as if the whole arena was a pulsing, living being, insatiable with excitement. It drowned out the pounding of blood in her ears and sent electrical charges through her body.

She risked a glance back. Was that Anna, staring straight ahead and with a fixed expression? Deep down she'd be as nervous and excited as she was. The next few days were crucial. Whether or not Anna would win a medal was down to her own performance and those of the other competitors – but her freedom lay in Kirsty's hands.

Endre was still in Scotland. Desperate though he was to see his sister, his presence might have complicated their escape – and as a coach Kirsty had access to areas Endre didn't. If all went well they'd be with him soon.

Kirsty took her seat in the stands. Anna was stronger looking and broader than when she'd last seen her, with the distinctive triangular shoulders and narrow waist of a highly trained swimmer. She nodded to the crowd as she was announced, then stepped onto her starting block. A hush descended and the atmosphere sharpened. Then the starter fired the gun. The sound transported Kirsty back to the Danube all those years ago. Two terrified girls trembling on a river bank and another gun being fired. A gun that pitched them into the water and a frantic bid for survival. This swim was for sport, and the glory of winning, but today could prove just as crucial as their wartime ordeal.

Anna powered through the water, her face a mask of determination, inching ahead of her competitors until her fingers touched the end a fraction before the others. When the cheer went up from the crowd, Kirsty felt buoyed up with pride. A new Olympic record. And the path to glory had been laid all those years ago at Lake Balaton.

She hurried down to the competitors' area as Anna came through from her race.

'Congratulations,' she said formally. It was important no one suspected a connection.

Anna's cheeks were flushed but she was strangely solemn for someone who'd just swum the race of her life. 'Thank you.' She leaned forward. 'Do you have a plan?'

'I do.' Kirsty had checked and fine-tuned the details. 'You

need to pretend to feel sick after the final. I'll meet you in the toilets nearest to your team's changing room.'

Anna nodded quickly and carried on.

Anna recorded a slower time in the semi-final and Kirsty wondered whether the tension surrounding her intended escape was affecting her. But she'd still qualified for the final. So far, everything was going well.

The final was scheduled for 3 August, three days later. As Kirsty tried to get off to sleep the night before, she went over the details in her head. She'd considered so many different options and this was the best she'd come up with. But it wasn't foolproof. There was still so much that could go wrong. Terrible scenarios flashed through her mind as she tossed and turned: Hungarian officials getting wind of their plans, Anna being sent back and imprisoned, Kirsty being arrested. *Keep calm*, she told herself. She'd be no good to Anna in this state.

She'd already briefed her deputy coach to take over in the event of her sudden disappearance.

The race was a closely fought one. Anna was in contention for the first two lengths, but seemed to tire towards the end, allowing three competitors to slip past her. She came fourth. Her team mate got the bronze medal. Perfect. Kirsty felt a pang of regret for Anna, whose dream of an Olympic win was over – at least this time. But all the attention would be on the other girl's success. Communists didn't like losers. Anna could sidle away unnoticed. It would be easier to execute their plan.

Her chest tight with nerves, Kirsty picked up her bag from the changing room and went into one of the toilets. There, she took off her British team tracksuit, replacing it with a drab skirt and blouse topped by a white overall. She was still wearing her plimsolls but they'd have to do. Then she fitted the brown, curly wig she'd bought from a Glasgow hairdresser the week before. She put her tracksuit in the bag, on top of the other item. After checking her appearance in the mirror, she ducked into the cubicle again to wait unnoticed. It was strange to be dressed as a cleaner once more. She hadn't worn a uniform like this since she was fourteen.

After about five minutes the door banged open. Kirsty tensed, her heart hammering against her rib cage. She held her breath as someone entered the toilet, locked the door, then relieved themselves. She seemed to take an age washing her hands and checking her appearance. Finally, the girl left. Kirsty let her breath out slowly.

The door opened again, more quietly this time. Anxiety sloshed in Kirsty's stomach. A whispered voice. 'Kirsty?' Thank God. Anna.

Kirsty thrust the bag towards her. 'Put this on.'

Anna took the bag into the next cubicle. Kirsty waited, her heart rate increasing with every second that passed, every foot-step in the passageway. But no one else came in. As soon as Anna emerged, now dressed in the British team tracksuit and with an auburn wig, Kirsty gave her a brief thumbs up, then ushered her through the door.

In the corridor, chattering competitors dressed in their national kit made their way to their various changing rooms. Anna and Kirsty kept their heads down as they threaded through the crowd. Anna still clutched the bag, presumably containing her team costume. They'd dump it when they were safely away. Their disguises wouldn't fool anyone who knew them, but they would probably convince strangers. They just needed to get lost in the melee.

'This way,' Kirsty muttered when they came to a junction. She led Anna up some stairs and along another passageway until they reached the entrance, where a few officials were checking people's passes as they entered the building. 'Keep your head down and try to keep going,' she whispered.

As a man in a black uniform approached them, fear surged up her body. She took a deep breath and tried to stay calm.

'Getting some air?' the official asked. He directed his question at Anna.

Anna nodded, but thankfully didn't speak. It wouldn't do to alert suspicion as to why a British coach was talking English with a foreign accent.

'Cat got your tongue?' the man said.

Anna darted an anxious glance at Kirsty.

Kirsty thought quickly. 'She can't speak. Bad toothache.' She rubbed her own cheek hoping Anna would understand.

Anna's eyes were wide with panic.

*Come on, Anna, come on.* Sweat dripped down Kirsty's back.

The man's polite expression faded. He stepped forward, his head to one side, scrutinising Anna.

Then Anna made a moaning sound and clutched the side of her face. Thank God.

'We're off to the dentist,' Kirsty said, grabbing Anna's elbow and steering her towards the door.

'Hope you get the tooth seen to.'

'Thank you.'

They walked rapidly out of the building.

'Down here.' Kirsty didn't dare relax yet in case they were

being followed. They hastened down the north London streets, the pavements baking from the August heat. How many times had she and Kirsty made their way through Budapest, terrified of running into Arrow Cross men, or Germans, or Russians? The last few years had consisted of one dangerous journey after another.

They took the tube to Euston, then finally boarded the train for Glasgow. There they discarded their wigs and she allowed herself to look at Anna properly. She gave her a little nudge. 'Scotland here we come.'

Anna managed the ghost of a smile.

The grimy London streets gave way to suburbia, then flat fields and farms, then cities and houses and factories and hills and lochs and mountains, for mile after mile, hour after hour.

They were alone in the carriage for the first few stops. Anna began to tell Kirsty the events of the last two years. The Russians had been far from the merciful saviours they'd hoped for. The Red Army constantly patrolled the streets. Anyone trying to escape the country was arrested, imprisoned, or even shot. Children were indoctrinated about Communism at school; all social groups were banned; the shelves in the shops were empty. Once again Jews were persecuted. 'Our people have learned to whisper – we're in constant fear of our conversations being intercepted,' said Anna.

Kirsty's eyes prickled with tears. 'I'm so sorry,' she said.

'What will happen when we get to Scotland?' Anna asked.

Kirsty had given their plans a lot of thought over the last few months. 'First you need to claim asylum,' she said. 'Then after a while, you'll be able to apply for British citizenship.'

'I haven't any money.'

'You don't need any, at least initially. You can stay with us.'

'But I'll need to work to pay my way.'

Kirsty grinned. She'd been waiting to tell Anna this. 'I've spoken to the Scottish Swimming Association. They'd be honoured for you to compete for us, once your citizenship comes through. In the meantime, Endre and I earn enough for us all.'

'But I must do something.'

'Don't worry, I'll keep you busy. I'll be your coach. Just as I was at Lake Balaton all those years ago. You can swim at the Hamilton baths. And I'll introduce you to the River Clyde. It's a lot colder than the Danube.'

Anna reached forward and hugged her.

Affection and relief surged through Kirsty. 'You'll need to get used to the cold. And not just in Scotland.'

'Oh?'

'All being well, you'll be going to the Helsinki Olympics in four years' time.'

Anna laughed but there was a fierceness in her expression. 'I was so cross with myself for coming fourth. I wanted to win for our people. For the thousands who never had my chances.'

That's what kept Anna going. Kirsty had seen it before: swimmers who had something to prove, or a mission to fulfil, often excelled. The drive to succeed that put them above the rest. 'Your time will come. And this time, you'll have the best coach in the world!'

They hugged again.

'Who'd have thought, when we were swimming for survival in the Danube, that you'd one day be competing at the Olympics?' Kirsty said. 'What a story that would make.'

'But would anyone believe it?' Anna smiled as she laid her head back against the seat.

More people piled onto the train at the next station. Kirsty thought of the times she'd been on trains over the last nine years. The frightening dash across Europe with Jean, just as war broke out; the even more terrifying wait at Jozsefvaros station, on a train which, she'd later discovered, would have taken them to Auschwitz had Raoul Wallenberg not saved them; the journey back from Hungary in 1945. And now, Anna's rescue.

She reached out to take Anna's hand in hers. 'Once again, we're two orphans on a train,' she said. 'Only this time we're travelling towards freedom.'

Ahead of them lay the purple hills of Scotland.

Ahead of them lay the rest of their lives.

# Author's Note

'The Orphans on the Train' was inspired by three remarkable women: a Scottish missionary and two Olympic athletes. The novel also combines two of my favourite activities: swimming and cooking. It was fun to research all these elements.

I've long been fascinated by people who excel in sport despite the odds, often demonstrating huge courage and determination. My inspiration for Anna was swimmer Éva Székely. As a Jewish girl in World War Two Hungary, Éva was banned from her local swimming team and excluded from competition for four years. Towards the end of the war, she lived with forty-one people in a crowded two-room 'safe-house' run by the Swiss. To keep herself fit, each day she ran one hundred times up and down five flights of stairs. I have Anna do something similar in my novel. You can read more about Éva Székely's remarkable story here: https://tinyurl.com/4wm3b7hd

I modelled Kirsty on Glaswegian swimmer Helen Orr Gordon. Helen, known as Elinor, grew up in Hamilton near Glasgow. As a female, she was only allowed to train for twenty minutes at a time, as ninety percent of the pool sessions were reserved for men. She also had to compete for space with children learning to swim. Rationing was still in place when she competed professionally and she had to surrender her ration book when she travelled so as not to be allowed more than her share of food. However, in my novel, Kirsty's journey to Budapest to become a cook was fictitious.

Helen Gordon and Éva Székely met in the 200 metres Olympic breaststroke final in 1952, gaining a bronze and gold medal respectively. In my story, Kirsty becomes a swimming coach, and Anna is the Olympian. I was interested to read that Greta Andersen, a Danish girl who won a gold medal in the 1948 London Olympics, didn't take up swimming until she was sixteen, which makes Anna's achievements plausible.

My character Jean Mathison is loosely based on the Scot Jane Haining, who was matron at a school for Jewish and Christian pupils in Budapest. She was advised to return to Britain after the outbreak of World War Two but refused to leave her pupils. She was arrested by the Gestapo in April 1944 and deported to Auschwitz-Birkenau in May. There she died two months later. In 1997 she was recognised by Yad Vashem in Israel as Righteous Among the Nations for having risked her life to help Jews during the Holocaust. You can watch a short film about her here: https://tinyurl.com/44t7za3t

The appalling shooting of Jewish citizens on the banks of the river Danube by Arrow Cross men is commemorated in the *Shoes on the Danube* memorial which poignantly depicts the footwear left behind by those tragic people. https://tinyurl.com/59m4tb29

Raoul Wallenberg saved thousands of Jews in Hungary during the Holocaust. In his role as Sweden's special envoy in Budapest in the latter part of 1944, he gave out protective passports and sheltered Jews in buildings he declared as

Swedish territory. On 17 January 1945, he was detained by the Soviets on suspicion of spying, never to be seen again. The 1985 film 'Wallenberg', starring Richard Chamberlain, powerfully dramatises his life.

Carl Lutz is believed to have saved 62,000 Jews from the Holocaust by issuing 'letters of protection'. He also helped 10,000 Jewish children emigrate to Israel after he became head of Switzerland's foreign interests' section in Budapest in 1942.

Another hero of this time was Arthur Weiss, whose business headquarters, known as the Glass House, sheltered thousands of Jews during the Nazi occupation and the Arrow Cross reign of terror. He was forced to give up his business activities in the summer of 1944 due to the Jewish persecution in Hungary. He disappeared on 1st January 1945, ironically only 18 days before the Glass House was liberated.

Where possible I've kept to historical dates as I think this makes for a more authentic and ethical read. However, essentially this is a work of fiction, and on rare occasions I have used artistic licence to tweak the timing of events in order to create more drama and interest. I've moved the air raid which Kirsty and Anna are caught up in from 1942 to 1943 to better fit my narrative. I have also moved the edict for the Jews to wear yellow stars forward by a week, and the provision of the yellow-star houses forward by two months. All these decisions were taken to make the story more intense and poignant, although the events themselves occurred as I depict them.

The treatment of Jewish people in Budapest, particularly during 1944 and 1945, was horrific. War brings out the best and worst in people. The Nazis and the Arrow Cross committed appalling crimes and caused immense suffering. But this terrible time also gave us unassuming heroes such as Raoul Wallenberg, Carl Lutz, Arthur Weiss and Jane Haining, to name but a few. In them we find the selflessness, courage and goodness that give us hope for humanity.

# Acknowledgements

Books are never written in isolation, and I'm so grateful to those who supported 'The Orphans on the Train' editorially, and to the experts who answered my many questions. Any unintentional mistakes are my own.

A big thanks in particular to the following: my wonderful agent Anne Williams, my brilliant editor Sherise Hobbs, her lovely assistant editor Priyal Agrawal, and the editorial, sales and marketing teams at Headline.

The amazing Cari Rosen for insights into Jewish culture and beliefs, and for so meticulously copy editing the manuscript.

Journalist Andy Bull whose article, *Holocaust survivor to Olympic gold: the remarkable life of Éva Székely* (the *Guardian,* 3rd March 2020) first drew my attention to this incredible swimmer, and led me to research World War Two Hungary.

My good friend and fellow writer Jacqui Pack for her generous and wise support for the novel.

Angela Ward of the Hamilton reference library and Garry McCallum of *Historic Hamilton* for helping me to research the town and its history.

The very helpful administrative staff at Scotland's International Development Alliance.

Ian Alexander for kindly sending me an electronic copy of his fascinating booklet on Jane Haining.

The informative staff of the National Mining Museum Scotland.

Jim Paterson of Clyde Commercial diving for his expert knowledge of the river Clyde – both above and below the water.

Richard Adair at GLUG (Glasgow underwater group).

Matthew from the Dunscore heritage centre for his kind interest.

Melinda Eveleigh from Cranleigh leisure centre for helpful advice on swimming tuition.

International swimmer Kelvin Jones for his fascinating insights into competitive swimming.

Wild water swimmers Alyson Wilson and Hannah Coleman for illuminating me on the joys of outdoor swimming when I was too much of a coward to leave the safety of my local baths.

My water-loving granddaughter Leonie for testing out some of the swimming manoeuvres for me.

Two Hungarians, Kitti Szabó and Orsolya Imecs, for kindly supplying correct translations (and their friends, Kerry Fisher and Claire Bethel respectively, for liaising between us).

Ákos Varga, a museologist from the Hospital in the Rock Museum in Budapest for answering my many questions so thoroughly.

Novelist Mason Cross for advice on Glaswegian dialect words.

'Grandfather Poet' David Bleiman for linguistic help on Scottish and Yiddish words and expressions.

Dr Dana Thompson for medical insights.

I am so grateful to you all, and I know the book is richer as a result of your generosity.

**TO SAVE HER CHILD, A MOTHER MUST MAKE AN IMPOSSIBLE CHOICE.**

Prague 1939. Young mother Eva has a secret from her past. When the Nazis invade, Eva knows the only way to keep her daughter Miriam safe is to send her away – even if it means never seeing her again.

But when Eva is taken to a concentration camp, her secret is at risk of being exposed.

In London, Pamela volunteers to help find places for the Jewish children arrived from Europe. Befriending one unclaimed little girl, Pamela brings her home.

Then when her son enlists in the RAF, Pamela realises how easily her own world could come crashing down . . .

**Available to order now**

## IN THE DARK NIGHT OF WAR, LOVE WOULD GUIDE THEM HOME.

### 1996

The war may have ended decades earlier, but for the elegant woman sitting alone now, the images live on in her memory: her sister's carefree laughter, the inky black of a German soldier's boots, the little boats that never came back. And the one constant through it all: the lighthouse that always guided them back to the island . . .

### 1940

For sisters Alice and Jenny life is just beginning when the Nazis seize control of the island of Jersey, driving the girls down separate paths. While Alice is forced by the enemy to work in the German hospital, Jenny is attracted to the circle of islanders rising up to resist the occupiers. And as the war tightens its grip, it will cause each of the sisters to make an extraordinary choice, experience unimaginable heartbreak and emerge forever changed . . .

**Available to order now**

**REVIEW**